EDGE OF VALOR

A TODD INGRAM NOVEL

JOHN J. GOBBELL

SEVERN RIVER PUBLISHING

Severn River Publishing
www.SevernRiverBooks.com

ISBN: 978-1-64875-526-2 (Paperback)

ALSO BY JOHN J. GOBBELL

The Todd Ingram Series

The Last Lieutenant

A Code For Tomorrow

When Duty Whispers Low

The Neptune Strategy

Edge of Valor

Dead Man Launch

Somewhere in the South Pacific

Other Books

A Call to Colors

The Brutus Lie

Never miss a new release! Sign up to receive exclusive updates from author John J. Gobbell.

severnriverbooks.com

Dedicated to the men and women who served in the American and Allied forces during what became known as a long, and sometimes bloody Cold War.

It took a while; your contribution may have not been immediately apparent. But you did, indeed, prevail.
Because of you, the world is a much better place.

Well Done.

Greater East Asia - 1945

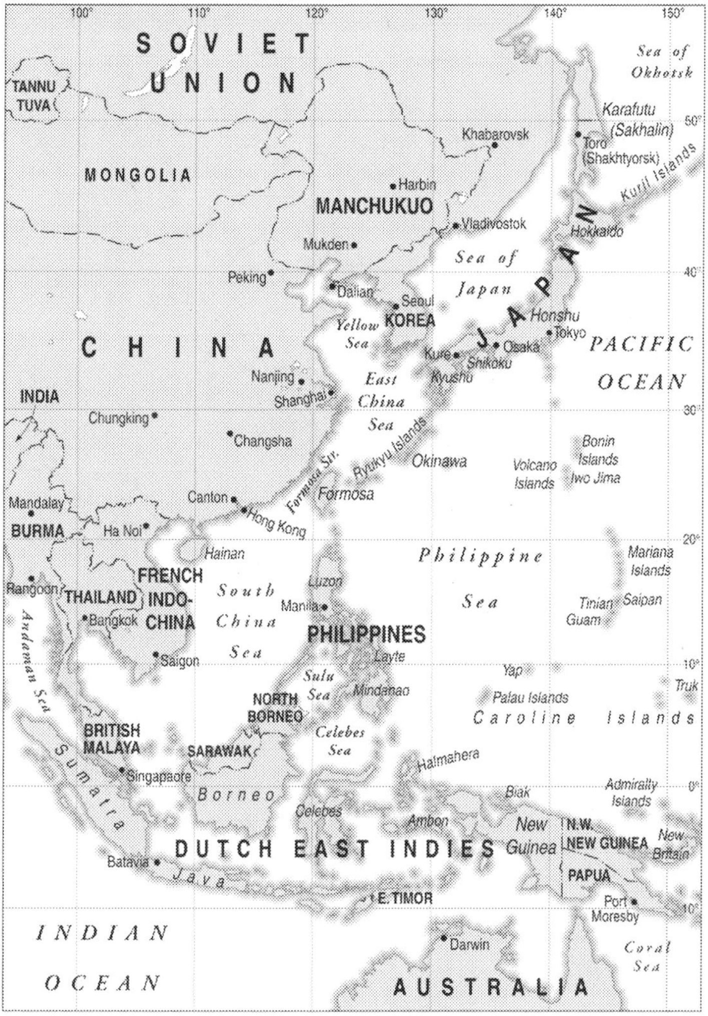

Okinawa Prefecture, Ryuku Islands, Japan - 1945

Tokyo and Environs - 1945

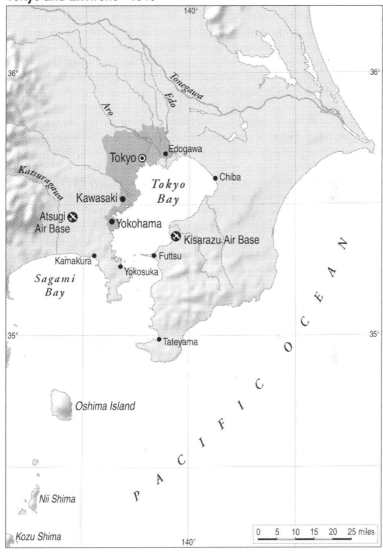

CAST OF CHARACTERS

U.S. Navy
USS *Maxwell* **(DD 525) (Crackerjack), attached to DESRON 77**
Cdr. Alton C. (Todd) Ingram, commanding officer
Lt. Cdr. Eldon P. (Tubby) White, executive officer
Lt. Thomas F. (Woody) Woodruff, operations officer
Lt. Julian Falco, gunnery officer, main battery director

DESRON 77
Maxwell (flag),
DesDiv 77.1: *Maxwell* (flag), *Snowden*, *Bertea*, and *Geiler*
DesDiv 77.2: *Wallace* (flag), *Cheffer*, *Beaulieu*, and *Truax*
Capt. Jeremiah T. (Boom Boom) Landa, commodore, Destroyer Squadron
77, aboard *Maxwell*

Eleventh Naval District, Long Beach, California
Cdr. Oliver P. (Ollie) Toliver III, case officer,
Office of Naval Intelligence (ONI)
Cdr. Walter (Walt) Hodges, supply officer
Long Beach. Naval Shipyard

Other U.S. Navy Personnel
Adm. William F. Halsey Jr., commander, Third Fleet
Vice Adm. John S. McCain Sr., commander, Task Force 38 under Admiral Halsey
Lt. Larry M. O'Toole, attached as Japanese-language interpreter to Manila peace talks and first Karafuto expedition

U.S. Army
SCAP Staff, Manila and Tokyo
Gen. Douglas A. MacArthur, supreme commander for Allied Powers (SCAP)
Gen. Richard K. Sutherland, General MacArthur's chief of staff
Brig. Gen. Otis (n) DeWitt, aide to General Sutherland
Col. Sydney Mashbir, Japanese-language expert and chief negotiator, Manila
Maj. Clive W. Neidemeier, State Department liaison
Ie Shima Air Base/Atsugi Air Base

Karafuto (Sakhalin) Expeditions
Note: Karafuto Island and Toro Airfield became Sakhalin Oblast and Shakhtyorsk Airfield respectfully after the Soviets captured them in August–September 1945.

First expedition: USAAF C-54, tail number 626384 (Hot Rod 384)
Second expedition: USAAF C-54 744326 (Apprentice 26)

U.S. Army Air Force (USAAF)
Maj. Marvin F. (Bucky) Radcliff, pilot and aircraft commander first expedition
1st Lt. Leroy Telford K. Peoples, copilot, first expedition; pilot and aircraft commander, second expedition
Capt. Jonathan L. (Jon) Berne, navigator first and second expeditions
Sgt. Leonard (n) Hammer, flight sergeant, engineer first and second expeditions
2nd Lt. Richard W. Lassiter, copilot, second expedition

U.S. Marines
GySgt. Ulysses Gaylord (Ugly) Harper, USMC, squad leader of thirteen
Marines, first expedition
GySgt. Horace T. Boland, USMC, squad leader of thirteen Marines, second
expedition
Office of Strategic Services (OSS)
Colin Blinde, agent,

San Pedro, California
Maj. Helen Durand Ingram, U.S. Army, Todd Ingram's wife; floor nurse,
Ward 6, Fort MacArthur Infirmary
Maj. Julian T. Raduga, MD, U.S. Army, psychiatrist
Fort MacArthur Infirmary
Cpl. Eddie Bergen, patient, Ward 6, Fort MacArthur Infirmary; previously
U.S. Army M-4 tanker on Okinawa
Emma Peabody, Todd and Helen Ingram's next-door neighbor on South
Alma Street

Hollywood, California
Laura West, pianist, NBC Symphony Orchestra
Maestro Arturo Toscanini, conductor
NBC Symphony Orchestra, West Coast Division
Roberta Thatcher, business manager, NBC Symphony Orchestra
Anoushka Dezhnev, Russian film star; mother
of Eduard Dezhnev

Soviets
USSR Navy
Captain Third Rank Eduard Ianovich Dezhnev
garrison commander, 21st Naval Regiment,
Shakhtyorsk Airfield, Sakhalin Island
Captain First Rank Gennady Kulibin
Dezhnev's immediate superior at
Shakhtyorsk Airfield, Sakhalin; later, commanding officer
of the (war prize) cruiser *Admiral Volshkov*

NKVD (Narodnyy Komissariat Vnutrennikh Del'), Soviet Secret Service, predecessor of the MGB and KGB
Karol Dudek, Polish assassin
Oleg Lepechn, agent, Shakhtyorsk Airfield, Sakhalin
Matvie Borzakov, agent, Shakhtyorsk Airfield, Sakhalin

Imperial Japanese Navy (IJN)
Captain Shiroku Fujimoto, commander minefields
of Tokyo Bay and environs
Major Kotoku Fujimoto, commander Toro Airfield,
Karafuto (Sakhalin), Imperial Marines

International Red Cross
Walter Frederick Boring, Geneva, Switzerland; representative assigned to
the northeast Asia sector

PART I

At the height of a kamikaze raid off Okinawa in April 1945, Rear Adm. Arleigh Burke of the U.S. Fifth Fleet heard a voice transmission from an unidentified destroyer that had just been hit, killing all of her senior officers: "'I am an ensign,' the voice said. 'I have been on this ship for a little while. I have been in the Navy for only a little while. I will fight this ship to the best of my ability and forgive me for the mistakes I am about to make.'"

—E. B. Potter, *Admiral Arleigh Burke*

We do not intend that the Japanese shall be enslaved as a race or destroyed as a nation; the Japanese Government shall remove all obstacles to the revival and strengthening of democratic tendencies among the Japanese people. But stern justice shall be meted out to all war criminals... Freedom of speech, of religion, and of thought, as well as respect for the fundamental human rights, shall be established.

Potsdam Declaration, Article 5, Conference of the Allied Powers, Potsdam, Germany, July 26, 1945

1

---

9 August 1945
USS *Maxwell* (DD 525), Task Force 38, North Pacific Ocean
twenty-three miles east of Hitachi, Japan

A lonely sun hung above the Japanese coastline as if governed by its own whim--it alone would decide when to set, and to hell with nautical predictions fabricated by mere mortals. The orange-red ball cast a miasma of reds and pinks around a circular formation retiring to the east, the day's deadly task now done. The group consisted of four cruisers and eight destroyers protecting the battleship Iowa in the center. Four F6F Hellcats, their combat air patrol, buzzed lazily overhead, watching, waiting.

The setting sun made everybody nervous. Bad things happened at sunset and sunrise. The desperate Japanese were hurling kamikazes after the Third Fleet. The damage had been great; ship after ship had been taken off the line for repairs; many had been sunk. Destroyers and carriers had borne the brunt. In many cases the destroyers, the "little boys," had been crumpled into junk as if smashed by a giant fist.

The *Maxwell* was again at general quarters after a long day's work. The crew had stood at their battle stations during sunrise. Then, during the day, Task Force 38 moved close to the Japanese mainland and the Iowa had hurled her 16-inch, 2,000-pound projectiles eight miles inland. Her target: the industrial section of Kiribati Prefecture, where Hitachi Industries' electronics works were concentrated.

The *Maxwell* and the rest of the task force had been close enough to pump out a few rounds as well. But as they retired for the evening the destroyers readied their 5-inch guns for the kamikazes' deadly retribution. Gun crews stuck the "common" ammunition with base-detonating fuses below into the magazines and pulled up antiaircraft projectiles with proximity fuses, stocking them in the upper handling rooms for immediate use. Now they were once again at general quarters to defend against the raid that was certain to come.

Cdr. Todd Ingram paced his bridge, tugging at the straps on his life vest. The *Maxwell* had made it through so far. Whether by luck or Divine intervention or skillful fighting and maneuvering, Ingram couldn't say. After the protracted Okinawa campaign coupled with Admiral Halsey's triumphant bombardment of the coast of Japan, he was too tired to think about it. For the past four months he'd averaged five hours of sleep a day. Along with the rest of the crew he'd lived from meal to meal and watch to watch, becoming a near automaton.

But over the past three days a different feeling had crept over Ingram--and, perhaps by osmosis, over the crew as well. Something awesome and horrific had happened at Hiroshima. Rumors flew around the fleet. The war could be over. Expectations of surrender grew into dreams--a good night's sleep, a week's worth of good night's sleep; a thick, juicy steak; plenty of beer; and course zero-nine-zero: home. But the good news didn't come; the pressure was still on. No sleep, no beer, no steak, no homeward trek; just more kamikazes and the incessant cracking of guns and the smell of cordite and the odor of death.

Lt. Cdr. Tubby White, the *Maxwell's* executive officer, clomped onto the bridge wearing khaki shorts, a T-shirt, and sandals. White had played guard at USC, but his well-muscled torso had grown to generous proportions since then; thus, his nickname. White's inverted belly button poked through his sweaty T-shirt. As exec, White's general quarters station was two decks below in the combat information center (CIC), a dark, cramped space full of heat-generating electronic equipment such as radar repeaters. There was no air conditioning.

Ingram and White had known one another since the Solomon Islands campaign of 1942–43 when they had served in the destroyer Howell. The Howell was sunk, and White went on to successfully command a PT boat in the Upper Solomons campaign and then a squadron of PT boats during General MacArthur's return to the Philippines. The Philippines campaign was just about done. PT boats were no longer needed, and Lt. Cdr. Eldon P. White was on the market, so to speak. Ingram scooped him up in an instant.

White walked up, waving a flimsy.

"What is it?" snapped Ingram.

White tucked the message behind his back. "Touchy, touchy."

"Damn it, Tubby, I don't have time for--"

Capt. Jerry Landa walked up and snatched the flimsy from behind White's back. "Insubordination, Mr. White."

White drew up to a semblance of attention. "Sorry, Commodore."

Ingram turned aside, trying not to laugh. These two had been at it for years. But they were so similar. Although Tubby White was heavier than Landa, their configurations were the same: portly. But Landa, with dark wavy hair, was far more handsome and sold himself to others with a winning smile, the main feature being upper and lower rows of gleaming white teeth. A pencil-thin mustache on top was designed to draw in the ladies and more than adequately did its job. The son of a Brooklyn stevedore, Landa went to sea at fifteen and worked his way up, obtaining his master's license at the age of thirty. At the war's outbreak, he immediately transferred to the U.S. Navy and a life on destroyers. He soon found himself in command, and it suited him well. A fearless and solid leader at sea, the unmarried Landa was flamboyant when ashore, doing more than his share of drinking. Often, junior officers were tasked with carrying their commanding officer back to the ship, where they pitched him into his bunk to sleep it off. Over the years Landa had acquired the nickname "Boom Boom," presumably because, when the party had shifted to third gear, he would stand on a chair--or whatever was convenient--and tell barroom jokes mimicking the sounds of human flatus. Oddly, Landa didn't like to be called "Boom Boom," although he enjoyed calling others by nicknames.

Ingram, on the other hand, came from Echo, Oregon, a small railroad and farming community in southeastern Oregon. Not muscle bound, Ingram still had an athlete's frame and weighed an efficient 187 pounds. He had sandy hair, and his deep-set eyes were gray with a touch of wrinkle in the corners, the result of lonely hot summer days in the endless wheat fields of eastern Oregon. A broad, disarming grin delivered from time to time was characterized by a chipped lower tooth, the result of a fall off a combine as an eleven-year-old. A graduate of the U.S. Naval Academy in 1937, he escaped the "Battleship Club" syndrome and went to small ships, initially minesweepers, where he rose to be the young skipper of the mine-sweeper USS *Pelican* (AM 49) by war's outbreak in 1941.

While others at home were still trying to overcome the shock of the Pearl Harbor attack and the devastating Japanese conquests in the Far East, Ingram was seeing the horrors up close. One of the worst was when the *Pelican* was bombed out from under him in Manila Bay in April 1942.

As different as they were, Ingram, Landa, and White had at least one thing in common: utter exhaustion. They were dead tired. None had slept more than three or four hours at a time over the past three months. There were dark pouches under their eyes, especially Landa's, and the skin on their faces had a grayish pallor and sagged. The corners of their mouths turned down and their eyes were more often than not bloodshot.

But for now, Ingram forgot their predicament as White and Landa glared at one another for a moment, reliving a heated argument that began in the days on the Howell when Landa had been the skipper and Tubby White a lieutenant (jg). Ingram was sure both had forgotten what started the argument and now merely relished mutual efforts to antagonize each other. The rancor grew worse when Tubby White openly referred to CIC as the Chaos Information Center, a joke that Landa would have gladly told himself had it not come from White.

White transferred off the *Howell*, but Ingram stayed on board as executive officer. He'd followed in Landa's footsteps--their personalities completely opposite, their thinking and actions beautifully synchronized. Now Landa was a full captain and commodore of Destroyer Squadron 77

(DESRON77) with tactical and administrative control of the eight destroyers now arranged around the modern fast battleship Iowa. It was Landa who had put the *Maxwell* in station seven, the position nearest the Japanese mainland.

At length, Landa dropped his eyes and read the message. "Holy smokes. This has to be it."

"It what?" asked Ingram.

The corners of Landa's mouth curled up. He looked at White, "You got this from radio central?"

"Yes, sir. Mr. Ross thought it was important enough for me to see it. He brought it down."

"And you read it?" asked Landa.

"Of course, . . . Commodore."

Landa's face glowed; his eyes glistened as if he were getting ready to tell one of his famous farting jokes. But he remained silent.

Ingram spread his hands. Enough. "Come on, Jerry!"

Landa handed over the message.

"I'll be a monkey's uncle!" He whipped off his helmet and waved it in the air. "Can't be long now. With the Rooskies on our side, how can we lose?" An hour ago, a fleet broadcast had announced that the Soviet Union, a supposed neutral to the Japanese, had instead declared war on them and had begun pouring thousands of troops across the Mongolian border.

Landa snorted.

Tubby White was more vocal. "Sheyatttt."

Ingram continued, "All in the spirit of comradely cooperation, I'm sure. After all, those fine Soviets have been defending our cause for years."

They stared at him.

Ingram grinned and clapped his hands. "Speaking of the spirit of comradely cooperation, how 'bout it, Commodore? Would you like to tell the crew?"

Landa unleashed his signature white-toothed smile and shook his head. "They're your guys."

Ingram nodded. This was the skipper's job. "Can't argue with that." He stepped inside the pilothouse and stood beside the 1MC--the ship's public address system--mounted on the rear bulkhead. The eight sailors and two officers in the pilothouse had their ears cocked in his direction. At a glance Ingram could tell the word had already leaked up from radio central via the sound-powered phone connected to Radford, the lee helmsman, on the engine room annunciator. They already knew what the message said.

No matter. Ingram nodded to Birmingham, the short, stout, heavily tattooed second-class boatswain's mate of the watch. "Okay, Birmingham," he said. "All hands from the captain. Use that." He pointed to the silver boatswain's pipe dangling on Birmingham's chest.

"Aye, aye, Captain." Standing on tiptoes, Birmingham pulled down the microphone. Then he flipped all the compartment levers and energized the 1MC. Taking a deep breath, he blew on his pipe. Birmingham's pipe echoed clearly and mournfully throughout the ship, giving one the feeling he had stepped back two hundred years in time. Still on tiptoes Birmingham barked, "Now hear this. Now hear this. Stand by for the captain."

Ingram stepped to the mike. "Good evening. I have in hand a fleet broadcast signed by Admiral Nimitz. A second atomic bomb was dropped today on the Japanese mainland. This one on Nagasaki in southern Kyushu."

There was a massive intake of breath in the pilothouse. All eyes were fixed on Ingram as he continued, "While it says nothing about an end to hostilities, it does caution us to maintain the utmost vigilance while negotiations are under way. The war is not over by any stretch of the imagination. And I can't emphasize enough that we must remain vigilant. On the other hand, and I may be stepping out on a limb, I do like the use of the word 'negotiations.' That's all I can say about this, so draw your own conclusions." He checked the plan of the day posted nearby. "Okay, absent any visitors between now and sunset, the movie tonight is *Guest in the House* starring Ralph Bellamy and Anne Baxter. Showtime is twenty-thirty on the mess decks. That is all." He flipped off the levers and walked out to the open bridge.

As he stepped through the pilothouse door, he heard Birmingham mutter in his fog-cutter voice, "I don't get it. What the hell's an atomic bomb?"

Landa and Tubby White were still on the port bridge wing pretending to snarl at each other. Landa said, "Short, to the point, but not exactly Knute Rockne."

"Well, you can't expect--"

"Bridge, aye." Anderson, Ingram's talker, wearing sound-powered headphones, raised his head and said, "Combat has six bogies, inbound, bearing two-eight-six true. Range twenty-five miles."

The dreaded words mesmerized the three officers for a moment. Ingram and Landa locked eyes, the question unspoken. How did they get in that close?

"Must be hugging the deck," muttered White. "See you fellas." He dashed through the pilothouse door toward the ladder leading down to CIC.

"Must be," said Ingram. They looked up to see the Hellcats swooping low, headed west, their engines snarling.

"I was so looking forward to a quiet evening with Ralph Bellamy," sighed Landa, moving away. As was their custom during action, Landa took a position on the starboard bridge wing with his status boards and talkers to issue instructions to his destroyers. From the *Maxwell*'s station in the number seven position he could see all of his "little boys" and send messages by flag hoist, signal light, or TBS--voice radio.

On the port bridge wing, Ingram took up a position between Anderson and Lt. Tom Waterman, his GQ officer of the deck. Athletic and, dark-haired, Waterman was balding at the age of twenty-three. The hair loss made him look twice his age but seemed to garner respect from the men who worked for him.

"There!" said Waterman, pointing aft.

Ingram raised his binoculars and spotted planes popping out of the mist at about 15,000 yards, flying low, no more than 50 feet off the deck. "Close," he muttered. Even so, he saw a Hellcat roar in aft of one. Almost immediately the Japanese plane burst into flames and hit the ocean with a splash. He squinted and tightened his focus. "Zeros."

All the men topside, from the bridge crew to the 40- and 20-mm gun crews, strained to see the incoming enemy.

Ingram called, "Batteries released. Heads up, everybody; here we go again." To Waterman: "Tom, tell main control to cut in superheat to all boilers and stand by for maneuvering bells."

"Yes, sir." Waterman ducked inside the pilothouse and gave the order.

Ingram heard the faint buzz of the oncoming Zeros' engines. They were flying impossibly low. Even so, the Hellcats ranged among them, their engines strong, authoritative. Machine guns rattled and another Zero hit the ocean with a loud explosion, its 500-pound bomb bursting on impact. The plume hadn't yet dissipated when Ingram yelled up to Falco, his gunnery officer in the main battery director. "Julian, shake a leg, damn it."

Falco's head popped out of the director; sweat rolled down his acne-scarred face. "On target and tracking. You ready, Skipper?"

"Wait one." To Anderson, "Does plot have a solution?"

Anderson keyed his sound-powered phone, asked the question, and nodded. "Yes, sir, plot reports solution."

Range now was about eight thousand yards. A flash of light was followed by a large column of water, and another Zero disappeared.

Ingram yelled, "Falco, mounts 4 and 5 commence fire." *We have to unmask batteries.* Ingram waited a moment as the after two 5-inch mounts belched out a round apiece. He called to Landa through the pilothouse hatches. "Jerry, how about a turn nine?"

"Negative." Landa, a radiophone jammed to his ear, waved Ingram off with a thumbs-down. He yelled something, but a second salvo obliterated his words.

"What?" Ingram shouted back.

Landa yelled, "Formation speed, twenty-eight knots. Stand by, execute." He hunched over the radio telephone handset to relay the same command to the other destroyers.

Ingram grabbed Waterman's arm. "Tom, make turns for twenty-eight knots and stand by for radical maneuvering."

"Twenty-eight knots, radical maneuvering; aye, Skipper." Waterman shouted the order through the pilothouse porthole, Radcliff spun up his enunciators, and the *Maxwell* fairly leapt out of her fifteen-knot wake.

The Zeros stood out clearly now. Three of them: one banking left, one banking right, and one boring straight in. Right for the *Maxwell*. Ingram felt as if cement had hardened in his stomach. They were targeting him, all three of them. An image of Helen flashed through his mind. Her large, brown eyes and glistening raven-black hair. Her olive skin. And then another image: Helen holding their baby, Jerry; the kid was smiling. And then she was smiling.

Suddenly, the Zero directly aft pulled up and then dove into the water in a fiery red ball of flame. A Hellcat flew through the pyre and then swooped to chase the Zero on the right.

Two to go: one on either side. The *Maxwell*'s guns were blazing, port and starboard, as the Zeros heaved out about three thousand yards and then turned and headed directly toward her. Ingram had a sinking feeling. *We've been through so much. So many others have suffered. Maybe it's our turn. Oh, God, keep us safe.*

The Zero to starboard exploded about a thousand yards away, nearly vaporized. Pieces no larger than a tire or a wing flap twirled though the air.

One to go. Ingram turned to look at the one to port. It wasn't there. "What the hell?"

"Sheyaaaat!" A lookout pointed up. The Zero had pulled nearly straight up to about a thousand feet. Now it was heading down at a steep angle for the *Maxwell*, its engine screaming.

Turn into it. Ingram shouted, "This is the captain. I have the conn. Left standard rudder. Make turns for thirty-five knots."

The helmsman spun his wheel; a flurry of replies answered Ingram's orders; and the Zero plunged down. No more than five hundred feet now.

Mount 53 belched out a 54-pound projectile. Milliseconds later, its proximity fuse triggered the round. The shell blew up in front of the Zero, tearing off its right wing. Men topside cheered as the Mitsubishi A6M, minus its right wing, twirled into a flat spin, trailing oily red flames and smoke as it descended a bizarre path.

Suddenly Ingram realized the Zero, its engine at an insane pitch, was still going to hit the *Maxwell*. He clenched his fists. "No, please."

The others topside saw it too. Men in the after-torpedo mount and the midships 40- and 20-mm gun mounts ran for their lives as the plane caromed down.

With a screech of tearing metal the Zero's left wing sliced through the number two stack. The rest of the plane splattered onto the starboard side of the main deck and spilled into the ocean leaving a hissing mist of dark smoke. Miraculously, its bomb had not gone off. The severed upper section of the number two stack stood in place for a moment, as if undecided what to do. Then, groaning and tearing, it tumbled over to starboard onto the main deck, exposing economizers that gushed shrieking steam from the lower section. The top half of the number two stack tumbled into the Pacific, following its foe to the bottom.

Ingram slowly exhaled. He yelled at the lee helmsman to be heard over the din, "Radford, tell main control to secure economizers for number three and four boilers."

Breathe. Looking aft, Ingram checked the sky. The Zeros were gone. The steam stopped spouting. He called, "Mr. Waterman. Take the conn to resume formation course and speed." To his talker he said, "Okay, Anderson, Damage Control Central, report damage."

Landa walked through the pilothouse. "Thought that little bastard had our number."

"I'll say." Ingram's right hand was shaking, and he felt like vomiting. Quickly, he stuffed the hand in his pocket.

The motion was not lost on Landa. He knew the signs. They'd been through it so many times. And they knew each other too well to say anything. Maybe later Landa would give Ingram some heat about this. Except . . . last June off Okinawa, Landa had peed his pants as a kamikaze dove on them, missing by only a hundred yards. He dashed into Ingram's sea cabin to change. Later he claimed it was spilled coffee. Maybe it really was. Everybody reacted differently. But in the end, they were just ordinary men.

"Bridge, aye." Anderson turned to Ingram. "Main control reports economizers secured on boilers three and four. They have twenty-seven knots available for steaming. No damage except number two stack."

Ingram and Landa walked to the starboard side. Already the repair party was out on the main deck clearing wreckage. "Any casualties," asked Ingram?

Anderson listened for a moment, smirked, and then said, "Yes, sir, there are."

"Well, what?" demanded Ingram.

"Mr. White in CIC," said Anderson.

"Mr. White? CIC? What the hell?" demanded Ingram and Landa in unison.

Anderson stood at near attention and said, "Mr. White reports thirteen guys scared shitless."

2

15 August 1945
USS *Maxwell* (DD 525), Kerama Rhetto, Okinawa Prefecture
Ryukyu Islands, Japan

Adm. Raymond A. Spruance, commander of the Fifth Fleet, had ordered the capture of the Kerama Islands well before the invasion of Okinawa, not only to protect the fleet's flank, but also to provide a staging area for supplies needed in the Okinawa invasion and for ship repair. The Keramas lay only twenty miles west of Okinawa's southern tip. Ship repair became the higher priority as kamikaze after kamikaze smashed into U.S. Navy capital ships, particularly the destroyers that formed the outer picket line. Too many had been sunk while on picket duty; those that survived were sent to Kerama for temporary repairs before steaming away to Ulithi and stateside--or, in the case of some of the blackened hulks lying about, to be towed home ingloriously by seagoing tugs.

The fifteenth of August was a day of mayhem and celebration. Shortly after lunch, Adm. William F. (Bull) Halsey Jr. had sent an "all hands" message to his entire Third Fleet that the Japanese had capitulated and the war was over, effective immediately. Pandemonium erupted throughout the Keramas, with whistles blowing, signal flags two-blocked, sirens wailing, and guns of all calibers firing. The same thing happened all over the western Pacific, the celebration extending well into the evening. But lest a last-minute kamikaze attack be hurled at a relaxing Third Fleet, the prudent Halsey sent a follow-on message to his airmen:

"INVESTIGATE AND SHOOT DOWN ALL SNOOPERS--NOT VINDICTIVELY, BUT IN A FRIENDLY SORT OF WAY."

Todd Ingram was a veteran of Japan's 1942 siege of Corregidor and later the Solomon and Marianas campaigns. He had seen death many times, sometimes up close. He had smelled it too, but the odor hadn't been as oppressive as it was here in Kerama Rhetto, a veritable junkyard of twisted metal and scorched superstructures. Some ships were so badly wrecked that it was impossible to tell what class they once were, let alone make an actual identification. Through the process of triage, a few had simply been beached to be later picked apart by salvage crews.

The *Maxwell* was second in a nest of five destroyers secured to the *Pluto*, a 12,000-ton repair ship whose crew worked around the clock patching up the ships in her brood. Directly alongside the *Pluto* was the destroyer *Richard W. North*. Her topsides had been mangled when five kamikazes had attacked her simultaneously from all compass points. Without air cover, she fought valiantly, knocking down three of them. But two found their mark--one forward, one aft--the conflagration unimaginable as the kamikaze's fuel tanks exploded and spread holocaust over the entire ship. The fires burned so hot that the 20- and 40-mm ammunition topside cooked off. Two ensigns who only six months before had been pulling fraternity stunts were the only officers to survive out of twenty-two. They brought the *North* in, one ensign conning from the fantail, his arm in a sling, the other down in main control in the forward engine room.

As fate would have it, the *North*'s after stack was the only piece of her superstructure that survived. The *Maxwell*, which lay second in the nest, was to be the lucky recipient. Third in the nest was the *Alphir*, her second 5-inch mount obliterated by a kamikaze. The *Manon*, fourth in line, had hit a mine. She rode on her lines all right, but the repair crew had yet to figure out if her back was broken. Last in the nest was the *Riffey*, victim of a collision with an oil tanker while refueling. The two smacked side-to-side in a lumpy sea, obliterating the port side of the *Riffey*'s bridge. Miraculously, no lives were lost, but they'd fired the *Riffey*'s skipper and Ingram was worried they would grab Tubby White for the spot. He was certainly qualified, although Landa refused to admit it. Ingram suspected that Landa and White enjoyed their jousting but secretly held the utmost respect for one another. Landa was career Navy while Tubby White was a Reserve who planned to transit back to civilian life as soon as possible. If White really was incompetent, Ingram thought, Landa would have long ago fired him.

The seventeenth was calm and sultry. With no wind, flags hung limply from their halyards. The celebration finally over, the crews resumed work. Blue-brown clouds of smoke from welding torches surrounded the nest, making it look as if the ships were trapped inside an Indian teepee. Worse, the odor of death hung in the air as the *Pluto*'s repair crews hacked at the *North*'s wreckage and recovered bodies, some trapped for days.

The odor got to Ingram. As long as this pall of death hung over his ship, he couldn't eat. Yesterday morning he had been up on the *Maxwell*'s foredeck when the workers recovered a body from the *North*'s forward 5-inch gun mount. The poor sailor's blackened chest was ripped open as if by a giant cleaver, the ribs and viscera exposed. Ingram had lain awake last night visualizing the horror at that wrecked gun mount. He knew he would never again order spare ribs in a restaurant. *Wind. Please, oh, please, God, just a little wind.*

At sunset the *Maxwell*, *Riffey*, *Alphir*, and *Manon* were at general quarters, obeying Halsey's instructions for vigilance. The ghosts on board the *Richard W. North* stood also at their battle stations, a duty they would silently bear into eternity. The combat air patrol buzzing over Kerama Rhetto ensured the ships' safety against unfriendly snoopers. Also helping were the 20- and 40-mm antiaircraft guns stationed on the surrounding islands.

Ingram and Landa leaned on the bridge bulwark looking aft, watching the *Pluto's* welders zap the final touches on the *Maxwell's* new number two stack. Landa had returned earlier in the day, intending to get under way that evening to rejoin his squadron still at sea guarding the *Iowa*.

Ingram couldn't get used to this relaxed GQ. Men were talking at their battle stations; a few even milled around the weather decks. A pall of tobacco smoke streamed up from the main battery director. At first Ingram felt rage. *They're smoking up there.* He wanted to yell at them to knock it off. The war was over, but his psyche still dictated a brink-of-disaster frame of mind. It was sunset. Surely a bomb would explode or a 5-inch 38 would crack in his ear at any moment. But all was quiet.

"Todd, damn it, relax," ordered Landa. He cuffed Ingram's shoulder. "Drink up." Landa had ordered coffee sent to the bridge, something unthinkable at general quarters in wartime.

"Okay, sure." Ingram removed his battle helmet but kept his eyes on the western horizon, occasionally raising his binoculars.

"Go on, damn it. Drink!"

Ingram took a sip. *Tastes good.* He took another.

"What do you think?"

"Beats the hell out of the stale macaroni and cheese we had for dinner. Where'd you get it?"

"Off the tender. CO passed out a pound to each of his cans today."

"We have enough to make some for the crew?"

Landa flashed his neon smile. "That's what *I* asked. The guy was a little embarrassed. Another five pounds will come over the gangway before we sail."

Ingram nodded. "Good. They deserve it."

Landa watched as the welders gathered up their gear. "Umm, not a bad job. It looks straight, at least. Could use a little paint here and there."

"We'll get after it," said Ingram, frowning at the smudges of greasy smoke left over from the kamikaze hit.

Landa lowered his voice. "So, you haven't told me. What do you think?"

"About the coffee? I *said* it was good."

"Come on." Landa patted the letter stuffed in his chest pocket, just in with the afternoon mail.

"Lemme read it."

"Negatory. Too much driveling stuff that would drive you nuts. I'm sure it's like when Helen writes--"

"Okay, okay. You've finally set a wedding date?"

"Well, no, but we're going to."

"And now you're getting nervous."

Landa flushed. "Absolutely not. I just have to think about the proper time, that's all."

Ingram allowed a smile. "Don't let me stop you."

For nearly two years Landa had been dating Laura West, a gorgeous platinum blonde pianist with the NBC Symphony Orchestra's West Coast Division. They were engaged, but the war hadn't cooperated with wedding plans. "So, what do you think?" he asked again.

Ingram said, "Okay, I'll tell you what I think. You are one lucky son of a gun. She's too good for you. If I were you, I'd have tied the knot six months ago before somebody could walk in and show her what a good husband is really about."

"I appreciate your confidence."

"Jerry, damn it, get it going before it's too late. Before some rich Hollywood 4-F drives up in his Cadillac with a diamond ring."

"She already has a Cadillac."

"But not the diamond ring."

Landa shrugged.

"You get my gist. Quit putting it off."

Landa rolled his eyes. "Okay. The minute we land stateside I will grab her and--"

"Excuse me, gentlemen." Radioman first class Leo Pirelli sauntered up, arrogant as always. It was something about how he looked directly at his superiors and how he carried his head.

"We're at GQ," snapped Landa.

Pirelli didn't miss a beat. "My apologies, Commodore." He played at clicking his heels. "I was out for a stroll, and--."

"Whaaaat?" said Landa. "You insubordinate--"

"To deliver this to Commander Ingram," Pirelli continued. "It's a priority message and I knew he'd want to see it now. Sign here, please, Captain."

Ingram signed. Pirelli gave a regal bow. "Good evening, gentlemen," he said and walked away.

As Ingram read the message Landa growled. "Todd, you gotta get these people under control. First that damned exec of yours is crapping in my soup. And now that candy-ass radioman is directly insubordinate to--"

"Holy cow," Ingram blurted. "You won't believe this." He handed the message to Landa:

BT
FROM: COMMANDING OFFICER, FIFTH FLEET
TO: COMMANDER ALTON C. INGRAM, 638217, USN
DATE: 16 AUGUST 1945
SUBJ: TEMPORARY DUTY, ASSIGNMENT
INFO: COMMANDING OFFICER THIRD FLEET
COMMANDING OFFICER DET B-27
COMMANDING OFFICER SERVRON 27
COMMANDING OFFICER, DESTROYERS PACIFIC
COMMANDING OFFICER, DESRON 77

1. UPON RECEIPT, YOU ARE TEMPORARILY DETACHED USS MAXWELL (DD 525).
2. YOU ARE TO PROCEED TO CO DETACHMENT B-27 WHEREVER IT MAY BE TO ARRIVE NLT 172400I.
3. FURTHER INSTRUCTIONS VIA COMDET B-27.
4. WHITE, ELDON P. LCDR, USNR ASSUMES TEMPORARY COMMAND MAXWELL.
5. AUTHORIZATION: COM5 BB-27117–5AT

BY DIRECTION
C. J. MOORE
BT

Landa's eyes grew wide. "Jesus. This is from Spruance. What did I ever do to him?"

"Commodore, in case you didn't notice, it's me he's after, not you."

"No, I mean I get Tubby White. What did I do to deserve this?"

"You'll get over it." Ingram reread the message. "Surprised he still remembers me."

Landa pursed his lips and made kissing sounds. "Yeah, please tell me sometime how you made his A list." Adm. Raymond A. Spruance had awarded Ingram the first of his two Navy Crosses in 1942 before sending him back to the South Pacific as executive officer of the USS *Howell* (DD 482). Jerry Landa had been the destroyer's CO.

"And I have until tonight to get there." Ingram turned to his talker. "Anderson, ask combat to check the OP-Manual Annex for the location of Detachment 27-B."

"Sir." Anderson pushed a button and relayed the order.

Only a moment had passed when Anderson said, "Bridge, aye." He reported, "Combat says Detachment B-27 looks sort of like a moving target. Today and tomorrow, it's located on Ie Shima."

Ingram called into the pilothouse to the quartermaster of the watch. "Townsend, you have the local chart up?"

"Right here, Captain."

Ingram and Landa clumped into the pilothouse and crowded around the chart table. Ingram found Ie Shima, a bean-shaped island about three miles off the west-central coast of Okinawa. He picked up dividers and stepped off the distance. "About fifty miles north of here."

A breathless Tubby White stepped into the pilothouse. "Todd, er, Captain. You're not going to believe this. Oh, and here's a copy for you, Commodore." He handed over copies of the message they had just read.

Ingram said, "Thanks, Tubby. Pirelli just brought up a copy."

White mopped his forehead, "One of these days I'm gonna bust him back to seaman deuce."

Landa said, "You better do it before I do, old son."

White ventured a look at Landa and then straightened up and faced Ingram. "Captain. The *Pluto* repairmen have finished gluing on the after stack. Ship is ready for sea."

Ingram said, "So I see. Very well, Mr. White. Do we have fuel?"

"Topped off, Captain."

"Provisions? Ammunition?"

"Done."

"Line handlers?"

"Standing by and ready to split the nest."

"Very well. Set the sea and anchor detail and plot a course for Ie Shima."

"Will do, Captain," replied Tubby White. "All we need is your permission to light off boilers three and four. Also, we have to finish passing the milk and ice cream."

"I thought we had our allotment," said Ingram.

White said, "Well, I spoke with the boys on the *Pluto*. They agreed to help us out with some extra."

Landa asked, "Anything about coffee coming over?"

White replied, "Ah . . . er, Commodore, I traded that for the extra milk and ice cream. I figured the crew would like--"

"Shit!" said Landa, slapping his hand on the chart table. "Why didn't you ask me first?"

"What? I didn't know. I didn't . . ." A sheepish White turned to Ingram. "Permission to light off boilers three and four?"

"Granted. Make sure you check the minefield plots for Ie Shima. Have a copy posted up here as well." Ingram slapped Tubby White on the butt. Eager to escape, White disappeared quickly around a bulkhead.

Anderson suppressed a snicker and the other men on the bridge turned away to hide their smiles. Landa looked to the sky, fighting to hold his temper.

Ingram said, "Jerry, he obviously didn't know you had ordered the coffee. It was for the crew that he--"

"I'll kill the son of a bitch," growled Landa.

"Well, you'll be dropping me ashore at Ie Shima, so I won't be around to see the bloodbath. Of course, by that time Tubby White will be the skipper, and if you do kill him, you'll be up on charges of mutiny."

"The fat little bastard."

Ingram faked a yawn.

"What the hell does Spruance--or Halsey, for that matter--want with you?"

A gentle breeze wafted through the nested ships, taking with it, at last, the odor of death. It was nearly twilight and a quarter moon climbed above the horizon. Ingram sniffed at the zephyr. *Thank you.* He shook his head with the realization that he looked forward to getting off the *Maxwell.* That made him feel guilty. But now, maybe, the nightmares would go away. "I wish I knew."

3

---

18 August 1945
Ie Shima Island, Okinawa Prefecture
Ryukyu Islands, Japan

Ie Shima was flat except for Mount Gusuku, a craggy two-hundred-foot peak that dominated the eastern end of the island. An airfield ran diagonally across the island's center. At one time the five-mile-long island's rich soil had been tranquil farmland. But the fighting for Ie Shima had been as bitter and protracted as it had been for the rest of Okinawa. Bomb and artillery craters pockmarked the once meticulously tilled fields and the white sand beaches.

Pulitzer Prize–winning journalist Ernie Pyle had been killed on Ie Shima the previous April. A war correspondent for the *Washington Daily News*, Pyle was already famous for his reports from the African and European campaigns. He was perhaps more famous--at least among the troops--for promoting the "Pyle Bill" in Congress, which awarded an extra ten dollars per month to infantrymen in combat. A victim of a tumultuous marriage and combat fatigue, Ernie Pyle was wedded to his job. With "his" beloved troops, Pyle moved to the Pacific theater when the Nazi regime collapsed. While touring Ie Shima by Jeep with a colonel and two others he was killed by a Japanese machine gunner. Still in his helmet, Pyle was buried with honors in the military cemetery between an infantry private and a combat engineer. He was the only civilian in World War II to be awarded the Purple Heart.

Ingram stepped off the shore boat near midnight and reported to a thin and balding major named Neidemeier in a deep bunker near the airfield. The bunker was full of squealing electronic machines that reminded him of a Bela Lugosi movie. Tired and half asleep, he paid scant attention as Neidemeier brusquely stamped paperwork, handed it to Ingram, and told him to stand by for orders at any moment. Then Neidemeier waved him off to a Jeep that took him to block A-355, a four-man tent somewhere out in the night.

Ingram barely managed to get the bedding laid out before collapsing into his cot as the tent's three other occupants snored peacefully. Not even the rumble of R-2800 engines being tested kept him awake. He slept soundly--and dreamlessly--until three o'clock the next afternoon, and then went in search of a late lunch. Along the way he discovered that the tents were grouped around an airfield. On one side was a huge boneyard of wrecked Japanese airplanes of all sizes. A few American planes were sprinkled among them. The other side consisted of a polyglot of American fighters and bombers squeezed into revetments. Quite a few transport aircraft were parked on the tarmac before a rickety control tower. Nearby, large tents housed operating personnel, a hospital, and a chow hall. Soldiers, sailors, and Marines were bivouacked there in four-man tents, including the one Ingram occupied in block A-355.

Fortunately, the chow line was open. He wolfed down meatloaf, mashed potatoes, and string beans. Then he found his way back to his cot and . . .

Ingram awoke to find a shadow looming above him. Someone--a nondescript private--was shaking him. "Zero six forty-five, Commander."

"Huh?"

He received no answer. The man was gone. Ingram lapsed back into sleep.

"Rise and shine, Commander." This time it was a major, one of two Army Air Corps throttle jockeys sharing his tent, shaking Ingram's shoulder. He wore a khaki flight suit. "Hi there. I'm Bucky Radcliff. Come on, Commodore, off and on. Today's the big day."

Ingram rubbed his eyes and sat on the edge of his cot. After two nights of solid sleep he felt better. "What's so big about it?"

Radcliff didn't tell him. "Chow at oh seven hundred. Japs at eight."

Ingram stood and stretched. "I have no idea what you're talking about."

Radcliff grabbed his shaving gear and walked toward the tent flap. "You know Major Neidemeier?"

"No. Well, yes, but . . ."

"Better go see him, Commander. I think he's going to tell you that we're going to be seeing a lot of each other." Radcliff walked out.

Ingram dressed, quickly shaved, and walked to the mess tent, where he feasted on scrambled eggs, juice, toast, and coffee. Then he walked over to Neidemeier's bunker. With daylight, he saw that it sprouted antennae of all sizes and was guarded by soldiers with submachine guns. He showed his ID and was admitted to the space with the squealing machines. A bank of radios stood against one wall. Four teletype machines clattered in a corner. IBM punch card and collating machines ground away on the opposite wall. It was hot, and people buzzed about a collection of old metal and wooden desks, waving papers in the air. They wore shorts and T-shirts with no rank or insignia devices.

Except for one man, a gray-faced major who sat at a desk in the middle of the room. His black Bakelite nametag was emblazoned NEIDEMEIER. Books, manuals, and papers covered the surface of the desk, some spilling onto the floor. Behind him was a row of filing cabinets marked Top Secret. He wore stiff khakis with flashy collar devices that looked as if he'd just retrieved them from a box of breakfast cereal. Chewing his fingernails, he looked up to Ingram. "You are Commander . . ."

"Ingram."

"That's right, you're Ingram."

"That's who I am."

Neidemeier narrowed his eyes. "I remember you now. Detachment B-27."

"What is a B-27, Major? The message was very cryptic."

"Oh, my God. Nobody told you?"

"Not a soul." Ingram didn't like the sound of this. He looked around. "Maybe you can let me in on it."

"Well, you're the last of my special assignments. Welcome to Project Sunrise."

Ingram really didn't like the sound of this. "Project Sunrise?"

Neidemeier fanned himself. "There are bugs out here. I hate bugs!"

"Where you from, Major?"

Neidemeier sat up straight. "State Department. Washington, D.C. Special appointment, you know."

"Yes, I know."

Neidemeier looked at Ingram.

Go along with it. "Sorry, Major. I don't know much about bugs. I've been at sea for the past eight months and we don't have bugs out there except for cockroaches."

"I hate cockroaches."

"Major, please. Project Sunrise?"

Neidemeier looked at his watch, an expensive one. "Oh, my God. Seven-forty. You have to move--now. Report to the flight line and Major Radcliff. He's the--"

"I know him; an Air Corps throttle jockey. You put us in the same tent."

"That's right." Neidemeier stood; the man was no more than five eight. "Get your gear. You're flying to Manila today."

"Manila? I don't need to go to Manila. I need to go back to my ship. They have--"

Neidemeier held up a hand and opened a file cabinet. Withdrawing a thick envelope, he handed it over to Ingram and said, "I'm just the messenger, Commander. Somebody up there likes you. A fat assignment. Now, grab your gear, get out to the tarmac, and report to Major Radcliff.

There, you board a C-54 for Manila." He held up a clipboard. "Sign here first."

Ingram signed. "For how long?"

"Two or three days. Then you'll return to your precious ship. And make sure you read your orders."

In spite of his derogatory remarks, Ingram suddenly realized how precious the *Maxwell* was to him. He actually missed her. "Where am I going, again?"

"Manila."

This doesn't make sense. Last time he was in Manila was before the war. "What the hell for?"

"All in due time, Commodore. It's all--"

"Commander."

"Ah . . . excuse me, Commander. As I said, it's all in your packet. You and a few others will be escorting sixteen high-ranking Japs down to Manila."

"Japs? The hell I will."

Neidemeier crossed his arms and frowned. "You're due on the flight line by oh eight hundred, Commander. I suggest you get going. And read your orders."

The packet was heavy in his hand. Ingram took a deep breath. "Fine. Yes . . . I have to gather my gear. You have a Jeep and a driver?"

"Of course. You can ride with me. I'm going too."

Neidemeier told the driver to pull up to a C-54 Skymaster aswarm with mechanics who were bolting the nacelle on the number three engine. High-ranking officers stood under the tail. Ingram spotted at least three generals and two admirals. Loosely gathered on the periphery stood a squad of Marine MPs looking sharp in class A uniforms. A group of Army Air Corp officers stood under one wing, Radcliff among them. Ingram pointed to Radcliff, and the Jeep driver pulled over and stopped. Neidemeier hopped out of the backseat and quick-stepped over to the senior officers, clutching a clipboard to his chest. Ingram unloaded his duffle and walked over to Radcliff.

"Good morning, Commodore," said Radcliff.

"Commander."

"Whatever." They shook hands. A smirk and glance at Neidemeier brown-nosing with the flag officers telegraphed Radcliff's disdain. "Here, say hello to my guys." He nodded to a tall, thin Army Air Corps first lieutenant. "Leroy Peoples is my copilot, but don't ask him to speak; he's from Arkansas and our next interpreter doesn't come on duty until fourteen hundred. So you should--"

"Very funny." Peoples extended a hand to Ingram. "Pleased to meet ya, Commander." Peoples' accent was thick indeed, but it fit his grin and easy manner.

Not missing a beat, Radcliff continued, "And this other guy is our navigator, who's pretty good when he's sober. Meet Jon Berne." Captain Berne, thick and beefy, looked more like he belonged in the boatswain's locker than in an airplane using trigonometry to solve intricate navigation problems at night over the ocean with the plane bouncing and rattling through a thunderstorm.

Radcliff nodded toward Neidemeier and said, "I see he's briefed you."

"Not really." Ingram patted his orders. "Have yet to read these."

"Shame on you."

"Yes, shame on me."

An Air Corps flight sergeant dressed in a flight suit with a label atop the pocket that said HAMMER walked up to Radcliff. "All set, Bucky--er, Mr. Radcliff. She's all gassed and we just finished the plug change on number three. She's as ready as she can get." He handed over a clipboard.

Radcliff signed it and handed it back to Hammer with a nod. He said to Ingram, "Well, believe me, Commodore. Neidemeier doesn't know squat. He's a State Department catch-fart doing dirty work for others. Stick with us. We'll take good care of you and seat you up front with all the good coffee and doughnuts. Maybe even some--"

Both pricked up their ears at a familiar rumble--distant at first--from the northwest.

Initially Ingram thought they might be kamikazes in a last desperate raid. *Where are the air-raid sirens?* The rumble grew to a roar as the dots in the distance took shape. With a sigh of relief Ingram recognized P-51s carrying long-range wing tanks. The Mustangs were arranged in two flights of six each. Each flight was grouped around a B-24 Liberator bomber.

Ingram and the others gasped in unison. Ahead of each B-24 was a Japanese twin-engine Mitsubishi G4M 2 "Betty" bomber.

"Oh, mercy, will you look at that," drawled Peoples.

The cigar-shaped Bettys broke formation and began to circle, one behind the other, as the P-51s and B-24s swarmed overhead. "What have they done?" muttered Radcliff.

"I wish I knew," echoed Ingram. Each of the Bettys was painted bright white with green crosses in place of the red meatball insignia formerly on the wings and fuselage.

A green flare whooshed from the control tower as the first Betty lined up with the runway. The plane was a tail dragger, and with lowered landing gear and flaps it flared over the threshold and made a perfect three-point landing, its engines softly backfiring as the pilot chopped the throttles. The Betty stopped, turned onto the taxi strip and pulled behind a Jeep displaying a large Follow Me sign.

"Hope the Japs can read English," quipped Radcliff.

"One wonders. I've seen them--"

"Oh-oh. Check this." Radcliff pointed.

The second Betty was on its final approach and had begun its flare, but the pilot had not lowered the flaps.

"Oh, Lordy," said Peoples.

"Deep shit," said Berne.

The Betty flared but still had plenty of airspeed. It landed long, touching almost halfway down the runway. It bounced high, hit hard, and ran the length of the runway and onto an extension made from coral patch, its wheels sinking in. The Betty shuddered to a stop in a cloud of white dust. A U.S. Army Jeep raced up behind it.

The first Betty rumbled up to the C-54, spun a 90-degree turn, and stopped, facing the runway. Then the pilot cut its engines. The second Betty taxied up, also spun around, and drew to a halt beside the first one, its propellers scything to a stop.

Ingram whistled. Each Betty had more than a few bullet holes. The elevators of one were bare metal without fabric.

"Newest thang in air conditioning," said Peoples.

Radcliff asked, "What do you think, Commodore?"

"I can't do that right now."

"Do what?"

"Think."

Radcliff sighed. "No wonder our Navy is so screwed up."

The others chuckled as sets of stairs were pushed under the Betty's aft hatches. The hatches opened and Japanese began to descend: high-ranking officers and a few civilians as well. Ingram counted eight from each Betty. They stood stiffly near their aircraft, nervously looking over at the American contingent.

Ingram wished he'd had time to read his orders, but even so he realized something profound was going on.

A tall, leather-booted Army Air Corps colonel whistled from under the tail. He pumped a fist up and down.

Radcliff said, "Showtime, gentlemen. Come on, Commodore, you can board with us.

4

19 August 1945
Ie Shima Island, Okinawa Prefecture
Ryukyu Islands, Japan

The forty passenger seats in the C-54 were quickly filled. The Japanese were dispersed throughout the cabin, each with an MP seated next to him. American officers took up the rest of the seats.

Radcliff had motioned Ingram into a seat up front on the aisle. He was buckling up when Neidemeier hustled up and took the window seat. Buckling his seat belt he asked, "Read your orders yet, Commander?"

Ingram took a look aft and asked, "Who are all these guys?"

"What guys?"

"You know, Japs."

"Read your orders and find out." Neidemeier dug inside his briefcase, pulled out some papers, and began to read.

Ingram's stomach jumped. The enemy was seated right behind him, and he couldn't do a thing about it. "Read my orders, aye." He lowered his tone. "By the way, Major Radcliff tells me we're going to have thunder-storms all the way down to Manila."

"He what?"

Ingram sensed he had hit a nerve. "He says there are two enormous fronts to punch through."

Neidemeier turned. His eyes darted around the cabin.

Ingram continued, "Usually, this flight would take four hours or so. But Radcliff is worried because we have a full planeload. He's not sure if we ..."

Neidemeier unbuckled and stood, looking aft.

Just then, the hatches thudded shut and the flight crew secured them.

A Japanese Navy captain in dress blues walked up front but found no seat. He looked at the MP behind him and shrugged. The MP, a Marine gunnery sergeant, said, "Full house. Looks like somebody snafued."

Flight Sergeant Hammer stepped from the cockpit. "Sorry." He pulled a jump seat down from the forward bulkhead and gestured to the Japanese captain. The captain nodded, sat, glanced impassively at Ingram and Neidemeier, and then looked away. The Marine gunny stood beside Ingram fidgeting.

"Hold on, Sarge," growled Hammer. He disappeared forward.

Number two engine began turning. It caught and fired.

"Get your gear aboard okay, Major?" asked Ingram.

Neidemeier swallowed a couple of times. His face was pasty white. "What? Yes. I don't suppose ..." He looked at the Marine gunny. He had two rows of campaign ribbons with plenty of battle stars. The gunny whistled softly and ignored him, looking at the overhead.

Ingram said, "Relax, Major. This C-54 is equipped with a Torvatron."

"A what?" gasped Neidemeier as number one engine rolled and shud-dered to life. Numbers three and four quickly followed. "Torvatron?"

"Shhhh." Ingram put a finger to his lips. "Top secret."

Uh huh." Neidemeier sat and fidgeted with the seatbelt buckle. "Never heard of it."

"Well, they used a Torvatron to navigate the B-29s to Hiroshima and Nagasaki. Now we have one and we're safe as bugs in a rug."

With a burst from the engines, the C-54 began rolling, braked right, and headed down the taxi strip.

"Where'd you hear that?"

Ingram nodded toward the cockpit.

"Major Radcliff?"

"Yes."

"He shouldn't be disclosing top secret information. He could be arrested. Maybe I should--"

Hammer popped into the doorway again. "Commander Ingram?"

"Yes?"

"Major Radcliff has a spot for you in the cockpit. He tells me the Nip--er, the Japanese captain--and the gunny are to sit where you are and the major is to take the jump seat."

Neidemeier barked, "That's ridiculous!"

Hammer said, "You wanna complain to the major, fine. He's in charge of this aircraft. You'll find him in the cockpit."

Neidemeier unbuckled and stood. "This is quite irregular. I--"

Ingram said, "Please, Major. World War II is over. Don't start World War III."

Neidemeier said, "I only meant--"

Ingram unsnapped and stood eye to eye with Neidemeier. He hissed, "Listen, Major. Don't make a scene. Either you get over there or I'm--"

Neidemeier held up a hand. "Okay, okay, I get it, Commander." He nodded to the Japanese Navy captain. "Do you know who that is?"

"No idea."

Neidemeier lowered his voice, "That's Captain Shiroku Fujimoto of the Imperial Japanese Navy. He was one of their best destroyer commanders. But they don't have any more destroyers, so guess what he's doing now?"

Ingram stared at Neidemeier. *How the hell does he know all this?*

Neidemeier said, "Mine defenses. Fujimoto is one of the IJN's leading mine defense experts. He's our ticket into Tokyo Bay."

"Who the hell wants to go into Tokyo Bay?"

"All in good time, Commander." Neidemeier gave a small grin. "All in good time. And it might become clearer when you read your orders. Now, Mr. Hammer here, as uncouth as he is, is correct. Captain Fujimoto outranks me. So, if you will excuse me . . ."

Neidemeier bowed to the Japanese Navy captain, gestured to the window seat, and sat down in the jump seat.

Ingram stepped aside to allow the Japanese captain to slide by him. With a wink at Ingram the Marine sergeant took the aisle seat.

The C-54 braked to a stop at the runway's head and the pilot began running up the engines, testing mags.

Ingram stepped into the cockpit. *Fujimoto . . . Fujimoto.* The name rang a bell. Radcliff, wearing headphones over a garrison cap, grinned and waved to a jump seat behind Peoples, the copilot. As flight engineer, Hammer sat behind Ingram at a console loaded with engine-monitoring levers and gauges. Now serious, Hammer made some small adjustments and noted them in his logbook. The navigator, Berne, was seated on the port side behind Radcliff at a small but efficient navigation table. He was bent over a chart making notes.

Radcliff said, "Welcome to the nuthouse, Commodore. Would you like a straitjacket?"

"No thanks. Just a parachute."

"Sorry, not enough to go around. Fight crew only. Passengers suck gas. But get this. You get to watch Leroy make the takeoff. So strap in tight, close your eyes, and pucker up while I read the last rites for all souls present. I can go on the PA if you think it's necessary. After all, you outrank me and--"

Stopping in mid-sentence, Radcliff held up a hand then touched his earphones. He spoke into the mike and then nodded. "Got that, Leroy?"

"Got it, Bucky." Peoples released the brakes. The C-54 waddled onto the runway, lined up with the center, and braked to a stop.

"Let 'er rip," said Radcliff.

"Banzai!" Lieutenant Peoples grabbed the throttles and ran up the engines to a mighty roar. The C-54 shuddered and rattled while the four Pratt and Whitney R-2000 engines strained in their mounts, developing 1,350 horsepower each. After a few seconds Peoples popped the brakes and the C-54 began rolling. Radcliff called off the speed, "Eighty-five, ninety, ninety-five . . ."

Peoples pulled the yoke back and the C-54 eased off the runway and easily gained altitude. "Gear up," he called. Then, "Climbing power."

Hammer reduced the throttles a bit. The engines' urgent tone became less strident as Radcliff slapped the landing gear lever to the "up" position, then drawled to Peoples, "Come on, Leroy. Quit showing off with this sideslipping shit."

"Huh?" Peoples face turned pink.

"Right. Get down to basics."

"Sorry, Skipper, forgot we have passengers aboard." Peoples eased the aircraft into a gentle left turn. "By the way, sir, could you please return the flaps to the full up position?"

Reaching for the flap lever, Radcliff said, "I'll put a man right on it."

Berne, the navigator, said in a falsetto, "Lieutenant Peoples, please try to remember we're not hauling Spam today."

Radcliff muttered, "Yeah, just a bunch of generals, admirals, and Japs."

"Yes, sir." Peoples called over his shoulder. "Oh, Captain?"

Berne growled, "How can I help you?"

"Ah, sir, you got a course for us?"

Berne said, "You sure you can handle all this at one time, Leroy?"

"Do my best, Captain."

"Okay, then," said Berne. "Steer course one-nine-three and try not to screw it up. Twelve thousand feet."

"Yes, sir, Captain Berne. One-nine-three, twelve thousand, and don't screw it up. Yes, sir." Peoples reached to set the autopilot.

Radcliff said to Hammer, "Chief, time to give the box lunches to the Japs."

"Right now, sir?"

"Might as well. And break out the orange juice, too. See that they're comfortable. Blankets, anything they want."

"Well, I mean, these are Japs! Shouldn't we--"

"Sergeant. Orders are orders," said Radcliff.

Hammer scratched his belly and stood. "What about our guys? All that brass. What do they eat?"

"Remember, this morning we all dined on eggs, bacon, toast, orange juice, and coffee.

Some of us alfresco, I might add."

"Al Fresco. I remember him," said Hammer. "He was in the 229th. We used to get drunk all the--"

Radcliff interrupted, "I repeat. The box lunches are for Japs only. And especially not that little turd Neidemeier."

Actually, Neidemeier is smarter than I give him credit for, thought Ingram.

"Japs only. Nothing for the little turd. Yes, sir. Orders is orders." Hammer walked out.

The plane droned on with Radcliff and Peoples checking their instruments and writing in logbooks. That done, they began talking politics: Radcliff hated Truman; Peoples loved Truman. Then their talk turned to women. Radcliff loved Jane Russell; Peoples disapproved of her. Berne folded his arms on his chest, put up his feet, tipped his cap over his eyes, and dozed.

The C-54 gained altitude and settled on course through smooth, bright blue skies. Six P-51s with long-range tanks gathered around, three on each wing.

With a sigh, Ingram opened the envelope and began to peruse his orders. As he turned pages the name kept ringing in his mind: *Fujimoto.*

5

19 August 1945
One hundred miles south of Okinawa Prefecture
en route to Nichols Field, Manila, Philippine Islands

"Amazing," said Ingram.

"What's that, Commodore?" called Radcliff.

"Just damned amazing," Ingram repeated.

"What the hell are you reading, *Esquire* magazine?" asked Radcliff.

"Orders, Bucky. Something completely unexpected."

"You mean the Navy is as screwed up as the Army Air Corps?"

"Worse."

"So, where are you headed?"

"Same place you are, Nichols Field."

"Swell. I already knew that. How bout when we get there? Say, you play poker? We need a fourth."

Ignoring Radcliff, Ingram tried to digest what he was reading. A State Department summary enumerated that General MacArthur had been appointed supreme commander of all forces in the Pacific. One of the general's first demands was that the Japanese provide a delegation to meet with his staff in Manila, hence the two white planes with the green crosses at Ie Shima. The number in the delegation--sixteen--was selected because the Japanese passenger version of their G4M2 could hold only eight people. Once in Manila, they were to negotiate a surrender ceremony to be conducted on board an American ship, yet to be named, in Tokyo Bay. More important, they were to discuss procedures for the immediate release of all Allied prisoners in the Pacific region.

So much for the background. Specifically, Ingram discovered, he was on this airplane to work with Captain Shiroku Fujimoto on clearing mines in Tokyo Bay, or Lower and Upper Sagami Wan. *That's the musical chairs guy sitting right out there*, Ingram thought. He wondered if the man spoke English. His eyes and expressions seemed to indicate that he was following the conversation. Maybe so. At any rate, the orders said Captain Fujimoto had been assigned an interpreter, Lieutenant Nogi Tanaka, who was supposed to be among the sixteen Japanese seated back in the cabin.

But why was the name so familiar? *Fujimoto . . . Fujimoto. And what about those sixteen people back there? Army, navy, diplomatic . . .* Ingram wondered how many of them knew about the atrocities he'd seen on Corregidor and the Bataan Peninsula. How many had been directly involved in the Bataan Death March? Or, more recently, the horrible stories filtering back from POW camps in the Japanese Home Islands or the ones scattered throughout Asia.

He wondered how many men back there knew about or were directly involved in his own experience. Had they ordered the raping and pillaging in the Filipino villages whose people had safely hidden his men in the long days of their escape through the Visayans and on to Darwin, Australia? Over the years he had suppressed nightmares about those times, often taking refuge in Helen's arms. Still, the visions flared in unguarded moments: a stretcher-bound Brian Forester bayoneted by a Jap soldier in Mindanao; another Jap soldier bayoneting a wounded Baumgartner on the pier in Penang. Those men had been helpless and worthy of compassion; instead, they were gutted by monsters begat by a monstrous political system.

Ingram stood and walked aft into the main cabin. Captain Fujimoto looked up and regarded him coolly. They locked eyes for two long seconds, then Fujimoto went back to the remnants of his box lunch, the Marine gunny looking on hungrily.

Neidemeier was perched on his jump seat across the aisle. Tucking his packet under his arm, Ingram knelt beside him and asked, "Where's the translator?"

"I see you've finally read your orders."

"Not all. Now where's the translator?"

Neidemeier sighed and nodded to a well-dressed Japanese civilian seated seven rows back. The man looked at Ingram for a moment, glanced at Neidemeier, then looked away.

"That's him?"

"Nogi Tanaka. I think so. Supposed to speak fluent English, Spanish, and Tagalog."

"You *think* so? Aren't you supposed to know who these people are?"

"Yes."

"And you don't know if this is the guy?"

"No."

"Why the hell not?"

"You see, the Japanese were instructed to provide sixteen of their top people. But this surrender has been such an embarrassment to them that people disappeared as soon as they were appointed. They just went away. Nobody wants to take responsibility."

"Then who are all these guys?" Ingram waved around the cabin.

"Good question. Whomever they could scrape up, I suppose."

"So the roster is not accurate?"

"It was as of yesterday afternoon. The thing is, we're not sure if these are their best people."

"So how did you make up this list?"

Neidemeier gave a thin smile. "Oh, no. It wasn't me. I'm not that good. This comes straight from OSS."

"OS--what the hell is an OSS?"

Neidemeier sighed. "You've been at sea too long."

"Come on."

"OSS: Office of Strategic Services. A secret government agency." He looked furtively from side to side. "Keep a secret?"

Ingram almost laughed. This airplane was full of people blabbing secrets. "Sure, ah . . . by the way, what's your name?"

"What?"

"First name; what do they call you?"

"Clive."

"Okay, Clive. I'm Todd. And yes, I can keep a secret."

"See that man back there? Blond American, young looking, in a green suit?"

Ingram craned his neck a bit and rose on his haunches. *There.* He spotted a very young man, a near teenager, with white-streaked blond hair that spilled across his forehead nearly to his eyebrows. He was seated next to an Air Force general, and they were engaged in an animated conversation, hands waving. "Young is an understatement. Looks like he should be fishing little red whistles out of Cracker Jack boxes."

"That's Colin Blinde. Don't let his looks fool you. A wunderkind. He graduated from Yale at the age of nineteen. And yes, he's our OSS man. Feeds me all this stuff, which he filters from the State Department. Then I translate it into militarese."

"If that means he's smart, I don't want any part of him."

"He knows a lot of people in high places. He's seated next to General Dexter, Curtis LeMay's second in command."

Ingram whistled.

"Speaking of high places," Neidemeier nodded to the Japanese captain across the aisle. "Your Captain Fujimoto over there. Originally, we were to have a rear admiral."

"An admiral was bumped by a captain?"

"No, no. We were supposed have Admiral Onishi."

"Who is . . . ?"

"Leader of the kamikaze corps."

"Well, where is he?"

"Committed hara-kiri. Onishi could have done wonders for us. Instead, he slit open his stomach and his throat. Then, in direct defiance of Hirohito's peace proclamation, our next choice, Admiral Matome Ugaki, flew off."

"To where?"

"Nobody knows. Ugaki was a samurai. He couldn't bear the shame of defeat. So he strips off all emblems of his rank, climbs into the observer's seat of a B5N, and takes off in glory on a kamikaze attack on Okinawa on the day peace was declared."

"What happened?"

Neidemeier shrugged. "Don't know. Ugaki's plane just . . . disappeared. Conjecture is the combat air patrol got him. Trying to arrange the surrender terms has been just one crisis after another. There was a palace coup. They tried to kill Hirohito."

Ingram was shocked. "Who would do such a thing? I thought the emperor was sacrosanct, a god."

Neidemeier nodded. "It's the army. They can't stand the idea of surrender. If they had their wish, they'd fight to the last bullet . . . the last drop of blood."

"I thought the atom bomb taught them otherwise."

"One would think so. But they stick their heads in the sand. And they're still all-powerful in Japan. Do you realize that they have more than a million men in the Kwantung Army in China?"

Ingram thought about that. "Maybe so. But they'd have to get to the home islands to fight us, wouldn't they? And without a navy or air force for transportation . . ."

"You have a point."

"And even in China they need to be supplied, don't they?"

"Yes. But keep in mind that the Kwangtung Army is not just an army. It's a political system and economic machine and military organization all wrapped into one. They are almost self-sufficient. Prime Minister Tojo came out of the Kwangtung Army."

"Well, let 'em rot in China," Ingram said. "Let's return to the subject. Who staged the revolt on the emperor?"

"Kwangtung fanatics--junior officers ranking no higher than major-- who tried to kill Hirohito." He looked back into the cabin. "But it was put down after only a few hours. They never got near him. I'll tell you," the major added, "these people are burning up their best and brightest even though the shooting has stopped. It's scary. We need them."

"What for?"

"Who's going to run the country and prevent a civil war or civil riots? The emperor can't do it by himself."

Ingram nodded.

Neidemeier waved. "So what we have with us today is a patchwork quilt of Japan's diplomatic and military staff. We pray their negotiations and commitments are binding. Otherwise, it's back to . . . God forbid."

Ingram thought about all the years at war--the death and horror and fear. Neither he nor anyone else was anxious to go back on the firing line.

Neidemeier gave a long sigh. "But we were lucky on one score."

Ingram's eyebrows went up. He had to lean in as Neidemeier spoke in a near whisper. "See that general three rows down on the right hand side?"

Ingram craned his neck to see a bemedaled Japanese general wearing a crisp uniform. His cap rested on a thin briefcase in his lap, and he sat very erect, looking straight ahead. "I see him."

"General Torashiro Kawabe, deputy to Imperial Army Chief of Staff General Yoshijiro Umezu, the top officer in the entire Japanese army. With Kawabe along, we may have some pulling power."

"Let's hope." As the plane droned on, Ingram suddenly understood that General MacArthur was not just going to walk into Hirohito's palace and take over. The peace process was not going to be easy. A lot had to happen: on both sides of the Pacific.

Hammer walked by counting a fistful of ten-dollar bills.

"You there," said Neidemeier, "what's that?"

Hammer's lips drew to a grin. "The Japs tipped us for their lunches. Ten bucks apiece. I have over a hundred and fifty smackers. Gonna give it to Bucky and see--"

Neidemeier stuck out his hand. "Give it to me."

"But Major, the Japs are tipping us. That means . . ."

"Please," said Neidemeier. "It's evidence."

Hammer's fists went to his hips. "Evidence of what?"

Ingram said, "It's okay, Hammer. Give it to Bucky."

"Yes, sir." A relieved Hammer quickly stepped through the cockpit door.

Major Neidemeier gave Ingram a fierce look.

Ingram said, "Forget it, Clive."

Neidemeier sputtered, "That's insubordination."

"Forget it. It'll be something for these guys to tell their grandkids."

Neidemeier snorted. "I'll bet they spend it on women."

"Women? Where, Clive? Manila? Tokyo? Those cities are wrecked. They'll probably lose it in a poker game." A moment passed as Neidemeier gained control of himself. Ingram flipped to the last page of his orders. "I'll be damned."

"What?"

He pointed to the signature line.

"Yes, Otis DeWitt. He works for General Sutherland."

"Now I know who sucked me into all this."

"You know him?"

"In a manner of speaking. I see he's a brigadier now."

"What's wrong with that?"

Ingram chuckled. "Otis DeWitt a brigadier general? What's this world coming to?"

Neidemeier said, "A little advice. Don't trifle with General DeWitt. He'll scour you."

"He's a pussycat."

"How can you be so sure?"

The day continued clear, with Berne giving the crew a course to fly over the South China Sea down Luzon's west coast. The landscape below was dotted with extinct volcanoes, and the terrain looked verdant and tropical. By late afternoon they had dropped to five thousand feet and arrived at the entrance to Manila Bay, an enormous natural harbor thirty miles across. Three of the P-51s accelerated ahead while the other three climbed and took station five hundred feet above the C-54. Ingram stood just behind Radcliff; Berne and Hammer were there too, all peering out the cockpit window.

Peoples was back at the controls. He popped the C-54 out of autopilot and banked left. Soon they flew right over Corregidor and into Manila Bay.

Ingram watched the tadpole-shaped island slide under the left wing. He hadn't been here since 1942. Unlike the Bataan Peninsula to the north and the Pico de Loro Hills to the south, Corregidor was brown and barren, devoid of greenery, a victim of the two-month Japanese round-the-clock artillery barrage prior to the invasion. Memories flooded: his ship, the minesweeper *Pelican*, had been bombed and sunk in a cove at nearby Caballo Island. Several of his men had died there. He and the remainder of his crew had taken refuge with 11,000 GIs and Filipino Scouts on Corregidor, a 3-mile-long island able to accommodate only 4,000. Many were escapees from Bataan and were terribly wounded. Ingram watched many die.

Corregidor did hold one bright spot in his memory. He had met Helen on Corregidor. He wondered what it was like now in the Malinta Tunnel's hospital lateral where she had worked so hard to save soldiers, amputating arms and legs without anesthetic as artillery shells thundered overhead. During the last two months before being evacuated by submarine she had worked in that putrid atmosphere with scanty supplies, limited equipment, and almost no food or sleep.

Radcliff seemed to understand. "Been there, Commander?"

"Yes, I have," Ingram said softly.

"Yeah." Radcliff waved a hand toward Manila, almost hidden beneath haze. Smoke rose from the hills to the left. He said to Peoples, "What do you think, Leroy? Can you find Nichols Field in all that goop?"

"Do my best, Bucky. The chart says ten miles south of town." Peoples looked a bit nervous, sitting forward, his back erect.

Radcliff keyed his mike, held up a hand as he checked in with the tower. "We're cleared to land. Altimeter 29.62. Runway two-four."

They set their altimeters, then Peoples said, "Roger runway two-four."

"That's it. Come a little bit more right and have at it, my man. And get us down to two thousand feet." Radcliff looked up at Ingram and winked.

"Roger, Skipper."

"And try not to screw it up, Leroy," said Berne.

"Shut up, Jon," said Peoples.

Berne crowded in. "Hey, you can't--"

Radcliff turned around and, giving Berne a cold look, chopped a hand across his throat.

Berne nodded and stepped back.

"Cavite." Ingram picked out the Cavite naval station off to the right. Ahead, a long runway appeared out of the dust.

"Voila, Leroy! You did it," cried Radcliff. "Hey, look at that."

The three P-51s that had gone ahead were buzzing the runway, three across, about fifty feet above the deck. The three in their escort above suddenly dove to join them.

"Damnation," said Berne as Nichols Field hove into full, clear view. An enormous crowd lined the runway from one end to the other--so many people that they seemed a solid mass.

Mostly Filipinos, Ingram guessed.

The P-51s had all joined up and now buzzed Nichols Field six across. At the end of the runway they pulled up, one at a time, and banked left to turn into their downwind leg while dropping landing gear, flaps, and bleeding off speed. They had timed their maneuvers to pull in behind the C-54 and land right behind it.

They were halfway through their downwind leg when Radcliff grabbed his earphones. Thirty seconds passed before he gave a terse, "Roger." Then he said, "The tower informs us there's a big crowd down there, estimated in the thousands. A Jeep will meet us at the end of our roll-out and lead us to a VIP area where our, ah, passengers will embark for the Rosario Apartments."

Radcliff looked around the cockpit, his gaze settling on Ingram. "Know anything about the Rosario Apartments?"

"Downtown," said Ingram. "Very posh. Two blocks from the Manila Hotel."

"Hotsy-totsy," said Peoples.

Radcliff said, "Ah, Leroy?"

"Yeah?"

"You mind if I take it?"

"All yours, Pop."

Radcliff grabbed his control yoke as Peoples released his. Then Peoples picked up his landing checklist. Berne and Hammer returned to their consoles as Peoples called out the list, all four making settings and barking answers.

With Radcliff flying precisely, they lined up on final. Peoples called the last item on the checklist and then said, "Wow-wee. Look at that crowd. You'd think it was county fair day."

Radcliff looked up at Ingram and said dryly, "Don't bother to sit and strap in Commodore. You're all goo and jelly if I stack this thing."

"Trust you with my life, Bucky." Ingram stayed on his feet, peering out the cockpit, enthralled at the sight.

"Suit yourself." Then, "Full flaps if you please, Mr. Peoples."

"Full flaps," said Peoples.

Radcliff chopped the throttles and eased back on the yoke. The C-54 kissed the runway with hardly a bleep.

The nosewheel settled and Hammer said, "Nice."

Peoples said, "Hey, Skipper."

"Yeah?"

"You were sideslipping back there."

"What about it?"

"Well, there was no crosswind."

"So what?"

"Why the hell can't I sideslip?"

"Someday, when you're skipper, you can sideslip all you want."

"Grandstander," muttered Peoples.

They laughed.

6

19 August 1945
Nichols Airfield, Manila
Luzon, Philippine Islands

Ingram followed the C-54's aircrew out the forward hatch. Hoisting overnight bags, they hobbled down the stairway and found themselves in the midst of the enormous crowd they had seen on their approach. Angry Filipinos bumped against them and shoved their way past, some shaking their fists, others growling. There were women with babies, many dressed in simple peasant clothing. All pushed toward the C-54's rear exit, where the Japanese delegates and their chaperones were debarking.

Neidemeier quick-stepped down the stairway and joined them.

Radcliff had to shout, "Where's our ride?"

Neidemeier yelled back, "Don't worry. Follow me."

"Which way?" Radcliff yelled.

Neidemeier pointed to the wall of humanity.

"These guys don't look too friendly," Hammer said. Like an offensive guard, he stuck out his elbows and led the way, people bouncing away from him. As they got farther from the plane the crowd thinned.

Neidemeier guided them to a line of trucks and stopped behind an open Studebaker six-wheeler. He flipped down the tailgate and waved them inside.

"This?" gasped Radcliff.

"This is it. No exceptions," Neidemeier said.

The truck was loaded with a half dozen beefy MPs. They stubbed out cigarettes and grudgingly gave up the forward end of the truck. Ingram, Radcliff, Peoples, Berne, and Hammer tossed up their bags and mounted the tailgate. Moving to the front, they looked over the cab. The tarp was off the top, and a breeze twirled from Manila Bay, cooling them in an otherwise humid evening.

The crowd had nearly swallowed up the Japanese delegates and their American chaperones trying to make their way toward a line of four-door Mercury staff cars painted olive drab. It was all the MPs could do to hold the crowd back.

What most amazed Ingram were the photographers. There were hundreds, it seemed, their cameras clicking, flashbulbs popping with the intensity of machine guns.

Also, there were quite a few off-duty American soldiers in the crowd, who chanted, "Banzai! Banzai!" With huge grins, they thrust both arms in the air and swept exaggerated bows toward the staff cars.

Berne muttered, "They should show respect."

"Can you blame them?" countered Radcliff.

"Ain't this the livin' end," groused Peoples. "We ride in trucks while Japs ride in limousines. I thought we won the war."

"Quitcherbitching," said Radcliff. "You could be back on Okinawa swatting flies."

"Yeah, yeah," said Peoples.

"Here you get three squares and nice, clean sheets."

"And here I get to swat mosquitoes instead of flies."

"Leroy, I can always get another copilot," said Radcliff.

"Yeah, yeah," said Peoples.

The photographers pressed in closer; camera shutters clicked, flashbulbs spiked in the deepening dusk. The crowd was right behind them. Like an inexorable tide they swept through the photographers and merged around the line of MPs ringing the Mercury staff cars.

"These people are really pissed off," said Radcliff. He turned to the MP sergeant. "Aren't you guys going to do anything?"

The sergeant sighed. "Looks like we're going to have to, sir." He blew a whistle, waved an arm over his head, and shouted, "Come on, ladies." The MPs jumped down and ran forward to join the MPs at the staff cars. Others dashed past from trucks behind.

"Why can't we am-scray?" asked Hammer.

"It'll be soon enough," said Neidemeier.

"Well, it better be soon or we'll all be dog meat," said Berne. He looked around and said, "Gotta get this for history." He pulled a 16-mm Bell & Howell movie camera from his bag and loaded a fifty-foot roll of film. Then he wound it up, put his eye against the eyepiece, and began panning the crowd.

"You do this often?" asked Ingram. Cameras, especially movie cameras, were supposed to be illegal, but many used them anyway.

Berne said, "We go to a lot of places. You know: Guadalcanal, Tulagi, Rendova, Leyte, Okinawa. Got into Tarawa a couple of times. So I get shots of wrecked airplanes, burned-out tanks, and pillboxes. Got some natives, too. Beautiful sunsets, that sort of thing."

"Color?"

"Yup." He leaned over. "Keep a secret?"

Ingram snickered to himself. Why was everyone blabbing to him about keeping secrets? "Of course," he said solemnly.

"A buddy of mine is with the 509th."

Army Air Corps mumbo-jumbo, Ingram thought. "What's the 509th?"

"You know, the 509th composite group: B-29s. The ones who dropped the A-bombs on Japan. Anyway, my buddy was a crew member on the *Great Artiste* and shot some footage with this little baby." He tapped his camera as he panned. "The *Great Artiste* is a B-29; it accompanied *Bock's Car* as one of the instrument planes."

"Wow! How did it turn out?"

"The guy blabbed. They confiscated his film. Nearly threw him in the stockade. Instead he's in hack for three months. I was lucky to get my camera back."

Just then Ingram spotted Captain Fujimoto. A staff car door was held open for him. He ducked his head and entered. No sooner had the Mercury's door closed than a rotten pomegranate exploded against the window, showering the car and bystanders with red juice.

Ingram looked away and asked, "Did he see it? You know, the blast?"

Berne flicked off the switch and examined his camera as if it were a holy object. "They let me talk to him for a couple of minutes. He said he couldn't sleep the first couple of nights. All he could see when he closed his eyes was this great pinkish flash. Then they were hit by a shock wave that tossed them around. After that, an enormous mushroom cloud boiled up above them. Amazing. They were at thirty thousand feet and this damned cloud zipped up to forty or fifty thousand feet, with weird lightning bolts flashing inside; all sorts of reds, yellows, and greens. 'The devil's caldron,' he called it."

Ingram thought of the pomegranate splattering against the staff car's window. "I can't imagine," he said.

"I can't either," said Berne. He went back to his photographing.

The next thing Ingram knew, Major Neidemeier was standing beside him. He looked around Ingram to see Berne photographing. "Say, what's he doing with that camera? That's not authorized."

"Don't worry. He's just--"

Neidemeier waved a hand. "He should be--"

Someone yelled up to Neidemeier. "Clive, what the hell are you doing out here? Why aren't you in Washington?"

Neidemeier shouted down, "Wanted to see it all for myself, General."

"Well, damn it all," the voice shouted up in a Texas twang, "git your ass back on that plane and skedaddle for the States. You're not cleared for this."

I know that voice. Ingram stepped to the side and looked down. There he was, Otis DeWitt, now a brigadier general with a star on his collar and aide to Lt. Gen. Richard K. Sutherland, MacArthur's chief of staff. Ingram had met him under far worse conditions when they were trapped on Corregidor three years ago, DeWitt a major, Ingram a lieutenant. General DeWitt certainly looked healthier than during their starving days on the "Rock."

With his weather-beaten face sporting a thin mustache, he appeared to be back to his normal weight of 180 pounds on a 5-foot 8-inch frame. Otis DeWitt wore his signature cavalry campaign hat and jodhpurs. Clamped between his teeth was a long, gold cigarette holder, the same holder he'd spirited away from Corregidor, Ingram supposed. A Lucky Strike was jammed in the end. Ingram cupped his hands and yelled down. "Otis, how the hell are you?"

"Watch what you say, Commander," whispered Neidemeier.

DeWitt jammed his fists to his hips and rocked back on his heels. "Welcome back, Commander. I needed you two days ago. Where the hell were you?"

Commander, huh? Same old Otis. "Got caught in a crap game. Sorry. Say, why don't we go downtown to the Chi Chi Club tonight and dig up some whores?"

Neidemeier covered his eyes and shook his head.

A corner of DeWitt's mouth turned up. "What would Helen say to that?"

"She'd kill me."

"She should. You don't deserve her."

"You're right about that, Otis. But guess what? We have a son."

DeWitt's craggy face softened. "I'll be damned. Congratulations. You named him after me, of course?"

"Not a chance." There was some commotion forward. The lead staff car began moving. "He's named after Jerry Landa, my boss."

DeWitt began walking forward. "Boom Boom Landa?"

"Yeah."

"Worthless son of a bitch." He turned and called back. "We have you bunking at the Rosario Apartments with the Japs."

"Great. Do I get to sleep with a carbine?"

"Naw, naw, we have guards out the ying-yang. Plus, I wouldn't trust a Navy guy with a carbine. You'd just shoot yourself in the foot."

"I appreciate your confidence, Otis."

"The pleasure's all mine. Now, instead of hookers, how about dinner tonight?"

Ingram glanced at Neidemeier. The major looked on in wonder. With a wink Ingram called down, "Don't think so, Otis. I already have a dinner date with General and Mrs. MacArthur."

DeWitt walked quickly toward the last Mercury. With a wave over his head he called, "Not to worry. I'll break it for you. Be ready at nineteen hundred. And wear something decent for a change."

"So you two do know each other," said Neidemeier dryly.

"We go a ways back."

"Maybe you can ask him to--"

Neidemeier's request was lost as the Filipino crowd pushed in with a mighty roar, the MPs barely holding them back. DeWitt sprinted for the Mercury, opened the door, and jumped inside just before the crowd began throwing rocks at the staff cars. The first Mercury in the line rounded a corner and sped away from the crowd as rocks caromed off its top and sides. Ingram spotted the silhouette of one of the Japanese looking stoically forward. Some Filipinos shook their fists; others spit.

The MPs jumped back into the Studebaker. The sergeant pounded the cab top and yelled, "Roll 'em, Freddie." With a clank and a grind of its gears, the truck heaved into position as the first Army vehicle behind the Mercurys. Soon they were racing through the crowds and out of the airport. They turned onto Dewey Boulevard and headed north for downtown Manila.

The exuberance of arriving in Manila disappeared quickly. The men's chatter stilled as the truck drove deeper into the city.

Radcliff waved at the wreckage. "The Japs fought to the last man. The dogfaces had to go in and flush 'em out, house to house."

Manila had been declared secure just a month ago, on 5 July. Even then, many Japanese soldiers had taken to the jungles north of the city to continue the fight. Some of the buildings still smoked; wreckage was strewn everywhere; dust hung heavily; and a putrid odor enveloped the city. At times Ingram had to cover his nose with a handkerchief. He'd smelled that odor before. Clearly, the Filipinos had not recovered all of the bodies from the buildings the Japanese had wrecked in their withdrawal. People staggered about, coated with a grayish morbid powder, their faces covered with rags to keep out the dust and the stench.

Ingram had lost his appetite by the time the Studebaker pulled up before the Rosario Apartments. The staff cars were parked in a neat row, and Ingram gave a thought to going inside, grabbing one of the Japanese, and wringing his neck. But that passed as he jumped down, grabbed his bag, and walked into the lobby.

Neidemeier followed him in. "We're bunking two to a room. The aircrews are all together, so you're with me. Hope you don't mind."

"Not at all, Clive. Why don't you sign us up? I could use a shower."

"Right away, Commander."

The apartment had two bedrooms with a connecting bath and shower. Ingram hadn't had a decent shower in months; the hot water didn't work but the cold was lukewarm. It felt wonderful, and he lingered for fifteen minutes, scrubbing every pore. He stepped out, skin tingling, as Neidemeier called, "Houseboy has your uniform. It'll be pressed and cleaned within a half hour."

"I hope he knows military pleats. Otis DeWitt is a stickler."

"Don't I know it."

Twenty minutes later Ingram went down to the cocktail lounge to find DeWitt already there, pacing. He looked Ingram up and down and said, "Your shoes need shining . . . badly."

"Mrs. MacArthur said she wouldn't mind. Now, if you'll excuse me . . ."

"And where are your campaign ribbons?"

"Back on my ship. Nobody told me I was being presented to the inspector general of the Army."

"Two Navy Crosses and six battle stars would have impressed even General MacArthur, let alone Mrs. MacArthur."

"Sorry. As I said, I didn't know."

"Come on, I have a table waiting in the dining room. But first I want you to see something." He led Ingram down a long hallway. They drew up to a set of double doors with four guards, each with a Thompson submachine gun slung on his shoulder. With a wink to Ingram, DeWitt said to one of the guards, a sergeant, "Everything okay?"

"Quiet as a two-man funeral, sir."

"Just need to check." DeWitt nodded to the door. The sergeant reached down and opened it a crack. DeWitt stuck in his head and then nodded to Ingram.

Ingram looked in and saw three long tables connected in a u. There were six guards inside watching over the Japanese, most of whom were now sitting back, smoking and chatting amiably. He whistled to himself. The table was set with silver and china. Three large silver platters held turkey carcasses. Serving dishes with remnants of mashed potatoes, peas, creamed spinach, turkey stuffing, and cranberry sauce were scattered about.

Ingram spotted Fujimoto sitting six feet away. Once again they locked eyes. This time, Fujimoto glanced toward the turkey carcass and then looked back to Ingram with a nod. Ingram backed away and slowly closed the door.

DeWitt had been watching. "What do you think? Thanksgiving with all the trimmings in August. Can you believe it?"

"Amazing. You'd think we'd be feeding them maggots."

"General MacArthur, with the full concurrence of the State Department, has decided to take another approach. He wants to treat the Japanese courteously. Show them good intentions. Be decent to them."

"Well, that's nice, Otis. Tell that to the guys on the Bataan Death March. Or the ones we left behind on Corregidor."

They rounded a corner and stepped into a small dining room that was about half full. "That will be dealt with," said Dewitt. "There will be war crimes trials. Even now they have their eyes on Yamashita and Tojo."

"Not enough, Otis. These bastards deserve every bit of--" He stopped short as a waiter approached. DeWitt announced himself, and they followed the waiter to a table in the corner. Once seated, DeWitt smoothed his mustache and asked, "First of all, tell me about Helen. Is she as beautiful as ever?"

Ingram allowed a grin. "Even more so. At least judging by the photos she sends. Our son, Jerry, is a pistol, crawling around, getting into pots and pans. A real terror, she says."

"She still a nurse?"

"Yes, they have her at the Fort MacArthur Army Hospital in San Pedro. You know, where the big guns roar?"

DeWitt's face darkened. "Damn things are useless." He waved in the direction of Corregidor. "Just like the ones on the Rock. Man, oh, man, did we learn a lesson."

Ingram tried to force away the memory. He'd been on Corregidor with DeWitt, had seen the bitter lesson firsthand. Corregidor's big World War I–style "disappearing" 12-inch guns were useless against aerial attack and Japanese artillery sighted in from Bataan.

"And you live there?" DeWitt asked.

"Huh?"

"San Pedro?"

"We rent a little house near San Pedro High School, about five minutes from work. And she's a captain now, so show some respect."

DeWitt chortled.

"I'll see her in a couple of weeks. I'm taking leave, you see. Jerry Landa is getting married and I'm his best man. His fiancée is Laura West."

"The singer?"

"Yeah, he lucked out."

"What's with you Navy guys? Marrying above your level. Must be all that gold braid shit you wear on your sleeves."

They sat in silence for a moment until Ingram asked, "What's up, Otis? I know I'm having dinner with you for a reason."

"Ummm."

"You've got too much on your plate with all these Japs to sit on your butt and talk over old times with me. So spit it out."

DeWitt took a deep breath. "Well, I could say it has to do with your question about how we're dealing with the Japs."

"Something about showing respect is the point you were trying to make."

DeWitt nodded and then asked, "Tell me, Todd, who's going to run the government if you grind them under your boot?"

"Who cares?"

"About eighty million Japanese do. If you leave the emperor intact, you have the machinery for a strong civil government."

"What about the military?"

"They're all washed up. We have these delegates here to help put together an interim government, get back our prisoners ASAP, set up a ceremony for the surrender in Tokyo Bay, and get the Japanese army and navy to lay down their arms everywhere." He paused. "Everywhere, that is, except . . ." He looked at Ingram, a glint in his eye.

Ingram knew that look. "Except where?"

"The Rooskies."

"What about them?"

"They haven't stopped fighting in Manchuria. In fact, they're enveloping Japan's Kwantung Army right now. We figure the Rooskies have the Japs outnumbered three to one, and yet the Japs are holding strong in some areas." DeWitt shook his head. "It's only a matter of time, though. A lot of their people were parceled out to fight the Pacific war. Now their army is made up of mostly conscripts and inexperienced garrison troops."

"Too bad for the Japs."

"Yes, except we've learned that Joseph Stalin . . . excuse me, Generalissimo Stalin, has designs exceeding the treaties we all agreed to."

Ingram felt a sinking feeling in his stomach. He tried to change the subject. "Where's our menus?" He looked around.

"That's all taken care of."

"What?"

"Turkey. We're all having turkey. Happy Thanksgiving." DeWitt patted Ingram's forearm.

As if on cue, two waiters laid a spread before them of Jell-o salad, ginger ale, and bread and butter.

"No wine?" Ingram complained.

"Same as the Japs," DeWitt said. "We need everybody on their toes. A meeting tonight, another tomorrow morning, then we send them on their way back to the land of the rising sun."

"Wonderful." Ingram started his salad. Delicious. Then he said, "What designs?"

"Huh?"

"You said the generalissimo has designs."

"Oh, that." DeWitt stared at Ingram for a moment.

"Come on, Otis; damn it."

"Okay, okay. It turns out Stalin wants to take back all of Karafuto--or Sakhalin Island, as the Rooskies call it. Plus," he waved his fork, "he wants the northern half of Hokkaido."

Located just south of Karafuto, Hokkaido was the northernmost of the four main Japanese home islands. "Jesus."

"That's right. Stalin wants his pound of flesh. Word we have from the State Department is that Stalin and Truman are circling each other like a pair of tall dogs, growling and snorting. Tell the truth, we don't know what's going to happen. It changes day by day. But right now the Rooskies are driving south on Karafuto and are pretty close to wrapping things up. That's when they plan to jump the La Peruse Strait and take Hokkaido."

Ingram said, "I thought we were through with fighting." He pushed away his Jell-o half eaten.

"Me too," said DeWitt. He took a last bite and said, "But maybe there's something we can do about it."

"I hope so."

"Well, you might be part of it. You're meeting with my boss in twenty minutes to talk it over."

Ingram gasped, "General Sutherland?"

"The one and only. Now, finish your salad. Here comes our dinner."

7

August 1945
Rosario Apartments, Manila
Luzon Island, Philippines

They walked down the hall to a door marked "Suite B." DeWitt nodded to one of the two guards and knocked. Hearing a muffled response DeWitt stuck his head in and said something. Then he turned to Ingram. "Go on in, Todd," he said, opening the door wider. "I'm right behind you."

General Richard K. Sutherland sat near the end of a cloth-covered table as Filipino waiters cleared dishes from what looked like a party of six. A blue cloud hung in the room. Ingram sniffed: cigars and cigarettes. To help things along, Sutherland smoked a Lucky Strike; a near-empty pack lay close to his left hand. Ignoring Ingram and DeWitt, Sutherland flipped pages in a thick report, fully engrossed.

A side door opened and a silver-haired Filipino wearing a starched white coat and gloves entered. He reached over the chair next to Sutherland and said, "The general forgot this." With a gold-toothed smile, he pocketed a corncob pipe and silently withdrew. DeWitt raised his eyebrows at Ingram.

Sutherland looked up. "Seats please, gentlemen. Just another minute." He returned to his reading as Ingram and DeWitt pulled out chairs. Sutherland looked to be in his mid-fifties with sandy hair and an average build. Like General MacArthur, Sutherland was a blueblood. His father had been a U.S. senator from West Virginia. He'd sent his son to Phillips Academy and then to Yale. Sutherland's hair was mussed; dark pouches hung under his eyes. No sleep and the jungles of New Guinea can do that to you, Ingram supposed.

Sutherland had been General MacArthur's chief of staff since 1937, and that job was taking its toll. More so since President Truman had named MacArthur the supreme commander of the Allied Powers (SCAP). Accordingly, events of the time weighed on MacArthur and his staff. And this man sitting before Ingram and DeWitt was making decisions in the general's name affecting tens of millions of people. Sutherland and his staff were stuck in a near-hopeless quagmire trying to deal at the same time with the U.S. State Department, the Japanese military, the Japanese imperial household, the transport home of tens of thousands of GIs, recovering thousands of emaciated prisoners of war, and occupying a nation of 80 million subjects loyal to Emperor Hirohito.

With a grunt, Sutherland laid down his half-finished report and checked his watch. "Damn, I'm due next door in two minutes." He looked up. "We're meeting with the Japanese delegation tonight and then tomorrow morning. And then we send them home tomorrow afternoon." He looked to DeWitt, "Otis, do you have that stuff on imperial Japanese protocol, traditions, and usage?"

DeWitt fired back, "It's done, sir."

"On my desk first thing tomorrow?"

"Yes, sir."

"Good." Sutherland fixed them both with a stare and then said to Ingram, "Always good to have the Navy around."

Ingram said, "Glad to help out, General."

"You'd think this was a time for celebration and thanksgiving, but it isn't, not with this." He closed the report and tossed it aside. "You know what this says?"

Ingram and DeWitt shook their heads.

"Of course not. Pardon my rhetoric. It says that Generalissimo Josef Stalin is demanding all of Karafuto and half of Hokkaido." He looked at Ingram. "Do you realize that Marshal A. M. Vasilievsky kicked the shit out of the Kwangtung Army?"

"That bad, sir?"

"And that Vasilievsky's three armies total about one and a half million men, most of them battle-hardened troops fresh from fighting Nazis on the European front. The Japs' ranks were decimated to bolster the Pacific war. All that remained were old men and untrained garrison troops. They had no idea about what they were up against and didn't have a chance against Vasilievsky's people." He tapped the report with a forefinger. "The Commies outnumber the Japs three to one in men and three to one in tanks. And these are big tanks, T-34s, against the little matchboxes the Japs slap together with American scrap metal." He looked at Ingram with tired blue-gray eyes. "Nope. The Japs didn't have a chance. The Rooskies beat them with what they learned from the Nazis: maneuver warfare." He ticked off his fingers: "Manchuria, the Kuriles, and now Karafuto."

Ingram stared back. *What the hell am I doing here?*

Unfazed, Sutherland continued, "Our intel as of twelve hours ago states that Stalin intends to keep going south from Karafuto. It appears he will order Marshal Vasilievsky to make an amphibious invasion of Hokkaido across the La Perouse Strait day after tomorrow."

"Jeepers," said Ingram.

"I wondered when you would wake up, Commander," said Sutherland.

"You have my attention, sir."

"Very well." Sutherland continued, "However, it turns out we have a president with balls. He challenged Stalin--excuse me, I mean the generalissimo--reminding him that the Commies are indeed entitled to Karafuto, or Sakhalin, as they call it, in accordance with agreements reached at the Yalta Conference. The Kuriles too. Hell, the Japs took it from the Russians in 1904. Why not grab it all back? So far so good.

"But, God bless the president, he stuck to his guns and told Stalin that

Hokkaido is not a matter of negotiation." Sutherland waved a radio flimsy. "This just in. State Department informs us that Truman told Stalin to go fly a kite. That all of the home islands are to remain under the jurisdiction of the Japanese in accordance with the Potsdam Declaration. Stalin signed the dotted line. The ink isn't even dry, so Truman has him over a barrel."

Sutherland took a long drag. "All this from a Democrat president. I am impressed, truly I am." Sutherland sat back and sipped coffee.

Ingram couldn't resist. "And?"

"We wait for the generalissimo's decision. In the meantime, we need you to do something for us."

Ingram glanced at DeWitt, who rendered a noncommittal shrug.

Sutherland said, "Here it is in a nutshell. Do you know anything about Walter Boring?"

"I haven't had the pleasure," said Ingram.

His sarcasm wasn't lost on Sutherland. "Of course not; you've been driving destroyers around the Pacific."

"Trying to do my best, General."

"And well you've done. Two Navy Crosses, and I was there to see Ray Spruance pin one of them on you." That was true. With ten other men, Ingram and DeWitt had escaped the horrors of Corregidor via an open boat through the Philippine archipelago. After reaching Australia they were taken to San Francisco, where Rear Adm. Raymond A. Spruance had pinned the Navy Cross on Ingram in an impromptu ceremony in the Pope Suite of the St. Francis Hotel. At the same time Sutherland promoted Otis DeWitt to lieutenant colonel.

"Thank you, sir."

Sutherland took a deep breath. "So we hope we have Stalin backing down and not invading Hokkaido. The fighting is winding down in Mongolia, China, the Kuriles, and Karafuto--I guess I'll have to get used to calling it Sakhalin. Even with all that, we need you for a special mission."

Here it comes.

"Take it easy, Commander. You'll be with us for only a couple of days. We'll have you back to your ship within a week."

A door creaked open at the other end of the room. A balding colonel stuck his head in the door. "Okay, General?"

"Right there, Sid." The door closed and Sutherland turned back to Ingram. "That's Sydney Mashbir, our chief translator; best in the business. I'm supposed to be conducting the meetings, but it's Sid who understands every nuance of their lingo. He'll sit beside me and catch it if they try to snow us."

Ingram blurted, "What will General MacArthur do?"

Sutherland gave a sly grin. "General MacArthur has retired back to his suite at the Manila Hotel, and as far as I know is watching a movie with his wife and young Arthur."

"Oh."

Otis DeWitt spoke quietly, "It's the imperial way, Todd."

Ingram must have looked bewildered because Sutherland leaned over and patted his forearm. "Gamesmanship, son. The general knows it better than anyone. Even better than Emperor Hirohito. And the delegates understand it. We have a simple list of demands, and it's really not necessary for the general to be there. They would try to sidetrack him with some stupid detail, and then it gets messy."

Ingram said, "I think I'll stick to driving destroyers."

Sutherland chortled. "That's the spirit. Now, back to Walter Boring." He paused for a moment and butt-lit another Lucky Strike. "Boring is a Red Cross representative who was inspecting Japanese POW facilities near Harbin, China, when the Soviets attacked suddenly. The Japs swept Boring up and carried him east just ahead of the Soviet invaders. Eventually, he ended up on Karafuto and was trapped in a pocket near Toro on the west coast where the fighting is still going on. So far, they're holding off the Russians, but it sounds like the end is near, a matter of a week or so. It's essential you get Boring and return him to us before the Soviets get him."

Ingram sat back. "Oh, sure," he snapped his fingers, "just like that."

"Mr. Ingram," barked DeWitt, "please remember where you are."

Sutherland raised a hand, "It's okay, Otis. I don't blame him. He doesn't fully understand the connection."

Ingram took a deep breath. "Sorry, General."

There was a rap on the door. Mashbir stuck in his head. "All set, General."

"Be right there, Sid." Quietly he said to Ingram, "Otis has the details, but basically it's this. Boring has information that's prejudicial to the security of the United States, especially if it falls into the hands of the Soviets."

"Jeepers. I thought they were our friends."

"Don't believe all you read, Commander, especially about Communists," said Sutherland. "Basically, you are to fly to the Toro airstrip on Karafuto and bring Walter Boring out."

"How do I find him?"

"He's with the Japanese, under their protection." DeWitt's twang notched up a bit. "It's like this, Todd. You fly into Toro, contact the garrison commander there, and have him hand over Boring and any documentation he may have."

Ingram raised his eyebrows.

"Documentation?"

"Can't talk about that, Todd. Safe to say that the Japanese have assured us that this can happen. They'll be waiting for you."

DeWitt grabbed Sutherland's pack of Lucky Strikes and plugged one into his cigarette holder.

Sutherland stood. "Please don't get up. I have to go, gentlemen. It's been a pleasure. See you tomorrow morning, Otis." He gathered his papers, then his near-empty pack of Lucky Strikes, and said to DeWitt, "You're welcome."

"Hell, it was my pack to begin with, General."

They both grinned. "So it was." Sutherland walked out.

Twirling his cigarette holder, DeWitt said, "Major Radcliff will take you there in his C-54. Colin Blinde will also go, and we'll send a squad of Marines just to help out." With great panache, DeWitt lit his cigarette and blew a long stream of smoke.

"Blinde? He's a fop."

"I know, I know. But he has back channels."

"Back what?"

"Someone reliable who tips us off to stuff."

"Oh, a spy."

"Spies can be shot. A back channel is far more reliable and much safer than someone hiding in the bushes and snapping pictures through the window."

"Why do you need a back channel to the Japs? Just point a gun at them."

"No, not the Japs. I mean to the Russians."

"What do the Russians have to do with this?"

"Just in case. That's all I can say."

"Fine. So, I just show up and ask for Walter Boring. Is that it?"

"Hopefully. Boring is a Swiss citizen, so they have no reason to hold him. And don't forget we're sending you in with Fujimoto." DeWitt blew a smoke ring. "And here's something Captain Fujimoto doesn't know. His little brother is the Japanese garrison commander there."

"How is that going to help?"

"Fujimoto is a mine-laying expert. If the Soviets come into play, he can trade information with them about the mines laid around Karafuto."

"Let me ask again, Otis. How can the Soviets come into play if they have yet to take the territory? And why me? Why not some flunky major like Neidemeier?"

"I don't know all the answers, Todd. We want you because you have experience with Japs. And Russians too, if it comes to that."

"Russians? Only once, and that was a long time ago."

"Well, suffice to say we're trying to cover all the bases."

Ingram drummed his fingers. "What can you tell me about Fujimoto?"

"He's one of those we need to help us in a peaceful occupation of Japan and to agree to our terms for a surrender ceremony. And you'll be accompanied by an interpreter, one of yours."

"One of my what?"

"Navy. Lt. Larry O'Toole. He rode down with you on the plane.

"There were a lot of people on that plane."

Well, I understand he's good, so give him lots of room."

"Okay. Now, what about the surrender ceremony? When is that?"

"A week or two. No later than the end of August. Then you'll see two hundred U.S. Navy ships anchored in Tokyo Bay, yours included--what is it, Todd?"

"It just hit me. Fujimoto acts like he knows me."

"I don't think he knows you, but he knows of you."

"You're speaking in riddles."

"His father was Rear Admiral Hayashi Fujimoto; his brother was Lieutenant Commander Katsumi Fujimoto, both recently of the Imperial Japanese Navy.

"You mean--?"

"Captain Fujimoto and his younger brother are the surviving males in the Fujimoto family, the other two having been dispatched by you with a torpedo in Nasipit Harbor on Mindanao. You know . . . the place where we . . ."

During Ingram's escape from Corregidor in a 36-foot launch, Katsumi Fujimoto, skipper of the destroyer *Kurosio*, tried to run him down off Fortune Island. In his zeal, Katsumi Fujimoto ran his ship aground, allowing Ingram to escape in the darkness. Months later, Katsumi Fujimoto was relegated to the command of a captured American service barge in Nasipit, Mindanao. While there, he renovated a captured flush-deck American destroyer. He took it out for torpedo practice one night with his father, Rear Admiral Hayashi Fujimoto, at his side. It was to be a night of great achievement for Katsumi, the family's oldest son. Instead, Ingram managed to launch a Mark 15 torpedo into the ship, sinking her with all hands.

"I remember, Otis."

Dewitt straightened in his chair. "Look, Todd, it's simple. How can Fujimoto be pissed at you if you reunite him with his little brother? It all works, you see."

"Jesus. You guys play for keeps."

"It's important, Todd." DeWitt's cigarette was nearly done. He took it out of the holder and crushed it in an ashtray.

"I think I can get you aboard ship to see the surrender ceremony."

"You're kidding."

"Ninety-two percent sure."

"Can I bring a guest?"

"Like who?"

"Like my boss and my exec?"

"Jerry Landa is a worthless son of a bitch."

"What did he ever do to you?"

"Tells farting jokes in the officers' clubs, for one thing. Embarrasses the ladies. He does that everywhere, I'm told."

"Otis, that's Jerry on the beach. He knocked that stuff off years ago, anyway."

"Wrong. Last performance two weeks ago at the Kadena O Club."

"You were there?"

"Only because admission was free. No tickets required to see that jerk. Likes to be called Boom Boom."

"He hates that name."

"Well, everyone was calling him that."

"Otis, let me tell you something. At sea, Jerry Landa is one of the best fighting sailors you'll ever find. I've served with him for almost three years now and trust him with my life."

"That's what I'm afraid of."

"What?"

"When Landa stops fighting, is farting all he knows in peacetime? You see what I mean?"

"Otis, I--"

DeWitt raised a hand. "Maybe I'm being too rough on the guy. I'll see what I can do. But just getting *you* in is going to be really tight."

"So, it's going to be a big deal?"

"A major deal. And it's growing by the minute. The world press is being invited. Representatives from all the Allied nations. Everyone wants in. Yes, a very big deal."

Ingram sat back as DeWitt fished out a new pack of Lucky Strikes. Just then, Sutherland burst through the door. "Otis, you don't mind if I--ah, look at that."

DeWitt stripped off the pack's cellophane and slowly counted out ten cigarettes.

Sutherland gave a deep mock bow and took them. "Thanks, Otis. I owe you."

"That's three packs so far."

Sutherland gave a great laugh. "There aren't many people who could talk to me like that, cigarettes or not. Look, I sent one of the waiters off to the PX for a couple of cartons. That satisfy you?"

"Very nice, General, thank you, sir."

"The Japs love these too. American cigarettes. Great for negotiating. They're going nuts in there."

"Glad to help out, General."

Sutherland produced a gold Ronson lighter and lit a Lucky Strike. Then he looked to Ingram. "How's it going? You got it?"

Ingram said, "Think so, General, except for one thing."

Both looked at him.

"This Walter Boring. What's he do? What's so big about him?"

DeWitt and Sutherland exchanged glances. At length, Sutherland said, "I'm sorry, we can't tell you that."

8

---

21 August 1945
En route to Ie Shima Island, Okinawa Prefecture
Ryukyu Islands, Japan

After a quick lunch, the convoy raced Ingram and the others back to Nichols Field for a 1:30 takeoff. This time there were no angry Filipino crowds, just a desolate, smoldering city and MPs waving them through traffic. Time was of the essence because the Japanese had to transfer to their G4M2s at Ie Shima for a flight back to Japan, and deteriorating weather was predicted.

Ingram was in the cockpit jump seat watching Peoples do the takeoff while the others laughed and taunted. They were comfortable with Ingram, so their language was crass, especially at ten thousand feet and on autopilot. Every few minutes the C-54 hit an air pocket and dropped a few hundred feet. The passengers in the main cabin cursed as the aircraft jiggled and bounced.

"I'm here." Major Neidemeier stood over Ingram. He'd agreed to switch to the cockpit jump seat while Ingram spent time with Fujimoto back in the main cabin. The plane shook. Neidermeier reached up and braced himself against the overhead.

Berne said, "Better not touch that, Major. It's high voltage."

"Jeeeez!" Neidermeier jerked his hand away.

Ingram stood. "It's okay, Clive. Here, sit." He checked the Bakelite tag on the spot where Neidemeier had braced. It was labeled AUX RAD 2. He looked at Berne, who shrugged.

Neidermeier sat and swiveled his head, his eyes becoming large.

"Seat belt," barked Radcliff.

"Okay, okay," said Neidemeier. He strapped in, getting more bug-eyed as he looked about the cockpit. "Look at all these dials and levers."

Radcliff turned around. "You buckled up?"

"Well, yes, I suppose so."

"Good. Don't move, and don't touch anything."

"Yes, yes, okay."

Radcliff went back to monitoring his gauges.

"All set back there?" asked Ingram. He took a step aft.

"They're waiting for you," said Neidemeier.

The plane bounced for a moment. Neidemeier groaned. He asked, "So now can you tell me about the Torvatron?"

"The what?" said Ingram.

"At Ie Shima you said this aircraft was equipped with the latest safety device, a Torvatron."

Ingram slapped his forehead.

Neidemeier asked, "Please, Commander, can it help us through this?"

"Well, I'm not sure about all the settings. I'm not a pilot, you see." *What the hell do I do now?* Ingram caught Hammer's eye.

Hammer picked it up. "Ohhhh, the, ah, Torv . . ."

"Torvatron," snapped Ingram.

"Yeah, the Torvatron."

Neidemeier turned to Hammer. "So, we do have one?"

Hammer looked back to Ingram, his face deadpan. "I think so."

"What do you mean you think so? Do we have one or not?"

"Well, yes," said Hammer, dropping his gaze back to Neidemeier.

"What's it do?"

Hammer fiddled with switches. "Kind of hard to say, Major. It's complex, and I'm not sure if we carry the latest mod."

"Wait a minute, Commander Ingram told me this aircraft was fitted with one of the newest safety devices: a Torvatron. And now you, the flight engineer, aren't sure if we carry the latest modification?"

"Well, I'm not sure if I can say any more," said Hammer.

Ingram tried to exit, but the plane lurched in a downdraft and he stumbled against Berne. "Sorry."

Berne looked up with a grin.

"Well, do we have one or not?" demanded Neidemeier.

"Well, I . . ."

Radcliff spun in his seat. "Indeed, we do, Major Neidemeier."

"Fine. Can you tell me what it does?"

Radcliff eyed Ingram. "Well, basically, the Torvatron is still classified top secret. That's why Sergeant Hammer can't respond. But I can tell you a little."

"Go on. I'm cleared for top secret."

Radcliff lowered his voice. "Okay, here's the dope. A Torvatron is a spheroid hydrofrezassbitz that's connected to the quavertine radiometer that governs all sigmoidographic information."

Peoples clapped a hand over his face. Berne fiddled with a sextant. Hammer suddenly became involved in a fuel transfer.

"Sigmoidographic? Like in a doctor's office?"

Radcliff looked from side to side, "Shhhh. Yeah, doctors' offices, same idea; used for people with a shitty outlook."

"Huh?"

"Right, the idea is the same, except a Torvatron is used for shitty weather. Like now, it's bumpy. So, what happens is we crank in a 17-degree offset to the tircumdittleflatter and then we--"

The plane hit another air pocket and dropped. Ingram grabbed the edge of Hammer's chair and held on.

"What was that?" wailed Neidemeier.

"Power supply interruption to the Torvatron," said Radcliff. "We'll be okay now." To Hammer: "Sergeant!"

"Sir!"

"Better go aft and make sure everyone's buckled in. Weather looks snotty up ahead."

"Yes, sir." Hammer unbuckled and walked out.

Neidemeier asked, "What do we do if we don't get the power back?"

Radcliff faced forward and tightened his seat belt straps. "Later, Major. I have work to do."

Ingram exited quickly.

Aside from the jiggling the main cabin was quiet. Except one could feel the tension as the plane bounced and bucked. Nevertheless, people tried to doze or read magazines. In the rear, two Japanese naval officers and a Japanese general were gathered around General Kawabe's seat. Four Marines stood in the aisles, watching closely. The conversation, although animated, seemed normal. Hammer walked up to them and soon had them in their seats and belted.

Fujimoto again sat in the front-row window seat. The aisle seat was empty, and the Marine gunnery sergeant across the aisle was fast asleep. An American interpreter, a balding Navy lieutenant with dark bags under his eyes, sat in the bulkhead-mounted jump seat just in front of Fujimoto.

Ingram nodded to the aisle seat. "May I?"

Fujimoto gestured to the seat and Ingram sat.

They turned to examine one another. Ingram marveled that he faced someone who just a week ago had been dedicated to killing him. Then it occurred to him that Fujimoto was probably thinking the same thing.

Fujimoto rattled off something in Japanese.

"He says you look tired, Commander," said the interpreter.

Ingram forced a smile, "So do you, Lieutenant."

The interpreter asked, "Does it show?"

"Ingram. Todd Ingram. Call me Todd."

"Larry O'Toole."

They shook hands. "You do look beat," said Ingram.

"No doubt about it. We went 'til 2:30 in the morning. Not much shut-eye, I'll tell you."

O'Toole had a legal device on his collar. Ingram asked, "You an attorney?"

"Who wants to know?" He faked a Brooklyn accent.

Ingram grinned.

"University of Notre Dame." He held up his left hand displaying a class ring. "Class of 1937--liberal arts. Law school, class of 1940." He pointed to Ingram's class ring. "Annapolis?"

"Class of 1937. Where'd you learn Japanese?"

"Grew up there. Tokyo. My dad worked for RCA. Lead engineer." With a look to Fujimoto he said, "I hope he's still there."

"You mean--"

"I went home to go to Notre Dame. Dad stayed. I have no idea what happened."

"Your mom?"

"Died in 1933 in a car wreck."

"I'm sorry."

"Gets worse. Dad took up with a Japanese girl later. I don't know what happened with the two." He bit a thumbnail.

"Everything go all right last night?" Ingram asked.

"As far as I can tell. There was a little trouble at the start with the wording of the surrender agreement--something to do with how the royal family is to be addressed; miniscule point but very tricky. I have to tell you, Colonel Mashbir is the greatest. The Japs were ready to give up at first. But Mashbir caught the error and changed it right there on the spot without permission from anybody. He just did it. And that was gutsy because the wording came directly from the State Department. Talk about playing with fire. He didn't even ask General Sutherland. The guy is amazing. The Japs agreed, and we moved on." O'Toole loudly exhaled. "I have to tell you, I thought I knew everything, but I learned a lot."

"So, the emperor retains control?" Ingram looked again at Fujimoto. He seemed intent on their conversation.

"Absolutely. But he's subject to the authority of the supreme commander."

"Ahhh."

O'Toole continued, "After that, it went okay until . . ."

"Until what?"

"Some real trouble came when we asked about the location of the POW camps. Like squeezing blood out of a rock. But it sounds like we have them now."

The C-54 slammed into an air pocket and dropped, shaking when it hit bottom. Beverages spilled; a Marine cursed.

O'Toole turned white and mumbled, "I hate airplanes."

Ingram felt a bit shaky himself. Neidemeier snored, and he'd not slept well last night. Air pockets didn't help. He mumbled back, "We're punching through a front. Don't worry about it."

"I do worry about it. A buddy of mine was a Hellcat pilot who . . ."

Fujimoto slowly held up his left hand. Both Americans gaped at the ring on his third finger. "I'm a Domer, too," he said, "although not quite Irish."

O'Toole gasped, "I'll be damned. University of Notre Dame." He squinted, "Class of . . ."

"Nineteen thirty-five," said Fujimoto. "Electrical engineering."

"Holy cow," said O'Toole.

"And after that?" asked Ingram.

Fujimoto shrugged. "The navy, of course. My father wanted me to go to Etajima, but I got lucky and scholar-shipped to Notre Dame." Etajima was the naval academy for the Imperial Japanese Navy. "Afterward, I returned to Japan, got into the swing of things, and grew up in destroyers, so to speak. Just like you." He fixed Ingram with a dark stare.

"You know who I am?"

"I do. I've known almost since it all happened in Nasipit. I had no idea we would meet face to face."

Ingram felt the blood draining from his face. Cursing the circumstances as well as the weather he muttered, "Me neither."

O'Toole asked, "You guys know each other?"

"In a manner of speaking," said Fujimoto.

"Well, if that's the case, maybe I can get some shut-eye. You clearly don't need an interpreter here." O'Toole started unbuckling.

"Please remain with us, Lieutenant," said Ingram. Then he looked to Fujimoto, "Look, I wish I could say I was sorry about all this. But your brother and your father were--"

Fujimoto held up a hand. "An explanation is not necessary. It was war. My father and my older brother are gone now. I have a younger brother, but I'm afraid he is lost too. I fear my country is lost as well: the fire bomb raids; your A-bombs, whatever you call them; the emperor's capitulation; mass suicides--our top officers are killing themselves as we speak. Tokyo, Kobe, Yokohama, Sasebo--so many cities devastated, to say nothing of Hiroshima and Nagasaki. Tens of thousands of women and children incinerated. The trouble is, I can view this like a Westerner and am therefore cursed with an understanding of both sides of the issue: my years in the States have done this to me--all that Catholic training. I hope my countrymen will forgive me, Mr. Ingram, because I love Japan deeply. And she is reeling." Fujimoto took a deep breath, "I understand you need the mines cleared from Sagami Wan."

"Yes. They're planning the surrender ceremony in Tokyo Bay for the last week in August. We need to get our ships in there."

Fujimoto sat up. "Indeed. I missed that part of the meeting. The ceremony is going to be on a ship, not ashore?"

"I can think of no more appropriate place."

Fujimoto's face grew dark. "Commodore Perry returns."

Ingram said, "They tell me it was at Admiral Halsey's request. They've already sent for Perry's flag, the one he flew when he entered Tokyo Bay."

Fujimoto stared for a moment. "We begin again."

"I hope so. Maybe in the right direction this time."

O'Toole's mouth hung open and he snored loudly.

"Poor guy has had it," said Ingram. He shook O'Toole awake. "Larry!"

"Huh?" O'Toole sat up and smacked his lips. "Oh, sorry."

Ingram said, "Look, go aft, grab an empty seat, and get some sleep. You'll be coming to Karafuto with us, so you need rest."

"Garden spot of the globe." O'Toole lowered his voice. "Let me ask you, Commander, is that trip necessary?"

"Ask General Sutherland. Now, go on aft and get some rest."

"As you say, sir." With a nod to Fujimoto, O'Toole stood and walked aft.

Ingram turned to Fujimoto, "We need your help in clearing those mines. Can you do this?"

"Of course. I have the charts. It should be fairly easy."

"Can you give them to me right away?"

"Can it wait? Things are in such turmoil."

"No, it can't. Admiral Halsey wants to send in the Third Fleet as soon as possible. We need those charts."

Fujimoto rubbed his chin. "Perhaps you can send someone back with us to Tokyo. We'll gather the charts and send them back with him."

"On those planes? They're wrecks."

"That's all I can offer."

Ingram drummed his fingers. It hadn't been Neidermeier's snoring that kept him awake last night. It was the orders Sutherland and DeWitt had given him--orders authorized by the office of the supreme commander: Gen. Douglas MacArthur. That's why he'd tossed and turned. All he wanted was to rejoin his ship and rediscover the promise of going home, of seeing Helen and Jerry and holding them close. He was tired of the threat of war, of war itself, of the dust and aftermath of war. Instead, they were sending him out among a vanquished and still-hostile enemy. He couldn't even write a letter to Helen; no mail service was available where he was going. "We'll have to think of something else."

9

21 August 1945
Ie Shima Island, Okinawa Prefecture
Ryukyu Islands, Japan

The C-54 bucked and bounced for hours on its way to Ie Shima. American and Japanese passengers alike snatched barf bags from seat backs. It was near dusk when the C-54 crabbed its way onto final approach. The cockpit door was clipped open, and Ingram heard a resounding cheer in the cockpit as Radcliff sideslipped the C-54 to a beautiful touchdown against a twelve-knot crosswind.

After the propellers stopped windmilling, a ground crew rolled ladders up to the hatches. Ingram stood to let the Marine sergeant escort Captain Fujimoto down the aisle. Fujimoto turned once and asked, "Are you sure you want to do this?"

"Orders, Captain. And if it's as you say, then it won't take long, will it? No more than a day?"

"I suppose not. But don't be surprised at what you see." Fujimoto ducked out the hatch, joined the other delegates on the ground, and headed toward their white-painted G4M2s with the green crosses.

Ingram found Clive Neidemeier taking deep breaths on the tarmac. His face was pasty, and Ingram could swear his cheeks had a greenish tinge. "Rough trip?" he asked.

Neidemeier snapped, "You needn't patronize me, Commander."

"What do you mean?" Ingram could hardly hide his smile.

"You know perfectly well what I mean. Those people are animals. I have never been so insulted. Torvatron indeed!"

"Sorry to hear that. Did you get sick?"

Neidemeier shook his head.

"Very good. A lot of people were puking in the main cabin."

"I'm sure Major Radcliff and his gang were expecting the same from me. But I didn't give them the satisfaction. They--"

A young man walked up to them. "Oh, here," said Neidemeier, "I don't think you've met Colin Blinde yet."

Blinde stuck out a hand, "Good afternoon, Commander. I've heard so much about you." Despite his youthful appearance Blinde's voice was deep and resonant, and his diction was clipped, efficient, like that of a lawyer addressing judge and jury in a packed courtroom.

Ingram caught a hint of aftershave as they shook. "Ummm, smells like home."

Blinde gave a deep laugh. "Actually, I just slapped it on to overcome the smell of all that"--he waved a hand--"vomiting. The general next to me puked like there was no tomorrow."

"Have to admit I felt a little shaky myself," admitted Ingram.

"But then you have your sea legs."

"Something like that. Maybe a drink of your aftershave would help smooth the waters."

"Not this stuff." Blinde smiled again, his teeth sure to give Landa a run for his money in a Pepsodent ad. "The people at Aqua Velva try to guard against that; they lace it with a bittering agent. It's called, uh," he snapped his fingers, "denatonium benzoate to discourage, ah, sipping."

Denatonium benzoate. It rolled off Blinde's tongue easily, telling Ingram this man was no dummy. For some reason it also triggered a caution light in the back of his mind. "Well, in spite of all that, a few of my sailors dared; they got very sick."

"They learned a lesson."

"Indeed, they stood before me at captain's mast for deliberately putting themselves on the binnacle list."

"Sick list?"

"Exactly."

An engine roared to life. They turned to see one of the Japanese G4M2's engines fire up, blue smoke blasting under the wing and stabilizer. Its Japanese passengers were boarding on the opposite side. The twin-engine bomber looked forlorn in its white livery. One aileron had a bullet hole, and there was a large fabric tear in the left elevator. To Ingram, the thing looked like . . . a hearse.

"That's your flight," said Blinde.

"Thanks, Colin. You want to ride with me? We could play Parcheesi on the way to Japan."

Blinde's smile was shallow. "I wish I could go. But there's too much to look after here."

Ingram noticed that the other half of the Japanese delegation still stood near the other G4M2. Mechanics swarmed over it. He asked, "What's with the other Betty?"

Neidemeier said, "Damaged from that rough landing yesterday, I'm told. Probably won't get out of here until tomorrow. You'll go with seven of the most important delegates in that plane there. The others stay until repairs are completed."

Ingram said, "Hey, Clive, give one of them my bunk. It's available."

Blinde continued, "The most important items are the surrender ceremony documents negotiated in Manila. That and our demands for locations of all POW camps. They promised it would all be at the Imperial Palace no later than noon tomorrow. If not, the Allied governments will be very upset. And the Japanese know it."

"Okay."

"We'd like you to have this." He handed over a holstered .45 with two magazines of ammunition.

"Great. When they organize a banzai charge against me I'll hold them off from the back of the plane," said Ingram dryly.

Blinde drew himself up. He was a bit taller than Ingram and had broad shoulders: an athlete's body, not muscular but well defined. "Commander, this assignment is extremely important. Especially, if we want to bring an effective end to the war and embark on a successful road to peace."

DeWitt and Sutherland had thrown all this at him late last night. Ingram had gone to bed in a daze and had slept little. His exhaustion was getting to him; his reserves were low. He replied, "Let me tell you something, pal. You scraped the bottom of the barrel when you chose me. I don't know why you did, but it was stupid. I have a far more important job--one, I remind you, that I'm trained for: ensuring the safety of my ship and crew and fighting my ship if necessary. And yes, going in harm's way."

Blinde covered his mouth. "Like Lord Nelson?"

"That's not funny."

"Sorry."

"You really need to go back to your roster and find somebody more qualified to . . . play spy."

"That's enough, Commander!" Neidemeier barked. "Keep in mind to whom you are speaking. Mr. Blinde speaks with the full weight of the State Department."

"I thought he was OSS."

"Well, that too."

"Oh, yeah? Please ask Mr. Blinde where he was when the kamikaze hit my ship. Or where he was when the Japs invaded the Philippines or Guadalcanal or Pearl Harbor, for that matter. I don't see any stars on Mr. Blinde's shoulder boards. In fact, I don't see any shoulder boards. I wonder if--"

Blinde held up a hand. "I get the idea, Todd. You are exactly right. The Navy did a magnificent job and you deserve a breather, and a commendation. We'll make sure you are returned to your unit as soon as possible."

"The unit is the USS *Maxwell*. And forget the commendation. That belongs to the guys who aren't coming back."

"Of course. The USS *Maxwell*." Blinde spoke soothingly, as if he did have shoulder boards full of stars. "Todd, there's a good reason for all of this. You'll find out when you get to Karafuto. Now, are your instructions clear?"

Ingram began strapping on the .45. "I'm to fly with the Japanese tonight to Kisarazu, Japan. I'm to make sure the minefield charts are accurate and complete. I am then to dispatch those charts via a soon-to-be-named Japanese destroyer to rendezvous with the Third Fleet, such destroyer to then lead the Third Fleet into Tokyo Bay."

"Good. And then?" prompted Blinde.

"Tomorrow morning Major Radcliff will fly into Kisarazu airfield to pick us up and take us to Toro Village on the west coast of Karafuto Island, where we'll meet the brigade commander and secure the release of Walter Boring, the Red Cross representative."

"And how are you going to ensure this is done?"

"Captain Fujimoto will accompany me. He doesn't yet know that his brother, Lieutenant Kotoku Fujimoto, is the brigade commander at Toro. Captain Fujimoto, perhaps using the radio, will ensure we have permission to land at the Japanese airfield there and help us accomplish our mission with the people on the ground."

The wunderkind clapped Ingram on the shoulder. "Very good, Commander. It should go without a hitch."

"I wonder," said Ingram.

"Yes?" asked Blinde.

"I introduce Captain Fujimoto to his long-lost little brother. They drink sake, sing "Home on the Range," and then turn over Walter Boring to me at which time I fly out in a blaze of glory."

Blinde drew a large smile. "Very good, Commander. Not sure about the blaze, but you have the right idea."

"What about the Soviets?"

"My information is that they're not there yet. Not for at least a week. Maybe two. So there's plenty of time."

"Your information?"

"That's our intelligence."

The other engine on the G4M2 wound up and fired. It looked as if all the passengers were on board. A man stood outside the aft hatch looking toward Ingram.

"Your stuff in there?" asked Blinde.

Ingram nodded. "A small duffle. Captain Fujimoto took care of it."

"Better get going. You have a long flight." Blinde stuck out a hand. "Godspeed."

Ingram shook it, then turned to Neidemeier. "Major, can you mail a letter home for me--for my wife?" He held out an envelope.

"May take two or three days. And I'll have to have it censored."

Ingram flared, "Listen Major, may I remind you that the war is over? You don't need to censor this. If you don't mail this now, I'm going to--"

Blinde snatched the envelope and said solemnly, "It'll be in her mailbox within . . ." he examined the address, "San Pedro . . . umm, thirty-six hours tops, Commander, maybe less."

"That quick?"

"Yes, that quick; by courier. Now, please, go."

"Okay." Ingram walked away.

He was almost to the plane when Radcliff caught up to him. "You're not climbing into that the piece of crap are you?"

"Haze gray and under way. Gotta go, Bucky. See you tomorrow?"

"Hammer is going over our little bus with a fine-tooth comb. It'll be in tip-top shape.

"Good. Bring coffee and doughnuts."

"Todd, I have to tell you," he pointed to the G4M2, "that number two engine leaks oil like a sieve, and look at all those bullet holes. You'll never make it."

Damn. Ingram was overwhelmed with an urge to turn back. He looked over to Neidemeier and Blinde standing under the C-54's wing, their hands on their hips. *Those bastards.*

"And the weather."

"What?"

"Are you listening?" Radcliff plopped his hands on Ingram's shoulders. "I said the weather, you damn fool. You'll have more than a bumpy ride. Predictions are for headwinds on the nose. It looks shitty."

"Bucky, let me ask you a question."

"Shoot."

"Would you fly in this if you were ordered to?"

Radcliff dropped his hands and gave a nod. "Yeah, I would. I can handle it. But those are Japs and that thing's a crate that belongs on a trash heap. Let them commit hara-kiri."

Ingram remembered something Sutherland and DeWitt had said: that these men carried plans for one of the most important paths to peace for all humankind. Blinde had said the same thing. That it was imperative that those instructions be followed to the letter. No tricks. He was there as a watchdog. He had no idea why they'd chosen him, but he knew he had to go. And yet, while tossing in his sweat-soaked sheets last night he'd had a dark premonition. Early that morning he had written the letter to Helen.

Ingram took Radcliff's hand and gave it a firm shake. "Thanks, Bucky. Gotta go. See you tomorrow. No excuses." He turned, walked up to the hatch, and climbed in.

10

21 August 1945
Ie Shima Island, Okinawa Prefecture
Ryukyu Islands, Japan

A Japanese rating closed the hatch and the G4M2 surged forward. The airplane bounced on the rough tarmac, and especially hard on the tail wheel not far from where Ingram stood. The passenger cabin was much louder than the C-54's. And being a converted bomber, it was cramped. Ingram looked around and saw three passenger seats on the starboard side and four to port. A jump seat was jammed between the last starboard seat and a narrow doorway with a curtain drawn across the entrance. *Probably the toilet.* Luggage was piled up the center aisle. Ingram guessed it was to distribute the weight.

The delegates turned and cast cold stares as Ingram looked about for a seat. It struck him that these were some of Japan's most prestigious officials: flag officers, diplomats, and a royalist. They looked at him with undisguised resentment, almost loathing. *What the hell?* Ingram felt an impulse to go for his pistol.

In sign language, the rating bowed and pointed to the jump seat. He was tall and slender with a thin moustache and crew cut. Even white teeth were disrupted by a gold tooth on his lower jaw. His slight build aside, the man looked like someone who could take care of himself. "You go." The man pointed to the jump seat. Then he stepped to the toilet compartment, drew the curtain open, sat on the commode, and buckled himself in.

The Betty had only one small window on each side. Ingram couldn't see outside and had no idea what they were doing. He sat on the jump seat and fumbled with the seat belt buckle.

The man seated in front of him turned. It was Fujimoto. He yelled over the roar of the engines, "Do you wish to change places?"

Ingram shouted back, "I can manage, thanks."

"Hang on. A difficult takeoff, they tell me."

"Why?"

"A weather front has moved in, which means headwinds. We took on a lot of gas, so we're going to need every foot of runway."

"Hail Mary."

"What?"

"Say a rosary."

Fujimoto gave a wry grin. "It's been awhile. Maybe later. Perhaps you should--"

The pilot firewalled the throttles and the cabin filled with loud rattling, tearing sounds as the G4M2 powered up to full rpm. The pilot popped the brakes and the plane began rolling. The tail lifted, but the Betty seemed glued to the ground. But each bounce of the landing gear seemed lighter as they gained speed. Suddenly, there was no more bouncing. Now airborne, the plane mushed along, clawing for altitude. Ingram spotted a large shrapnel hole near the bottom of the fuselage. Peering through it, his gut turned to cement when he saw whitecaps no more than thirty feet below.

Fujimoto turned and looked down through the hole as well. He shrugged and faced forward as if to say *we all have to go sometime.*

Ingram shouted. "How long's the flight?"

The pilot reduced the throttles from takeoff power to climbing power. Fujimoto didn't have to yell as loud now. "Four hours or so."

I can handle that. He nodded toward the passengers. "Are they angry with me?"

Fujimoto shrugged. "Just that you're here. They didn't plan for you."

"I don't get it."

"Your weight. There are too many of us. Like I said, we need every drop of gas." He turned and put his head back against the seat.

Ingram leaned back and tried to wedge himself in, but the aluminum seat was small and bit into his butt. His back was cramping. He tried to sleep but awakened each time the plane bounced and jinked, sometimes far worse than the C-54. Once in a while someone crawled over the luggage pile, entered the commode, and took care of business.

Darkness fell and the bouncing and stomach-grabbing downdrafts got worse. Once during a downdraft, the starboard engine sputtered and quit. Someone yelped; another cursed. Not quite windmilling to a stop, the engine started again with the pilot nursing it back to life and revving it to cruising power. Ingram couldn't see the faces of the other passengers, but he could feel their collective relief.

Surprised to find that he had slept for a while amid all the bouncing and shaking, Ingram awoke to a cabin darkened save for one small bulb near the forward section. It cast a dim light, making the cabin's features stand out like a macabre horror movie. The people in the seats in front of him might just as well have been zombies strapped to their seats as they jiggled along. Suddenly, another figure appeared. This man was dressed in a fur-lined flight suit with goggles perched on his forehead. He spoke to the delegate in the forward seat. They motioned the rating forward, and the three were soon engaged in an intense conversation.

"What's going on?" asked Ingram.

"We'll soon find out," said Fujimoto.

The flight-suited man disappeared forward into darkness. The rating crawled aft over the luggage, speaking with each of the delegates as he moved past. One--he looked like a general--stood and shouted at the man. But the rating moved on relaying his message. He spoke to Fujimoto last and then turned to the luggage pile and began tossing the bags toward the hatch.

Fujimoto stood and began helping.

"What?" called Ingram.

Fujimoto grunted as he wrestled with the bags. "Headwinds. We may not have enough gas to make Kisarazu."

Lightning flashed, illuminating the passengers. The plane rocked to starboard; the pilot righted it. The passengers stood now, helping pass their luggage aft.

The rating opened the hatch and clipped it back. Wind roared in, chilling the cabin and making Ingram wish he'd brought a parka. Then the rating knelt and began tossing bags into the night.

The others towered over him passing bags. Ingram felt as if he were glued to his seat, blood frozen in his veins. My God. Helen! Not now, after all this. He'd survived the war and now there was a chance he'd end up in the Pacific with the enemy--his former enemy--after all.

"Wait!" Ingram jumped and held up a hand.

They stopped. The rating grabbed his shirt. "*Iko, iko!*"

Fujimoto said, "We're losing speed and fuel, Commander. We have to act quickly."

"Act after you assure me the documents are safe," demanded Ingram.

Fujimoto shouted forward. Someone shouted back. "All secure, Commander. Don't worry, it's as important to us as it is to you."

Ingram looked forward. One of the civilians held up two oilskin-wrapped packages. Another held up a large mailing tube. *Have to go with that.* "Okay. Finish it up."

Two minutes later, the bags were all gone save Ingram's small bag, which had been unceremoniously plopped on his jump seat.

The rating began securing the hatch. "Hold on," shouted Ingram.

He unzipped his bag, dug out a foul-weather jacket, rezipped the bag, and handed it back to the rating. In an instant it was out the hatch and gone into the night.

With effort, the rating pushed the hatch shut and secured it. He walked forward and a civilian delegate handed him the two oilskin packages and the mail tube. He accepted them with a bow and then walked aft and sat near the hatch. He looked at Ingram, smiled, and nodded at what lay in his lap. He drew up his knees and hugged the packages close. To Ingram's surprise, the man flashed thumbs-up.

Fujimoto turned and said, "Thank you for sacrificing your luggage."

"I'm as interested in living as you are," Ingram said, wriggling into his foul-weather jacket.

Fujimoto brushed away an imaginary piece of dust. "I don't think so."

"What the hell do you mean?"

Conversation stopped as the left engine sputtered, bucked in its mount, then roared back to life.

Jeepers. Ingram checked his watch. They'd been in the air well over four hours. Plenty of time to make landfall in a normal flight.

"My life is over," said Fujimoto.

Ingram thought about that. *Fujimoto's life is over? So what?* He felt the same way. For the past three and a half years, life had been fleeting--a very long, dark, and terrifying path. He'd been scared, speechless, and numb. But that was war, and in a way he had been resigned to it. Now, with the war supposedly over, the threat was gone and he'd just let go, allowing tendrils of peace to seep into his system, giving him a sense of well-being, of finally returning home and being with Helen and Jerry. Now this. No, he'd never get used to being scared. His heart was pounding and his arteries felt as if they were filled with battery acid, electrifying every cell.

"Nonsense. You have a lot to live for."

Fujimoto waved a hand. "My country is dead. My father is dead. Dead are my two brothers. My mother died in 1936 from cholera. There is nothing left. So . . . when I fill my obligation to you and my country I intend to commit seppuku."

"What's that?"

"Suicide. The honorable way."

The engine sputtered again but caught almost immediately. Strangely, the air became smooth and it was suddenly light outside. Moonglow.

"Oh, hara-kiri."

"That's what you call it."

Ingram pointed to the enlisted rating at the hatch. "Why does he have all the diplomatic stuff?"

"Yakushima is a strong swimmer. Tried out for the 1936 Olympics in freestyle but fell short by two-tenths of a second. Can you imagine? If he had made the Olympics, he most likely would be someplace else, serving in a more honorable position. But for that two-tenths of a second we would not have his services tonight. All our diplomatic material is entrusted to him for safekeeping in case we go into the water."

"I see." Ingram looked over to Yakushima.

The man bowed his head.

"It's the best we can do. I'm sorry," said Fujimoto. "Should the plane go down, we fear that your people will think it a trick of some sort. That we collectively committed seppuku and destroyed the documents as a gesture of defiance."

Ingram thought about Japanese trickery from Pearl Harbor to Okinawa. But he put it aside and said, "I don't know about that, but there is something you should know."

In the dim moonlight, Fujimoto's eyes were dull.

Tell him now. What does it matter? If we crash, he'll die happy; if not, then maybe I'll have his cooperation. "You do have something to live for. Your brother is alive."

"Yes." He brushed it off as if Ingram were telling a bad joke.

"Seriously. Lieutenant Kotoku Fujimoto of the Imperial Marines is the brigade commander at Toro Village on Karafuto."

"What is this?" Fujimoto's voice fairly boiled. He sat up straight, his lips curled.

"I need you to go up there with me tomorrow and get him out. And somebody else," said Ingram.

Fujimoto spat, "How dare you? After what I tried to--"

The port engine sputtered. Then it quit. Then the starboard engine stopped as well. The only sound was wind whistling through the airframe, a sound somehow louder than the roar of the engines had been. Someone in the forward part of the plane shouted. The bomber took a down angle. But it was a smooth descent, with the light seeming to get a bit stronger.

People babbled. Someone moaned. A civilian tried to rise in his seat, but another, a dark hulking shadow, pulled him down and yelled at him.

Ingram braced himself against the bulkhead and pulled his seat belt strap as tight as possible.

Fujimoto turned and said in a near-conversational tone, "Were you joking?"

"Not in the least."

"Then you have made me very happy."

Ingram looked at Yakushima, then at the shrapnel hole. Whitecaps whizzed past. The ocean loomed close. Then closer.

The G4M2 hit and bounced. They were airborne for three luxurious seconds, then they bounced again; and hit hard. The plane slewed to a grinding stop on the right wing. Water gushed over the top of the fuselage.

Immediately, water sloshed in the cabin. Everyone shouted. They jumped up at once. Yakushima popped the hatch. Clutching the documents, he catapulted out and disappeared into the night.

Ingram unbuckled and stood. Water swirled around his legs. His knees! *Get out!*

A general shoved Ingram back into his seat and pushed past. Fujimoto pulled him up. A screaming civilian tried to climb over them. Fujimoto elbowed him in the face and then shoved Ingram out the door.

Hands grabbed him as he pitched out. Yakushima. *What the hell?*

Yakushima was upright, water sloshing around his thighs. With a smile, he eased Ingram forward to sit on the wing.

Bright moonlight. Land. The beach was twenty yards away. Small waves lapped onto the sand. In the distance were a few houses, one with a light in the window. And beyond, Ingram made out a sight not available to Americans for the past three and a half years: moonlight glittering off the snow-capped peak of Mount Fuji.

The plane rested in light surf. *Son of a gun. Might as well be in Malibu.*

Fujimoto sat beside him. They watched as the rest of the open-mouthed passengers piled out.

The two pilots exited the cockpit hatches, slid down the wing, and mingled with them. Soon everybody pumped the fliers' hands, laughing and babbling at the same time.

Miraculously, a flask was produced and passed around.

It came to Fujimoto and he took his swig, "Ahhhh. It's been awhile." He offered it to Ingram.

"Thanks." Ingram took a drink. Pure fire. The brandy burned gloriously on its way down, shoving aside demons. He passed it to one of the pilots. With a grin, the pilot bowed and tipped the flask toward each of those gathered around. Then he raised it to his mouth. An admiral began chanting, then two of the generals. Soon all were chanting as one pilot and then the other chug-a-lugged the remaining contents.

Fujimoto looked at the star-speckled sky. "Perhaps a new beginning, Commander."

11

---

21 August 1945
1627 South Alma Street
San Pedro, California

"Noooo!" Helen sat bolt upright in bed. Her skin was clammy; her nerves jangled. Instinctively she reached for Todd. *Not here.* VJ Day was five, no six, days ago. She wanted Todd. *Come home. It's time.*

For a brief moment a warm feeling seeped through her. Maybe he *was* here. He'd just gotten up to make the coffee and was plowing around in the kitchen, clanking with dishes, filling the percolator. *And yet, he's not here.* She thumped the bed's left side just to make sure. *No, not here; not yet.* She grabbed his pillow, hugged it close, and lay back.

Early morning light crept into the room. A glance at her alarm clock told her it was 6:17. Whoops. It hadn't gone off. She picked it up and found she'd forgotten to wind the alarm last night; it was set for six o'clock. She cranked it up for tomorrow, then set the clock down and stared at the face.

Where are you, darling? Be well. Be safe. Come back to us soon. I love you. Then she said the Lord's Prayer and added a blessing for Todd.

A screech from the baby's room: Jerry. With a sigh, she got up, put on a robe, and looked out the window: bright sunlight caressed their Alma Street house. Another hot one today.

The Fort MacArthur Infirmary was busy as always. Patients still flooded in from the Okinawa and Iwo Jima campaigns. Plus, there was a residue of hard-case GIs from previous campaigns dating back to 1942: burn cases were the slowest to heal, and those needing prosthetic limbs.

Ward 6 was a special area for those who couldn't cope. Some called it combat fatigue; some called it cowardice. The seriously wounded said nothing against the patients in Ward 6. Sometimes they commiserated. The brain, the mind, has a right to be wounded or ill, just like the stomach or a decayed tooth. All needed professional help.

Many in Ward 6 feared change, especially sudden change--a loud sound, a flash of light, an unseen voice. Some trembled at unexpected phenomena such as wind or rain rattling the windows, especially at night. Lightning and thunder were the worst for these GIs. They pulled the sheets over their heads. Other things rattled their nerves. A door opening down the hall sending a sudden shaft of light bursting into the room evoked a stark recollection of a grenade or a bomb explosion or a fuel tank going up.

Late that afternoon Helen lay on the floor beside Cpl. Eddie Bergen's bed trying to coax him out. He'd been in the courtyard enjoying the sun when a fog clamped down on San Pedro. Eddie had walked inside, crawled under his bed, went fetal, and closed his eyes.

Helen recalled his record. Eddie was a tanker, a 75-mm gun loader on an M-4 Sherman tank crawling around Okinawa. The Japanese had taken out roughly half the tanks on Okinawa, and Eddie's tank fell unfortunately into that category. The 30-ton M-4 had clanked up to a cave entrance and began to train the mount inside and blast away. Instead, it hit a land mine. The charge was so powerful that it blew the Sherman on its back, leaving a six-foot-deep crater. Eddie was shaken but relatively uninjured. The tank caught fire, but Eddie scrambled up for the belly escape hatch, somehow making it out first. But he didn't jump. With

Japanese bullets clanking all around him, he reached in and pulled out Steve Marcus, the machine gunner. Then Eddie pulled out Rich Casenilli, the driver. He had both of the tank commander's wrists when a 7.2-mm round caught him in the butt and knocked him off the tank. He started to scramble back up, but ammunition began cooking off inside. They had to drag him away. The tank commander, Sgt. Orville Diggs, one of his best friends, was incinerated as those rounds went off. In tortured dreams, day and night, Eddie heard Orville's screams as the tank went up--first the gas, then the ammo. He slept in fits, getting a few minutes, maybe a half hour, at a time.

Drugs didn't help. Orville Diggs' screams came back the moment Eddie nodded off. They'd sewed up Eddie's butt and shot him with the new miracle drug, penicillin. The wound healed nicely. But wonder drugs couldn't heal Eddie's mind.

Eddie stretched out: a good sign. It meant he was about ready to come out and return to the real world.

"Hand me a cigarette?" Eddie asked. Eddie smoked like a forest fire. It was Helen's best weapon.

"Come on out and get one, Eddie." She took a Lucky from the top of his bed stand and waved it.

"Aww, come on," he pleaded.

"Eddie, you're sweating," she said.

"Hot under here," said Eddie.

"Fire hazard under the bed, Eddie."

"Please?"

"And look at this." She waved a Donald Duck comic book before him. Donald Duck was what had lured him out last week when the hospital commander, Colonel Ledbetter, marched in with six men, drew them to attention, and politely stood by while Helen coaxed Eddie from underneath the bed. He crawled out, stood, and wrapped his arms around himself as if he were in a straitjacket, then jumped under his covers and went fetal again. A moment passed. Colonel Ledbetter gave a polite cough and then he and his staffers gathered around Eddie's bed. Among them was Sgt. Melvin Letenske, Colonel Ledbetter's adjutant.

While Helen stroked Eddie's head and held his hand, Colonel

Ledbetter read the citation awarding Cpl. Eddie Bergen the Bronze Star and the Purple Heart.

Eddie teared up.

Colonel Ledbetter became misty-eyed too, and had to fight his way through the rest of the citation. Finally, it was over. He thrust out his hand. Letenske handed the medals to him. The colonel took a step toward Eddie's bed. But Eddie cringed, again drawing his arms around himself. Judiciously, Colonel Ledbetter pinned the medals on Eddie's pillow. Then Ledbetter stepped back, congratulated Eddie, saluted, and marched out with his staffers.

The last man was no sooner out the door when Eddie lit up a Lucky Strike and grabbed his Donald Duck.

Others said Helen was being too easy on Eddie. Even Dr. Raduga, the psychiatrist, advised her to tone down her commiseration. But Helen knew what Eddie was going through. Nightmares brought it all back. She had endured capture by the Japanese, and torture; the cigarette burns were still evident on her legs and the balls of her feet. At times, those horrible nightmares swirled in her sleep: Corregidor, Malinta Tunnel, Japanese artillery pounding mercilessly around the clock, sewer lines stopped up, one-third rations, no medical supplies, no anesthetics, amputations on screaming patients, their vacant eyes, the hopeless, ravaged eyes of the dead. But Marinduque Island, where the Kempetai had captured and tortured her, was far worse. She saw what they did to the Filipinos: the senseless and wanton raping of young women, hanging men upside down over a bonfire and laughing at their screams. At times she still felt like crawling into a hole. Todd had had it just as bad. Yes, she knew what Eddie was going through.

Again, Helen waved the Donald Duck comic. "It's brand new. There's a new guy, Uncle Scrooge."

"Hell, yes." He smiled and reached.

She drew the comic book back. "Out here, Eddie. You know the rules. No reading under the bed."

Eddie crawled out, almost like he was scrambling through the hatch of his M-4.

He's nimble today.

Eddie stood to his full five-foot, six-inch height. "Any more of that cake left?"

"I think so. You want some?"

"Yes, please, Mrs. Ingram." He took the comic book with one hand and lit a cigarette with the other.

"On its way." Helen headed for the kitchen. She looked back just as she walked through the door. Eddie had taken a chair by the window. The fog had cleared, and full sunshine cascaded through the blue smoke hanging over Eddie. Helen watched as he settled down with his comic book. That was a first.

In the kitchen, she wolfed half a slice of the chocolate cake, grabbed a piece for Eddie, and then headed back.

Sergeant Caparani stuck his head out his door as she went by. "Captain, can we see you for a moment, please?"

She stopped. "Okay."

"In here please, ma'am."

A man in Army fatigues sat before Letenske's desk. His nametag said Watson, but he bore no sign of rank or service affiliation.

"What can I do for you?" she asked.

"Are you Captain Helen D. Ingram?" the man asked. He snapped open a briefcase.

"That's correct."

"And you have ID?"

All Helen had was Eddie's cake. "No. It's back in my ward. Today it's Ward 6."

Watson said, "Well, then. You wouldn't mind--"

"What do you need, Mr. Watson?" Helen asked briskly.

Letenske said sotto voce, "I think he's a courier, ma'am."

Helen tensed. A damned courier. That could mean new orders or some other official correspondence that could transfer her out of here. Which she didn't want. Suddenly, she knew exactly how Eddie felt. *Never disrupt the status quo. Just let me remain here and greet my husband when he returns home. I can't move. I don't want to move. I won't move.* She thought about Eddie and crawling under her bed at home and taking a comic book with her.

With a nod to Letenske, Watson asked, "Are you going to get your ID?"

"We'll vouch for her, Mr. Watson," said Letenske. He nodded to the inner door. "Of course, you're welcome to speak with Colonel Ledbetter. But you'll have to wait. He's in surgery right now."

Watson blinked and made a decision. "Very good. If you'll sign right here, ma'am?" He handed over a clipboard.

Helen signed, and Watson passed over an envelope wrapped in cellophane. It was elaborately stamped and dated yesterday. She opened it while they watched. "Todd!" she squealed. Embarrassed, she looked up. Letenske wore a big grin. Watson scratched his head. "My husband," she explained. "It's dated yesterday. How did you--"

"I'm just a courier, ma'am. Picked it up in Hawaii this morning. Got in half an hour ago. And now," he stood, "I must continue on to Washington, D.C. A bunch of stuff for delivery."

"The courier business is intense these days?" asked Letenske.

Watson flushed. "Well, yes, as a matter of fact." He reached for Helen's hand. "I'm glad you're hearing from your . . ."

"Husband," she said.

"I wish you all the best." Watson walked out.

Sunlight poured through the window. Eddie was still engrossed in his Donald Duck. He accepted his cake with a distant, "Thanks," and kept reading.

Helen said a hurried, "You're welcome," then rushed to her desk at the end of the ward and sat to read Todd's letter:

My Dearest,

I'm sort of writing this on the fly since I am TAD to an operation that sounds very important. So important that I'll have a lot of fun telling Jerry about it in years to come, with me embellishing at every turn of the road. I wish I could say more but it sounds like a big deal. I can tell you that Admiral Ray Spruance personally ordered me here, so that should be justification in and of itself.

Things on the ship are fine. She's repaired now and ready for sea. Predictably, Boom Boom and Tubby White are going at it, almost in public. I'm never sure if they do it for show or if they truly hate each other. Can't tell you how many times I've had to break it up, though.

Speaking of Boom Boom, tell Laura that I pressured him to get things going, to set a date and get married. It's time those two grew up. Separately, they're the finest people you could find. Together, they're like a couple of fighting ten-year-old siblings--I'll never figure it out. Anyway, please advise her to get off the dime and pick a date. I'll do the same with Boom Boom. Maybe we'll have a ceremony yet.

I'm guessing we'll be back by early December. Everybody's in a rush, but I have to tell you, I have plenty of points. Too bad I'm career--first in, last out. By the way, I never told you this, but after our little Mindanao adventure I left a power of attorney in your name with your dad in case something goes haywire, so don't worry.

I'm beginning to sleep now, bit by bit, absent the specter of Jap air raids or torpedo attack. Strange feeling, waking up in the morning feeling rested and not looking over my shoulder. It's been so long. Hope it continues.

Only trouble with all this is that I think of you each and every waking moment. Jerry too. I bet he's turning into a handful just like his old man. So don't worry, I'll be home soon to give him some real competition.

I love you so,

Todd

She sat back, letting the glow work its way through her. Home. Something we can hang on to. No more shooting, no air attacks, no ripping blasts in the night. Yet this letter was different. The war was already over when he wrote it. It should have been more upbeat, more forward looking, more . . . she couldn't put her finger on it.

She reached for the phone and gave the switchboard the number for Laura West's home in the San Fernando Valley.

Laura picked up on the second ring. "Hello?"

"It's Helen."

"Hi ya, toots."

"Guess what I have?"

"A fifth of scotch?"

"Not likely." Liquor was scarce. Worse, Laura had taken to the bottle after her first husband, Luther Dutton, was killed in the Solomon Islands. Jerry Landa and Helen had brought her out of that. And she'd fallen for Landa. All to the good, but then she slipped into it again when Todd was trapped on a Japanese submarine. Now, she seemed to be doing fine. At least Helen hoped so. Laura was unpredictable. "You working hard?"

"Yes, Toscanini is combining the East Coast and West Coast orchestras. More work, and the pay is not bad. We're scheduled for the score on three movies, so it looks like I'll be here for a while."

"That's wonderful. Congratulations."

"Trouble is, the old guy is still trying to run his hands up my dress."

"Oh."

"What do you have, toots?"

"A letter from Todd."

"Wow! What's he say?"

"Well, the war is over. Jerry loves you and is anxious to set a wedding date."

"That's good news." She paused for a moment. "I have news for him; you too."

Something nagged at the back of Helen's mind. She couldn't pin it down. What was it?

"Hey, toots, you there?"

"Yes, sorry."

"You all right?"

"Yes, sure."

"Is Todd all right?"

"Yes, yes, of course. The war is over. Boom Boom is all right too. That's why I'm calling." She blurted, "You two *should* get married. It's been so long. You should set a date."

Laura sighed, "Well, I tell you, toots, I'm ready. I'll send a letter today saying Arturo waits behind the door with a lupara."

"What's a lupara?"

"An Italian shotgun. For a shotgun wedding. I think the Black Hand, or the Mafia uses them. And that's what I'm trying to tell you."

"So, tell me."

"I'm pregnant."

She squealed, "Laura!"

"How 'bout that, toots?"

"I had no idea."

"I'm finally showing. You're the only one to know except Roberta." Roberta Thatcher was the NBC Orchestra's business manager.

"Three months?"

"About that, maybe a little more. Last time Jerry was here for that special conference last May."

"We'll have a baby shower."

"Maybe a wedding too, huh? Say, toots."

"Yes?"

"You'll be my best girl?"

"Wow. What an honor. Of course. What a time we'll have."

"You bet! Hope and Crosby will be there. Maybe even Sinatra."

Laura always thought big. She was a beautiful woman and a very talented pianist. She could sing too, but Toscanini hated that. Laura was given to gross exaggerations and prattled on constantly about the A-list celebrities she knew. Once Helen got around that, she loved to listen to her talk. Fact or fiction, she didn't care. It was all great fun. "Maybe Gene Kelly too?"

"Gene's on a shoot in New York City right now, but I know his agent really well. He'll fix it up. I'll have him stand beside you at the wedding reception. I'll rent the ballroom at the Beverly Hills Hotel. We'll have it catered by--"

"Hang on a second, Laura." Sergeant Letenske stood over her desk. She covered the mouthpiece. "Yes, Sergeant?"

"Staff meeting. The colonel needs us just for ten minutes."

"Right now?"

Letenske shrugged.

"Okay. Be right there."

Letenske walked off. Helen said, "Duty calls, Mom. By the way, are you all right? Do you need any, ah, . . . medicines or anything?"

"Got anything for morning sickness?"

"Afraid not. Sorry. Try Seven-Up."

Laura sighed. "That's an idea. Okay, toots. You stay out of trouble, and no hanging out at Shanghai Red's."

Helen had no intention of hanging out at Shanghai Red's, an infamous waterfront dive in downtown San Pedro located, ironically, in the same block as the police station. The joint was a magnet for merchant and Navy sailors, and fights--including a number of stabbings--were common. The latest to hit the papers involved two prostitutes arguing over a john. Insults were hurled, and suddenly one was atop the other with a switchblade, disemboweling her on the dance floor. The downtown business association had once again clamored to close the place, but strangely, Shanghai Red's remained open for business as usual. Laura and Helen had gone there once for thrills and, even though it was a quiet evening, had an eyeful. "No, not likely," she said. They said their goodbyes and Helen hung up.

Something swirled in her mind. Then she found herself leaning against the doorjamb. To her surprise, she felt like sagging to the floor but caught herself about halfway down. *What?* She stood, took a deep breath and shook her head. *What's going on?*

Sergeant Letenske popped out of a door and walked past. "Captain, you okay?"

Helen rubbed her cheek and took a few faltering steps. "Yes, of course. You go on ahead. My leg fell asleep."

Letenske moved on.

She grabbed a memo pad and began walking. Then it hit her. Todd's letter. A single sentence buried among all the others. ". . . *after our little Mindanao adventure, I left a power of attorney in your name with your dad in case something goes haywire.*"

She stopped and leaned against the wall. Power of attorney? Mindanao? That was two years ago. *Todd, why are you telling me this now? Haywire? Oh, God.*

"Okay, Captain." Letenske ducked through another door.

Oh, my God, power of attorney.

12

22 August 1945
Kisarazu Air Base
Chiba Prefecture, Japan

P-38.

Ingram sat up. You could tell the sound of a Lockheed P-38 by the growl of the turbochargers. Louder and louder. One, two, three, four of them zipped right overhead. Rooftop level.

He'd slept on a tatami in a relatively undamaged section of the officers' quarters. It must be late; he checked his watch: 9:37. *Jeeez!* He jumped up and ran to the door. The two Japanese guards who stood on either side glanced at him then looked nervously up to the windy, overcast sky. Sure enough, the planes circled around to roar in again at deck level. Four Army Air Corps P-38 Lightnings with drop tanks. In single file they blasted overhead with throttles firewalled, turbochargers whining. No sooner had they zipped over the top than he saw the silver glint of a C-54 lining up for the runway.

It was side slipping. *Radcliff.* It was his signature. Or maybe it was Leroy Peoples, the Bucky Radcliff wannabe, doing the side slipping this morning.

"They're well escorted." Fujimoto had slept in the room next door. He was in working greens now, ready to go. He barked an order at the guards. They bowed and moved away.

"I'll say." Ingram felt woozy, the aftereffects of yesterday's adrenaline rush. A fisherman had found them and alerted the air base. An hour later, a truck bounced up and took them to Kisarazu. The rest of the delegates were taken on to Tokyo while a still soaking Ingram and Fujimoto met with the mine-group staff. Within two hours they developed a thick portfolio of charts and instructions governing the minefields in upper and lower Tokyo Bay. The plans seemed complete to Ingram. After two more hours of deliberation he nodded his approval and had copies sent off to the Third Fleet. Fujimoto dispatched them via courier to the destroyer *Sagari* to rendezvous with destroyers of the Third Fleet. The *Sagari* would lead the fleet back into Tokyo Bay--a sacrificial lamb. Following her would be eight minesweepers in line abreast, then destroyers, then cruisers, and finally the battleships. Hospital ships, troopships, and other auxiliaries would enter later, perhaps the next day.

"Sleep well, Commander?" asked Fujimoto.

"Well enough." Ingram ran a hand through his hair. Three hours of sleep wasn't enough, but it would have to do. The P-38s had shocked him to consciousness as well as any alarm clock. "Good to see Major Radcliff is on time."

Kisarazu Air Base looked far worse in the light of day than it had last night. The hangars showed extensive bomb damage. The tower was barely distinguishable, just a single wall that protruded up like a decayed, broken tooth. Wrecked planes were strewn everywhere: some tail-high, a few on their backs, most a blackened mess. Thankfully, the craters in the main runway where Radcliff was now headed had been filled. Yokohama, eighteen miles to the west across Tokyo Bay, was an amorphous hulking landmass in the gloom.

Watching the C-54 touch down, Ingram asked, "Can we perhaps have some coffee or tea for them?"

"Of course. But first, take a look." Fujimoto pointed out into Tokyo Bay, where a destroyer was headed south, out to sea. The waves were choppy; the wind was up. Water peeled off the destroyer's graceful bow as she pulled a fifteen-knot wake. Forward, she had beautiful lines: a proud, high superstructure, raked mast, and funnels. Twisted wreckage littered the after part of the ship all the way to the fantail. "The *Sagari*."

"So, our instructions got aboard?"

"Ummm."

"She's awfully beat up. Do you think she'll hold together long enough to get the job done?"

"Commander Watanabe is a good friend and fine seafarer. He'll get the job done."

"Okay." Ingram headed for the door. "Where can I wash up?"

Fujimoto pointed toward a set of double doors. "In there. To your right." He paused. "Commander?"

"Yes?"

"The weather out there is quite poor. It's part of what we flew through last night. We have word that a typhoon may be headed our way. If this is the case, then the, ah, ceremony will be delayed by a few days."

"What are you telling me?"

Fujimoto straightened. "A typhoon. We may have to wait."

Ingram ran a hand over his stubble beard. *What next?* Admiral Halsey's Third Fleet had run into two typhoons within the last eight months. Ships had been lost, men washed overboard. Boards of inquiry were under way along with time-consuming finger pointing and name-calling. Now, with the war supposedly over, Halsey would of course wait out a typhoon. "What about the weather north of here?"

"Seems all right as far as we can tell."

The C-54 pulled into a revetment about two hundred yards away and braked, its propellers wind-milling to a stop. Immediately, a dilapidated fuel truck pulled under one wing. Its engine wheezed and backfired, and black smoke gushed from the tailpipe. "You sure they have good av-gas?" Ingram asked.

"One hundred octane. Just about the last of our reserves. We're fortunate."

Ingram stood for a moment stroking his chin. *Let Hammer figure out if the gas is good or not.* "Very well. Please see that Major Radcliff and his crew have something to eat. I'll be along shortly."

"Of course."

Ingram's sleep last night had been disturbed by a lingering worry that Fujimoto would try to commit suicide. He was glad that he hadn't. "Are you packed and ready?"

"Yes."

"I'm pleased to see you're still here, Captain."

"Thank you."

Radcliff, Peoples, and Berne were the first out. Ingram wasn't surprised to see Colin Blinde step down the ladder next, looking dapper and Ivy League as usual. Lieutenant O'Toole brought up the rear, packing pistol, carbine, bayonet, web belt with grenades, and a wide grin.

Blinde walked up to Ingram and stuck out his hand. "Good morning, Commander. Everything go all right last night?"

Ingram was sure Blinde by now knew exactly what had happened. "Wonderful flight. They did a marvelous job."

Blinde began another question just as Lieutenant O'Toole walked up.

Ingram said, "Well, look who's here. The spirit of South Bend. Glad to see you, Lieutenant. You have enough protection there?"

O'Toole was not at all embarrassed. "Mister Blinde said I could carry anything I wanted."

Peoples said, "Jarheads gave him all that."

Blinde had brought along a squad of Marines with full field packs, radio equipment, food, and ammo. Ingram was particularly glad to see a long-range radio transceiver that would permit them to stay in touch with Okinawa and whoever else was directing the operation. All were armed with either M-1 carbines or Thompson submachine guns as well as pistols and bayonets. They fanned out around the C-54 and stood guard. Although it was quiet, and nobody threatened them, they held their weapons ready, fingers on trigger guards. Two Marines stood over the refueling crew along with Flight Sergeant Hammer. The Marine squad leader was the same gunny who had accompanied Fujimoto to Manila. And now, with eyes like a rattlesnake, he instantly picked out Fujimoto and watched him from a distance.

Blinde said, "They'll give us some comfort, don't you think?"

"Definitely," said Ingram. "What's the situation up there?"

"The Japanese are just about finished in China and Manchuria, and now the Soviets are overwhelming their Fifth Army on Karafuto. The Japs still control Toro and Toyohara. But they are wavering."

It hit Ingram. "Are we walking into a firefight?"

Blinde shook his head. "We have at least two or three days. Everything will be fine. Don't worry. We'll be back home tonight." His teeth gleamed in a smile. "Restroom?"

Ingram pointed toward a doorway. "Like an indoor benjo ditch."

"Pardon me?"

"You'll figure it out."

As Blinde walked off, Ingram waved the others toward a table under a lean-to beside the officers' quarters. "Breakfast, gentlemen. Captain Fujimoto has made a spread for us." They sat to find *katsuboshi*, salami-shaped sticks of dried bonito fish; *miso*, bean paste that tasted like cardboard; thin, watery soup; and tasteless tea.

Ingram sat with them, his eyelids feeling like sandpaper. He kept nodding off. The tension of the previous day's flights and the shock of crash-landing in the surf and tromping ashore last night were taking a heavy toll. The ride into town and the protracted meetings with the Japanese mine-group staff further drained his reserves.

"We gonna carry you on the plane, Todd?" asked Radcliff.

Ingram's head jerked up. He had nodded off again. "Huh?"

Radcliff focused on Ingram. "You okay?"

"Who, me? I just need a little sleep."

"I mean, that Betty bouncing around in the surf. You sure it didn't whip you around? Bruise or break something?"

"Bucky, I'm just tired."

Radcliff said, "I have to admit that Jap was one smart pilot."

Peoples chimed in, "I'd still be cleaning my underpants if it'd been me."

Ingram said, "Thanks for reminding me. Anybody have an extra pair? My stuff went out with the Japs' luggage."

"We'll work on it," said Radcliff.

Right," said Ingram. "Let's go." He pushed up from the table. "You ready, Mr. Blinde?"

"Of course."

Ingram looked to Fujimoto. "Captain?"

Fujimoto stood and hoisted an overnight bag. "*Hai!*"

Radcliff asked Ingram, "Is he armed?"

Ingram nodded to Fujimoto, who said, "Of course not. Do you wish to search me?"

Radcliff looked him up and down. "Holy smokes. He speaks perfect English."

"Courtesy of the University of Notre Dame," said Ingram.

"Son of a gun. Is he Catholic?" asked Radcliff.

Fujimoto's eyes glistened for a moment. "No, just Irish."

Ingram and O'Toole snickered.

"Nobody likes a wise guy," Radcliff muttered. "Nevertheless." He eyed Ingram.

Ingram gave a slight shake of his head. *No, he's not armed.*

They moved off, O'Toole and Fujimoto bringing up the rear. Ingram asked, "What's the weather look like?"

"Bumpy," said Radcliff.

Ingram groaned.

"We can handle it. Don't worry. You'll sleep like a baby. We're out of the bad stuff."

They walked under the C-54's wing just as the ancient fuel truck rattled away. "They didn't pump molasses in the fuel tanks, did they?" asked Ingram.

"Hammer checked it. It's what it's supposed to be. Even so, he and the jarheads watched them like hawks," said Radcliff.

The Marine gunny spoke to Blinde for a moment, then Blinde dashed up the ladder and out of sight. The gunny walked up to Ingram. "Good morning, Commander. Mr. Blinde says you're in charge; is that correct?"

Ingram blinked.

"Sir?" asked the gunnery sergeant.

"Well, Gunny, now that you remind me, I suppose so. My name's Ingram, Todd Ingram. And you are . . ."

"Harper, sir, Ulysses Gaylord. And no comments about the middle name if you please, sir. But I tell you that because my initials are sort of my nickname."

Ingram tried it out. "Ugh?"

", they call me Ugly, sir. My friends do, anyway."

"Thanks, Gunny."

"I always call the Navy my friends. At least I try to."

"Likewise, Ugly. Now, are your men fed? Do you need some chow before we shove off?" He pointed to the lean-to.

"It's okay, Commander. We have this thermos of coffee and some rats on the plane. So, we're good for now."

"Rats? And did you say coffee?"

"The United States Marine Corps at your service, Commander, with a five-gallon thermos of America's finest."

Ingram smacked his lips. "That sounds better than sleep. Thanks, Ugly."

"Glad to help the Navy, Commander."

It was going to be one of those days. Ingram asked, "Okay, you ready to head north?"

"Say the word, sir."

"Board your men, Gunny. We leave momentarily."

"You want anyone to stay out here while you start up?" asked Harper.

They looked to Fujimoto.

"That won't be necessary." Fujimoto shouted an order and the few remaining Japanese cleared the area.

Harper said to Ingram, "They're Japs, Commander. I don't trust them. Lemme leave a couple of guys on the ground until we start rolling."

O'Toole stepped close. "Sounds legitimate to me, Commander."

"No," Ingram said. "The guy has a million reasons to kill me, and so far, he's played it straight up. If we can't trust him now, we'll never get this operation off the dime. Board your men, Gunny."

"Aye, aye, Commander." Gunnery Sergeant Harper turned, put two fingers to his lips, and whistled shrilly. "All aboard!" he shouted.

Instantly, his men picked up their gear, walked to the plane, and climbed the ladder.

At a nod from Radcliff, Hammer pulled the chocks and carried them on the C-54. Then Radcliff turned to Ingram, "All set?"

"You bet. How far is it?"

"About 950 miles."

"We have enough gas?"

"Plenty for a round trip."

Ingram asked, "You want me to dig up that Jap pilot to give you some pointers?"

"We can handle it, right, boys?" said Radcliff.

Peoples said, "I'm not so sure. Don't forget the right inboard generator is crapped out."

"Huh?" said Ingram.

Berne chimed in. "And I forgot to tell you, we lost hydraulic power about fifteen minutes out."

"Yeah, yeah," said Ingram. He could almost smell the coffee from here. He turned and said, "After you, Captain."

Fujimoto followed the last Marine up the ladder. Ingram went up next.

Radcliff kept it going. "That's right. And I'd forgotten the Torvatron is on the fritz."

"What's a Torvatron?" asked O'Toole.

Radcliff wrapped an arm over his shoulder and pushed him to the ladder. "It's this new hush-hush black box we use for controlling cosmic rays."

"No kidding?" O'Toole started climbing. "Cosmic rays. Isn't that what they have in x-ray machines?"

"Yeah. Make you glow in the dark."

"Wow!"

"But cosmic rays make the magnetos crap out. Then there's no spark and the engines stop."

"Jeeez."

"Don't worry."

"Should I? I mean what's the Torvatron do?"

"Well, I can't tell you much, but you see the frizazbitz interacts with the .

. .

13

22 August 1945
Toro, Karafuto Prefecture, Japan

For centuries Karafuto was under the control of warring Chinese or Mongolian tribes. Later, the Russians expanding into eastern Siberia and the Kamchatka Peninsula made their presence known. By the nineteenth century the island, called Sakhalin Oblast by the Russians and Karafuto Prefecture by the Japanese, was under divided control: tsarist Russia ruled the northern mountainous portion, and Japanese settlers occupied the southern half, with pockets of Chinese settlers scattered throughout. Without official borders to separate the groups, firefights broke out from time to time.

Then the newly minted Imperial Japanese Navy defeated the czarist navy--and Russia--in 1904 in what became known as the Russo-Japanese War. The Treaty of Portsmouth, Maine, that ended the war in 1905 granted to Japan everything south of Karafuto's fiftieth parallel. Also granted to Japan were the Kurile Islands, stringing all the way from Karafuto up to the

Kamchatka Peninsula. With a formal border finally fixed, an uneasy peace fell into place.

Years later, the Soviets extended their "friendship" to the Japanese by agreeing to be neutral in the Pacific war. The nonaggression pact was an easy decision for both countries. The Soviets needed to throw all their resources against the invading Germans without worrying about Japan on their eastern flank, and the Japanese wanted to commit a majority of their forces and resources into their conquest of the western Pacific and Southeast Asia without worrying about an attack from the Russians.

The geopolitical profile changed with the fall of Nazi Germany in May 1945. At the July Potsdam Conference in Germany, President Harry S. Truman suggested privately to Generalissimo Joseph Stalin that now would be a good time for the Soviets to consolidate their position in the Far East. Stalin realized it was indeed a rare opportunity and swiftly capitalized on it. On 9 August 1945, the day of the Nagasaki bombing, Stalin sent Marshal A. M. Vasilevskiy across the Manchurian border with three armies totaling more than 1.6 million troops rushed from the European front. Over the previous four years these battle-tested troops had learned the hard lessons of "maneuver warfare" from the Germans.

Standing against them was Japan's once-vaunted Kwangtung Army, reduced by the demands of the Pacific war to 600,000 men, most of them raw recruits or garrison troops. The army's equipment was even more depleted. The Japanese had only 1,200 light tanks to put up against 5,600 of the Soviets' powerful T-34s. Moreover, the Soviets had 5,300 aircraft on hand compared with the 1,200 available to the Japanese, of which only 50 were serviceable frontline fighters. The Imperial Japanese Navy had for all intents and purposes ceased to exist; thus, no help was forthcoming from the sea.

The Soviet Manchurian campaign was brilliant and dazzling. In just twelve days the Soviets defeated the Japanese on the Asian mainland. Now they intended to finish the job by thrusting down Sakhalin and seizing the entire island.

Truman had done a shrewd thing urging Stalin to take on the Japanese in Manchuria, amazing for one who had been in office for such a short time. The Soviet attack made things far more convenient for the United

States, which no longer had to worry about an attack from Japan's Kwang-tung Army on the Asian mainland, and thus had more military options to utilize in order to force Japan's surrender.

But President Truman and his advisers had not anticipated Stalin's outlaw intention to cross the La Perouse Strait and seize Hokkaido, the northernmost of Japan's home islands. Hokkaido was reported to be poorly defended. The pickings would be easy.

The C-54 flew almost due north at seven thousand feet. Their course took them over Honshu up to the Sea of Japan, and then farther north along the west coast of Hokkaido. They reached the La Peruse Strait at about noon. The coastline of Karafuto, which they would soon parallel, slowly rolled into view.

The cockpit was crowded. Radcliff and Peoples were in their seats. They'd taken it out of autopilot with Peoples doing the flying and concentrating on the course. Hammer was at his flight engineer's station, and Jon Berne was squeezed against his navigation table. Ingram was perched on the jump seat, and Colin Blinde stood over Berne, constantly watching the navigation plot. Their attitude matched the gray overcast. Conversation was sporadic, the cockpit devoid of the usual banter.

Radcliff turned to Berne. "How far, Jon?"

"About a hundred fifty miles, give or take," said Berne.

"Give or take. That's what I like. Accuracy. Good job, Jon," said Radcliff.

Blinde stood over Berne. "Still have them?"

In addition to navigating, Berne operated the CW radio, keeping in touch with Okinawa via Morse code. "So far, so good. A medium signal but clear enough."

"Excellent," said Blinde. Now here's what--"

"Hey, Mr. Blinde," said Peoples. "You have a frequency for the Toro tower?" He reached up and spun a dial. "We should be able to pick them up, but so far I ain't got nothin'."

"Oh?" said Blinde.

"Well, yes, Mr. Blinde," said Peoples, "there are these things called barometer readings and altimeters and wind direction and landing instructions from airport towers. People don't like others barging in without being invited. It's best if you--"

"I understand, Mr. Peoples. Try 121.5 kilocycles."

"Tried that, but there's just a bunch of Japs talking."

"Why didn't you tell me?" Blinde turned to Ingram. "We should get that interpreter up here."

Ingram said, "We better have Fujimoto too."

"Getting kind of crowded," said Radcliff. "You sure we need both?"

Ingram said, "Fujimoto could give us a slant that O'Toole might not pick up. I say two mouths are better than one."

Radcliff said, "Okay. Tell you what, Mr. Blinde. Will you please go and ask Lieutenant O'Toole and Captain Fujimoto to come in? You'll have to take a seat back there in the meantime."

Blinde said, "But I--"

"Mr. Blinde," said Radcliff. "There simply isn't enough room. We'll let you know what happens. Now, would you please summon those two?"

Blinde looked at Ingram.

"Time's wasting, Mr. Blinde," said Ingram.

All eyes clicked to Blinde. "Fine. Sure, why not? I'll get them for you." He walked out.

O'Toole came in first, followed by Fujimoto, both gawking at the cockpit flight controls.

Radcliff said, "Good afternoon, gentlemen." He nodded to Ingram. "Commander Ingram will be your tour guide."

Ingram said, "Okay, what we need are landing instructions from the Toro tower and assurances that it's safe to land. We're unsure of the military situation, and I want to be certain that it's all okay before we set down."

He looked at Fujimoto. "Captain, can you be our go-between with the tower? I figure they'll trust you before they'll trust Americans trying to impersonate Japanese."

"What am I supposed to say to them?" asked Fujimoto.

Ingram said, "Just ask them what Leroy--Lieutenant Peoples--needs for landing instructions. That's all. Except that I'll need your sense of how safe it is around there too."

Fujimoto rubbed his chin. "I suppose I can do that. The information you need isn't that complicated?"

Peoples offered, "Actually, no. We could probably land this thing without all that, but it's nice to know they have the front door open for us."

"I see," said Fujimoto. "All right, I'll give it a try."

"Good," said Ingram. "And Lieutenant O'Toole will back you up as needed." He looked to Berne and nodded.

Berne stood, handed his headphones to Fujimoto and stood back.

"How 'bout me?" asked O'Toole.

"We'll fix you up." Berne rummaged in a drawer, dug up a single earphone, and plugged it into a jack.

O'Toole and Fujimoto nodded to one another, with Fujimoto closing his eyes and concentrating on the traffic. Suddenly, he burst into a long string of Japanese. Ingram heard the phrase "C-54." The name "Fujimoto" was repeated several times. Once, he seemed to be spelling something.

"Lots of talk," said O'Toole. "I think we have the Toro tower, all right, but it doesn't sound like they're controlling aircraft; more like army stuff about tanks and fuel supplies. Right now, it's a credibility thing. The captain here is demanding that his brother get on the line. Then we . . . wait one."

Fujimoto was yelling. He turned and looked at the others, raising his arms in frustration, his eyes raised to the overhead. "Shit," he yelled.

Chuckles ranged around the cockpit. Then Fujimoto bent to it again, yelling into the microphone.

Ingram asked, "Larry, should you do the talking?"

O'Toole shook his head rapidly and motioned Ingram to silence as Fujimoto burst into another long harangue in Japanese.

Radcliff yanked Ingram's sleeve and said quietly, "Todd, I got this strange feeling. We were supposed to just get in there and get out, right?"

Ingram felt uneasy himself. "That's what I was told. But Fujimoto's brother is the garrison commander. It should be all right. Let's decide when we get there."

"You're the boss." Radcliff called over his shoulder, "Jon, how far?"

"Wish I could tell you, but Fu Manchu here is standing in front of my chart."

Fujimoto turned and gave Berne a cold stare.

"Lieutenant Berne," barked Ingram.

"Sorry," said Berne.

Radcliff said, "Jon, off the top of your head, please."

"Fifty miles, no more," muttered Berne.

"That must be it, then," said Peoples. "Smoke on the horizon."

They all looked forward to see a column of smoke rising near the Kara-futo coast. Then another.

Ingram asked, "Bucky, is it all right if Mr. Blinde takes Sergeant Hammer's chair for a few minutes?"

"Frigging musical chairs." Radcliff looked at Hammer and said, "Send him up, okay, Chief?"

Blinde was no sooner settled in the chair than Fujimoto gave a long laugh.

"It sounds like we have him," said O'Toole.

Radcliff called over his shoulder, "Mr. O'Toole, please tell the captain we need landing instructions."

"Yes, sir." O'Toole spoke to Fujimoto in Japanese.

Fujimoto covered his mike and said, "It's Kotoku, my brother." He looked at Ingram. "He really is alive." He went back into a long discourse in Japanese.

They were almost on the smoke column. Berne elbowed Fujimoto aside and took his seat. After a moment he pronounced, "Toro should be just ahead. Ten miles, no more."

"Sure enough," said Radcliff in disgust. "And everything so clean and bright." The area was obscured by smoke. Two or three dark columns rose near the beach, flames erupting from one of them.

They were over a rugged coast where many small boats churned up the water. "Lookie that," said Peoples, pointing off to port. A number of ships were gathered in a large and ominous formation. There was a lot of activity inshore. "LSTs? Kinda like Okinawa," said Peoples. "We got LSTs up here, Bucky?"

"Dunno."

"We don't, but the Reds do," said Blinde.

Ingram scanned further out and saw several larger Soviet units--cruisers and destroyers.

Radcliff saw them too and nodded to Ingram. "There's some pretty heavy tonnage out there. What do you think?"

"Shore bombardment."

"Uh, uh. I don't like this," said Radcliff.

"You want to turn around?"

"It's your show, boss man."

"Well, then, let's press on. It seems quiet for now," said Ingram, not meaning a word of it.

Radcliff sighed. "Okay. I got it, Leroy." Peoples raised his hands as Radcliff took the control column. "Let's try five thousand feet and see if we can make sense of any of this." He eased the throttles back a bit and pushed the yoke forward, putting the C-54 into a shallow descent.

"What's going on, Captain?" Ingram asked.

Fujimoto shot an irritated glance, then went back to talking. It seemed more like babbling.

Radcliff said, "Todd, tell that Jap to start giving me some landing instructions or I'm going get that Marine gunny up here to shove a bayonet up his--"

Blinde said, "No need for that, Mr. Radcliff. It's his brother, you see. They haven't spoken in more than three years."

Ingram said, "I don't give a damn about that. What I care about right now is the safety of this aircraft and the men in it."

"Take it easy, Mr. Ingram. You'll get what you want. Please keep in mind that this is a matter of national security."

"All I care about right now, Mr. Blinde, is *our* security. Mr. O'Toole," he said sharply.

"Yes, sir?"

"Tell Captain Fujimoto in his language that he will do as we say or we'll remove him from the cockpit."

"Well, I--" said O'Toole.

At five thousand feet Radcliff leveled off and said, "You better tell him something, Lieutenant, or that Marine gunny is going to be up here making us a Jap cocktail."

"*Hai!*" Fujimoto covered his mike and said, "Gentlemen, I have it. Barometer 31.15; wind, northwest at five knots; use runway three-four. They have us in sight and advise us to stay away from the coast and the western end of the runway.

"There it is," said Peoples. He pointed down. Through smoke and haze, the runway hove into sight. It was oriented on a 340–160-degree axis, the end of the runway about two hundred yards from the surf line. The tower was on the runway's southern perimeter. To the northeast lay a green forested area. A large, jagged mountain range stood out farther north.

"Okay, let's try the downwind." Radcliff eased the C-54 into a right bank and pulled the throttles back a notch. "Flaps. Gimme flaps."

"How much?" asked Peoples.

"This is so screwed up," muttered Radcliff. "Gimme fifteen degrees."

"Fifteen degrees? Yes, sir. I'll put a man right on it," said Peoples reaching over and pulling the flap lever.

"Cowl flaps! Come on, you guys. Mr. Blinde, I'm going to need my flight engineer. Leo, get up here!" shouted Radcliff. "Leroy, where's the checklist? Let's get it going."

Blinde rose as Peoples began calling his list. Hammer slid into his chair and chimed in with his settings as Peoples read them off.

Soon they were down to one thousand feet, with Fujimoto, Blinde, and O'Toole gawking out the cockpit window. Radcliff gave a plaintive look to Ingram, then concentrated on flying his downwind leg.

Ingram said, "Gentlemen, it's too crowded in here. Could you please take a seat and buckle up for the landing?" The three shuffled out, leaving the atmosphere in the cockpit much lighter.

Radcliff looked out his side window and saw they were well past the end of the runway. "Base leg," he announced, easing into a left turn. "Gear down; twenty-five-degree flaps." He increased power a bit as the flaps came further down.

They were turning onto final approach when Berne grabbed his earphones. "Japs are shouting. This doesn't sound right."

Radcliff said, "Almost committed, Todd. About twenty seconds to go or no-go."

"Mr. O'Toole," yelled Ingram. "Come back up here, please."

"Sir?" said O'Toole.

Ingram handed him the loose earphone. "Quick. Tell us what's going on."

Two hundred feet. "Ten seconds, Todd. Still time to chicken out," said Radcliff.

"Holy shit!" shouted O'Toole. "He says they're killing people in there. Russians."

"I need a decision, you guys," pleaded Radcliff.

Something rattled against the fuselage. The plane bucked. Smoke puffs ranged all around. "Flak," shouted Peoples.

"Too late; we're committed," said Radcliff.

Ingram said to O'Toole, "Get aft and buckle up, Larry."

"You bet," said O'Toole, exiting the cockpit.

"Damn it, come on, baby," coaxed Radcliff.

The C-54 bucked. A horn sounded. Peoples looked out his window. "Fire! Number three! Shit. Oil pressure dropping on number four! Damn. Now it's zero."

"Better cut four," said Hammer. "Recommend fire bottle on three!"

"Do it," said Radcliff. He muttered, "No go-around now. Hang on for a hard landing. I need lots of rudder . . . Leroy. Help meee . . ."

"Got it, boss." Peoples helped stomp in left rudder, keeping the plane from twisting to the right.

"Fire?" asked Radcliff.

"Working on it," said Peoples, yanking the fire bottle lever.

Radcliff called, "Jon, you better tell Okinawa what's going on."

"Trying, Skipper," said Berne, tapping his key.

"Here we go. Full flaps, Leroy," said Radcliff.

Someone screamed aft. Blinde popped into the cockpit. "Machine gun. Mr. O'Toole is hurt."

"Get back there and help him," shouted Ingram.

"First aid kit on the port bulkhead," called Hammer.

They were over the runway's threshold. "Where's my flaps, Leroy?" asked Radcliff as he chopped the throttles.

Peoples gasped, "Lost hydraulics. Emergency pump, Chief!"

"Gettin' it," puffed Hammer. He was on his knees yanking a red handle back and forth.

"Fire's out, Bucky," said Peoples.

"That's something." Radcliff eased the yoke back. The C-54's nose rose a bit and the plane floated. "We're gonna be long." He pleaded, "Come on, come on."

The plane finally stalled and bounced hard on the mains. Radcliff let it roll for a moment, eased the nosewheel down, and then tried the brakes. "Hey, they work!"

"Thank the chief," said Peoples.

Hammer rose. "That's all you get, boss. We may be losing fluid and I'd rather not pump anymore out."

"Come on, girl, come on," urged Radcliff. The runway rushed past. Ingram saw burned-out aircraft, the rising sun painted on scorched wings. There were a few hangars as well, all reduced to rubble.

"Sheeeyat," said Peoples. "You can do this, Bucky."

"Please, old girl," pleaded Radcliff.

"Looking better, Bucky," said Peoples.

The C-54 slowed, and slowed some more, finally braking to a stop two hundred feet from the runway's end.

"Nice job, boss," said Hammer.

"I'll say," said Berne.

Peoples said, "Bucky, you forgot something."

"Huh?"

"You forgot to sideslip."

They all laughed.

Berne said, "I think we took machine-gun fire back there."

"Don't I know it?" said Radcliff.

Blinde stuck his head in the cockpit and shouted, "Lieutenant O'Toole is dead, and Captain Fujimoto is wounded."

"What?" said Ingram. He stood looking at Blinde.

"Hey, Todd, check this." It was Radcliff pointing outside the cockpit.

Ingram turned to see two half-tracks pulling up and pivoting to block their path. A red star was painted on the side of each. Each one packed a quad .50: four .50-caliber machine guns pointed right at them.

14

22 August 1945
Toro Airfield
Karafuto Prefecture, Japan

Everybody was yelling.

"Quiet!" shouted Radcliff.

Peoples gasped, "Did the Japs shoot at us?"

"No, that stuff came from the beach," said Radcliff.

"Which means they have at least two more guns at the other end of the runway," said Ingram.

They started yelling again.

"Pipe down," said Ingram. He turned to Radcliff. "Did you see them back there?"

"Saw one son of a bitch from the corner of my eye just as we flared. He was shooting straight at us. And there must be others because they caught us on final approach."

Ingram doubled his fists. *From one war to another in one easy lesson.* He turned to Berne. "Any luck with Okinawa?"

"Trying to raise 'em."

"When they answer, tell them the Russians are shooting at us and we have one dead. And that we need help. Quick!"

"Yes, sir." Patiently, Berne tapped his key.

"And let me know when you get an answer."

"Yes, sir."

Gunnery Sergeant Harper burst into the cockpit. "What's up, Commander?"

"Sergeant Harper, are you and your men ready to deploy?"

Harper said, "Yes, sir, we're already cocked and loaded. Just those two half-tracks right now. Can't see what's behind us, though."

"Are your men okay?"

"No injuries. Couple of my kids, first time in a firefight. Scared shitless."

"Aren't we all?" said Ingram.

"But Lieutenant O'Toole is dead."

"We heard." Ingram thought for a moment, shook his head. *O'Toole was a good man. A good sailor. No time. Let the dead bury the dead.*

"And the Jap is wounded."

"How serious?"

Harper said, "Hit in the shoulder. Piece of shrapnel. I think we can fix him. That is, if you want. Otherwise we can just toss him out on the runway."

"No, we'll probably need him, especially now that Lieutenant O'Toole is dead. Please fix him up."

"Actually, Mr. Blinde is looking after him."

"That's good. I need to know if the runway behind us is clear of the other half-tracks. I want to get us back to the tower and the protection of the Japanese," said Ingram. He marveled at what he'd just uttered. *Protection of the Japanese.* "Do you have any grenades?"

"Enough to make life shitsville for our Commie friends out there," said Harper. "Mind if I take a look?"

"Go right ahead."

Harper squeezed past Ingram and craned his neck to look out the windshield. "Those are M-16s, made in the good old U S of A."

"Brought to you by the miracle of lend-lease," said Radcliff.

Harper rubbed his chin. "Four guys per vehicle: a driver; guy next to him looks like a radio operator or commander or both; then two gunners to operate the quad .50."

As if they'd been listening, the gunners on the half-track on their right trained their quad .50 right at the cockpit, then raised the muzzles.

"What the hell?" said Radcliff.

The quad fifties fired. All four of them. The muzzle flashes momentarily blind them. The bullets whizzed right over the cockpit with a thunderous noise.

"Sheeeyat," said Peoples.

The Russian gunners grinned. One of them stood and drew a finger across this throat. *Cut your engines.*

"Think you can take 'em out, Ugly?"

"Okinawa just rogered our message, Mr. Ingram," said Berne.

"Good," said Ingram. "Keep talking to them. Make sure they know those Commies are shooting at us."

"Roger, Commander."

Harper said, "Yeah, we can take them out. But we better do it before they start shooting again."

"Okay. Get ready at the hatches, port side. It may be tough debarking, so we may need a diversion."

"I have one," said Radcliff. He spoke for a minute.

When Radcliff finished, Ingram and Harper looked at one another. "Sounds good," said Ingram. "Okay with you, Sergeant?"

"I say let's give it a shot, Commander," said Harper. A thin smile revealed tobacco-stained teeth. "Better than sittin' here on our butts." He nodded out the window. "But we should hop to it. Looks like Ivan is calling in his troops."

A glance told them a man was hunched over a field radio, speaking into a microphone.

"Yeah, check that." Radcliff nodded out the window.

A skirmish line of troops was forming near the beach, perhaps five hundred yards distant. They began walking toward the runway.

"This is getting tricky," said Peoples.

"Let's do it!" said Ingram. "And Gunny, tell Mr. Blinde I'll be right there. Will thirty seconds be enough?"

Harper headed for the door. "Give me sixty. But I need ladders."

Hammer stood. "I can fix you up. Okay, Skipper?"

Radcliff said, "Go, Chief."

The two disappeared out the hatch.

"Sixty seconds, then we go," Ingram shouted after them. He checked his watch, then looked at Radcliff. "Sorry about this mess, Bucky."

Radcliff said to Peoples in a loud voice, "Let this be a lesson to you, Leroy. Never, I mean never, volunteer for anything."

Peoples replied, "You mean we're not getting time and a half?"

Berne said, "Would you believe we are about to shoot at our allies?"

"They shot first," said Radcliff.

"Twenty seconds," said Ingram.

He stood in the doorway and looked aft into the cabin. The Marines were bunched against the two port-side doors, about six to a door, portable aluminum ladders poised. He caught Harper's eye and they exchanged a thumbs-up.

Ingram checked his watch. Time! "Go, Bucky."

"Roger." Radcliff reached over and advanced the two port-engine throttles. With a roar, the engines revved up and the C-54 began swinging clockwise, the port number one engine heading directly for the half-track off to their right.

"Jeeez, you were serious boss," said Peoples.

Berne crossed himself.

"Trust me, boys," said Radcliff.

The Russians looked up in panic as the C-54's outboard propeller, driven by a 1,350-horse Pratt & Whitney R-2000 engine, scythed right at them. Three of the four jumped out the sides. The driver frantically kicked the starter and worked the choke.

Ingram felt a concussion off to his left. Smoke billowed from the half-track on their port side. The Marines must have exited safely. The three Russians on the runway raised their weapons and began shooting. They were cut down immediately by a burst of gunfire from under the right wing.

The driver in the other half-track got his vehicle going, but it bucked and bounced as he yanked the steering wheel to the left. The half-track stalled, and the driver gave up and jumped out the door.

Berne stood and looked out the left cockpit window. "You got it, boss. We're okay."

The driver stood about twenty feet away watching as the propeller cleared the M-16 by no more than two feet. Then he took off toward the skirmish line.

A red flare rose from among the troops in the skirmish line. They were closer, perhaps three hundred yards.

Ingram said, "Bucky, roll for the tower and the Japs. Try to find a revetment where Hammer can do something with those two engines."

"I had the same idea."

"You should be safe there. Get Fujimoto to talk to the Japs."

Radcliff looked up. "Only chance we got. I wonder if he's okay."

"Wait one." Ingram ran aft, finding Fujimoto stretched out on the floor. Blood was spattered over his khaki shirt.

Blinde knelt beside him pressing a battle dressing onto his left shoulder. Ingram asked, "What do you think?"

"I think he'll be okay. But I'm not a doctor," said Blinde.

"Hurts like the blazes," said Fujimoto. His face was pale and sweat beaded his forehead. "You have morphine?"

"Not now. I need you," said Ingram.

"Are you serious?"

"Please."

Fujimoto grimaced. "My every waking moment is filled with favors for you."

"Lieutenant O'Toole is dead. We're going to try for the tower. I need you to translate and negotiate with your soldiers. Okay?"

"I'll try." Fujimoto tried to sit up, groaned, and lay back. "Maybe later," he gasped.

"Thirsty?"

Fujimoto nodded.

Ingram looked across the aisle and saw Lieutenant O'Toole splayed on the floor, his gaze fixed at the ceiling. Blood ran from the back of his head.

"He was a good man," said Fujimoto. "A Domer."

"That he was," agreed Ingram. He looked up, "Anybody have some water?"

Sergeant Hammer came up the aisle and handed over a canteen.

Blinde grabbed it and held it to Fujimoto's mouth. The wounded man drank for a moment, water dribbling down his chin.

Ingram said, "You going to be all right?"

"Like I said, I'll try. How are things going out there?"

"To tell you the truth, I think we just started World War III."

"How nice. And this time everyone is mobilized. No time wasted."

Ingram said, "Not this guy. I'm ready for home."

Fujimoto closed his eyes and nodded.

Ingram turned to Blinde. "You have a weapon?"

Blinde patted a shoulder holster hidden under his jacket. "Thirty-two automatic. It was my mother's."

"What?"

"Pearl handle."

Ingram snorted. "About as much stopping power as a BB gun."

Blinde stuck his nose up a bit. "Better than nothing."

"I hope so." Ingram stood. "Okay, I'm off."

Ingram and Hammer walked back to the cockpit. Ingram let Hammer past and then asked, "Runway clear?"

"As far as we can see," said Radcliff.

"Good. Fujimoto looks all right--a little loopy, but okay. Blinde is helping him for now. I think he'll be okay when the time comes.

Radcliff called, "All right. Watch it out there, Todd. Looks like the bastards on the skirmish line are taking potshots at us."

"You're kidding!"

"Yeah, Harper and his boys are behind the half-tracks."

Ingram turned to Berne, "Any more from Okinawa?"

"Not a peep, sir."

"Damn it. Okay, keep trying. Gotta run, Bucky. Now get going."

"No argument from me. Good luck."

Ingram jumped out the port-side hatch and quickly scrambled down the ladder. Harper and six of his men knelt twenty yards away behind the empty half-track.

Two bullets grazed the concrete beside Ingram and zinged off into the distance. Radcliff goosed his engines, the roar incredible. The C-54 swung all the way around and began waddling back toward the tower.

Ingram ran up to Harper and crouched beside him. "They're shooting at us!"

"No shit."

"Well, come on." Ingram leapt over the side of the half-track and got into the pointer's seat of the quad .50. Harper followed five seconds later. "How do you work this thing," Ingram yelled.

"Should be a foot treadle on your side. See it?" shouted Harper.

Ingram looked down. "Yeah." He mashed it with his foot. A long burst roared out.

Bullets from the Russians began clanging against the half-track's armor-plated sides and the armor "flaps" on the sides of the gun mount.

"Okay," yelled Harper. "I'll train right to left. You hose 'em down. Give it just one- to two-second bursts. Should scare the living crap out of them."

Harper cranked the mount to the right. Ingram peered through his sight, found his hand wheel, and dropped the gun barrels right on the skirmish line, now two hundred yards distant.

"Now!" yelled Harper.

Ingram hit the treadle. The mount roared. Dust and concrete filled the air. Bodies dropped. An arm spun away from a cloud of red mist.

Harper trained a bit left. "Again!" he shouted.

Ingram fired at the Russians, now in full retreat and running frantically. Two or three dropped. The rest kept running.

Harper trained a little more left. "Give it to the bastards."

"That's enough," said Ingram.

"What?" demanded Harper.

"Let's save ammo, Sergeant. Now get over to that other half-track. See if you can start it and then follow me."

It dawned on Harper what they had done: they were now in possession of one, possibly two, M-16 half-tracks. "Not a bad way to even the odds, Commander."

"Not bad at all, Sergeant. Now get over there and see what you can do."

"Yes, sir." Harper leapt over the side and ran for the other half-track. He soon waved back. "Nine innings for this one, Commander. Electronics are all toasted."

"Okay, let's go. But grab some ammo off that mount, if you can."

"Yo!" Harper passed ammo cans to four of his Marines. In sixty seconds they were running back to Ingram's half-track and clambering aboard.

Harper stayed behind to splash a five-gallon can of gasoline in the cockpit. Then he jumped out with grenade in hand and shouted, "Fire in the hole!" He pulled the pin, tossed a grenade in the damaged half-track, and ran for the other.

The explosion set off the fuel tank, and they all felt the heat of the blast. "Just to make sure the Commies don't get it running again," Harper said.

"Good riddance," said Ingram.

Harper pointed to one of his men, a redheaded corporal. "Ely, think you can drive this thing?"

The corporal grinned, "Have more hours in one of these than an M-4."

"Then get this damn thing started and follow that airplane." He pointed to the steering wheel.

"You bet, Ugly." The corporal jumped in the driver's seat, hit the starter, and got the half-track going. He clanked it into gear and took off after the C-54. They soon caught up with the plane and passed it on the left side, waving to Radcliff as they went by.

Within two hundred yards of the tower Ingram noticed an irregular line of pillboxes and machine-gun nests well camouflaged with netting and brush. Further back were three artillery pieces, about 75 mm, he guessed. A few helmets bobbed up to look at him, but for the most part the defenders remained hidden behind sand berms and brush.

The half-track pulled up to the tower, a rickety three-story wooden building with all the windows shot out; Harper and his men jumped to the ground. "Fan out," he ordered. "Uh, Commander, I'd recommend you stay here until we sort things out."

They quickly formed a perimeter, with the C-54 taxiing into the middle. Ingram jumped from the half-track and walked over to the pilot's window.

Radcliff slid open his cockpit window and stuck out his head. "What's going on?"

Ingram gave a shrugged and mouthed, "Wait one."

The starboard hatch opened, the aluminum ladder dropped, and Hammer was down in an instant. Quickly, he ran under his starboard engines. He drew out a flashlight and shined it into the opened cowl flaps of number four, the outboard starboard engine.

Ingram walked over, finding it quieter on this side with both engines shut down. "What do you think?"

Hammer whipped off his cap and said, "If I was a bettin' man I'd say there's a chance with this one. Simply because we lost oil pressure, which means an oil leak. Can't tell, though, until I get the cowl off both of these and have a look-see."

"Uh, Hammer, what if you get just one running? Can we still get out of here?"

"Pretty sure we can take off on three engines."

"How about only two engines?"

"Not a chance."

"Oh."

"I'm hoping we can at least fix number four. That way we won't have too much torque from the port side."

Ingram pointed off to the right. "Is that a revetment over there?"

"Looked like it from the cockpit, but there's a lot of junk in there. Could be stuff from burned-out aircraft."

Berne walked up, a perplexed look on his face.

"What is it, Jon?"

He held up a notepad and flipped pages. "This from Okinawa, sir." He read aloud, "'Remain steadfast. Trying to send another C-54 but requires permission from USSR consulate. Under no circumstances are you to fire on USSR troops. Remember primary goal is to secure Boring.' It's signed 'Neidemeier for Flannigan.'"

"Flannigan? Who's Flannigan?"

"Ask him," said Berne. He nodded to Blinde, who was climbing down the ladder.

Ingram waited for Blinde to walk up and then demanded, "Who is this Flannigan guy?"

"My boss in Washington, D.C." Blinde stared at him. "He's not going to be happy about what happened back there. We've really stirred up a hornet's nest."

Ingram stood close. "Mr. Blinde, I don't have the time or the inclination for games. Those sons of bitches killed one of mine and wounded another. They shot at us on final approach, which could have resulted in a crash, probably fatal to us all. And they have seriously damaged this aircraft."

"You don't understand. Someone was supposed to--"

"Supposed to what?"

"Meet us. Welcome us. Someone from the Red Army."

"Fine, Mr. Blinde. Just fine." Ingram waved around him. "Take a look at what's happened here. Instead of meeting us as you promised, your Russian friends fired on us, which could have killed us all, including your dead little ass. As a result, I'd say those people are not our friends. And since this whole snafu is my responsibility, I'm going to take every precaution, which includes killing more Communists if that's what's required. So, not that it matters, I ask again: Who is this Flannigan guy?"

"OSS."

Ingram whipped off his hat. "What the hell is a Washington, D.C., bureaucrat doing screwing around with a firefight eight thousand miles away?"

"The war is over, Commander Ingram. That's when the bureaucrats are supposed to take over," said Blinde.

"Well, look around you, Mr. Blinde. I'd say the war isn't over. In fact, peace hasn't even been declared. So, in the meantime, I'll take my orders from General MacArthur, the supreme commander out here. Not from some Washington bureaucrat."

"What I meant was--"

"Now, I want you back on that aircraft and tending to Captain Fujimoto. Is that clear?" Ingram stood close. "And don't get any ideas about having Captain Berne send messages. I decide what goes out and what doesn't."

Berne moved up. So did Harper and Hammer. Blinde looked at them and then said, "As you wish." He walked back and boarded the C-54.

Ingram turned to Berne. "Jon, send a message back to Okinawa that I intend to carry out my mission while protecting my people and my equipment to the best of my ability. If that means killing Communists, then that's what I'll do. Send a copy of that to MacArthur's headquarters and CinCPac in Guam."

"Todd?" Radcliff stood in the doorway. "What gives?"

Ingram yelled up. "Head for that revetment, Bucky. The Marines will clear it out for you. Then Hammer can get to work."

"Roger." Radcliff disappeared inside.

Ingram motioned to Harper.

"Sir?"

"Gunny, send four of your men over to that revetment and have them clear out the junk as best they can. For the time being, this aircraft is our only ticket home, so I'd like to set up a perimeter to protect it while Hammer tries to fix one or both engines.

"What about the Japs, sir?"

"Speak of the devil." Ingram waved toward the tower.

Four Japanese soldiers emerged from a low berm. Walking in front were two officers with holstered pistols, one of them wearing a sword. Behind were two soldiers with rifles slung over their shoulders.

The officer with the sword walked up to Ingram. "Commander Ingram?"

"That's right."

"I am Major Kotoku Fujimoto, Imperial Japanese Marines. Is my brother aboard that airplane?"

15

---

22 August 1945
Toro Airfield
Karafuto Prefecture, Japan

Kotoku Fujimoto resembled his brothers, but he was shorter and stockier. A black patch covered his left eye, and his left arm was in a sling. A Fu Manchu mustache made him look older than what Ingram guessed would be twenty-three or twenty-four. But he wore his khakis well and carried his sword with authority.

Major Fujimoto clasped a hand behind his back. "Commander, we do not have much time before the Russians counterattack."

"Counterattack? Who attacked whom?"

"Well, to their way of thinking, you attacked them. So, they counterattack. In any case, they have done this before. We've been through it with them for the past two days." He waved to the burned-out junk in the revetments. "I anticipate they will attack at dusk. It's their nature."

Ingram sputtered, "Your English is excellent."

"A family custom. Our father insisted. Although Katsumi, my oldest brother, was a bit off his game in that department."

Ingram knew this. "Oh?"

"He didn't like anything to do with English or Americans."

Ingram felt a hot flash of anger. "Did you go to Notre Dame also?"

"No, Etajima. I decided to become a marine when they threw all that engineering nonsense at me."

It had been the same at the U.S. Naval Academy. Midshipmen who preferred not to suffer math and physics courses could take the Marine "option" if they wished. "Things never change," muttered Ingram. "Yes. Your brother is aboard."

"May I see him?"

"Of course. But he's been wounded. Courtesy of our Communist friends."

"Is he--"

"He'll be fine, but he's lost some blood. A shoulder wound. Do you have a doctor?"

"We have a fairly decent field hospital here and a doctor. Let's get him off the plane and over there."

"I'm sorry, but I can't allow that," said Ingram.

"What?" Major Fujimoto stood rigid.

There was a roar from the C-54 as Radcliff taxied into the revetment and spun the aircraft around. The port-side props were still spinning as Hammer and a couple of Marines pushed a small platform under the outboard starboard engine. He scrambled up and began unbolting the cowl. Radcliff cut number one and two engines and it became quiet.

"What is your damage?" asked Fujimoto.

Ingram shrugged. "Could be an oil line. We're not sure yet. The inboard engine is the one that worries me."

Fujimoto whipped off his cap and wiped his forehead. "Have your flight mechanic speak with my sergeant here. We may be able to give you materials."

"Thank you."

"About my brother, can I . . ."

"Major, please go aboard now. Spend time with your brother. And please send up your medical officer. Believe me, I'd give a thought to leaving him here with you, but we need him to help us clear the mines in Tokyo Bay."

"You need to get in there so soon?"

"We need to get in there to secure the capital and, more important, to secure our prisoners of war. There are many in the area, I'm told." Ingram didn't want to tell him about the surrender ceremony planned for Tokyo Bay.

Fujimoto nodded. "I see."

Ingram decided to add, "And to secure your people from fighting among themselves. We hear there are a number of hotheads there who want nothing more than to lead palace revolts and suicide charges."

"So I have heard." Fujimoto studied Ingram for a moment. Then he turned to his officer and gave instructions in Japanese. The officer, a lieutenant, bowed and walked quickly back toward the brush--and disappeared.

Ingram blurted, "Amazing."

"You like our camouflage, Commander?"

"Where did he go? I can't see a thing."

"Believe it or not, I have five tanks, thirteen artillery pieces, twenty-five machine-gun nests, and ten pillboxes around here. All in all, I have about one thousand men hidden.

Ingram nodded slowly. These were brave men. But a handful of tanks and guns and a thousand men weren't nearly enough to withstand the onslaught of the Soviet hordes. "Communications?"

"Not bad. We have some wireless. But all that aside, you should be out of here by sunset."

"Depends on how repairs go."

"They had better get the engine repaired soon; otherwise the Soviets will shell it to bits."

"They have artillery?"

"All around us. Plus, the ships anchored out there. They have been quite open about it and expect us to surrender, especially since Toyahara fell yesterday."

"Where's that?"

About two hundred kilometers east of here. It is the capital of Karafuto. Our commander there sent out a general surrender order last night. But I have not yet decided."

"Why not?"

"Those people, the Mongols, are animals--monsters from the central steppes of Asia. No wonder the Germans tried to wipe them out. They are violent, lawless, and uneducated. Did you hear what they did to Mukden?"

Ingram shook his head.

"Raped every woman and child and then killed them all. They did the same in Harbin."

"Ever hear of Nanking, or Peking, or Singapore, or Manila?" Ingram retorted.

Fujimoto flushed. "Touché. Yes. That is true. But I am not going to let them do that to us. May I ask a favor?"

"If I can."

"Please don't tell my brother about the impending attack."

Ingram raised his eyebrows.

"I don't want him upset if he is wounded."

"All right," said Ingram. "But he's a grown man and a full navy captain."

"Yes." Fujimoto checked his watch. "Coming up on fifteen hundred. That gives you about five hours. If you remain after that, you will be fighting on the side of the Japanese. Isn't that a twist?" He laughed. "And now, if you'll excuse me, I will go and see--"

"Major Fujimoto, do you have a Swiss Red Cross representative with you? A man by the name of Walter Boring?"

"Are you here to take him?"

"That's my mission."

Fujimoto rubbed his chin. "He came to us in terrible shape."

"What happened?"

"Since he arrived he has been in a sort of trance--nearly catatonic. Doctor Osuga can tell you more."

"What happened to him?"

"He is not a military man. He was in Mukden when the Soviets attacked. They have been nipping at his heels ever since, and he has been passed from command to command. A plane brought him here, but it was shelled just as it landed. That must have driven him around the bend because he can barely communicate now. He's in my command bunker if you wish to see him."

Just then, a uniformed man with red-trimmed badges and medical bag walked up and bowed. The lieutenant followed close behind.

Fujimoto said, "This is Doctor Osuga. And Lieutenant Nakayama is my executive officer."

Osuga and Nakayama bowed. In clear English Osuga said, "Hello, Commander."

Ingram said, "How do you do, Doctor." He nodded to the C-54. "Let's get you up there."

"Thank you."

With two Marines watching closely they walked to the ladder and Ingram called, "Bucky!"

"Yo!" Radcliff poked his head out the hatch. Berne stood behind him.

"Can I send these two up? This is Major Kotoku Fujimoto, the garrison commander and the brother of Captain Shiroku Fujimoto, our guest for the past couple of days. With him is Doctor Osuga, who will try to patch up Captain Fujimoto."

Radcliff beckoned, "Send 'em up."

As the Japanese mounted the ladder, Ingram asked, "Anything from Okinawa?"

"Not a peep," said Berne.

The realization sunk in that there would be no rescue plane today. Ingram's heart skipped a beat. Finally, he managed, "The State Department must still be wrestling with the Soviet Foreign Office for permission to fly in another C-54. I think we're on our own, Bucky."

"Looks like it."

"Jon, send a message to Okinawa that we expect a Soviet counterattack at dusk. You can add that we're currently garrisoned with the Japanese, who are cooperating."

Looking over Radcliff's shoulder, Berne said, "Okay, Todd."

"And let me know when they roger the message."

"Yes, sir." Berne disappeared.

Fujimoto and Osuga reached the top of the ladder. Radcliff stood aside to let them pass.

Ingram asked, "How's Hammer doing?"

Radcliff tilted a hand from side to side. "We may be okay with number four. Looks like an oil line was shot out. He's replacing it now. Number three looks dicey, though. Took a shell right in the starter motor. So, for sure we won't be able to get a ground start. Maybe windmill it if we get off the ground."

"When we get off the ground," Ingram corrected.

"Roger that," said Radcliff.

"How long before he tests it?"

"Pretty soon."

"No kidding?" Ingram looked over to engine four. Hammer and Peoples stood on a platform, surrounded by cowling and tools. He couldn't see their faces. Both were shirtless and muttering as they clanked and tinkered at the engine. Oil dripped everywhere.

"I'll let you know when we're ready to test, Todd."

Ingram said, "Okay, I'm off to secure our guest."

"Who?"

"Walter Boring."

"Oh, yeah."

"It's why we're here, Bucky."

Radcliff gave him a look that said *bullshit*.

Hammer walked up. "I think we can give it a go."

"You sure?" said Radcliff.

"Only way to tell is to give it a shot. Can I have a bottle?"

"Right." Radcliff ducked back and reappeared with a fire extinguisher.

Peoples walked up, oil smeared all over his torso. "Try not to flood it, Bucky."

"Damn it, Leroy, I know how to start an engine."

"I wonder at times," countered Peoples.

A muttering Radcliff ducked from the hatchway and soon appeared at the copilot's window, sliding it open. "Gimme a minute." He looked down and checked switches and gauges. "Everything away from the engine?"

Hammer said, "Everything except the cowl. And that's right here under the wing."

"Okay. Clear prop!" yelled Radcliff.

The starter motor wound up to full rpm; Radcliff engaged the propeller. Out of curiosity, Ingram asked, "How far does he wind it?"

"Twelve blades should do it," said Hammer.

Radcliff gave a thumbs up and watched closely as the propeller slowly turned.

Ingram tried to keep up. Twelve blades for a three-bladed propeller meant four complete revolutions before Radcliff switched on the magneto.

The blades swung gracefully through the air. Suddenly the engine coughed. Flames gushed out the exhaust stacks. A plume of blue-black smoke followed. Then it began to catch, a few cylinders at a time. It sputtered and backfired. Then all fourteen cylinders caught, and the engine roared to life.

They grinned at one another as Radcliff ran it for a couple of minutes to smooth it out. Finally, Hammer drew a finger across his throat. Radcliff nodded and cut the engine. Radcliff barked, "Secure the cowl, Chief, and get ready to get the hell out of here."

"What about number three?" Hammer asked.

"Do what you can, but I want to get out of here at a moment's notice. Right, Todd?"

"You bet."

"Okay, let's get at it," said Hammer. He went over to the work stand and with Peoples helping began replacing the cowl.

Ingram called up, "Bucky, can you send Mr. Blinde to the hatch?"

"He's right here." Radcliff stepped away and Blinde appeared. "Yes? What is it?"

"Sorry to bother you," Ingram said with exaggerated politeness. The sarcasm earned a cold stare from Blinde. "We're going after Mr. Boring now," he continued. "Do you wish to come?"

"The radio. I have to stick close. Big things are happening. Can it wait a few minutes?"

"No. I want to get out of here. What's so big?"

"Soviet intentions. Could affect what we're doing here." Blinde turned an ear toward the cockpit. "This sounds important." He moved away.

Major Fujimoto appeared in the doorway and climbed down, the doctor right behind. "Congratulations. What about the other engine?"

Ingram said, "We're going to check. But I'm told we can take off on three engines if we must."

"How about fuel. Do you need any?"

Ingram shrugged. "Ask the pilot."

Fujimoto walked under the cockpit and called up to Radcliff.

"Do you need fuel?"

Radcliff said, "We could use some. Especially if we hit headwinds. Hold on. Weather report." He moved inside.

Fujimoto turned to Peoples, "You see, with all our aircraft gone, we have fuel we won't be needing. What octane do you burn?"

Peoples drawled, "Any old rotgut."

"I beg your pardon?"

"One hundred, Major," said Hammer.

"We have a few barrels."

Peoples smiled and said, "Damn fine."

Fujimoto said, "What does that mean?"

Ingram said, "He means we'll take your one hundred octane, Major. Thank you. Now, how do I find Walter Boring?"

16

22 August 1945
Command bunker, Toro Airfield
Karafuto Prefecture, Japan

Major Fujimoto's command bunker was deep in the brush, about one hundred yards south of the runway. With Sergeant Harper and three of his Marines in trail, Ingram followed Fujimoto, Captain Osuga, and Lieutenant Nakayama as they picked their way through dense shrubs and trees. Along the way Ingram counted two tanks and a pillbox with a 37-mm cannon.

Low branches slapped at Ingram's face as he caught up to Fujimoto. "How is your brother?"

"The doctor tells me he needs blood."

"Well, with the engine fixed we can get him back to Kisarazu and take care of that."

"I hope so." Fujimoto drew up for a moment. "My brother told me about your role in the fate of my father and brother Katsumi." His right hand rested on his sword.

Ingram's hand went to the .45 hanging from his web belt. They eyed each other for a moment.

Harper leveled his carbine. "Knock it off, Tojo." The other Marines stood back and readied their weapons as well. Osuga and Nakayama were rooted, their eyes wide.

Ingram waved them down. "We were on opposite sides of the table then. You would have done the same." The sun went behind a cloud, rendering the moment darker.

Fujimoto's hand slipped off the sword. "Shiroku is terribly conflicted. He wants to kill you, but his Catholic education has left him in a quandary. "The worst part is," he pawed the ground with his split-toed sandal, "after your escape from death last night, he feels different toward you--an American, a sworn enemy. He feels almost . . . a kinship."

"We were lucky," said Ingram. "We had a damn good pilot." There was an awkward silence. "And you?" Ingram asked. "Where do you stand?"

Fujimoto looked down for a moment. "He made me promise to help all I can."

"Thank you," said Ingram. "Let me add that if there's any way, you're welcome to come back with us."

"And leave my men? That is one thing I will not do. Even my liberal brother understands that."

"What if--"

Fujimoto barked, "Commander Ingram. Imagine your ship is mortally wounded and going down. What do you do?"

"Last man off," Ingram said quietly.

"Exactly." Fujimoto turned and walked away.

The bunker had been carefully dug about fifteen feet below ground level; the walls and ceiling were reinforced with logs, dirt, and sandbags. Most of it consisted of a large room about twenty feet square. The floor was hardpan dirt, and off to one side were a small galley, a benjo, and two bunkrooms with curtains across the doorways. The main room had a large map table in the center, radio equipment against one wall, and a small dining table against the other wall. A wooden ladder led to a cupola atop the bunker that offered a clear view above the brush line.

Several men in the bunker wore earphones. Fujimoto barked a question in Japanese. Three men stood, and each shook his head. Fujimoto turned to Ingram, "All quiet. I don't like it." He pointed to a doorway and drew aside a curtain. "In here."

The bunkroom was small, about four feet by six, with room for bunk beds, a desk, and a locker. A number of boxes and a heavy-looking crate covered the top bunk. The lower bunk was rumpled and dark.

Fujimoto barked a command. The lights went on and revealed a human shape under a blanket. It stirred and gave a low moan. Dr. Osuga knelt beside the bed and pulled the blanket back to reveal a man with gray-white hair in disarray. Heavy stubble grew around his jaw and mouth. He smacked his lips, revealing yellow teeth. His eyes fluttered, and he gave a long, wailing moan. "*Wasser.*"

Fujimoto uncorked a pitcher, poured a cup, and handed it to Osuga. The doctor raised it to Boring's mouth and poured. The man tried to swallow, but a lot of water burbled out and ran down his chin. He began choking.

Fujimoto whispered, "A seventy-year-old man. Apparently, he went through several artillery barrages before he came to us. Now he can barely hear; he is severely dehydrated and frightened nearly to death. The Red Cross had no business sending him."

Ingram wondered what age he would have to achieve before he would be considered too old for a war zone. It seemed he'd been doing this all his life. *Tired.*

Fujimoto must have caught on for he smiled for a moment. Then he said, "Dr. Osuga will give him a sedative."

"Can he travel?"

Dr. Osuga said, "*Hai.*" Then he dug into his black bag and pulled out a syringe. In a moment it was prepared, and he jabbed it into Boring's arm.

The man's eyes popped open at the pain.

Ingram leaned close, finding the man's breath horrid. "Mr. Boring?"

The old man's eyelids fluttered and then opened. He focused on Ingram and studied him for a moment. "*Ja, ja. Amerikaner?*"

"Yes, I am an American naval officer. We're taking you home."

"Home?" He croaked.

The odor was terrible. Ingram had to draw back. "To America; to Switzerland."

Boring let out a long sigh and then said in clear English. "Make sure you bring the crate." He pointed to the bunk above him.

"What's in it?"

Boring waved to Fujimoto and Osuga. "Send them away."

"Why?"

He nodded. "It's very important. Please."

"Very well." Ingram turned to Fujimoto. Would you two leave us alone for a moment?"

Fujimoto looked at Osuga. They shrugged and backed out.

Ingram leaned close, trying not to breathe. "They're gone. What is it?"

Boring gasped, smacked his lips, and then spoke. "In Harbin, I found irrefutable evidence of Japan's vast biological and chemical warfare program."

"What?" Ingram drew a breath and with great willpower held his bile. This was a surprise. He hadn't heard the Japanese were conducting this kind of research. The Germans, yes; the horrifying data was leaking out after their capitulation three months ago.

"Since the mid-1930s they have been experimenting on live prisoners. Chinese, Koreans, Manchurians; even Americans, British, and Australians-- anybody they could lay their hands on. Thousands of them taken from death camps scattered from here to Singapore. They deliberately infected them with viruses or bacteria, watched them die, and then hacked open their bodies to see the results. Sometimes they hacked open the bodies of live prisoners. No anesthetic, no regard for pain."

Ingram sat back and drew a deep breath. Overwhelmed, he shook his head.

"Do you want proof?"

Tired. "I suppose so."

He pointed his chin at the bunk above. "Look up there. In that crate . . ." He wheezed for a moment then went on. "Those are what I was able to grab as the Japanese ran before the Russians. It cost me dearly, but I got them. As much as I could. My hosts," he waved outside the room, "think these are Red Cross records." Boring's voice was fading.

Once again Ingram held his breath and leaned close.

Boring wheezed, "The ones who died were frozen in freezers or left outside in the dead of winter. Stacked like cords of wood. Each one was categorized and numbered. They called them 'logs.' At their leisure, they brought a 'log' inside for study and analysis."

Boring gave a long, rasping cough and said, "They tried to cover all this up. Burned the buildings, burned the bodies in gasoline-fed fires. But the Russian attack was so swift they couldn't get it all done. Give them to Mr. Blinde. Make them . . . pay . . . make . . . them . . .'" Osuga's sedative must have begun working, for Boring's head dropped to the pillow and his eyes closed.

There was a knock outside. "Commander?"

"One moment." Ingram stood and took down the wooden crate. It was relatively small, and the lid was loose. He pried it open and found hundreds of photographs bound with rubber bands. He grabbed a stack labeled 17 June 1943 and slipped off the band. He managed to get through the first five of what must have been twenty photographs. Of those five, he knew they would occupy his dreams for the rest of his life. Some bodies were headless. Others had severed limbs. Many of the torsos were neatly sliced open. One decapitated man's shirt had a corporal's stripes; a faded USAAF was printed over the pocket. One photo showed a stack of bodies neatly arranged like a cord of wood, just as Boring had said. *Logs.* Snow was scattered over the top of them and on the ground.

"Commander!" The rap was insistent.

Ingram ripped open the curtain to find Sergeant Harper. "What?" he said sharply.

Harper blinked, then said, "Things are popping out there. Mr. Blinde and Mr. Radcliff recommend we take off now."

"What's going on?"

"We hear mechanized stuff near the beach at the west end of the runway. I figure they'll dump artillery in here and then send in tanks."

"Okay. Get your men to lift this man on a litter and put him aboard. And make sure you take this." He pointed to the crate and boxes on the top bunk.

"Can do, Commander. And there's one more thing."

Ingram looked down at Boring. "Yes?"

Harper leaned out and whistled up his men. Then he came back in. "We got word a Russian Jeep pulled up to the tower under a white flag. It carries a Russian officer. Sounds like a Russian navy commander. And he's asking for you."

"What? For me directly?"

"He asked for Todd Ingram."

17

A screech split the darkness. Helen jolted upright, her heart pounding. After a moment she realized it was only Fred, her lanky gray tabby cat, harassing Bubbles, her obese ten-year-old Russian Blue longhair. It was a game they played. Fred would roll on his back and try to wrap his arms around Bubbles' neck. Bubbles would spurn Fred's advances with a growl, a screech, and a swat of her paw. Fred loved it and did it again and again until Bubbles tired of it and simply ignored him. Bubbles had been a present from Laura West, who had unwillingly inherited the twenty-pound cat from Henry Shackleton, a down-on-his-luck French horn player who moved away to take a job with the Cleveland Symphony Orchestra.

Helen reached for the clock: 10:15. She'd been asleep for only an hour. Jerry stirred in his crib. Then he smacked his lips and cooed for a moment. *All right. Sleep tight, my love.* With a sigh, she whipped back the covers, stepped into her slippers, and grabbed her robe. Moonlight spilled into the living room, but the bedroom was dark. As she fumbled for the wall switch something whipped against her ankle.

"What?" She spun, disoriented. The room felt wrong. Nothing was where it should be. She pitched through the door to the living room and fell on the hardwood floor. "Damn it!" The furry thing rubbed against her ankle again: Fred. Then he strolled up to her face. They touched noses. Helen reached out and petted him. "I love you, too, you little schmuck." Fred had the temerity to purr.

Helen sat up and took stock. *Nothing broken.*

Bubbles lay under the piano bench, brilliantly lit by moonlight as if by a single spotlight in an opera house. She blinked and rolled onto her back, barely visible feet protruding from her corpulent body.

"It's wartime, Bubbles. How can you be so fat?" Helen braced herself to rise.

Bubbles blinked and purred. Then she rolled upright, worked herself to her feet, and waddled toward her feeding dish, her ample tummy swaying from side to side as she disappeared into the darkness. "Don't eat too much," Helen called after her.

Bubbles looked back, but all Helen could see were two large orange-yellow eyes.

Bam! She threw herself against the living room wall. Those yellow eyes tracked her, watching every move, every twitch, as Helen felt her way toward the bedroom. She found only empty space. "Noooo."

Suddenly Eddie Bergen leered at her, his face a twisted grimace as he crawled from the turret of his burning tank. But the fire was too much. Eddie screamed, and his face turned to wax dripping off a blackened skull. Eddie writhed horribly and sank back into the M-4. The tank lurched and bounced as ammunition cooked off inside.

Then Eddie was under his bed, sucking his thumb. The doctor and honor guard had to lure him out with comic books, so they could give him a medal.

Helen crawled into the bedroom on hands and knees. But, she couldn't get up; wouldn't get up. Her mind whirled. There he was, standing before her, wearing his white seersucker suit. Lieutenant Tuga, a cigarette carelessly clasped between a thumb and forefinger. Desperately, she ran a hand over faded burn marks, her arms, her feet; miraculously, the ones on her face had almost disappeared.

The memories had been harder and harder to suppress. The Kempetai, the Japanese Gestapo: Tuga and Watanabe on Marinduque Island. Watanabe looking over Tuga's shoulder, their expressions detached, uncaring. Tuga pushed the glowing cigarette against her skin. It sizzled; the pain incredible.

Sometimes Tuga would blow on the cigarette butt, making it hotter before pushing it into her skin again.

She screamed.

The baby screamed.

It burned everywhere: the palms of her hands, her breasts, the balls of her feet; everywhere nerves were concentrated.

Little Jerry was screeching. His wailing told her that he was terrified. Helen came back to herself at last. She rose, picked him up, and held him close. "I'm sorry, baby. My fault. Go back to sleep."

Wet. He'd wet his diaper. Scared stiff. She clicked on the light and busied herself changing him and putting everything right. After some cuddling and tickling Jerry was cooing again. She wrapped him in a blanket, clicked off the light, and held him close.

In the darkness she saw Eddie Bergen in the doorway. Quickly she clicked on the light. Nothing. The baby slept on, and she held him tightly. As close as she could to her heart.

Emma Peabody awoke with a belch. The damned alarm clock was ripping into a peaceful world with the 7:30 imperative. Time to get up and go next door to take care of Jerry. Again, she belched. Too much beer last night--it stayed with her. She made her own in the basement, and this new batch was particularly good--a dark lager with an unpronounceable Bavarian name.

Sunlight streamed into the window. Emma rose and stretched. Damn, that *was* a good batch. Maybe she'd have another sip or two this afternoon. But for now, it was up and off to work. She slipped on a housecoat, washed her face, and walked into the kitchen and started the coffee. There was a smile on her face as she looked forward to the best time of the day. Playing with Jerry was more a joy than a job. He was crawling like a gorilla now, getting into cupboards and redistributing pots and pans with enthusiastic clamor.

Emma Peabody looked up to the picture of her late husband, Leo. They were unable to have children, but they had everything else, especially love. Leo worked as an engineer for the Southern Pacific, Emma for the phone company. Then both retired and Leo happily went to work in their basement, setting up a brewery, building a photography laboratory, and starting a shortwave station.

But a heart attack stopped it all. At a young sixty-four Leo was gone, leaving Emma with no children, only the house and the basement.

Having the Ingrams living next door had given Emma back her life. They became great friends, and Helen actually paid Emma Peabody to babysit. To mother a child. To watch him laugh and throw things around and grow up--something denied to her by a quirk of nature.

She stepped into her house slippers and walked out the back door. Soon, she was through the fence and on Helen's back porch. She knocked. "Hello?" She flipped open her pocket watch. It was Leo's, a retirement gift from the Southern Pacific Railroad in appreciation of thirty-six years of service, thirty-two of them as an engineer. The watch was a genuine Bulova pocket timepiece featuring a twenty-one-jewel movement with a gold case and long gold chain. Accurate to within one one-hundredth of a second each day. It had seemed ironic. Leo didn't need such precision after he stopped driving the monstrous 4–8–8–2 cab-forward engines for the SP. The watch read 7:42. Emma rapped again. "Better get a move on darlin'. You're gonna be late."

Nothing.

This doesn't feel good. Emma Peabody reached into her pocket and pulled out the house key Helen had given her for emergencies. She rapped again, loudly. "Helen!! You there? Yoo-hoo!"

She put her ear to the door. A baby cried. *That's it.*

Emma shoved the key into the lock and turned it. The crying was loud, and she was overwhelmed by the odor of cat pee. Helen hadn't let Fred and

Bubbles out. She quickly walked through the kitchen. Everything cold. No coffee. No breakfast. Emma dashed into Helen's bedroom.

The baby crawled on the floor toward her, screaming. Emma scooped him up. "Jerry! What's wrong?"

Helen's bed was empty, unmade. Jerry's bottom was wet, and the screaming was a sure sign he was hungry. She lay him on his changing table and began to unpin the diaper as he writhed, his little fists wiggling in space.

A low moan, a squeak.

Emma picked up the baby, stooped, and peeked under the bed. Her heart skipped a beat. "Darlin' what are you doing?"

Helen was squeezed against the wall. She blinked.

"Dear girl, come on out of there."

Helen focused. She gave a thin smile. "Hi, Emma. I had a bad night." Her grin was almost sheepish.

"Well, get out of there and tell me about it."

Helen wiggled out and said, "Give me a minute."

"Take all the time you want."

Helen sat on the bed and pinched the bridge of her nose. Then she looked at the clock. "My God!"

"Don't worry about it, dear."

"I have to." She stood.

"Where you going?"

"Shower and to work."

Emma cradled little Jerry. "If you must. But I think you should see somebody."

Helen wasn't listening as she turned on the faucets.

Emma made coffee, toast, and scrambled eggs while Helen showered and dressed. Then, gulping her breakfast at the same time, Helen described what had happened last night.

"So, you're okay, now?" asked Emma.

"Much better. The shower was therapeutic, as was the breakfast. Thank you." She patted her tummy and stood, gathering her things.

Emma sipped coffee. "You're lucky, you know."

"Yes?" Checking a small mirror, Helen adjusted her cap.

"You have a hospital and staff full of doctors who can help."

Helen leaned down and kissed her son on the forehead. "Can't do that," she said, checking her watch. "Ye gads."

Emma's eyebrows went up.

"Do you realize what happens if some snoop finds out I'd been seeing a shrink?"

"You need help."

"Not that kind of help. People gossip. They think you're gooney. They steer away from you."

"So, phooey on them."

"They'd think I was crazy. Men with butterfly nets would come and get me."

Emma sighed. There was a certain truth to that. Even in civilian life, seeing a psychiatrist was stigmatic. But when you need help, you need help. "Darlin' you can't do this all by yourself."

Helen slipped into a windbreaker and opened the front door. "Oh, but I can. Now that I've identified the problem, I know how to treat it."

"But--"

Helen put a finger to her lips. "Not a word to anybody. Promise?"

Emma was riveted by Helen's eyes. They exuded confidence, warmth, and femininity. Unlike the pale, trembling woman she had seen thirty minutes ago, Helen could now be a *Vogue* centerfold or a Coca Cola poster girl. It was hard to look away. Her ebony hair, pulled into a ponytail, glistened in the morning light. Her smile was beautiful, engaging. In her Army uniform she looked radiant; her silver captain's "railroad tracks" sparkled.

"Okay?" she asked again.

18

Ingram and Fujimoto broke from the brush to see a Russian command car with two white flags on its front fender parked beneath the C-54's nose. An officer walked unsteadily back and forth, a cigarette dangling from his lips. Three other Russians sat stiffly in the command car, fully aware that they were the focus of Harper's well-armed Marines and a number of Japanese soldiers. Ingram waved to Harper at the edge of the brush. The sergeant set his end of Boring's stretcher down and then fanned out his men.

The Russian looked up and smiled. Flicking away his cigarette, he shuffled toward Ingram, hand outstretched. "Todd, how the hell are you?"

Ingram knew that voice and that walk. "No!"

"Hey, come on, it's me."

"Eduard?" He couldn't believe it. It was the flamboyant Eduard Dezhnev, once naval attaché to the Soviet consulate in San Francisco. But the FBI had caught him and his control, Sergei Zenit, in a sting operation and had them deported, persona non-grata.

"That's right. Good to see you, comrade." He grabbed Ingram's hand, pumped it, and then gave him an awkward bear hug. "You're looking great."

Ingram pulled away. Dezhnev had gained weight since the last time Ingram saw him. His 5-foot 11-inch frame now carried about 190 pounds instead of the 160 Dezhnev had weighed when Ingram knew him in San Francisco. His dark red hair was still combed straight back, his face was fair complected, and his broad shoulders exuded confidence. And he was walking better, without the limp he'd had two and a half years ago after losing the lower half of his left leg in a skirmish with German E-boats in the Gulf of Riga.

Dezhnev caught him looking. "New prosthesis--American, actually. Mail order, and not bad--I walk almost normally."

"Waste of time. I thought by now they would have tied you to a chair and put a bullet behind your ear."

Dezhnev gave a broad grin. "You have it all wrong. There's a war on. They need me. Look, I'm a captain third rank now."

"I'm so impressed."

Colin Blinde walked up. "Good to see you two have met up. I wondered what would happen."

"This is a farce, Colin. What's he doing here?"

Blinde stammered, "I thought you were old friends. You know, from your San Francisco days."

"Yes, San Francisco," said Dezhnev loudly. He pointed to his gleaming belt buckle, which featured the outline of a series of buildings. It was stamped with the legend ALCATRAZ. "Remember?"

"No, I don't remember."

Dezhnev scratched his head. "Must have been while you were gone. Toliver and I had a night on the town. Went to Wong Lee's and then strolled through Chinatown. He bought this for me." Oliver Toliver III, now a lieutenant commander in naval intelligence, was a shipmate and close friend of the Ingrams. He had been one of the eight, including Otis DeWitt and his then girlfriend Helen Duran, who had escaped Corregidor with Ingram in a 36-foot launch.

Dezhnev stuck out his chest. "Gold plated, too. Ollie had that done for me." Toliver came from a wealthy family.

"You should melt it down and sell it," said Ingram. He turned to Blinde. "You knew about this all along?"

Blinde said, "Ahhh, yes. It was meant to be a surprise. A backup if things went wrong. Something to smooth the waters, so to speak. I just wasn't sure if Captain Dezhnev would be in this spot. We knew he was in the area."

"Peachy keen," said Ingram. "And things did go wrong."

Dezhnev said, "Look, Todd. I can explain. We have all this--"

Ingram turned to Harper. "Get that man aboard, Sergeant. We leave momentarily. Please ask Major Radcliff to step out here, and I'd like your men to set up a perimeter around the plane." He added quietly, "Stick the crate and boxes in the cargo hold."

"Yes, sir," said Harper. He whistled, and several of his men hustled the stretcher carrying Boring from the brush to the C-54. Another stretcher followed with Boring's crate.

Dezhnev said, "Is that one of your men?"

Blinde said, "You see, Captain--"

"Yes, that's one of my men. He was shot when your people fired on my plane, Captain Dezhnev." Ingram nearly spat the last word. "He was treated at the field hospital here. Now we're trying to get him home."

Dezhnev rose on his tiptoes to watch Harper and his men carry their loads to the C-54. "Yes, of course. Perhaps our doctor could examine him. We have whole blood. Everything you need. Here, let me--"

"No need to bother, Ed," said Ingram. "American doctors can do just fine."

Dezhnev took a step toward the C-54. "No, I insist. We can do a much better job right here."

"We have it all set, Ed. He'll be in good hands by this evening."

Dezhnev persisted, "Our doctor really must examine him. I have to show proof that--"

"Not to worry, Ed. I'll vouch for him."

"And I'll need to examine that crate. It's contraband."

"Nonsense."

"You are standing on territory of the Union of Soviet Socialist Republics and are taking equipment that belongs to us. I demand that you turn it over."

Blinde muttered under his breath, "Ixnay, Commander."

Dezhnev said loudly, "Ixnay? Ixnay? What sort of charade is this?"

Ingram said, "Colin, I want you to meet Eduard Dezhnev, captain third rank, Bykovo graduate, stage actor, expert in colloquial English, and consummate bullshitter."

"You forgot, NKVD, Todd," said Dezhnev.

"Oh, so you've been elevated? Now they've taught you how to pull fingernails?"

Dezhnev rolled his eyes. "Please, Todd, you're making it difficult."

Time. Play for time. "No need to shoot up my airplane, Ed."

Dezhnev pulled a face. "You killed eight of my men."

Ingram said, "After you fired on an unarmed American transport on a peaceful mission, killing a U.S. naval officer, injuring another man, and crippling this aircraft. Then your M-16 blocked our path on the runway and threatened to fire on us. Yes. We killed a few of yours, Ed, and I'm hoping your superiors will find you at fault and finish the job they failed to do three years ago and shove you down a hole."

Dezhnev wiped a hand over his face. "I came in a gesture of peace, Todd, for you. We demand the surrender of this garrison and everything here, including your airplane."

"My airplane? What do you intend to do with it?"

Dezhnev didn't answer that. "You'll be guests of the Union of Soviet Socialist Republics, of course. You'll be interned in Vladivostok and treated well while you're there. In no time you'll be returned to your loved ones."

Radcliff walked up. With an eye on Dezhnev he asked, "What's up, Skipper?"

Ingram said, "Excuse us, please?"

Dezhnev said, "Of course. Take your time while I get to know Major Fujimoto a little better."

Ingram, Blinde, and Radcliff walked away--ten paces.

Before Ingram could say anything, Blinde hissed, "Why are you treating Captain Dezhnev like a schoolyard thug?"

"Because that's what he is. What do you know about this guy?" replied Ingram.

"That he is the area commander."

Ingram said, "I can't believe your spy buddies haven't shown you the file."

"What file?"

"The FBI file. That son of a bitch betrayed our friendship. He spied on the United States while working in the Soviet consulate in San Francisco."

Blinde said, "That's all diplomacy. Half of it's gobbledygook. You're not cleared for those levels. You don't know."

"Let me put it on a personal level for you. Dezhnev knowingly tipped the Japs via radio of my wife's whereabouts while she was hiding out on Mindanao awaiting rescue. The bastard did his best to turn her in--to screw us."

"You have no proof. Look, this is important. We must keep the Soviets happy and--"

"Mr. Blinde. Our mission is to rescue Walter Boring, and we are doing that. Isn't that right, Bucky? Is he on the airplane?"

"Yes," said Radcliff.

"Can we take off, Bucky?"

Radcliff said, "Normally, yes."

"Normally?"

Radcliff glanced down the runway. "That's a five-thousand-foot strip, which would be marginal to okay for a three-engine takeoff. But now that piece of crap is parked out there eating up the last seven to five hundred feet. Dicey."

"How dicey?"

"Very dicey to maybe not."

"You're saying we can't take off?"

Radcliff tilted a hand from side to side.

"Decide, Bucky."

Radcliff looked up to the sky, threw up his hands, and asked, "Is this important enough to die for?"

Ingram said, "Extremely important. They used the phrase 'prejudicial to the security of the United States.' And I believe it."

"It has to do with what's in the cargo hold and that guy they brought on board?" asked Radcliff.

Blinde said, "Commander, you've said enough."

Ingram nodded toward Radcliff. "Mr. Blinde. If this man is about to die, he should know why, don't you think?"

"Under normal circumstances, yes."

"Are there any abnormal circumstances when you die, Mr. Blinde?"

Radcliff said, "Okay, you guys. Quit the bickering. I can do it."

Ingram and Blinde looked at one another. Ingram asked, "You sure?"

Radcliff said, "I'm sure, Todd. Look, I just said I can do this. What more do you want?"

Ingram said, "All right, let's do it then."

Blinde nodded.

Ingram said to Radcliff, "Get back aboard and wind 'em up. And ask Berne to inform Okinawa of our intentions."

"Got it." Radcliff trotted back to the C-54.

Ingram and Blinde walked back to Dezhnev and Fujimoto, who stood silently ten feet apart. After a pause, Dezhnev spoke first, "Are you aware, Major, that Toyahara has fallen? The capital of the Karafuto Prefecture and the headquarters for Japanese military operations on the island are no longer in your hands."

Fujimoto said, "I am."

"You have orders to surrender, then." A statement.

"It has been left to my discretion, Captain," said Fujimoto.

Dezhnev said, "Major, we can squash you like a grape." He waved a hand toward the sea. "On a moment's notice I can have twenty T-34s charge down this runway in line abreast, roll over your stupid pillboxes, and grind your troops into the soil. You'll all be dead within twenty minutes."

Ingram muttered, "Now that's what I call negotiating."

Blinde said, "There's more to this than meets the eye."

Dezhnev said, "I don't follow you, Mr. Blinde."

Blinde said, "Isn't it true that the Soviet Union intends to invade Hokkaido?"

Dezhnev paused. "Marshal Vasilevskiy doesn't disclose his plans to me."

Ingram had heard the name somewhere. "Who is Marshal Vasilevskiy?"

Blinde said, "Marshal Vasilevskiy is the theater commander. He reports to Stalin."

"Generalissimo Stalin," corrected Dezhnev.

"Yes, the generalissimo," said Blinde. "Well, let's take a hypothetical case. Let's say that the Soviet Union does plan to invade Hokkaido. Maybe even as early as tomorrow. But Major Fujimoto and his people here are tying up his right flank. And Marshal Vasilevskiy needs the tanks that are here for his amphibious operation tomorrow or the next day." He turned to Fujimoto. "I'm sorry Major; you seem to be interrupting Marshal Vasilevskiy's plans."

Ingram said, "Gee, too bad. Maybe Marshal Vasilevskiy will have to shoot Captain Dezhnev here for incompetence."

"I appreciate your goodwill, Todd," said Dezhnev.

Just then, number two engine rolled. After three turns it coughed, rattled, and then roared to life.

Jon Berne walked up. "'Scuse me, Commander. I have a message for Mr. Blinde." He waved a message pad in the air. "Priority."

Blind grabbed the pad and began reading.

Number one engine rolled, sputtered, and shot out a stream of blue-black smoke. Then it rumbled into life.

They waited for number four engine to start and settle down. Ingram spoke loudly. "Look, Ed. The Japanese have surrendered to us. You can consider them our prisoners. We'll round them up and--"

Dezhnev said, "Sakhalin is Soviet territory. Major Fujimoto must surrender to me. I'll give him just four hours. Then my T-34s will roll."

Fujimoto's hand went to his sword, "Not before I have your head on a stake."

Ingram shouted, "Gentlemen, please. I'm sure--"

Blinde waved the pad in the air and shouted, "I have here a State Department communiqué saying that Generalissimo Stalin has ordered Marshal Vasilevskiy to stand down from his Hokkaido invasion."

The others stared dumbly.

Blinde said, "Gentlemen, this means the war is over. Truly. There is no reason to keep fighting."

Dezhnev said, "I don't believe you."

Ingram said, "What if it is, Ed? This means you can take your tanks and put 'em back on flatcars."

"Ridiculous. Even if it's true, you all are still my prisoners. I'll need confirmation before I can release you."

"Then get it." Ingram took Dezhnev's elbow and guided him to the command car. "And then you can pop open your vodka bottles, Ed, and enjoy life. Now move that thing before I chop it up with my propellers. We're not waiting. We have wounded aboard."

Dezhnev looked into the distance and seemed to make a decision. Sticking out a hand, he said, "We could have been friends, Todd."

Ingram said, "You crank out such bullshit, Ed. But yes, I agree. We could have been friends. In another time."

"Maybe once again?"

"Maybe."

"I'm sorry about San Francisco. I was under orders. I always liked you. We had so much fun."

"Until you got serious and tried to turn in Helen, to say nothing of espionage against the United States."

"I'm sorry. Truly I am." Something in the way Dezhnev said the last part told Ingram that it was true. At least that Dezhnev believed it was true. "How can I make it up to you?"

Ingram gestured at the Japanese. "By letting these people pack up in peace and go home."

"I'm sorry. These people are my prisoners." He stiffened slightly, puffing out his chest; a shaft of sunlight glinted off his golden Alcatraz belt buckle.

The C-54s Pratt & Whitney R-2000s rumbled under their cowlings, softly backfiring.

Dezhnev looked first at Ingram. "Go, then," he said. To Fujimoto he said, "You have two hours to surrender, Major. If not, then we will attack."

Ingram said, "You said four hours, Captain."

"Now it's two." Dezhnev bowed. "Goodbye, Todd. Perhaps we will meet under more favorable conditions sometime." He turned, signaling his driver and twirling a finger in the air. The command car started. Dezhnev climbed in and the car sped down the runway trailing dust.

Ingram turned to Fujimoto. "I'm sorry. I'm afraid I made a mess of that."

"I too am sorry. I would have liked to spend more time with my brother."

"I wish I could help." Ingram waved toward the Soviet lines. "Your chances are not too good."

"I know, but surrender or no surrender, did you see that man's eyes?"

Ingram nodded.

"He has overwhelming force and he wants to use it. I think it is his first fight. And he is afraid to lose. He needs a victory. War or no war."

Ingram recognized the truth in what Fujimoto said. He offered, "Last man off the ship?"

"I'm afraid that is me this time."

Ingram looked up. "Why don't they use airplanes?"

"We're not much of a target, really. They stopped bombing last week when they took out our remaining aircraft. I think they want to do an Attila the Hun number and rush in with swords flashing."

"Okay. Good luck." Ingram held out a hand.

Fujimoto took it, saying, "To be honest, Commander, I don't think they intend to let you out of here either. But rest assured that if anything happens while you are trying, we will open fire and stall them."

"Reveal your positions?"

Fujimoto shrugged. "We have to start sometime. But were I Dezhnev, I would attack now rather than wait two hours. I think that is what he will do. It is the Soviets' nature."

"Go on up and say goodbye to your brother."

"I've already done so. Goodbye, Commander." Fujimoto saluted, then turned and walked off into the brush. He shouted and waved a hand over his head, and his soldiers melted into the brush with him.

Ingram looked around. Aside from him, the only ones remaining were Harper's Marines and Hammer, who was pulling safety pins from the landing gear and picking up wheel chocks. Ingram whistled, pumped a fist over his head, and pointed to the forward hatch ladder. They all ran for it and quickly boarded.

19

22 August 1945
Toro Airfield
Karafuto Prefecture, Japan

Captain Fujimoto stood at the forward hatch. Ingram was astounded he had gathered the strength to crawl there and then pull himself to his feet. Radcliff released the brakes, and the C-54 began moving. To Ingram's amazement, Major Fujimoto stepped from under the wingtip. The brothers saluted one another and then waved, Major Fujimoto with his hands over his head. Captain Fujimoto struggled to raise an arm.

Radcliff spun the C-54 to the right, leaving Major Fujimoto in clear view for a moment. Hammer left the hatch open until the brothers lost sight of one another. Then, almost reverently, he eased it closed and clipped it. Two Marines helped Captain Fujimoto back to his stretcher. Hammer and Ingram looked at one another with the same thought. Then both looked out at the right wing. Number three engine remained defiantly quiet, robbing them of 1,350 desperately needed horses.

"Time to get to work," said Hammer.

Ingram followed the flight sergeant into the cockpit and strapped himself in.

Peoples called off the checklist. "Controls."

Radcliff replied, "Free and clear."

"Electrical panel."

"Clear," said Hammer.

"Fuel transfer valves."

Hammer said, "Off."

"Master switches."

"On," said Hammer.

Radcliff eased the nosewheel tiller again, turning the C-54 to the right and sending it lumbering down the taxi strip.

Peoples said, "Bucky, you taking off already?"

"Why?"

"Hell, we're going kind of fast. I can't tell if we're taxiing or doing a loop-de-loop."

As if to confirm, the plane shook as it banged over potholes. "In a hurry, Leroy."

"Why?"

"Cause I think that Commie wants to do us in."

"What if--"

"Leroy, damn it. The checklist."

The plane lurched sickeningly over a pile of rubbish.

Peoples said, "Battery switchers and inverters?"

"On and checked," said Hammer.

"Booster pumps?"

"Fifteen pounds."

"Trim tabs?"

"Set," barked Radcliff.

An explosion erupted on the taxiway a hundred yards ahead.

Ingram realized it was Dezhnev opening up with his artillery or his tanks. "Keep going, Bucky."

Another round hit off to the right, sending up a great column of rocks and dirt.

"Gettin' closer," muttered Hammer.

"How far, Bucky?" asked Ingram.

"Another couple hundred yards, give or take."

"Get on the runway if you can. I'm thinking they don't want to damage the runway."

Radcliff muttered, "Okay, boss. I'll try anything once." He threw the C-54 into a laborious left turn and had it rolling onto the main runway. No sooner had it turned than an explosion ripped the taxi strip right where the plane would have been.

Ingram cursed the day he met Eduard Dezhnev.

"Tail wheel," yelled Peoples.

"Locked," the three yelled back. The C-54 had no tail wheel.

"Vacuum."

"Check."

"Altimeters."

"Toro reports 30.15," said Berne.

They twirled their altimeter knobs.

"Instruments."

"Checked," said Radcliff.

"Checked," said Hammer.

"Radios."

"All set," said Berne. "We have Toro tower on VHF and Okinawa on CW."

"Flaps?" said Peoples reaching for the handle.

Radcliff said, "It's okay for now, Leroy. Just leave it there until I tell you. Then I want full flaps."

"Huh?"

Radcliff said, "What is it about the English language you don't understand, Mr. Peoples? Or do they teach you something different in Arkansas?" He threw the C-54 into a graceful 180-degree turn at the runway's end. "I'm tellin' you no flaps."

Peoples said, "Bucky, where did you learn to fly? Don't you want--"

Radcliff said, "Seriously, Leroy. I got it. Just call out our speed and hit full flaps when I tell you. Can you do that?"

"Yes, sir. Don't forget: opposite rudder."

"Well, I'm going to need you to work with me on this, old son."

"Name it."

"I'm going to go with full power on engines one and four."

"And then we--"

"You got it. After we start rolling, we feed in engine number two as quickly as possible. By that time my hands will be busy, so you're the one to do that. Okay?"

"Yes, sir."

"Good. And don't forget to call our speed."

"Have I ever forgotten before?"

"Shit. Leroy!"

They felt more than heard three rapid thumps. Smoke puffs and foliage debris blew out of the underbrush nearby. "Japs are shootin' back," said Radcliff.

"Well, let's not hang around to see who wins," said Ingram.

"Right. Here we go." Radcliff stomped on his brakes. Then he advanced the throttles on engines one and four, the outboard engines, to full power. The C-54 roared and rattled and bucked as it stood in place, the crew's eyes riveted on the rpm to and manifold pressure gauges. "Tighten up, everybody," shouted Radcliff.

Berne faced forward, locked his seat, and drew the belt snug. Ingram did the same and from the corner of his eye saw Berne pull rosary beads from his pocket. Ingram wished he knew the prayer.

Radcliff popped the brakes. An explosion slammed into the ground fifty feet to their left. Thick black smoke gushed past the windshield. "Wow!"

But the C-54 was moving. Peoples advanced the number two engine's throttle as the C-54 lumbered along. The plane rolled faster, but not before it had gobbled up a thousand feet of runway. Radcliff gradually fed in left rudder to offset the asymmetrical pull of the port-side engines.

"Forty-five," said Peoples.

Hammer slapped a hand over his eyes, but his fingers were splayed.

"Fifty-five," said Peoples. Fifteen hundred feet gone.

Ingram rose a bit to peer out the windshield. The M-16 was still there. Spaced on either side were two T-34 tanks. Miraculously, their turrets pointed off to the side. They were shooting at something else.

Ingram had felt terror before, and this was just as he remembered. He wanted to defecate, urinate, and vomit all at the same time. Perhaps he was thinking too much. Always before he had had something to do. Now he just had to sit and watch it happen, feeling as if he was wired to a transformer sending a thousand volts through his body. *Helen, I love you. I love Jerry. Take good care of him.* The Lord 's Prayer came to him, and he said it while watching Berne's fingers move over his rosary beads.

"Sheeeyyat, Bucky."

"Come on, Leroy, speed, damn it!"

"Seventy-five ... eighty ..."

Three thousand feet gone. The M-16 and the tanks grew large in the windshield. The top hatch of the tank on the left popped open. Then the hatch on the right flipped open.

"The bastards are bailin' out," said Peoples. Indeed, four men scampered from the top hatches, jumped to the ground, and ran away.

"Leroy!"

"Eighty-five."

Land and runway whizzed past. They were almost on the Russian armor now.

"Ninety-five."

"Full flaps!" yelled Radcliff.

Peoples shoved the handle and Radcliff pulled back on the control column.

The C-54 staggered into the air and mushed in surface effect. The two tanks and the M-16 whipped past below. Moments later they were over the Russian lines looking down on surprised upturned faces, tanks, trucks, and armored vehicles--hundreds of them. Then the surf. Then gray, quiet ocean. And ships, Soviet warships.

"Can you believe this?" shouted Peoples.

Hammer and Berne yelped and shot their fists over their heads.

"Quiet. Gear up, Leroy."

"Coming up, boss. Talk to me about flaps."

"What's our speed?"

"One oh five."

"Jesus, we shouldn't be flying," muttered Radcliff.

"What do you want, Bucky?" asked Peoples.

"I dunno. Milk 'em up. Try flaps thirty and pray we stay airborne. And gimme some trim, my foot's getting tired. But not too fast."

"Bitch, bitch, bitch." Peoples cranked in rudder trim to ease the pressure on Radcliff's rudder pedal.

Berne pocketed his rosary then clamped a hand over his earphones. "I'll be damned."

"What?" said Ingram.

Berne called out. "Toro tower says, 'Sayonara.' They're signing off now."

"Tell them thank you," said Radcliff.

"Hey, look at this," Radcliff said two minutes later. "We've gained all of six hundred feet." But their speed was holding at 135. He turned to Hammer. "Okay, Chief, give it a try."

"Really?"

"No time like the present."

"Yes, sir." Hammer pushed some levers. "Here we go." He hit the button to unfeather engine number three. "Fire in the hole."

Peoples looked out the cockpit window. "She's rolling."

"Hurry up, our speed's dropping," said Radcliff.

Peoples flipped engine three's magneto to "all." The engine caught.

"Glory, glory," said Hammer, adjusting the throttle. "All yours, Skipper."

"Okay, Leroy, let's reset the trim." With all four engines running, the C-54 flew smoothly.

Radcliff said, "Jon, if we keep flying in this direction we should hit Peking about dawn tomorrow morning. What do you think we should do?"

Berne said dryly, "Well, it would be a good thing if you could fly course one-nine-one. That way, we won't be tried and executed for wasting one of the taxpayers' fine aircraft."

"Makes sense to me. Think you can handle that, Leroy?"

"Got it, Pop." Peoples took the control column and eased in left rudder to come to the new course.

Radcliff turned to Ingram and said loudly, "How you doin,' Todd?"

Ingram shouted back, "More underwear to clean."

They laughed.

Ingram leaned forward and said quietly to Radcliff, "That was a very nice job, Bucky."

"Thanks. Challenging, huh?"

"So how are we doing now?"

Radcliff said, "Climbing like a homesick angel."

20

The mess tent was cramped and hot. There was just one long table on a packed-dirt floor. At the insistence of Brig. Gen. Otis DeWitt, the tent flaps were closed, and a guard was posted outside. Two anemic fans attempted with very little success to clear the heavy cigarette smoke.

DeWitt leaned back and blew a smoke ring. "He was in good shape when you found him?"

Ingram yawned again. Two hours' sleep hadn't made a dent in his exhaustion. "I'd say no. He looked like death warmed over, and he sounded like it too."

"What did he say?" asked Neidemeier.

"He was incoherent," said Ingram.

"Are you sure?" Neidemeier pressed.

Ingram looked around the table at Otis DeWitt, Clive Neidemeier, and

Colin Blinde, the latter gushing Aqua Velva from every pore. Bucky Radcliff kept nodding off, his head propped on his fist.

Almost all the other men in the tent were as tired as he was. On their arrival at Kisarazu they had sent Captain Fujimoto to a hospital and transferred their cargo to a new C-54 flown in by a replacement crew. Then they bucked and bounced through headwinds back to Okinawa, not arriving until 5:30 in the morning. DeWitt had called an 11 a.m. meeting in spite of everyone's exhaustion--everyone except Clive Neidemeier, who, with eight solid hours of rack time, bored in like a pit bull.

"Commander, please, this is important," pleaded Neidemeier.

"Don't you think I know that, Clive? I've told you everything I can."

"But none of this makes sense," replied Neidemeier. "How did Walter Boring die?"

"Captain Dezhnev shot him in the head?" said Ingram.

Radcliff snickered. Otis DeWitt groaned, and Blinde's eyes popped wide open.

Neidemeier's face grew red. "This is no time for trifling."

DeWitt waved him down. "It's okay, Clive. Commander Ingram is just joking. Right, Commander?" He blew another smoke ring.

Ingram said, "Yes, Clive, I was joking. Dezhnev stabbed him in the chest."

Neidemeier sat back and rolled his eyes. "All right, have your fun. But please keep in mind this is an official inquiry." He nodded to a staff sergeant taking notes in a corner. "You should be more--"

", Todd," DeWitt broke in, "I'm wondering why you keep mentioning Captain Dezhnev. Do we speak of our old friend?"

Ingram nodded. "One and the same. Eduard Dezhnev. Our San Francisco buddy."

"Small world," said DeWitt.

"Bullshit," said Ingram, looking at Blinde.

Blinde's eyes popped open. "Ahh, yes. We knew about Commander Ingram's friendship with Dezhnev. That's why we asked for him."

DeWitt gave a broad grin, a rarity. "Friendship?"

Blinde replied, "Well, that's what it sounded like to us. But the FBI wouldn't let us have Dezhnev's file. We weren't aware of difficulties following your initial meetings."

Radcliff mumbled, "I wouldn't trust the son of a bitch as far as I could throw him."

Neidemeier said, "Major, could you stay with us long enough to make sense out of what happened?"

"Doing my best, Major Fingermeier," said Radcliff.

"Neidemeier."

"Ummmm."

Again, DeWitt had to wave Neidemeier down. "How is Ed?" he asked Ingram. "Same old regular guy?"

The tent flap rustled, and a man walked in. He was Navy, a full commander's oak leaves on his collar. Tall, lanky, and tow-headed, he was--

"Ollie!" Ingram jumped up to greet his old friend Oliver Toliver III.

They shook hands and then hugged, slapping backs. "What the hell are you doing here?" asked Ingram.

"Plane was late." Toliver reached over to Otis DeWitt. "General? Good to see you again."

DeWitt rose and likewise bear-hugged Toliver. "You're a sight, sonny boy. You look great. Heard you got yourself shot up, but I sure as hell can't tell."

Toliver gave a wan smile. "It still grabs me once in a while. And the trip out here! That damned plane bounced and jumped all over the Pacific." He nodded toward Radcliff. "I don't see how you guys do it." He pulled out a chair and sat heavily.

DeWitt introduced the others to Toliver and sketched out their past connection. In May 1942 the Yale-educated Toliver had served as Ingram's gunnery officer in the minesweeper USS *Pelican* (AM 49) at Corregidor. Without fuel and unable to move, the *Pelican* was sunk from under them in Manila Bay. Along with DeWitt, Ingram and Toliver managed to escape Corregidor in a 36-foot launch the night the Japanese invaded the island. They made it through the Philippine archipelago and all the way to Darwin, Australia, a remarkable voyage of 1,900 miles.

The following October, Toliver was back in action as gunnery officer on the destroyer USS *Riley* (DD 542). But the *Riley* was blown out from under him by a Japanese type 93 torpedo at the Battle of Cape Esperance. Toliver's hip was broken in the explosion, and he was shipped back to San Francisco. A specialist at the Stanford Lane Hospital nailed it back together. But Toliver was still cursed with frequent pain and a distinct limp. The doctors recommended Toliver be placed on limited duty and not return to combat. He'd served on the Twelfth Naval District staff in San Francisco as a gunnery liaison officer before signing up for the regular Navy and joining the Office of Naval Intelligence.

Which was ironic. Toliver was wealthy. His father was Conrad Toliver, a founding partner in the Manhattan law firm of McNeil, Lawton, and Toliver, which served as corporate counsel to six of the thirty firms constituting the Dow Jones Industrial Average. Conrad fully expected his son to finish law school and join him in the firm. He dreamed of showing off his young son as a World War II poster boy who would strut around the firm's richly appointed offices in full uniform, his medals clanking. And beautiful medals they were. Ollie had been awarded the Distinguished Service Medal, a Purple Heart, a Combat Action Ribbon with three stars, and a Navy unit commendation. It would have been so good for business. Conrad was very unhappy when he discovered his son had shipped over to the regular Navy.

Neidemeier asked, "General, is he cleared for this meeting?"

DeWitt shot back, "Cleared? He's supposed to be running this damn meeting, but it looks like he's spent too much time in Pearl chasing women."

Toliver toasted DeWitt with a water glass and drank deeply. Then he turned to Neidemeier. "Major, the Office of Naval Intelligence is as interested in this as you are. Plus, I know Eduard Dezhnev, and as you heard, Commander Ingram and I are old shipmates and friends. In fact, Dezhnev, Commander Ingram, and General DeWitt all spent a lot of time together. Right?" He looked at Ingram.

Ingram couldn't help it. "Wong Lee's café." He grinned. Wong Lee's had been a favorite hangout when they were all in San Francisco. "How is Suzy?" Suzy Lee, Wong Lee's daughter, had co-managed the café along with her mother while her father was trapped on Mindanao with Helen. At the time, she had been a junior at Stanford.

Toliver grinned, "She graduated . . ."

"Hot damn!" exclaimed DeWitt.

"And she's running Wong Lee's down in Los Angeles."

"Waste of a good education," said DeWitt.

"Well, yes and no," said Toliver.

"What?" said Ingram?

"We, uh, we're getting kind of serious," said Toliver.

"Ollie, that's great," said Ingram. "What now?"

Toliver raised his eyes to the rest of the group, who looked on open-mouthed. "Maybe we should move on."

"I agree. We're wasting time," growled DeWitt. "I was asking Todd if Dezhnev has changed much."

Ingram said, "Still the same old blabbermouth. You'd think he was Bob Hope. Thanks to his Bykovo training, he's fully Americanized."

"Bykovo? What's Bykovo?" asked Neidemeier.

Ingram said, "If I told you Major, you would crap in your pants."

"Commander, please! This is a--"

Once more, DeWitt had to reel in Neidemeier. "What he means, Major, is that you're not cleared for that area. It's strictly 'need to know.'"

Blinde said dryly, "Clive, Bykovo is a Soviet training camp near Moscow where, over a period of nine months, top-grade military officers are immersed in language and cultural training, so they can be inserted into the United States without fear of detection. That's all you need to know."

"Oh."

Toliver looked at Neidemeier and then over to Ingram. *Who is this guy?*

Ingram grinned and said, "Well, Captain Dezhnev must have taken some postgraduate courses because he's in the NKVD now. How's that for being a regular guy?"

"Impressive," said DeWitt.

"We knew this," said Blinde.

Ingram said, "Otis, I'm tired. I'd barely hit the pillow when your guys woke me up."

"I'm sorry, but General Sutherland is anxious for a report," said DeWitt.

Ingram drew a long breath then looked around the room. "Tell you what, Otis. Just you and I talk. Okay? I'll blab like I was vaccinated with a phonograph needle. Let everyone else go get some shuteye."

Radcliff groaned and buried his head in his arms.

DeWitt said, "Guess we'd better."

"I'll stay," said Blinde.

"Absolutely not," said Ingram.

"I think we should let him," said DeWitt. He nodded to the stenographer and Neidemeier. "You're excused. But please stay close by for the next twenty-four hours in case we need you." Then he said, "Major Radcliff!"

Radcliff raised his head. "Huh?"

"You're excused for now, too."

"Huh?"

Ingram leaned over and patted Radcliff's elbow. "Go, Bucky. Hit the sack."

"Oh, man. What'd you do that for? I was dreaming about this sweet little--"

"Go, Bucky."

"Yeah." Radcliff shuffled to his feet and walked off like a zombie. The others followed, and the stenographer drew the tent flap behind them.

DeWitt looked at Ingram and said, "Todd, I have no doubt that you all exhibited unparalleled acts of heroism in carrying out your mission. That landing, Sergeant Harper and his men--"

"Should get medals," said Ingram.

"Your rescue of Boring. And then that amazing takeoff. Major Radcliff has real guts."

"I'd add 'command presence' to Radcliff's citation. When the chips were down, it was all his show." Ingram leaned forward, "I have to tell you, Otis. I wasn't that scared even during our escape from Corregidor. Bucky Radcliff was really something to watch."

DeWitt butt-lit another cigarette and said, "I have no doubts as to Major Radcliff's capabilities. Nor do I have any doubts of yours, Todd. Do you know the difference?"

"Speak English, Otis."

"The difference is that Radcliff, like you in the 51 boat, had something to do. Aboard the C-54 you were just strapped to a seat, awaiting your fate."

"Damn near crapped in my pants."

Toliver said, "Todd, quit being so damned modest. Otis is right. It was me, not you, who damn near crapped my pants back then."

"Okay, okay," said Ingram.

"All that said, I really must know two things. One, did you speak with Walter Boring? And two, do you have any idea how he died?"

Blinde added, "There's a third question, General. Did Commander Ingram examine any of the cargo brought back with us?"

"I've already told you, no, no, and no."

DeWitt stubbed out his cigarette, sat back, and turned to Blinde. "Colin, I thought we were getting plans for some new Jap secret process for titanium production or something like that. Isn't that the information Boring had?"

Blinde looked at Ingram. "No, it's not, General."

"Well, what the hell is it?" demanded DeWitt.

"Commander Ingram knows."

"Go shit in your hat, Colin," said Ingram.

Blinde sighed, "We're a bit compromised here with cards on the table. So, I guess you should know, General."

"Yes?"

"The Japanese were involved in human experimentation."

"Holy cow. Like the Germans?"

"Worse; far worse," said Blinde. "They started in the early 1930s and over the years expanded to several experimentation units throughout China and Mongolia. But Harbin, known as Unit 731, was the headquarters. Walter Boring's timing was unfortunate. The Red Cross decided to send him in at the same time the Russians invaded. It was a mess."

DeWitt was aghast. "Are you telling me they experimented on live people?"

Blinde said, "All the time. Everything from germ and biological warfare to excessive-cold experiments to high-altitude experiments to small-caliber ballistics experiments. They did everything. But they couldn't afford to have any of it become public knowledge, so they tried to burn everything when the Russians came. Walter Boring recovered partial records of what went on in these camps."

"Whom did they experiment on?" asked DeWitt.

"Chinese, mostly," said Blinde.

"Americans, too," said Ingram.

"Nonsense," said DeWitt.

"Americans, Australians, Brits, New Zealanders," said Ingram.

Blinde nodded, "They hated B-29 crews especially. The ones they were able to shoot down. Many were sent to the camps for 'work.'"

The image of the headless USAAF sergeant popped into Ingram's mind.

"They'll stand to justice with the rest of those butchers," said DeWitt.

Blinde said, "I don't think so."

"What?" demanded Ingram and DeWitt.

"A bargain was struck. A month ago. Through back channels," said Blinde.

"What sort of bargain?" asked DeWitt.

Blinde drummed his fingers. "The Japs would give us all their research and data."

"In return for?" asked DeWitt.

"In return for total amnesty and no prosecution whatsoever," said Blinde.

"You sick sons of bitches," said DeWitt.

Blinde spread his hands. "General, I'm sorry. This was not my decision. I just do what they tell me. But I am convinced that this stuff is so hot that it will not only advance our war-fighting capabilities but will also give us a huge advantage over the Soviets if we can keep it from them. That explains the desperate NKVD measure with Dezhnev and his people."

"He did try to kill us," said Ingram.

DeWitt steepled his fingers, "Manila. I was out of the room for a couple of hours. Maybe that's when they discussed it."

"General, it went much higher than that. This was discussed weeks ago. Certainly not at Manila."

DeWitt looked up. "So that's it?"

"I'm afraid so," said Blinde. "This got messy because of Mr. Boring's condition and the Russian interference. You weren't supposed to know any of this."

"Ummm," DeWitt mused. "Okay, we still don't know how Walter Boring died. I guess we'll have to wait for the autopsy report."

"They'll do a toxicology examination?" asked Blinde.

"Of course."

"Save them the trouble."

"Why?"

"He died from potassium cyanide poisoning."

"Holy cow," exclaimed Ingram.

"Did you ...?" asked DeWitt.

"Yes, of course I did it," said Blinde. "I crushed a cyanide capsule between his teeth. Death was near instantaneous, and painless. He was so far gone he would have died on his own, but I couldn't take the risk. Those Marines were trying to help him. Giving him water and setting up an IV."

Ingram and DeWitt sat back, dumbfounded.

"He was a blabbermouth," Blinde said. "He blabbed to you, Commander. In the airplane cabin he told me that you had talked in Major Fujimoto's bunker, that he told you what he'd seen in Harbin. Before that, he blabbed to Major Fujimoto; he blabbed to a Russian negotiator in Harbin before he was whisked off by the Japs. That's how Captain Dezhnev and his people got wind of him. Think of it. The NKVD doesn't just rush around the countryside for nothing. They play for keeps. They wanted Walter Boring and all the information in his possession. That was Eduard Dezhnev's assignment."

DeWitt said, "Maybe it's just as well we keep it quiet. If it ever goes public, it will create a furor the world has never seen."

"Ummmm."

Ingram asked, "Do you suppose General MacArthur and Sutherland are aware of all this?"

"Ummmm."

Ingram said, "Are you sure that's not so bad, Mr. Blinde? Maybe the world should know about Unit 731."

"Never," Blinde said. "At least not now. We have it, the Soviets don't, and that's the way it has to be. Had Boring been allowed to return to the Red Cross he would have blabbed to them. Like you, Commander Ingram, I have my instructions. We had to put a stop to that. And now, I have to know what he said to you and what you saw in that crate."

"You're putting the screws on me?" demanded Ingram.

"No, nothing like that. What I mean is--"

"Who in the hell do you work for, Mr. Blinde?"

After a moment, he said, "For my country."

Ingram barked, "No. I mean who? Army? Navy? Coast Guard? ONI? Who do you represent?"

Blinde shrugged. "General DeWitt has a copy of my orders."

DeWitt said, "Like I told you, Todd. OSS."

"Whatever that means," said Ingram. "I guess it means he has a license to go around killing people."

DeWitt said, "Todd, now don't go getting--"

"Tell me, Mr. Blinde, where are the boxes and crate now?"

"On their way to Alexandria, Virginia, for analysis."

"Okay," said Ingram. "Mission accomplished. So, what else is there?"

Blinde sighed. "It sounds like the cat's out of the bag as far as you're concerned. But I need your sworn word to keep your mouths shut."

Ingram was tired, and it took little effort for him to say, "You have mine." He glared and added, "I want to put Major Radcliff and his crew in for DFCs. Also, I want to recommend Bronze Stars for Sergeant Harper and each of his men."

Blinde said, "I'm sorry. That isn't possible."

"What the hell? Do you mean to tell me that--"?

DeWitt said, "I think he's right, Todd. This stuff is too hot."

Ingram doubled a fist. "Look, you little backwater--"

DeWitt barked, "Hold it, Commander. That's enough!"

Toliver doodled on a notepad.

Ingram had overstepped, and he knew it. "Okay."

"I'm sorry," said Blinde.

DeWitt picked it up with, "There's no doubt you all did an outstanding job, and you have the thanks and gratitude of General MacArthur and his staff. If there was a way, he would gladly endorse your recommendations, which would include a Silver Star and maybe even another Navy Cross for you."

"Otis, it wasn't me. Those guys put their lives on the line."

"I know they did. And they deserve recognition. It sounds harsh, but that's the way it has to be. I wish I could say more, but you're done here, right, Colin?"

"Done," said Blinde. He looked at Ingram, "You'll sign a security statement?"

"I said I would," said Ingram. He didn't like the sound of it.

Blinde said, "Good. And you too, Commander Toliver?"

Toliver said, "Not on your life, cheese ball."

Blinde said, "But--"

"What do you expect, Mr. Blinde?" said DeWitt. "He's with the Office of Naval Intelligence. His rank is full commander."

Ingram piped up. "Yeah, congratulations, Ollie. When did that happen?"

"Six months ago. Washington, D.C."

They looked at Blinde, who said, "Oh, all right."

DeWitt said, "Done, then. I'll have the recorder prepare a statement for Todd to sign before he shoves off." He stood, gathered papers, and began stuffing them in a briefcase. "I have a launch standing by to take you back to Kerama Rhetto and your ship."

Ingram was suddenly overcome by outrage at the hypocrisy that was occurring on both sides. The Japanese had been conducting horrible acts of savagery over the years and were getting away with it; and his fellow Americans, who were protected by the flag under which they fought, had agreed to look the other way. Again, the photos rushed back into his mind. What had Boring called the corpses? "Logs."

"What?" asked DeWitt. "What logs?"

Ingram's blood boiled. The Japanese had labeled thousands, perhaps tens of thousands, of helpless butchered people "logs." They'd sewn tags to their coats, dragged them into an operating theater, and hacked open their bodies while stoic interns stood by, drawing diagrams or clicking off photos. And now, the United States was going to look the other way, so it could improve its war-fighting capability. He stood and braced himself.

"You okay, Todd?" asked DeWitt.

"Tired." He took a deep breath then leveled his eyes on DeWitt. "Okay, we're finished." What was done was done. And apparently the Harbin activity was all over. No more human experiments. Time to get on with it. Time to get on with life. Silently, he thanked God for the chance he had been given. Far better than what had happened to the poor people in Harbin and the millions of others killed in Asia and Europe.

But he knew he'd be dreaming again. Worse dreams than the ones after his escape from Corregidor. One way or another, he would be going home soon. Helen and his baby boy would be his to have and hold. "Maybe the war really is over."

"I beg your pardon?" said DeWitt.

"Okay, Otis. No medals. Right?"

"That's what I said, 'no medals.' Sorry."

"Well, then, there is one thing you can do for me."

"What's that?"

21

Helen straightened Eddie Bergen's pillow. He seemed to be doing better. He had even allowed a barber to sit him in a chair and cut his hair. Eddie's color was good, and he smiled a lot more. But he still smoked his Luckies constantly and read Donald Duck and Scrooge McDuck comics. But that was normal, she reasoned. A lot of GIs read comic books. They'd littered every Army post to which she'd been assigned. Eddie was engrossed with Huey, Dewey, and Louie in Scrooge McDuck's rock-solid treasury building with ten-foot-thick walls. The little ducks were sitting on a mountainous pile of gold coins, tossing them in the air.

Eddie ignored her as she lifted his wrist and checked his pulse: seventy-four. Not bad. She noted it on his chart and said, "Eddie, it's noon. Time to eat. You hungry?"

"Huh?"

"Eddie. Put that down before I throw it in the trash."

Eddie set the comic aside. "Sorry, Captain. It just came in with this morning's mail."

"You saw Dr. Raduga this morning?" Dr. Julian Raduga, the infirmary's psychiatrist, looked the part: he always wore a starched white lab coat and black bowtie. On the long side of thirty, he had pomaded brown hair and a Van Dyke beard.

Dr. Raduga's ward was growing rapidly as GIs flooded in from POW camps in the Pacific. Unattended patients could often be seen wandering the halls at three in the morning, some wearing nothing but a diaper, some weighing less than one hundred pounds, their thousand-yard stare riveting passersby. Getting an appointment with Dr. Raduga was like trying to get tickets to a Bob Hope radio show.

Eddie nodded. He'd been lucky.

"How did it go?"

"He asks stupid questions."

"Like what?"

"Wants to know if my father beat my mother."

"What did you tell him?" *Careful, Helen*.

"All the time. Especially when he was drunk.

Her heart went out to him. "Oh, Eddie."

He said, "But my mom usually got me out of there. She would send me outside to Larry's room over the garage."

"Who's Larry?"

"My uncle. Dad's brother."

"But why didn't . . .?"

A shadow swept across Eddie's face.

Time to stop. Helen faked a yawn and patted her tummy, "Sorry, Eddie. My stomach's growling. How about you?"

"Yeah, okay." He picked up Uncle Scrooge. "Peanut butter and jelly again?"

"I heard it's turkey sandwiches."

"Really? Peachy keen."

"See you later, Eddie." Helen headed for the dining room thinking about Eddie's progress. He was doing well. She, on the other hand, wasn't. Two nights ago, at two in the morning, Fred had knocked a glass liberty bell off a shelf in the living room and it shattered on the floor. She'd jumped out of bed terrified, panting and shaking. It took fifteen minutes to control her breathing. Then, without thinking, she crawled under the bed. She was there ten minutes later when Jerry started crying. His diaper needed changing. She got up, changed it, and fell into bed exhausted.

A psychiatrist. A shrink. It was such a delicate subject. The last thing she wanted was someone discovering she was seeking psychiatric help. If she was going to do this, she had to do it quietly, discreetly. And she should do it now. Todd would be coming home soon. She wanted to give him a proper welcome, a sailor's welcome--*in* the bed, not curled up into a ball under it.

Last night she swallowed her pride and called Laura West. A true friend, Laura didn't miss a beat and suggested Dr. Robert Behrman, a Beverly Hills psychiatrist who attended some of the movie colony's most famous. But Behrman charged $100 per hour, and his office was a two-hour drive up Sepulveda Boulevard. That would kill most of a day *and* her ration of gas, and it would definitely kill her bank account. Next, she thumbed the Yellow Pages and found a psychiatrist in downtown Long Beach. His receptionist finally divulged that Dr. Sullivan charged $25 per hour. Still too much.

That left Dr. Raduga. She mulled the name over and over in her mind. Outside of seeing him hurrying down the hall from time to time, she hardly knew the man. She did know she needed help.

"Ooof!" Someone stepped from an exam room and bumped into her.

"Oh, Helen." Capt. Martha Brubaker had been the floor nurse on the obstetrics floor the night Helen went into labor. Brubaker had practically delivered Jerry by the time Dr. Gaspar showed up. Brubaker stopped. "How are you doing? I don't get to see much of you, and of course, your little . . ."

"Jerry. He's a handful, Martha, and doing fine. Sleeping through the night. Misses his dad."

"And how *is* your husband, that handsome naval captain? 'Boom Boom?' Is that what you called him?" They stopped, Brubaker partially blocking her path. Obviously, she wanted to talk.

Play along. Helen laughed. "Oh, no. He's not my husband. He's my husband's best friend, Captain Jeremiah Landa. We named the baby after him. Jeremiah Ingram." She didn't add that at the time her son was born her husband was a prisoner aboard a Japanese submarine en route to the submarine pens in L'Orient, France.

"How sweet. And the father is . . ."

"His name is Todd. He's fine. He's still out there, a destroyer skipper. He's like a million other guys who want to get back to his family. But it's hurry up and wait, as usual."

"So, he's not career?"

"Oh, he's definitely career. But he's been overseas for such a long time. I'm sure the Navy will wake up and give him stateside duty."

"Let's hope so. I--oh, hi, Mel." Brubaker waved as Sgt. Melvin Letenske poked his head out the dining room double doors and smiled.

"Hiya, gorgeous. Got a date tonight?"

Brubaker laughed. "It's Captain Brubaker, Sergeant."

"Well, Captain, you got anything going tonight?"

"Let me check with my husband first."

"You're married?"

"Come on, Mel." She waved her gold wedding band.

Letenske grinned. "He's one lucky son of a bitch." He looked at Helen. "How about you, beautiful?"

"That's Captain Ingram, Sergeant."

Letenske got on one knee. "Pardon me, Captain. But you look like you need company tonight."

Helen and Brubaker exchanged glances. "Can you believe this?" said Brubaker.

"Mel, you know better than that," said Helen.

"Well, if you change your mind, I know this neat little place over in Wilmington called Louie's. Fantastic Italian food. We could--"

"Sergeant!"

"Sorry, Captain. Can't blame me for asking." Letenske ducked back inside and the doors swung closed.

Brubaker reached for the door handle and muttered, "That man is horny as a two-peckered goat--you first, honey." She opened both doors and stood back for Helen to enter.

Helen stepped in and--

"Surprise!"

The room was full of staff, some in lab coats, some in operating gowns, some in uniform. A smiling Colonel Ledbetter stood before her. Letenske was at his side with a clipboard. Both wore their class A uniforms. She recognized Dr. Raduga in the back.

"Surprise!" they yelled again.

A photographer knelt before her and clicked his shutter. The bulb flashed. Helen covered her face for a moment. She felt as if she'd been given an electric shock. "What?" Frozen. She couldn't move.

"Helen, this is for you, honey," said Brubaker.

"What?"

"Come on, dear, can't keep the colonel waiting." She placed a hand under Helen's elbow and gently pushed.

"Let go." She shook off Brubaker's hand.

The photographer blasted out another shot. Then he unscrewed the flashbulb and replaced it with another. "Another, okay, ladies?"

"This is all so . . ."

"Nurse Ingram," said Colonel Ledbetter. "You're out of uniform."

Helen turned to Brubaker, "What is this?"

Brubaker hissed, "Get on with it, honey. You've been promoted to major and you'd better respond." She gave Helen a withering look and took a step back.

"Martha, I'm sorry," said Helen. She walked up to Colonel Ledbetter and said, "Sorry, sir. This is too much of a surprise."

Colonel Ledbetter was also an MD and usually a serious man. But he wore a genuine smile as he held out his hand. Sergeant Letenske passed over a citation.

Staged. This whole damned thing has been staged. Why couldn't they just do this quietly?

Colonel Ledbetter did a creditable job of reading the articles of promotion. People clapped and cheered as Letenske, with great panache, stepped close and handed a box of gold oak leaves to Colonel Ledbetter. He whispered to Helen, "Don't forget about Louie's."

Helen knew Letenske was a hero. He had led his dogfaces through the North Africa, Sicily, and Italian campaigns, and he carried a piece of shrapnel in his head from a German mortar near Anzio. He had two Purple Hearts atop a chest full of medals. This was supposed to be soft, recuperative duty for him. But he pushed it too far at times.

She threw Letenske a hard stare and then looked around the room as Colonel Ledbetter fumbled at pinning on her collar devices. Martha Brubaker stood close by, beaming. Eddie Bergen shuffled into the room wearing his bathrobe, slippers, and a wan smile. There were other patients from her ward as well, and of course the doctors and nurses she worked with.

Finally finished, Colonel Ledbetter smiled and stepped back. "Congratulations, Major." He extended his hand.

"Thanks." Helen took it.

Martha Brubaker stepped up and gestured toward the back of the room. "Helen, the kitchen staff fixed a cake."

Indeed, they had. Flaming candles adorned a large, square three-layer chocolate cake arranged on a long table. Finger sandwiches and a large bowl of iced lemonade stood nearby. For the first time she saw the long butcher's paper sign on the back wall: "Congratulations Helen." She forced a smile. "Jeepers. Thanks, everybody. Let's dig in. Wow!"

"Make a wish first," said Letenske.

"Awww, come on . . ."

"Make a wish," they chanted. "Wish, wish, wish."

Helen took a deep breath and blew. Fifteen of the twenty candles went out. Five sputtered and burst back into life. They all laughed, realizing the candles came from a joke shop.

The turkey sandwiches were good. Too good. People ate their fill, became sleepy, and began drifting back to their workstations or beds, as was the case with Eddie Bergen.

Helen was still dishing up cake when Sergeant Letenske slithered up. "Thought it over, Major?"

"Thought what over?"

"You know, Louie's."

"Mel, I know some Marines who would be most happy to take you out back and teach you a lesson."

Dr. Raduga moved alongside, took a plate of cake, and nonchalantly began eating.

Letenske stood straight. "Send 'em in. I can teach them a few things."

Brubaker piped up. "Nothing like the lessons Helen learned in Mindanao."

Letenske's eyes bulged. "Holy crap."

Helen muttered to Brubaker, "Don't do this."

"Go fly a kite." Brubaker turned to Letenske. "Yeah, she was on Mindanao. So, watch it, buddy boy. And her husband's a destroyer captain."

Letenske said to Helen, "Mindanao? I got buddies on Mindanao. When were you there?"

Helen gave a deep sigh. "Okay, I was there. But it was under new management. So, I didn't see any of our boys."

Lentenske's eyebrows went up.

"We were up in the mountains, away from all that."

"With the resistance?"

"You could say that."

"You were killing Japs?"

"Well, we needed food."

"Man, oh, man. I bet you did learn some lessons."

"They taught us some awful lessons, and then we taught them some awful lessons. Let's just say it wasn't pleasant."

Letenske put aside his cake and said, "Ma'am. I owe you an apology. I never knew you were there."

"Actually, nobody is supposed to know."

"They should." Letenske reached out and shook her hand. "My uncle Jim," he went on, "he was at Bataan. The Death March, we think. We don't know."

"I'm sorry. I was there, too." *Damn it. Why did I say that?*

"Bataan?"

"No, Corregidor."

"How did you get out?"

"Submarine."

"My God. Mindanao and Corregidor?"

"No. Corregidor, then Mindanao."

"Not great tourist spot these days."

"Just as bad in North Africa, Sicily, and Italy."

Letenske nodded. "Well, it's over. Maybe we soon find out about Uncle Jim, huh? Excuse me." He walked over to two young nurses.

Brubaker moved away too, leaving her alone with Dr. Raduga.

She set aside her plate.

"No good?" he asked.

Helen regarded him. He had deep blue eyes. "Well, I had a large slice."

Raduga took another bite. "My mother is a good cook. She makes this when I'm home. But I think she uses more sugar and . . ." he smacked his lips, "eggs, I think."

"Sounds delicious."

"I couldn't help but overhear about your involvement overseas. You had an . . . interesting time."

"It was awful. Except . . ."

He finished the last bite and picked a crumb from his beard.

"Except I met my husband out there."

"The destroyer skipper."

"You have good ears."

"That's what they pay me for." His eyebrows went up.

Helen thought it over and panicked. "I have to be getting back." She made to move away.

"I have eyes too."

"I beg your pardon?"

"When you came in. You looked like you were being stood before a firing squad."

Helen exhaled. That was how she had felt. "I guess I overreacted."

"An understatement."

"What do you know?"

"I don't, but you do."

She stood silently, her lips pursed.

"You're Eddie Bergen's floor nurse, aren't you?"

"Yes."

"You're doing a great job. He talks a lot about you."

Go for it. "Okay, yes. I think something in Eddie Bergen triggered something in me. I'm doing weird things."

"Such as?"

"Yesterday morning I heard a loud noise and I hyperventilated. The night before, I awoke terrified and crawled under my bed. You're right. When I walked in here I was scared to death. Goosebumps. Hot flash. I wanted to run and hide." She looked at him. "I think I need help. But I don't want anyone to know. Can you help me?"

"I think so. Make an appointment."

"With all these POWs coming back, what chance do I have of getting in to see you?"

"I'll put you at the top of the list."

"You're kidding."

"This happens to doctors and nurses, believe it or not. It gets to them. It gets to all of us. Nothing to be ashamed of. We need you. We need you healthy, so we can all get on with our jobs. You're critical to our success in the psychiatric ward."

"You're kidding."

"Go back to your desk and book in with Alice. I'll clear it with her."

"You'll keep it absolutely secret? Nobody must find out."

Raduga put a finger to his lips. "Top secret. I promise."

"Okay."

"It won't be easy."

Helen sighed. "I can imagine."

Dr. Raduga put down his plate. "That was good. Congratulations, Major. Now, go call Alice."

22

26 August 1945
Tokyo, Japan

Kokutai.

With the A-bombs and the Soviet invasion of Mongolia, the Kuriles, and Karafuto, indecision became rampant in Emperor Hirohito's officer corps and cabinet. Some urged fighting to the last man; others agreed that the end was near, if not upon them, and urged cooperation. Finally, the emperor stepped in and influenced his government to accept the surrender terms of the Potsdam Declaration. He won acceptance on 14 August, and on 15 August Hirohito's recorded voice was played over radio station NHK for his subjects and the world to hear. It was an extraordinary measure. No one outside Hirohito's inner circle had ever before heard his voice. But he wanted his subjects to hear the message of surrender directly from him in order to emphasize his acceptance of it.

Near hysteria gripped the nation afterward. Rebels, mostly young officers, hatched implausible plots to take over the government and direct Japan back to fighting to the last man. Either from bushido pride or outright devotion to their emperor, many of the officer corps committed suicide. The most notable suicide took place on 15 August, the day of the emperor's broadcast. Popular Vice Admiral Matome Ugaki, once Admiral Yamamoto's chief of staff, took off in a B5N single-engine torpedo bomber to attack the American fleet off Okinawa. He left behind a suicide message that said "I alone am to blame for our failure to defend the homeland and destroy the arrogant enemy. . .

"Long live His Imperial Majesty, the Emperor!"

Ugaki's plane disappeared to the southeast and was never seen again.

That evening, Admiral Takijiro Onishi, founder of the kamikaze corps, committed seppuku in the classic style at home. He penned a haiku just before he raised the dagger: "Refreshed, I feel like the clear moon after a storm."

There were several revolts in the palace itself, many of them led by overzealous officers of the rank of major and below. Gunfire broke out. Emperor Hirohito and his family were sometimes forced to take refuge in their underground bunker. At one time a fire was set. But with great skill, Hirohito's chamberlains, army and navy loyalists, and in some cases the dreaded Kempetai put down the revolts.

Smaller revolts continued outside the palace over the next few days. A glaring example occurred on the afternoon of 22 August when ten young men wearing white *hamchimaki* headbands occupied Tokyo's Atago Hill, which lay within sight of the boarded-up American embassy. They called themselves the Sonjo Gigun--the Righteous Group for Upholding Imperial Rule and Driving out Foreigners. In pouring rain, they linked arms against approaching police while singing the national anthem. Suddenly they shouted, "*Tenno heika banzai!*" and detonated the hand grenades they had been carrying. The men lay dead, their epitaph written on a suicide note that read, "The cicada rain falls in vain on defeated hills and streams."

Another insurrection roiled up at Atsugi Airfield, southwest of Tokyo, where General MacArthur was soon scheduled to land and assume his new role as supreme commander. Led by navy captain Ammyo Kosono, the revolt went on for several days to the sounds of "Gunkan Kaigun," the Imperial Navy's marching song. Kosono's airplanes showered Tokyo with leaflets inciting revolution until loyalist troops arrived from Tokyo and put down the rebellion by force of arms. Several people were killed on both sides. When finally captured, Kosono was completely crazed; he had to be wrestled down and carried off in a straitjacket. With that, all aircraft at Atsugi were defueled, and their propellers were removed to ensure no one as demented as Kosono could again defy the emperor's wishes.

General MacArthur set a positive tone in the way his staff treated the Japanese emissaries at the Manila meetings of 19–21 August. The Japanese were astounded at the Americans' fair and polite treatment and grateful for the fine food and lodging--luxuries they hadn't enjoyed for a long time. The swift series of meetings went well, and over a short period the Japanese revealed the disposition of all troops and ships; the location of airfields and naval bases, including those set up for deadly *kaiten* midget submarine raids; and ammunition dumps and minefields. First and foremost was the identification of all POW camps and methods to get food and medicine to the prisoners and ways to secure their immediate release.

MacArthur's top priority was to conduct a surrender ceremony on board a U.S. Navy ship in Tokyo Bay in hopes that a peace treaty would soon follow. Indeed, American statesmanship, beginning with the Potsdam Agreement, specified that cordial relations must be established with the Japanese in order to bring them back as responsible partners to a peaceful and productive family of nations.

But the outside world, especially the Western world, didn't realize that endemic in the Japanese psyche at all levels was the preservation of *kokutai*, their national essence. With everything lost, that is what they were fighting for; that is all that remained. With *kokutai* in place, they would be tractable. But *kokutai* was possible only if Emperor Hirohito remained on his throne.

General Douglas MacArthur was one of the few Westerners who realized the significance of *kokutai*. He intended to play it to his advantage by protecting Emperor Hirohito because he knew the rewards would be boundless. To do that, he needed to get to Japan quickly. In the meantime, Emperor Hirohito had his hands full.

General MacArthur and General Sutherland originally planned to occupy Japan on 26 August. Admiral Halsey's enormous Third Fleet was en route to Tokyo Bay when a typhoon began brewing across their path. Having learned his lesson with two previous typhoons, Halsey decided to stand clear and wait it out. The occupation of Japan was delayed. Some viewed this as a blessing because it gave the "hotheads" in Japan more time to cool down.

By 26 August near panic had seized Japan. The Soviets still rattled their sabers on Karafuto and threatened invasion. Rumors abounded. There were reports of Chinese forces landing in Osaka. Elsewhere, thousands of American soldiers were rumored to be raping women and looting in Yokohama. Women were told, "Don't go out in the evening. Hide all your valuables such as watches and rings. If rape is attempted, don't yield; show dignity and cry out for help if at all possible."

Word spread quickly when Oxford-trained General Shizuichi Tanaka, wearing full uniform, shot himself at his desk. A man of culture and discipline, Tanaka took responsibility for lives lost in the Tokyo firebombing raids and for the burning of the Imperial Palace.

The night passed uneasily but quietly.

Kokutai.

23

27 August 1945
USS *Maxwell* (DD 525), Task Force 38
Entrance to Sagami Bay, Japan

Midnight weather reports indicated the typhoon would get worse, not better. So, before it really kicked up, Admiral Halsey decided to get it over with and enter Sagami Bay, the lower portion of Tokyo Bay, on the morning of 27 August.

The morning dawned sunny and cloudless. A forty-knot gale roared from the southwest, tearing the tops off cresting waves and gathering them into a white, foamy, confused sea. With the wind on her port quarter, the *Maxwell* pitched in troughs, sometimes disappearing from the view of the ships around her. Then she would rise and roll drunkenly, the helmsman cursing as he spun the wheel to keep the stern from sliding to starboard and the ship from broaching. Green water occasionally cascaded over her transom, pooping her and sweeping away anything not tied down. It was dangerous back aft, and Ingram had ordered all the weather deck hatches to be secured; anyone having to travel outside did so on the 01 deck above the main deck.

Ingram, Landa, and Tubby White were huddled on the *Maxwell's* starboard bridge wing casting occasional glances at Mount Fuji, just off the port bow. The ship had been at general quarters since dawn, and they had spotted Fuji almost immediately. As the *Maxwell* neared Sagami Bay, the snow-capped peak grew larger against a sharp blue background. They also kept close watch on Admiral Halsey's flagship, the battleship USS *Missouri*, two thousand yards on the *Maxwell's* beam. Spray flew through the "Big Mo's" upper works as she plowed through the waves, a mighty fortress. Earlier, a FOX broadcast had announced that the *Missouri* had been chosen as the site for the surrender ceremony, in honor of President Harry S. Truman's home state. After the minesweepers did their job in Tokyo Bay, they were to move in with the ships attending the surrender ceremony, tentatively scheduled for the morning of 2 September 1945.

Ingram marveled at his presence here. Originally, DESRON 77, including the *Maxwell,* was assigned to Admiral Spruance's "Big Blue" of the Fifth Fleet. Consisting of all but one of the carriers, the Big Blue was now steaming fifty miles offshore, ready to oppose any Japanese trickery. But DESRON 77 had been reassigned to Admiral Halsey and his Third Fleet, now poised to enter Tokyo Bay in force. Today, the *Maxwell* was in a position of honor, steaming at fifteen knots in an AA defense circular formation on the two-thousand-yard circle off the *Missouri's* port beam. Four destroyers were arranged concentrically at four points of the compass, the other three being the *Snowden, Bertea,* and *Geiler.* Another four destroyers steamed on the outer four-thousand-yard circle: the *Cheffer, Beaulieu, Wallace,* and *Truax.* Landa was commodore of DESRON 77 and was again riding in the *Maxwell.*

"Smoke on the horizon, dead ahead," announced Richard Dudley from atop the pilothouse, his binoculars raised. The tow-headed seaman second class had reported from San Diego boot camp while the ship was recuperating in Kerama Rhetto. Lookout duty was a challenge today. His teeth chattered, his cheeks were bright red, and the hood of his parka was pulled up. "Looks like a can coming out; maybe a Jap." He pointed.

"Very well," said Tom Woodruff, Ingram's GQ OOD.

Ingram pulled a face at Tubby White. White immediately reached for a telephone handset.

Landa was on it too, not missing a chance to jump on Tubby White. "Mr. White, can you tell me why a seaman deuce can--"

Before Landa could finish, White barked into his handset, "Mr. Guthrie. I'd like to know why our taxpayers' radar didn't pick up a Japanese destroyer coming out of Sagami Bay."

Landa fumed and sipped coffee while Tubby White listened.

Finally, he said, "Well, damn it, let us know next time. What? This time of day? Hell no, you can't make popcorn. There's still a war on, whether you like it or not. Now give me an ETR. Yes, that's right."

White hung up and turned to Ingram. "Power supply on the surface search radar blew about two minutes ago. They're drawing tubes and should have it back up in ten minutes."

Landa rolled his eyes and turned his back, muttering something about "while Rome burns," and walked over to join Woodruff.

Ingram said, "Tubby, those tubes blow all the time, especially when we're in a seaway."

"I know."

"Well, then, get Mr. Guthrie on the ball and have him set up a ready box of power supply tubes instead of having to draw them from stores. Besides, I don't like guys walking around topside when it's blowing like this. If that was the air search trying to spot a kamikaze we'd be dead fish on a fork by now."

"Sorry."

Ingram didn't let up. "Popcorn?"

White sighed. "I let them do it on the midwatches." Ingram still had some catching up to do since returning from Karafuto. Overall, he felt Tubby White had done a good job as interim commanding officer. Landa had offered no real objection to it, but the two had escalated their spitting contests to exquisite levels. By now, though, even the lowest man in the crew realized that 90 percent of their act was put on.

Ingram said, "Tubby, you can't let up. What if the Japs try a trick?"

"I know. Our guys have been at it for so long, though. I thought they deserved a break."

"Give 'em a break when we start steaming home. Right now, I'm interested in staying alive." After Karafuto, Ingram had strong opinions about that. Glad to return to the relative safety of his ship, he felt physically fine after four days of square meals, hot showers, and clean clothes. Except he didn't sleep well. The photos he had seen in Fujimoto's bunker kept worming into his mind in the middle of the night. The headless Air Corps corporal stacked with all those other frozen bodies.

He wasn't sure how to handle the Unit 731 images, but he knew he had to find a way to live with it. He took solace in a bottle of belladonna he'd had for two years. It helped some but also made him feel logy. There were only six tablets left. Time to speak with the doc.

Anderson, Ingram's GQ talker, piped up with, "Combat reports surface search radar back on the line, Captain."

"Very well." Ingram nodded to White. "Congratulations."

"Right." White made to move off, but Ingram waved a finger. "And Tubby."

"Yes, sir." White recognized Ingram's tone. He knew more was coming.

"Ask Mr. Woodruff when he last rotated the watch. That lookout on the pilothouse looks like he's frozen solid." Technically, Ingram was wrong. The ship was at general quarters, and watches did not rotate. Yet, men exposed to the elements had to be cared for lest they become ineffective or even fall ill.

"Yes, sir," said White stiffly. Once again, he made to move off.

"And Tubby?"

White stopped. "Yes, sir?"

"Just one ass chewing per day. So, you're all done until tomorrow."

White moved off with, "Gee, thanks."

Clack, clack. The signal light went into action on the after part of the bridge. The signalman was acknowledging a light flashing from the *Missouri.*

Landa sauntered back from the open bridge. "This could be it."

He was right. It was a tactical signal from the *Missouri* to COMDESRON 77 ordering the formation to change from circular formation to a single column ahead of the *Missouri.*

Ingram smiled inwardly. The *Maxwell* was slated to move from the position of honor, off the battleship's port beam, to what he called the position of horror at the head of the column. The ships' positions had been discussed at a presailing conference four days ago, and the other skippers had given Ingram a hard time. But few could ignore the fact that if there were mines to be hit, the *Maxwell* was a prime candidate. The Japanese destroyer would be first. But Ingram wasn't worried about Japanese mines. Many of those had already been swept. The big worry was the influence mines laid by B-29s over the past few months. The worst variant of these were pressure mines, and hundreds were scattered around Sagami and Tokyo Bays. But there was no known method to sweep pressure mines. The only consolation was that they did have disarming devices, but those weren't set to activate until February 1946. Ingram hoped the issue would be resolved tomorrow, when twenty-three minesweepers moved into Tokyo Bay and concentrated on anchorages around Yokohama, Yokosuka, and Tokyo.

Ingram stood back and watched Landa and his staff executing their signals. It was a sweet dance he'd seen many times as Landa and his staff ordered a flag hoist to DESRON77 to comply with the formation specified on the OPORDER. The signalmen worked furiously bending flags on the starboard halyards. Soon the flags were hoisted halfway up to the dip, the "ready position," where they crackled in the breeze. When all the destroyers acknowledged by flying the same hoist at the dip, Landa shouted, "Execute." The signalmen yanked their halyards, ran the flags all the way up to the top, two-blocking them.

Ingram kept a close watch on Lieutenant Woodruff and the bridge watch, making sure the engine and helm orders were proper and followed exactly. He also kept a keen eye on the other ships. Screen changes could be dangerous; collisions were possible as destroyers ran for new stations like a bunch of Keystone Cops.

Now the fun began. The tin cans cracked their throttles and did what destroyers with 60,000 horses trapped in their hulls are built to do: their OODs let them out of the barn and held tight for the ride. The tin cans charged ahead of the Big Mo like Kentucky thoroughbreds. Their bows knifed the high seas, burying their noses deep in troughs, only to rise again and sprint on as water spewed off the weather decks. The *Maxwell* roared toward her number one position at twenty-two knots. At the precise moment, Woodruff cut her speed to fifteen knots, dropping the *Maxwell* perfectly on station.

The bridge watch moved with a calmness and professional sangfroid honed by countless hours of maneuvering and battle. Strange to think that as recently as nine months ago some of the *Maxwell's* crew had been enjoying civilian life as librarians, grocery clerks, and car salesmen. Lieutenant Woodruff had been in postgraduate architectural school at the University of California, Berkeley. But here they all were, executing this once difficult maneuver easily--almost enjoying the pounding the *Maxwell* took as she hurtled to her station like a crazed stallion.

The Japanese destroyer wheeled around directly before the *Maxwell* and assumed her position one thousand yards ahead. Ingram lifted his binoculars and examined the enemy ship with professional interest. It was the *Sagari*, the same ship he had seen exiting Sagari Bay five days ago. She had a raked mast, raked twin stacks, and a clipper bow; as ordered, her guns were depressed, giving her a sad, droopy appearance. She was rusty, and her aft section was still blackened.

But appearance didn't matter. The Japanese destroyer was there to lead them through minefields to a safe anchorage in Sagami Bay. Four American naval officers were on board to make sure everything went well. Ingram gave a silent prayer. There went four brave Americans who stood among a skeleton crew who could overpower them at a moment's notice. Anything could go wrong very quickly. They were first in line and would most likely be seriously injured or even killed if the *Sagari* hit a mine. Those four men and many others today and over the next few days were accepting things on faith. Hopefully cool heads would prevail. Too many Americans had seen the enemy's morbid tricks and endured kamikaze raids and the harsh fighting in the islands across the Pacific. Indeed, American sailors were trigger-happy and looking for an excuse to squeeze their triggers at the slightest provocation.

Steady on mates, and God bless.

By 1130 the *Maxwell* was anchored in eighteen fathoms of water one thousand yards off the coast, near Kamakura. The ship was close to the beach, the wind had dropped to a tolerable ten knots, and calm descended, the tension evaporating like ice on a Coca Cola bottle. The boatswain's mate of the watch piped away the noon meal, his whistle echoing over the ship's PA system. Ingram and Tubby White stayed on the bridge where they'd called a condition III watch. The rest of the crew headed for chow and maybe a nap. Guards armed with M-1s were posted: two on the forepeak, two on the fantail. Two more were positioned atop the pilothouse with BARs. Ingram was headed for the ladder to the main deck when he heard the *clack, clack* of the signal light.

Chief Signalman Tiny Overman was on the signal bridge rogering a flashing-light message from the *Missouri*, anchored six thousand yards out. Curious, Ingram walked over as Overman flipped his shutters.

"That for us, Chief?"

"Yes, sir," said the sandy-haired signalman. He clacked his signal light once, acknowledging he understood a word received. Then he called it to an apprentice who stood by writing on a message pad. "Unclass," he barked. Then he flicked his signal lantern. For a quick second Overman glanced at Ingram. "It's gonna be a long one. And it's addressed to you, Skipper. Go have chow. I'll run it down as soon as we get it all."

Then he clacked again, calling out, "Date time group . . ."

For me? What the hell? Overman had his hands full, so Ingram turned and went down the ladder to the wardroom. "Thanks, Chief."

24

28 August 1945
USS *Maxwell* (DD 525)
Anchored one thousand yards off Kanagawa Prefecture, Sagami Bay,
Japan

The night passed peacefully, with two destroyers patrolling outside the anchorage to bolster security. Personnel boats patrolling inside the anchorage searched for enemy swimmers, small boats, midget submarines, or any other mischief an enemy might put together. The morning dawned clear and bright, and sunlight glistened off the dew that had collected on the ships overnight.

The water was calm, and the *Maxwell* tugged gently at her anchor as the sun rose higher. Boilers 1 and 4 and generator 2 were on the line providing power. A condition III watch remained in effect on all ships, with radars energized along with a full bridge watch and skeleton crews in CIC, sonar, and all gunnery stations, where live rounds lay in their trays, ready to ram and fire.

Before chow, off-watch sailors flocked to the bridge for "hour-glass liberty," scanning with binoculars the Japanese shoreline a half-mile away. The firecontrolmen granted access to the Mark 37 gunfire control director atop the bridge, which offered a fine view. Men lined up all the way down to the main deck taking turns for a twenty-second sweep of the black sand beaches of the Japanese Rivera through the stereoscopic rangefinder. On occasion, a shouted "owwww-wieee" indicated that a sailor had managed to focus on a woman.

Wesley Sipes was a second-class radioman who had lived in Yokohama for five years when his father was a dispatcher for American President Lines. He still remembered some of the language and bits about the countryside. With his curious tourist seated at the rangefinder, Sipes would start at Kamakura, explaining that in AD 1250 Kamakura was the fourth-largest city in the world with a population of 200,000. Rich in political history, Kamakura was perhaps best known as home to the massive thirty-eight-foot-tall bronze statue of Amida Buddha. Enclosed since it was built in 1252, it survived an earthquake and tsunami in 1923 that destroyed the surrounding temple. To this day, Sipes would tell his guest, it still sits outside, exposed to the elements. Sweeping from the rangefinder from left to right, Sipes would go on to say that Kamakura was also the site of the emperor's summer palace. More than one sailor muttered something about sending over a few 5-inch rounds for Hirohito's wake-up call.

In the wardroom, a well-rested Ingram joined Jerry Landa and the off-watch officers at breakfast. He listened to stale jokes as they dined on powdered eggs and milk and good toast made from bread baked by the cooks during the night.

Landa scraped his plate with the last piece of toast, then sat back and raised the message again. "Who is Marvin Radcliff?" he asked Ingram. "And are we really invited to the surrender ceremony?" The message Ingram had received from the *Missouri* yesterday was an invitation from General Sutherland to attend the ceremony; it was countersigned by Brig. Gen. Otis DeWitt. Ingram and Tubby White had been so busy setting up watches and securing the ship in the anchorage that Ingram hadn't paid much attention to the message last night.

"Marvin?" Ingram laughed. "Let me see."

Landa passed it over. "Nice that you got us invited."

"Well, of course. This is probably one of the most momentous events of the twentieth century."

"I appreciate that, Todd," he said. "But again, who the hell is Marvin Radcliff?"

"It's Bucky. Bucky Radcliff. He was the C-54 pilot."

"Ahhh. He sounds like my kind of guy."

The PA announcer crackled with, "Officers' call, officers' call."

"Excuse us please, Captain?" The officers stood.

"Of course." Ingram nodded as they shuffled out. Tubby White had excused himself earlier and was already back on the quarterdeck.

Landa said, "Interesting that they picked the Big Mo. I guess it's that she's the newest one of her class."

"And named for Harry Truman's home state."

"Um, politics rears its ugly head. I bet they kick Halsey off his ship with MacArthur and Nimitz coming to town. There just won't be enough room for all that brass."

Ingram said, "I wouldn't be surprised."

"Look there," Landa pointed. "Does that really say 'Otis DeWitt'? That little turd is a brigadier general now?"

"That's right. He works for General Sutherland. What did he ever do to you?" Ingram recalled DeWitt's description of Landa. It was obvious the two had had a run-in. Ingram didn't want to get into the middle of whatever it was. On the other hand, he did want Landa to attend the surrender ceremony--along with Tubby White, the C-54's cockpit crew, and Sergeant Harper and his Marines. It was his price for keeping quiet about the incident at Toro Airfield. DeWitt had put on a great sputtering act of denial but finally agreed to do his best. And he had come through.

Landa said, "Ran into the little jerk one night in the officers' club tent at Naha. Started getting official with me."

"That's Otis."

"How well do you know him?"

"We took a boat ride together."

"Come on, Todd."

"All right. I met him on Corregidor. And then he ended up on the *51* boat with me."

"No foolin'?"

"All the way to Australia."

"I'll be damned. I can't see it in that officious little peckerhead, but he must have something to have survived that."

"That's why General Sutherland hired him. And now Otis is paying us back because of what we did for him up north. See?" Ingram pointed to the message. "He's invited the whole C-54 crew along with Sergeant Harper and his Marines."

"And me."

"And you."

"But you added Tubby White."

"I did."

Landa rolled his eyes. "This must be Ingram's revenge. First, I have to be polite to Lieutenant Commander White. Then I have to say 'yes, sir' and 'no, sir' to Brigadier General Dewitt. This is bullshit."

Ingram did his best to cover a smirk.

Taylor Jefferson, a yeoman first class, appeared at the doorway and knocked. "Excuse me, Captain. A boat pulled up with our mail about a half hour ago."

"Finally caught up with us?" said Landa.

"Yes, sir. We got a ton. It's going to take us a while to sort it all out. But there was a special delivery letter for you, Commodore." He walked in and handed it over.

"Thanks, Jefferson." Landa took the envelope and said, "Son of a gun, it's from Laura. What the hell have I done now?" He began tearing the envelope open.

While Landa read, Ingram sipped coffee, savoring the moment. Surrender ceremony! The war really was over. No more kamikazes, no more banzai raids. No Communists from the north. The only thing to worry about today was when to refuel. They'd brought in a tanker and--

"Holy shit!" Landa stood and walked about the wardroom.

"Everything okay?" asked Ingram.

"I'll say! Get a load of this. I'm gonna be a father."

"That's great!" Ingram stood and offered his hand. "Congratulations."

"Yeah, thanks. Cigars come later." He lowered the letter. "She wants to get married. Like right now."

"So?"

"Yeah. I think I can work it out. Grab two or three weeks' leave and go tie the knot. Why not? What do you think, Todd?"

"I have a shotgun in the gun locker that says you better do it."

"Yeah, yeah," Landa said absently. "Maybe I can bring it off. Hey, maybe take you along too. Get your dead butt out of here for a while."

"Hold on, I'm taking my men home on this ship."

"Just a little leave, Todd, to laugh your ass off while I get married. You'll be right back."

"I suppose I could."

Ingram headed for the door as Landa sat to finish reading his letter. "Please excuse me, Commodore, I have to go figure out how we gas up. And congratulations again."

"Yeah, yeah." Landa scanned the final page. "Aww, shit."

Ingram could have sworn Landa's face had turned the color of the page he was reading. "What?"

Landa looked at him.

"Jerry, what the hell is it?"

"It's personal, Captain. Now, please, don't let me interfere with your fueling schedule."

"Jerry, can I help? I mean--"

"Todd, seriously, it's nothing I can't handle. I'll let you in on it maybe later. Now go."

"You sure?"

"Positive. Now, please go."

"Yes, sir." Ingram walked out.

25

30 August 1945
Hot Rod 384,
en route to Atsugi Air Base, Japan

Leroy Peoples was flying, so Radcliff handled the radios. "Atsugi Tower, this is Hot Rod three-eight-four, heavy for you, twenty miles out, angels ten with four souls aboard. What do you have?"

The voice crackled in their earphones, "That you, Bucky?"

"One and the same."

"I thought they fired you." The voice belonged to Reid Callaghan, a C-54 pilot and friend of Radcliff's who had been tapped at the last moment for. flight controller duty at Atsugi.

"No, they kept me and fired you, Reid," said Radcliff. "What's it like down there?"

"Same as last time, Hot Rod. Planes everywhere. MPs strutting up and down with their chest sticking out. Brass screeching all over the place. It's like Coney Island. But instead of New Yorkers it's full of GIs and Japs."

"Japs giving you any trouble?"

"So far they're being pretty decent. One guy even gave me a cup of tea."

"Well, watch your back."

"You got that--"

"Radio discipline!" A harsh voice interjected.

Leroy Peoples turned to Radcliff and mouthed, "Who the hell was that?"

"Damned if I know," muttered Radcliff. This was their second run from Okinawa today. They'd been up since four this morning planning routes and landing and takeoff patterns. Hot Rod 384 was part of a massive train of C-47s and C-54s flying in the entire Eleventh Airborne Division, which was going in to occupy Atsugi Air Base and its environs. Radcliff's plane was one of the few carrying just cargo: two disassembled Jeeps, six barrels of aviation gas, several crates of small arms, ammunition, food, and medicine. Most of the other planes carried troops.

Callaghan announced crisply, "Hot Rod three-eight-four, wind is south-southeast at eight knots; barometer is two-niner point six; be advised major aircraft traffic this area: friendly, but lots of them. You are cleared for runway one-niner. Upon landing, stand by for special taxi instructions. Over."

"Understand two-niner point six, runway one-niner. Special taxi instructions upon rollout. Roger, Atsugi. Thanks, out." Radcliff clicked off and said, "You wanna take it in, Leroy?"

Peoples gave him a long look. "Not if you're going to torch my ass again."

On the return trip to Yonatan Airfield this morning Radcliff had asked Peoples to land the plane. About ten miles out, everything was on track; the gear was down and locked, the flaps were coming down. All of a sudden Radcliff yanked out a gleaming Ronson cigarette lighter, clicked it on, and cranked up the flame. He held it close to Peoples' face, almost under his nose.

"Sheeeeyat! What the hell you doin'?" Peoples shouted. "Ah cain't see."

Radcliff held the flame closer, "Come on, Leroy, you can do this."

"Ouch, shit, that hurts. Knock it off, damn it!" He tried to bat the lighter away, but he couldn't do that and hold the control yoke at the same time.

Peoples held on, yelling at Radcliff to stop and jerking his face from side to side.

"Leroy, we're almost there. Wing and a prayer. Come on."

People's left eyebrow sizzled, but he kept the yoke in a death grip.

With two miles to go, Radcliff pulled the lighter away.

"Damn. What the hell are you doin', partner?"

"Training exercise, Leroy."

"Well, where the hell did you--*arrrgh!*"

Radcliff had clicked the Ronson again and jammed the flame under Peoples' nose.

"Come on, the plane, you stupid redneck," yelled Radcliff. "You have fifty GIs back there. Fly the damned plane." That wasn't true, of course. There were just the four of them deadheading back from Atsugi.

"Arrrrgh!" shouted Peoples. He pulled up a bit with some wind shear, but then settled down. "Stop it, damn you, Radcliff. Shit, flaps thirty."

"Flaps thirty. Over the threshold, Leroy. Come on!"

Peoples jerked his head back and forth away from the lighter.

Radcliff followed every move, sometimes singeing more eyebrow.

"Ughhhh!" Peoples grabbed the throttles and eased them back.

The C-54 settled beautifully on its mains. Radcliff pulled the Ronson away and shut it off as Peoples put the nosewheel down.

"Nice," said Radcliff. "Right boys?"

"Outstanding," said Hammer.

"Very good," said Berne.

They gave a thumbs up to Radcliff.

"Assholes," Peoples muttered on the rollout. He moped and pouted while they reloaded and gassed the plane. Five minutes before takeoff on the second trip the crew learned that Hot Rod 384 would be flying into Atsugi right behind Gen. Douglas MacArthur's plane, the *Bataan*, a specially converted C-54 made to look like an ordinary cargo plane. Hot Rod 384 was to maintain a strict two-minute distance from the *Bataan* all the way to Atsugi. Radcliff assigned the takeoff to a now muted Leroy Peoples. Exactly 120 seconds after the *Bataan* took off, Radcliff said, "Go!" Peoples took off and held the proper interval all the way to Atsugi.

Now, as they descended into their pattern, Radcliff glanced over his shoulder at Hammer and Berne. Both nodded vigorously. He turned to Peoples. "Leroy, I have news for you."

"What?" he snarled.

"Why, Lieutenant Peoples, what ever happened to that cheerful, 'Yes, sir. What's that, sir?'"

"Stick it."

Hammer and Berne laughed.

"Okay, Leroy. No more games. It's all over. You passed your aircraft commander qualifications. You're now fully qualified for the left seat."

"No shit?"

"I mean it. You did well. You're the ninth guy I've done this with. Seven passed. Two panicked and I couldn't pass them." He held out his hand. "But you did the best of all of them."

They shook. Peoples grinned and said, "Thanks, boss. You mean I'll get my own airplane?"

"Gear coming down," announced Radcliff. "Yeah, sooner rather than later. Look at all this. One C-54 nonstop into Japan every two minutes. And everywhere else we have occupation forces. But be careful, Mr. Aircraft Commander. You might soon be flying your own C-54 with a snot-nosed right-seater to lead to the potty every five minutes, but right now you're two minutes behind the Big Cheese, so don't screw it up."

"No cigarette lighter?"

"That's all done. You passed the test."

"Can I do a sideslip?"

Radcliff ran a hand over his face to cover his grin. "Leroy, it's your airplane. You can sideslip all you want."

"My airplane?"

"All yours, Leroy. Congratulations."

Peoples sat erect and broke into song, "Amaaaazing grace, how sweet the sound . . ."

Hammer made a show of plugging his ears. Berne slapped a hand over his eyes.

Peoples continued loudly and horribly off-key, "that saved a wretch, like meeeeee . . ." Holding the note, he sang, ". . . flaps thirty, pleeez . . ."

"Flaps thirty," grunted Radcliff.

The threshold flashed beneath. Peoples shrieked at the top of his lungs, "Ah once was lost, but now am found . . ." He pulled back the throttles and eased back on the yoke.

Radcliff fought an impulse to clamp his hands over his ears.

First Lt. Leroy Peoples painted Hot Rod 384 onto runway one-niner and then, with the nosewheel settling, finished, "Was blind, but now ah see."

Guy is a natural, thought Radcliff.

Reid Callaghan broke into the concert with, "Hot Rod three-eight-four."

In a voice that could shatter glass, Peoples started on the second verse. "T'was Grace that taught . . ."

Radcliff barked, "Leroy!"

"Yes, sir?" Peoples asked innocently. He continued humming.

"Three-eight-four," Radcliff said. He made a show of clicking off and whispered, "You forgot to sideslip."

"Damnation!"

"Hot Rod three-eight-four, turn left next taxiway. Follow the guy on the bicycle to the tower. Taxi up and stop behind C-54 *Bataan*. Over."

With that, Peoples stopped humming. The two pilots looked at each other, then Peoples said, "You want it, boss?"

"Naw, that's okay, Leroy. You take it. Just don't rear-end the general's beautiful airplane. My insurance has lapsed due to insufficient funds."

Peoples muttered, "First a damned flame thrower up my ass, and now this."

The bicyclist, an MP, led the C-54 through streams of taxiing C-54s and C-47s. It seemed as though one popped up every hundred feet or so, their engines running. "Here we go," said Peoples. They followed the MP to a taxiway that led in front of the tower. They had pulled to within fifty yards of MacArthur's plane when another MP stood before them and crossed his wrists over his head.

"That's it, Leroy. Shut her down. Chief, break out the pins and wheel chocks. Looks like they'll be offloading us here."

"Roger." Hammer rose and clumped aft.

"Hey." Peoples pointed.

A man wearing the Philippine marshal's combination hat was exiting the *Bataan*. A corncob pipe was clamped between his teeth and he wore working khakis without a tie, just like the uniforms in Hot Rod 384. The five stars glistening at the general's collar points were the difference. He paused on the stairway platform and looked about for a moment. Then he descended toward a group of waiting officials. Camera flashbulbs popped as they crowded around to shake hands.

He did that alone. Amazing, thought Radcliff.

"That's him, isn't it?" asked Peoples. "General MacArthur?"

"Damn right." Radcliff felt a lump in his throat. America had been waiting for this moment since December 7, 1941. He couldn't believe his luck at being able to see it from such a great vantage point.

"Damn, look at all them reporters," said Peoples.

Photographers rushed in, dozens of them, popping flashbulbs off their cameras. Just behind them a crowd of cheering civilians pushed in. White-gloved police stepped in to keep people from engulfing the general and his party. The police made room for two men in top hats, who walked up, removed their hats, and bowed. The general shook their hands and they spoke for a moment.

A company of Japanese troops, fully armed, stood alongside a line of dilapidated cars and trucks. But they faced away from the MacArthur party, keeping the growing crowd at bay. The general continued to converse as more Army personnel descended the ramp from the *Bataan*. Among them Radcliff recognized Gen. Richard Sutherland and Brig. Gen. Otis DeWitt.

"You getting this, Jon?" asked Radcliff.

Berne snapped his fingers. "Damn. It's in my bag." He shuffled aft to retrieve his movie camera.

Radcliff looked back to see that a working party had drawn up under their cargo hatch. A forklift raised a man to open the cargo door and prepare for offloading. Just below, another man climbed the boarding ladder to the cockpit.

They were still gawking as General MacArthur's party headed toward the convoy of dilapidated passenger cars. There was a polite cough behind them. Radcliff turned, and his eyes bugged out. *Holy shit. A brigadier!* "Ten-shun!"

It was Otis DeWitt. "Now, how in the hell can you guys stand at attention in this little cramped outhouse, Major?"

"Sorry, General. I only meant--"

"I have about fifty-five seconds to deliver this to you, Major." DeWitt pointed out the cockpit window. "See that? Gen. Douglas MacArthur has just deplaned and now stands on Japanese soil. Can you imagine? Sort of a replay of when Commodore Perry sailed into Tokyo Bay ninety-two years ago. But unlike Perry, the general walked in here unarmed. We've been told to leave our weapons on board. No reason to be afraid of all those Japs out there. Look at their cars--straight from a demolition derby. That's what supposed to take us into town. Pray for our souls." He patted Radcliff on the shoulder. "Anyway, General Sutherland is a man of his word. He congratulates you all on a great job up at Karafuto."

Hammer walked into the cockpit and quietly sat at his station.

Radcliff nodded and said, "That's okay, General. We didn't expect that--"

"Like I told you in Okinawa, we can't give you medals. But we can invite you to the surrender ceremony aboard the USS *Missouri.*"

"You're kidding," said Radcliff.

An MP sergeant ran under the cockpit window and waved. Radcliff slid open his side window. The sergeant shouted up, "Ready, General."

DeWitt hollered out the window, "Right there, Sergeant."

DeWitt handed a packet to Radcliff. "These are your orders and passes. Special seats. It's gonna be really tight--lots of people from all over the world--but you'll have a good view. Congratulations, fellas." He extended his hand to each of them in turn.

Radcliff asked, "General, how about Todd Ingram?"

"Yes, he'll be there. In fact, you're in his party. Now I gotta go. Time to skedaddle into Yokohama. No, no, damn it, don't get up. Hell's bells. You can't anyway." Otis DeWitt walked out and exited the airplane.

Radcliff opened the packet. Orders for all four of them spilled out. "Here you go boys, congratulations." He passed them around.

"Humpff," went Peoples.

"What?" said Radcliff.

"We gotta step onto some Navy rust-bucket and watch these guys whompin' on a bunch of Japs?"

"Leroy, let me ask you a question."

"Shoot, boss."

"Do you plan on having grandchildren?"

Peoples rubbed his jaw. "Well, now that you mention it, yes. It's a fine old tradition in the Peoples family. Kids all over the place."

"Well, hang on Leroy. With all that coon-dog stuff you spread around, this is gonna be the best story you'll ever tell them."

PART II

ADMINISTRATIVE MESSAGE

ROUTINE
DTG: 02091741Z SEP 45
FROM: CINCPACFLT
TO: ALNAV-PACFLT
INFO: CNO
SECNAV
JOINTCHIEFS
SECSTATE
SECWAR
THE PRESIDENT

//UNCLAS//N5370
MSGID/GENADMIN/CINCPACFLT //

SUBJ: DEPORTMENT, EVERY MAN'S DUTY

IT IS INCUMBENT ON ALL OFFICERS TO CONDUCT THEM-

SELVES WITH DIGNITY AND DECORUM IN THEIR TREATMENT
OF THE JAPANESE AND THEIR PUBLIC UTTERANCES IN
CONNECTION WITH THE JAPANESE. THE JAPANESE ARE STILL
THE SAME NATION WHICH INITIATED THE WAR BY A
TREACHEROUS ATTACK ON THE PACIFIC FLEET AND WHICH
HAS SUBJECTED OUR BROTHERS IN ARMS WHO BECAME
PRISONERS TO TORTURE, STARVATION AND MURDER.
HOWEVER, THE USE OF INSULTING EPITHETS IN CONNEC-
TION WITH THE JAPANESE AS A RACE OR AS INDIVIDUALS
DOES NOT NOW BECOME THE OFFICERS OF THE UNITED
STATES NAVY. OFFICERS IN THE PACIFIC FLEET WILL TAKE
STEPS TO REQUIRE OF ALL PERSONNEL UNDER THEIR
COMMAND A HIGH STANDARD OF CONDUCT IN THIS
MATTER. NEITHER FAMILIARITY NOR ABUSE AND VITUPERA-
TION SHOULD BE PERMITTED.

C. W. NIMITZ, FLT ADMIRAL, USN

26

2 September 1945
USS *Missouri* (BB 63)
Tokyo Bay, Japan

The minesweepers had cleared what they could, allowing more than two hundred ships of the U.S. and Allied navies to anchor in Tokyo Bay. Battleships, cruisers, destroyers, amphibious and auxiliary ships lay quietly in their berths, some teeming with life and sending men ashore, others still waking up, feeding their men before quarters were called at 0800.

Conspicuously absent from the line of capital ships in Tokyo Bay were the carriers. Fearing a trick or a counterattack by hotheads in the Japanese military, Fleet Admiral Nimitz had ordered Adm. Raymond Spruance to lay offshore with his Task Force 58, the Big Blue. These deadly carriers and escort carriers could, at a moment's notice, wipe out any kind of Japanese military effort with hundreds of fighters and bombers. Admiral Nimitz, who had flown in from Guam on his Coronado aircraft, allowed four carriers into Tokyo Bay. All were escort carriers: two from the U.S. Navy and two belonging to the Royal Navy.

A few bombed-out hulks of the once proud Imperial Japanese Navy littered the harbors of Tokyo Bay. One of these, a titan with empty fuel bunkers, was the battleship *Nagato*, now dockside at the Yokosuka naval shipyard. At 42,850 tons *Nagato* was the world's first battleship fitted with 16-inch guns. On 7 December 1941 she had served as Admiral Yamamoto's flagship during the raid on Pearl Harbor. After suffering damage at the Battle for Leyte Gulf, the *Nagato* was taken to the Yokosuka shipyard for repairs. But Yokosuka's yard workers couldn't restore the ship quickly enough. Worse, the Japanese Navy simply didn't have enough fuel to waste on such a dinosaur. She was converted to a floating AA platform until, on 18 July, Admiral Halsey's carriers caught her with two bombs and a rocket that took her out of the war entirely.

A few POWs escaped from local camps and made their way to friendly picket boats off the shores of Kamakura. They described the horrible conditions in the camps and made it clear that a large number of prisoners needed immediate attention. On hearing this, Admiral Halsey sent the USS *Benevolence* (AH 13) in ahead of schedule and docked her at the Yokosuka naval shipyard on 29 August. Within twelve hours she had taken on a full load of 794 POWs from surrounding camps, with hundreds more en route.

Surrender ceremony preparations had been under way for days. The star of the show in Tokyo Bay would be the 52,000-ton USS *Missouri* (BB 63). When Fleet Adm. Chester Nimitz flew in from Guam on the twenty-ninth, he made the *Missouri* his flagship and Admiral Halsey politely shifted his flag to the battleship USS *South Dakota* (BB 57). Surrender ceremony preparations began in earnest when the *Missouri* moved into Tokyo Bay on 30 August. Admiral Halsey started off by making sure the *Missouri* anchored in the same spot where Commodore Matthew Perry had dropped his anchor ninety-two years previously. And then came the real work. Most of the ship's crew was pressed into service. There were innumerable errands to be run ashore and to ships anchored about the bay. Nimitz and Halsey decided the ceremony would take place on the 01 deck, a showplace sometimes called the "veranda deck." The veranda deck's starboard side lay under the Big Mo's massive number two 16-inch gun turret, which would serve as a backdrop. Shipfitters and welders were detailed to build a large platform outboard of the 01 deck to support journalists, photographers, and other special visitors.

An enormous task was the chipping away of the dark gray paint on the battleship's main and 01 decks to expose bare teak that hadn't seen the light of day since the *Missouri*'s commissioning. With extra hands laid on from other ships, the "deck apes" got it done. Then, in the time-honored tradition, they holystoned the newly found teak, bringing the hard wood back to life.

No detail was left untouched. The flag that flew over Washington, D.C., on 7 December 1941 was flown to Tokyo and broken on the *Missouri*'s foremast. At Admiral Halsey's instigation, the U.S. flag flown by Commodore Matthew Perry when he entered Tokyo Bay in 1853 was flown out from the U.S. Naval Academy. They mounted it in a special frame on a veranda deck bulkhead overlooking the spot where the ceremony would take place.

The actual document of surrender was flown out from the State Department accompanied by an Army colonel. There were two copies: one bound in leather for the United States, the other bound in canvas for the Japanese. Foreign Minister Mamoru Shigemitsu and General Yoshiro Umezu would be the two principal signatories for Japan: Shigemitsu for the government of Japan and Umezu for the military. The Allied signatories to the surrender agreement were to be Gen. Douglas MacArthur, as supreme commander of the allied powers (SCAP); Fleet Adm. Chester Nimitz, for the United States; and for Britain, Admiral Sir Bruce Fraser, who had steamed into Tokyo Bay on board his battleship, the *Duke of York*. Other delegates were General Hsu Yung-Chang for China, Lieutenant-General Kuzma Nikolayevich Derevyanko for the USSR, General Sir Thomas Blamey for Australia, Colonel Lawrence Moore Gosgrove for Canada, General Jacques Leclerc for France, Admiral C. E. L. Helfrich for the Netherlands, and Air Vice-Marshal Sir L. M. Isitt for New Zealand.

General MacArthur insisted that two special guests attend, both recently rescued from Manchurian prison camps. Shaken but somewhat rested and wearing fresh uniforms were Lieutenant-General Arthur E. Percival, who commanded the British Army that surrendered to the Japanese at Singapore in February 1942, and Lt. Gen. Jonathan W. "Skinny" Wainwright, the defender of Corregidor when it fell in May 1942. Activity was frantic when later in the day food and bathrooms were prepared for civilians and special delegates. General MacArthur and Admiral Nimitz also had large guest lists, many of them from the world press.

General MacArthur insisted the ceremony start at exactly 0900--no sooner, no later. Timing was critical. So was the sound system. Communication specialists tested and retested the ship's PA system. Movie cameras were positioned. A special radio network was set up to broadcast the ceremony to listeners around the world.

A dress rehearsal was conducted during the afternoon of 1 September that simulated the delegates' arrival and places during the ceremony. Most of the personnel on the veranda deck were to be flag officers standing in ranks. Three hundred of the Big Mo's sailors were rounded up to act as stand-ins for the admirals and generals. Grinning boatswain's mates and gunner's mates with Popeye-like forearms stood on the deck markings where generals and admirals would stand. Eleven crewmembers stood where the Japanese delegates were to be posted. The planners even went so far as to simulate the faltering steps of Japanese foreign minister Mamoru Shigemitsu, who walked with great difficulty on an artificial leg and cane, his real leg having been blown off by an assassin's bomb years before in Shanghai.

Some sailors, particularly the career ones, resented seeing their well-honed fighting machine turned into a circus. As the day wore on, there was a lot of horseplay and the inevitable breakdown in discipline. But at the back of every mind was the worry that the Japanese would try one last trick, and they would be unprepared for it. It was all strange and different. They wondered if it could come back to haunt them.

By sunset everything was ready--at least for the morrow's activities. But there was a more difficult issue yet to face: How were Americans and their Allies to set aside their hate and resentment for all the lives lost, the horrible wounds, the time lost from loved ones, and the irreparable damage done to priceless buildings and works of art throughout Japan's once-vaunted Greater East Asia Co-Prosperity Sphere? For some, there would be a lifetime of resentment and pain, of nightmares, and sadly, in some case, of drunkenness and suicide. But clear thinkers, the real statesmen who worked so hard in the background, hoped better times would begin on 2 September 1945. At least, that is what they planned: that the tone would set a new beginning for Japan, her neighbors, and the world.

But tonight, there was still mistrust. Japan technically remained at war with the Allies, and the men in the anchorage felt it acutely. After years of battle, people were edgy. Nobody knew what tomorrow would bring. Rumors persisted--would a flock of kamikazes appear? What sort of trick would the Japanese pull at the last minute?

Hardened by years of fighting and hate, the men on the ships in Tokyo Bay followed their instincts. All lights were doused at sunset, and darken ship was strictly enforced. Fleet Admiral Nimitz, the senior officer present afloat (SOPA), ordered condition III watches set. Guns were loaded and ready to fire on predesignated targets ashore. The younger men fell asleep easily and began snoring. But sleep wouldn't come for many of the veteran sailors, Marines, and sailors. They had seen too much on the long road across the Pacific. Many didn't want to sleep for fear of the horrible night-mares that struck in the middle of the night: the cold sweats, the quick breathing, the pounding heart, the curses of others growling at them to shut up.

Steady on, mates. God be with thee.

27

2 September 1945
USS *Missouri* (BB 63)
Tokyo Bay, Japan

The morning dawned overcast over Tokyo Bay. There was no wind, leaving the water a flat slate gray with barely a ripple. Seagulls ranged about the fleet crying to one another, perhaps sensing a change in the air. To the west lay Tokyo, its firebombed silhouette barely discernible against the morning mist. To the southwest was the once-busy port of Yokohama, also a bombed-out relic. South of Yokohama was the Yokosuka naval base, a prize the U.S. Navy would soon claim. To the eastern side of Tokyo Bay lay the scenic Miryra Peninsula, its trees and craggy hills likewise shrouded in morning mist.

The *Maxwell*'s motor whaleboat was fully loaded. In the back sat Cdr. Alton C. Ingram, the ship's commanding officer; Lt. Cdr. Elton P. "Tubby" White, the executive officer; and Capt. Jeremiah T. Landa, commodore of DESRON 77. Seated forward were members of the U.S. Army Air Corps: Maj. Marvin F. Radcliff, 1st Lt. Leroy Telford K. Peoples, Capt. Jonathan L.

Berne, and SSgt. Leonard Hammer. Representing the U.S. Marine Corps were GySgt. Ulysses Gaylord Harper and his twelve-man squad. The uniform of the day, as prescribed by SOPA, was working khakis, no tie, for officers, and working whites or utilities for enlisted. No ribbons and no weapons were to be displayed.

Standing high in the stern, the tiller between his legs, was Boatswain's Mate Second Class Alvin Birmingham, the motor whaleboat's coxswain. Birmingham's shoes were shined, his hair was clipped, and he wore crisp undress whites. His hat rode low on his forehead, an inch above the eyebrow, telling everyone that this was Birmingham's boat; that he was the coxswain and that today he was proud to be part of a major event in history. Similarly dressed was the bowhook, Richard Dudley, the seaman deuce GQ lookout with sharp eyes. A third member of the boat's crew was her engineer, Fireman Third Class Louis T. "Sherlock" Rathbone, also in starched whites, who handled the whaleboat's four-cylinder Buda diesel.

With all the men on board, the whaleboat was at capacity and wallowed in the wakes of the boats crisscrossing the busy bay as it drew closer to the *Missouri* on what should have been a placid Tokyo Bay. But wakes merged and slapped at them as they drew closer to the *Missouri,* causing them to buck and heave. Ingram figured they had maybe twelve inches of freeboard, meaning water would slop in the boat from time to time. But the bilge pump could handle that.

He felt good about today and was especially happy for the people who surrounded him. A promise is a promise, and Otis DeWitt had come through, inviting everyone Ingram had asked, down to the last private, first class.

For convenience, Ingram had brought them on board last night and threw a special dinner. After that, he gave them bunks. The ship's regular crew, officers and men, did not gripe when they were asked to give up their bunks. The weather was balmy enough, so they could sleep outside on the 01 level. But Ingram kept the galley open and stocked with sandwiches and Kool-Aid for anyone who couldn't sleep. Predictably, the Marines went back again and again.

Later that night, the usual epithets drifted through Ingram's porthole: "Hey, jarhead, you can piss off the fantail or you can use the head right through that hatch, take your pick"; or "Outta my way, squid"; or "Stupid birdman." They all loved it.

The boat crunched into another trough, with Birmingham swinging his tiller to avoid the worst of it. Water flew over the bow and misted over the starboard side. Three Marines were seasick and were heaving over the side. First Lieutenant Peoples, who had turned a dark shade of green, held valiantly to what had been a fine breakfast.

Jerry Landa and Tubby White were making stilted conversation about the boat's extended fuel capacity when another wave slapped the bow, throwing up a wall of water. Most of it flew overhead, but a handful hit Radcliff squarely in the face.

Radcliff muttered, "I knew there was a reason I didn't join the Navy."

Berne and Hammer hooted.

Ingram threw over a clean towel.

Radcliff blotted his shirt and muttered. "Obviously your revenge for you sitting in my jump seat."

Landa said dryly, "Only trying to help. Word's out that you haven't taken a shower in three weeks."

Radcliff gave a wry smile. "See you on the next MATS flight, Captain."

Landa asked, "You mean you'd stick me in the cargo hold?"

"If there's room."

Landa and Radcliff traded grins as the whaleboat drew to within five hundred yards of the *Missouri*. Birmingham wove through traffic as though he were on the Pasadena Freeway. He dodged through a line of destroyers that, like sleeping greyhounds, laid to behind the *Missouri*'s starboard side, brown stack gas lazily drifting up into the morning. One by one, they offloaded VIPs on small boats to head for the *Missouri*'s quarterdeck, situated forward on the starboard side.

Birmingham's destination was the port-side quarterdeck, where lesser guests were boarding. Again, they fought the slop and wakes thrown up by craft ranging from 26-foot motor whaleboats to giant 51-foot personnel boats to LCVPs and tank-carrying LCMs. By Ingram's count there were at least fifty circling, waiting to disembark their passengers.

Birmingham called to Ingram, "We're in luck, Captain." He pointed to a sailor wagging semaphore flags near the quarterdeck. "That's us: Dog five-two-five."

Ingram said, "Sounds good to me." He turned to Peoples. "You ready to head in, Leroy?"

"Uhhhhghhh," said Peoples.

"I'll take that as a yes. Take her in, Birmingham. And then find a spot under that boat boom up forward. With any luck they'll let you up to see some of the action."

"Yes, sir." Birmingham gave a four-bell signal for full speed.

The *Missouri* grew more and more massive as they drew close. *This is a big ship, and she is beautiful,* thought Ingram. To someone used to living on a little destroyer, the battleship's 52,000 tons seemed like 500,000.

Birmingham rang three bells, and Rathbone backed the whaleboat, perfectly stopping it at the landing. Landa was first out, followed by Ingram, then Tubby White, and then the rest.

The OOD, a full commander, stood at attention with a gleaming brass telescope tucked under his left arm, throwing salutes like a Marine gunny on a parade ground. The instant Landa stepped on board, the *Missouri*'s messenger of the watch rang four bells and the PA system echoed with, "DESRON seven-seven arriving."

Ingram was next up, with the messenger announcing, "*Maxwell* arriving."

The rest of Ingram's party followed close behind, and within thirty seconds the messenger was announcing new arrivals.

Twenty young sailors stood before them. One of them, a young blond gunner's mate, second class, wore a nametag that said his name was Hopkins. He walked up to Ingram. "Are you the *Maxwell* party, sir?"

"That's right."

"Everybody here?"

"All set."

"Then please follow me."

Although things were pretty basic on the battleship's main deck, Ingram was glad Hopkins knew his way around. Time and again he eased his party through a group of sailors like a linebacker, shouting, "Gangway."

As they walked, the bell rang on the PA system announcer called, "Commander, Third Fleet, arriving."

Halsey had stepped on board.

Everyone on the main deck paused momentarily, as if expecting him to walk around a corner.

"The big hitters are in town," said Ingram, dodging a giant deck-mounted ventilator.

"I'm waiting for Harry Truman," said Landa.

Again, the bell gonged on the PA system. "Supreme commander of the Allied Powers arriving."

MacArthur had just stepped on board. Ingram had been with him in the Philippines and Corregidor. In those days, which seemed an eternity ago, he had seen the general just once; now he would see him again, both having traveled a long and hazardous route through the Pacific.

The party climbed a ladder to the 01 deck and drew up near the port side of the massive number two gun turret. Pointing to another ladder, Hopkins said, "Up there is where you'll be, gentlemen, atop this turret. You'll have a perfect view of the deck below. Captain Murray made sure you have front-row places to stand. Your numbers are taped on the deck."

Landa whistled. "Numbers?"

"Yes, sir. You'll find someone up there with spot assignments. He'll have your number assignment," said Hopkins.

"What'll they think of next?"

"Between you and me, Captain, best thing they can think of is sending us home," said Hopkins.

"Now you're talking," said Peoples. He smiled, the color returning to his face.

Radcliff said, "Easy, Leroy. Now that you're an aircraft commander they won't let you rest until you've flown the last buck private out of the war zone."

"Life isn't fair," said Peoples.

Hopkins said, "Please excuse me, gentlemen. If I don't get back soon the watch commander will cancel my leave for the next ten years."

"Go, son, go," said Ingram.

Hopkins backed up, saluted, and then walked off past a group of officers. Ingram recognized General Sutherland in the pack. He was speaking with a civilian. Sutherland looked up, caught Ingram's eye, and beckoned him over.

Ingram said to Tubby White, "Get everybody up there, Tubby, and check them in. We'll be up in a minute."

"Got it," said White.

With a nod toward Sutherland, Ingram said to Landa, "You want to come? I may need you to keep me out of trouble."

Landa said, "You sure you want me? As you know, I'm an expert at pissing off senior officers."

"Please remember that General Sutherland walks in the highest circles and will be most happy to assist you in your climb to the top."

Landa laughed at that one.

They walked over, and Ingram said, "Excuse me, General, good to see you again." He introduced Landa.

"Good Morning, Commander," said Sutherland, offering his hand. "And good morning to you, Captain Landa." They all shook hands.

Now that he was closer, Ingram was surprised to see that the man Sutherland had been speaking with was Colin Blinde.

Blinde didn't miss a beat. "Haven't seen you since Yontan, Todd. How you doing?"

"Sleeping better."

"That's something," said Blinde. He raised an eyebrow at Landa.

He's trying to decide which end to kiss. "Please say hello to Captain Landa, my squadron commander."

"The one they call 'Boom Boom'?" Blinde thrust out his hand.

Landa gave Blinde a fish grip and a cheesy smile. "So, this is Mr. Aqua Velva," he muttered to Ingram with an exaggerated sniff.

"Shhhh." Ingram stifled a grin.

Sutherland said, "We begin . . ." he checked his watch, "in six minutes. And I have to join the general." He turned to Ingram. "I wanted to make you aware of something, Commander."

"Yes, sir?" said Ingram.

Sutherland asked, "Did you know that the Soviet Union will be signing the surrender agreement along with the other Allied countries?"

Ingram said, "To be truthful, General, I hadn't thought about it but, okay, that makes sense."

"And that Lieutenant-General Kuzma Nikolayevich Derevyanko will be signing the surrender agreement for the Soviet Union?" Sutherland said.

"Yes, sir."

Sutherland's eyes bored in. "As a signatory, General Derevyanko was allowed to bring five guests as part of his official party."

Ingram kept silent. He had an idea of what was coming.

Blinde said, "Yes, we get Captain Third Rank Eduard Dezhnev as a member of General Derevyanko's entourage. They boarded about twenty minutes ago. Now they're wandering around the ship."

Ingram seethed. The man who only days ago had tried to kill him, and who had tried to kill both him and Helen three years ago, was now on board this ship and corrupting this magnificent moment in history. Jaw muscles twitching, he gave Blinde a hard stare.

Blinde said, "Don't look at me; it wasn't my idea to let him aboard."

"Oh? Who approved the Commie list?"

"Well, I--"

"Colin, I've got some Marines here who would love to stuff Dezhnev into a garbage can and drop it off the fantail. That son of a bitch tried to kill us. You too, if you didn't notice."

Blinde shook his head. "I know, I know. But here, today, it's diplomatic immunity and all that. Also, you should know they've got him rigged with a camera--a German Zeiss--and he's snapping pictures of everything from gun barrels to radar antennae to toilet seats."

"How sweet," said Landa. "Maybe we should send him up to the flag cabin and have him photograph our classified files."

"He is being watched," said Blinde. "Actually, they made me responsible for his safety today."

"Who is 'they'?" demanded Ingram.

"Well, that's part of--"

"Gentlemen," interrupted Sutherland.

Ingram took a deep breath. "Yes, sir. Thanks for letting me know, General. I promise I won't try to kill him. At least not this morning."

Sutherland said, "That's the spirit, Commander. We can't afford an international incident at this stage. But you should also know that his station is on top of the gun turret where I understand you will be."

Landa said, "Now this gets interesting. Maybe we can help him over the side, like on the New York subway." It was a twenty-foot drop to the veranda deck.

Sutherland gave a polite cough as more admirals were gonged on board. "I must join our party. But I wanted you to be aware of this and to ask that you be discreet."

Blinde said, "That means nothing physical, Todd."

Ingram said, "Shut up, Colin."

"What?" Blinde took a step back.

Landa looked away to cover a snicker.

Sutherland seemed unfazed. "I know you'll conduct yourself accordingly. Now, please excuse me, gentlemen."

Blinde shrugged and nodded to the rungs running up the side of the great gun turret. "See you up there."

"Topside," corrected Landa.

"Yes, topside," said Blinde. He began climbing.

"Okay," Ingram nodded to the ladder, "your turn, Boom, Boom."

"Very funny. You go ahead. I have to hit the head. Be right there."

"Good luck finding one in this mess."

"I'll figure it out."

28

2 September 1945
USS *Missouri* (BB 63)
Tokyo Bay, Japan

Ingram mounted the ladder and made his way through the noisy crowd that seemed to take up every square foot atop the gun turret. Tubby White beckoned from the starboard side, and Ingram walked over to join the rest of his group. They stood loosely, joking, gawking, and pointing things out. He was particularly glad to see the Marines standing alongside a proud Gunnery Sergeant Ulysses Gaylord Harper. A few had cameras and were making full use of them.

Ingram shook Harper's hand, "This is your day, Ugly, you and your boys. Thanks for it all."

Harper's chest puffed a bit. "You too, Commander.

White walked over. "Your spot is there, Skipper." He pointed to numbers fixed on the deck in tape. "You're number sixteen, the commodore is fifteen, and I'm fourteen."

Ingram took his spot and looked about. "Amazing." Situated behind a row of chairs, space number sixteen offered a fine view of the veranda deck below and the single stand-up microphone where the speaker would conduct the ceremony. Outboard of the veranda deck was a temporary platform jammed with photographers and their camera equipment. Row upon row of officers, most of them admirals and generals, lined the after part of the veranda deck and the area directly below Ingram on the inboard side. A lonely table covered with a green baize table cloth stood in the middle of the deck, a single chair on either side. On the table were two open folios, each easily twenty by twenty inches. A pen and inkwell stood sentinel beside each.

Below, on the forward part of the main deck, sideboys in dress whites were mustered in ranks around an accommodation ladder on the starboard side waiting for the Japanese. Officers in working khakis, the uniform of the day, stood at the end of the ranks waiting to escort the Japanese to the veranda deck. Sailors in undress whites were jammed into every available corner; not a square foot of horizontal space remained. Sailors lined the main and 01 decks, the decks above, the main bridge, the flag bridge, lookout stations, gun tubs, and antennae platforms; they crouched atop the main battery director and 5-inch gun mounts. Two men had found a space inside the 16-inch gun turret's massive rangefinder. Some, like big-city flagpole sitters, had slid out onto the Big Mo's yardarms, eighty feet above the main deck.

A group of Japanese photographers and newsmen, unlike their jocular counterparts, stood stiff and silent on the outboard platform, staring straight ahead.

Ingram spotted Jerry Landa speaking with Otis DeWitt on the veranda deck just below. Interesting to see those two conversing. The last he'd heard, DeWitt and Landa regarded each other as social misfits. What sort of small talk could they be making? Then Toliver walked up and shook hands with them. Landa pointed to Ingram standing atop the gun turret. They waved up to him. As Ingram lifted a hand to wave back, General Sutherland walked up and joined them. Then, to Ingram's amazement, Admiral Halsey walked out of a hatch and joined the group. Landa seemed to be doing the talking. Sutherland rubbed his chin. Toliver began talking, waving his arms as DeWitt stood patiently. Soon Admiral Halsey brightened at something. With a grin, he raised a finger and began talking. The other three nodded; something had obviously been decided.

A microphone blared, "Testing, testing."

Halsey flicked his wrist, checking his watch. Clearly there were things to do. He clapped Landa and Sutherland on the shoulders and stepped back into the hatch with Sutherland, DeWitt, and Toliver close behind.

Landa climbed the ladder and took his place with a grin. "Found the head."

"Oh, yeah? Looks like you were telling farting jokes to some high brass," said Ingram.

Landa gave a thin smile.

Tubby White said sotto voce, "Don't look now."

Ingram turned to see Eduard Dezhnev limp up with another Soviet and take spots behind Radcliff and Peoples.

Leroy Peoples said, "Mercy me. I thought we'd seen the last of this critter."

Dezhnev was dressed in a Soviet naval infantry uniform featuring a Sam Browne belt and polished boots. His companion, another captain third rank, was similarly dressed. Draped around Dezhnev's neck were an elaborate Zeiss camera, its hard leather case, and an exposure meter. He looked like a tourist photographing the Golden Gate Bridge. Incongruously, just beneath the camera and exposure meter glinted Dezhnev's rogue belt buckle from Alcatraz, light glistening off the golden edges.

"Too bad he's not in the front row," said Jon Berne, who stood beside Peoples. "We could pitch him over the side. But you can't win 'em all." Berne raised his movie camera and began slowly panning from left to right.

Dezhnev caught Ingram's eye and, with a slight smile, tipped two fingers to the brim of his hat. Then he raised his camera and began rapidly clicking. One or two of the shots included Ingram and Landa.

Aqua Velva wafted down the line as Colin Blinde walked up and took the space to Dezhnev's left. He flashed Ingram and Landa a broad smile and shook Dezhnev's hand.

"Wheooow!" Landa held his nose. "Smells like a Shanghai whorehouse."

Berne and Peoples held their noses and began coughing loudly. Then

Berne spun around, apparently responding to something Dezhnev had said. The two spoke for a moment; Berne smiled, then Dezhnev. Peoples turned and started speaking to Dezhnev and his companion. They all shook hands, Blinde smiling along with them.

Ingram began to grind his teeth.

Radcliff muttered, "Well, if it isn't Benedict Blinde."

Berne handed his movie camera to Dezhnev, who examined it with great interest. He held it up, looked through the eyepiece, and began panning as if he were really shooting. In exchange, Dezhnev absently lifted the camera strap over his head and gave his Zeiss to Berne.

Peoples winked at Ingram and Radcliff, then leaned over and pretended great concentration on Berne's examination of the Zeiss.

An OS2U Kingfisher flew down the *Missouri*'s starboard side. Its canopy was wide open, and a man with a giant camera hung from the aft cockpit. Berne nudged Dezhnev and pointed.

Dezhnev said, "*Da, da,*" and began shooting, the camera's chrome windup key slowly turning. He stopped and waited as the Kingfisher did a slow 180-degree turn and headed for a pass down the port side. Dezhnev kept the Kingfisher in his eyepiece as it swooped by. While Dezhnev was occupied, Berne slipped the Zeiss to Peoples, who unsnapped the back and flipped it open. He held camera and film open to the sky for a moment, exposing the thirty-six-shot roll. He would have gotten away with it, but Dezhnev heard the Zeiss' back cover snap shut. He looked up in time to see Peoples' Cheshire cat grin as he slipped the Zeiss back to Berne. Dezhnev's face darkened, and his eyes narrowed.

Peoples said, "Oops, sorry."

Blinde said, "See here," and reached for Dezhnev's camera.

"My camera, please," said Berne.

"Mine first." Dezhnev thrust out his hand.

Blinde made another move for Dezhnev's camera, but Berne turned away. "I said, gimme back my camera."

Dezhnev sputtered, "My film . . ."

"Give . . . it . . . back," said Blinde.

Landa said quietly. "Damnation. I believe we have an international incident."

Dezhnev's face grew red. He doubled his fists and then visibly relaxed and held out the Bell & Howell. The cameras were exchanged.

Radcliff, Peoples, Berne, and Hammer immediately closed ranks, standing shoulder to shoulder and making it difficult for Dezhnev to see, let alone take a shot. Dezhnev tried to move sideways, but Gunnery Sergeant Harper squeezed in with his Marines.

"Please," said Dezhnev.

Harper turned, "Something wrong, Ivan?"

Blinde said, "Gentlemen, please."

Radcliff said, "Take a hike, Benedict." He caught Ingram's eye and they exchanged winks. *Justice.*

"Attention on deck." A commander stood at the microphone.

Ingram checked his watch: 0900.

The chattering crowd fell silent and drew to attention. Their joking ceased. Faces became solemn and hard, registering retribution and revenge. To a man, their eyes were fixed on the table with the instruments of surrender laid out upon it.

The shrill whistle of a boatswain's pipe echoed from the accommodation ladder. The sideboys snapped to attention. A man in a top hat laboriously worked his way up the quarterdeck accommodation ladder. Proceeding with great difficulty, he finally gained the main deck.

"Who?" whispered White.

"Shhhh . . . it's Shigemitsu," Landa replied softly as Japan's foreign minister limped with obvious difficulty across the deck.

Ingram pointed and whispered, "Amazing."

"What?" rasped Landa.

"They're saluting." Indeed, all officers and enlisted in ranks were saluting the Japanese party as they crossed the main deck. The Japanese officers returned the salutes.

Shigemitsu hobbled to the veranda deck ladder and once again struggled to work his way up. At one point Col. Sydney Mashbir reached out to help, but Shigemitsu shrugged it off and finally stepped to the veranda deck on his own. He took a place ten feet before the great table and a Japanese general stepped up beside him. Two ranks of five and four Japanese delegates took positions behind them. Four of the delegates were in civilian attire; seven wore uniform with ribbons. No swords or any other weapons were in sight.

Landa said softly, "Alongside Mr. Shigemitsu is General Umezu, representing those friendly folks who brought you World War II."

The ship's chaplain, a four-striper, stepped up to the microphone. The PA system echoed: "Let us bow our heads . . ." The chaplain said a prayer and then blessed the proceedings against a backdrop of clicking shutters, popping flashbulbs, and grinding movie cameras. Then he stepped away. The Americans snapped to attention as the national anthem rang through the ship.

There was an awkward silence. Seagulls squawked, waves slapped the *Missouri's* hull, an LCVP diesel growled down the port side, and aircraft droned in the distance. Then Gen. Douglas MacArthur, Fleet Adm. Chester W. Nimitz, and Adm. William F. Halsey Jr. stepped through a hatch and strode to the podium. They turned and faced forward. MacArthur was at the microphone, with Nimitz and Halsey just behind him. Halsey's expression was reminiscent of a cowhand ready for a barroom brawl.

General MacArthur raised a single page of notes and began, "We are gathered here today . . ."

Ingram was captivated by MacArthur's eloquence. It was almost as if he were on stage, his oration that of a Shakespearean actor. Further, it was how the general formed his sentences and how each phrase struck home efficiently and to the point. Ingram was particularly moved by the general's expressed desire to "conclude a solemn agreement whereby peace may be restored. The issues, involving divergent ideals and ideologies, have been determined on the battlefields of the world and hence are not for our discussion or our debate."

Period. This man is not just some blundering footsoldier looking to grab headlines. He's telling us the Japanese are not to be tortured, or shot, or beheaded, or even pilloried. He's telling the onlookers to put aside their thirst for blood. There is great respect and tolerance here, almost as if they are signing a tariff or trade agreement.

"It is my earnest hope," MacArthur continued, "indeed the hope of all mankind--that from this solemn occasion a better world shall emerge out of the blood and carnage of the past, a world founded upon faith and understanding, a world dedicated to the dignity of man and the fulfillment of his most cherished wish for freedom, tolerance, and justice."

MacArthur paused. A gust of wind whistled through the upperworks. Then, as if cued by a stagehand, the clouds parted, and a shaft of sunlight broke through. The crowd drew a collective breath as the sun glinted off Mount Fuji in the distance.

At that, MacArthur continued, "I now invite the representatives of the emperor of Japan and the Japanese Imperial Headquarters to sign the instrument of surrender at the places indicated."

Foreign Minister Shigemitsu hobbled forward. An aide pulled out the chair, and he sat. Then he picked up the pen and looked at the document . . . and looked at the document. Seconds passed, and he kept looking . . . scanning, poring over the document.

"What the hell?" muttered Landa.

The crowd's mood darkened. *Is this guy reneging? Another Jap trick?* A few looked anxiously to the sky. Admiral Halsey looked furious, as if he were ready to walk over and throttle Shigemitsu.

"Sutherland," MacArthur barked, "Show him where to sign."

29

2 September 1945
USS *Missouri* (BB 63)
Tokyo Bay, Japan

Lt. Gen. Richard Sutherland stepped from ranks and walked to the table, taking possibly some of the boldest and significant steps in the history of diplomacy. He leaned over and pointed to the spot where Minister Shigemitsu was to sign.

"Ah!" Shigemitsu jolted up as if he had been shocked but immediately bent over, lifted the pen, and scratched his signature on both copies.

The crowd exhaled. *Halfway there.*

Pushing on his cane, Shigemitsu rose and hobbled back to his place at the head of the Japanese delegates.

The crowd drew another breath as stiffly, General Yoshiro Umezu stepped up to the table. Ignoring the proffered chair, he leaned over and signed his name on both documents.

Done. Another sigh whispered across the ship as the entire company exhaled. Some looked around. Halsey seemed a bit less peevish. Ingram and Landa exchanged glances. *History*.

General Umezu stepped back into ranks.

General MacArthur, now flanked by Gen. Jonathan Wainwright and Lieutenant-General Arthur Percival, stepped up, sat at the table, and signed the documents as supreme commander of the Allied Powers. General Sutherland stood just behind them. Ingram spotted General Willoughby and Otis DeWitt among several American admirals and generals standing two rows back.

Ingram was shocked by Wainwright's appearance. He was famously thin--his nickname was "Skinny"--but this man looked positively shriveled. His skin was yellow, and his weight could not have been above 110 pounds. Percival didn't look that much better, a testament to the cruelty of Japanese imprisonment for more than three years. It was a wonder either man could stand at all. Yet, both remained braced to attention as the supreme commander of the Allied powers used five fountain pens to ink his name. He passed the first two pens to Wainwright and Percival; of the others, one would go to West Point, one to the Naval Academy, and the last was for his wife, Jean.

MacArthur stood and Nimitz took his place. Halsey and Adm. Forrest Sherman moved up behind him, and Nimitz signed for the United States of America.

One by one, representatives of the rest of the Allies signed, beginning with General Hsu Yung-Chang for China. Admiral Sir Bruce Fraser signed for the United Kingdom. After that, Lieutenant-General Kuzma Niko-layevich Derevyanko stepped from the front row, sat, and penned his name for the Soviet Union.

On the veranda deck below, Dezhnev stepped from the ranks, dropped to a knee, and took his photos.

"Jerk," said Radcliff. "How'd he get there?"

"Wonder if we can shove a chair down on his head?" asked Landa.

A Navy captain seated in the row before them turned. "Sssssst! These are our friends."

"Not as of two weeks ago," said Ingram.

The captain turned in his chair, "Young man, what is your name and unit?"

Landa said, "May I introduce Commander Pigshit of the USS *Hoghumper*."

The captain stood and looked Landa up and down. "And you are ...?"

The crowd quieted. Some of the flag officers looked up to the commotion as General Sir Thomas Blamey sat and signed for Australia. Otis DeWitt looked up wearing a perturbed expression as General Blamey rose and gave the seat to Colonel Moore-Cosgrove, who sat, picked up the pen, and signed for Canada.

The two captains stood face-to-face; Ingram and Landa took in the man's collar tab: supply corps. Landa said, "Sit, pork chop, before you piss off every flag officer in the western Pacific."

"I ..." The supply officer looked down to see Otis DeWitt staring right at him. Toliver too.

"Too late, loser." Landa pointed. "See that BG down there? That's Otis DeWitt. He works for General MacArthur. By sundown he will have pulled enough strings to make sure the Navy Department busts you to ensign. For the next five years you'll be counting toilet paper rolls in Barstow, California. Now, sit!"

The man sat.

Peoples snickered.

Landa scowled.

General Jacques Leclerc finished signing for France, and Admiral C. E. L. Helfrich signed for the Netherlands with a flourish. Last to step up to the table was Air Vice-Marshal Sir L. M. Isitt, who signed for New Zealand.

Isitt stood and resumed his place in ranks. The ship remained silent as General MacArthur stepped back to the mike and paused. A gull squawked; a 51-foot personnel boat growled down the port side. High above, at the yardarm, the flags of MacArthur, Nimitz, and Halsey fluttered as a zephyr lifted them. Above them, at the top of the foremast, the Stars and Stripes stiffened.

General MacArthur said, "Let us pray that peace now be restored, and that God will preserve it always. These proceedings are now closed."

Sutherland fussed with the folios then handed Shigemitsu his copy.

The Japanese turned, and Colonel Mashbir led them back toward the ladder to the main deck. A great rumbling arose to the east. The noise grew louder and louder. Everyone looked up. Ingram shaded his eyes as he counted at least twenty B-29s approaching in formation with more on the way, their great Wright R-3350 engines hammering the sky.

"Holy cow," said Landa.

B-29s, tens of them. Following behind were hundreds of carrier planes: Corsairs, Hellcats, Avengers, and Helldivers, most of them in tight formations, swooping in from the east Like Vulcan's thunder. Ingram felt the noise through his feet as the armor-plated deck vibrated beneath him.

"Hell of a show," said White.

Berne stood fast, his camera grinding. Ingram looked down to see Dezhnev clicking away on the veranda deck. The crowd was breaking up as men headed for the gangway and their boats. The Japanese were lined up at the accommodation ladder and headed down to their boat waiting below. Once again, he saw the side boys and officers at the quarterdeck saluting the Japanese. And once again the Japanese returned the salutes.

Tubby White looked at him, "Military courtesy?"

Ingram nodded. "Strange," he said, "what the stroke of a pen can do."

Men gathered in groups on the 01 deck and chatted as they awaited their turn to descend the ladder to the main deck. The officers seated before Ingram's group rose and turned to head down the turret ladders. The supply captain made to step past Landa. "Excuse me."

"Of course, Ensign. Don't forget to wash your underwear."

The man gave Landa a sour look but moved on.

Ingram followed Landa down the ladder and said, "Jerry, you really know how to make friends. I am so happy to serve under your mentorship and influence. What would we all do without you?"

When they reached the bottom, Landa took Ingram aside. "Can I speak with you for a moment?"

Landa didn't look to be in a light mood. And Ingram knew Landa's moods well. "Pardon?"

"It's personal, Todd."

"Okay." Ingram turned to White. "Take them aft, Tubby, and group up on the quarterdeck near the big gun mount, port side. I'll be right along."

"Yes, sir." White's eyebrows rose.

Ingram shrugged. "Don't know."

"See you back aft." Signaling with a hand over his head, Tubby White collected the Air Corps crew and Marines and walked them toward the fantail.

Ingram turned to Landa. "What?"

"You're going home."

"Come again?"

"You're going home. Now. Your plane leaves in three hours."

"What the hell are you talking about?"

Otis Dewitt and Toliver walked up. "Okay?" asked DeWitt.

"Okay what?" demanded Ingram. "What are you guys doing?"

DeWitt said, "Todd, it's about--uh, hello, Colin."

Blinde had somehow merged with the group. "Good morning, gentlemen."

Ingram whispered to Landa, "He's supposed to be going aft with the others."

Landa grunted.

DeWitt made introductions, then said to Blinde, "How'd you like the ceremony, Colin?"

"Very fitting, indeed. The general put just the right touch on it, I thought."

Landa took a deep breath, once again inhaling Aqua Velva. Toliver must have sniffed it too, because he flashed a quick smile to Landa.

"How can we help you, Mr. Blinde?" Landa asked.

The "Mr. Blinde" was not lost on Colin Blinde. "I . . . ah, I just wanted to say hello."

"Mr. Blinde. Please be informed that this is a classified conversation."

Blinde gave a broad smile. "Oh, that's all right. I'm cleared for top secret."

Silence. They stared at him.

Blinde gave a short laugh. "Except in the case where I don't have a need to know, I see. Please forgive me, gentlemen. Really, I was just trying to say hello. I'll be waiting in the back with the others." He moved away a step.

Ingram said, "Thanks, Colin. Just walk straight aft on this deck. They should be beside number three gun turret. I'll be along shortly."

"Okay, thanks, Todd." Blinde walked off.

"Jackass," snorted Landa.

"Easy, Commodore," said DeWitt. "Blinde is well connected in the State Department. He can be either a king maker or a career wrecker."

"He's a turd."

"Commodore," barked DeWitt.

"Sorry, General, . . . uh, where were we?"

DeWitt said, "As I was going to say, this is about Helen. And fortunately, I can help. Correction." He nodded to Landa and Toliver. "We can help."

Ingram took a step back. "Speak English, will you?"

Landa took a letter from his back pocket and separated its pages. He removed a page and handed it over. "Take a look at this, Todd. It's from Laura, the letter I got a few days ago."

The perfumed onionskin rattled in Ingram's hand as he read:

-4-

...*came together nicely. And so Arturo still chases me around the podium, but he's letting me play. I think he really likes my work. It's a game. I think he's too old for sex, but he puts on a big show trying to make everybody think he can still do it.*

On a serious note, I've been keeping in touch with Helen and am really worried about her. About two weeks ago, she phoned and almost broke down. I had to coax out of her that one of her patients at Fort MacArthur was wounded seriously; he was a tanker I believe on Okinawa. He lost his crew in a fire and he was seriously burned. He became a head case taking refuge under his bed with all the nightmares.

She told me he went completely fetal at times. Now, it's happening to her. She's going fetal under her bed. She's keeping it from Mrs. Peabody, but I'm worried now about little Jerry and how he's getting by with all that. I just don't know. She asked for the name of a shrink and I gave her the name of one or two here in Beverly Hills, but I think that's too expensive for her.

Last, I could get out of her was that she may try a guy at Fort MacArthur.

Well, that may be what she ends up with, but I think she really needs a husband. They've been through so much together. So, if there is anything else you can do, please let me know...

Ingram looked up, searching their faces.

Landa nodded.

"Let me read it again," Ingram said, turning his eyes back to the letter. This time through he dwelt on the part about nightmares and the fetal position. Guilt swept over him as he recalled how many times had she been there for him in rough times. Every time. And now, she was going through it with nobody to help. He had pills. He had belladonna; he had all sorts of stomach tranquilizers and headache pills to get him through. And he had his job and his ship and his crew. Worse, he admitted to himself, he had his pride and tried to suppress what bothered him. Helen did it too, and she buried it deep. But she was taking care of nut cases in San Pedro and raising their son with nobody to really lean on. After all she'd been through in the Philippines, the stress was bound to pile up. Those horrible last days on Corregidor alone should have been enough to break her, to say nothing of being tortured by those Kempetai ghouls on Marinduque Island.

He looked at DeWitt and Landa and Toliver. "I . . . son of a bitch. I don't know what to say."

DeWitt said, "Well, I do, Todd." He put a hand on Ingram's shoulder. "You're going home to take care of her. You've both had enough."

Stark images swirled through Ingram's mind. He shook his head. "How about you, Otis? And you, Jerry? You guys deserve to go before me. Plus, I have a ship to take care of."

Landa said, "No arguments, Todd. You're going home. You have a beautiful wife and a fine young baby to look after. Thirty, sixty days and you'll be back. In the meantime, Tubby White gets to be captain and I get to yell at him, which is the real reason you're going. You're a pain in the ass and I can't intimidate you as easily as Tubby. So, you see it all works out."

Ingram's head swirled. "I don't know . . . how?"

DeWitt stepped close and spoke in a low tone. "Keep this under your hat, Todd, but Admiral McCain is very ill. Admiral Halsey held him over for the ceremony but is sending him back to the States tonight on Admiral Nimitz's flying boat. You're going on that plane. Maybe you two can sing western songs together. I understand he likes that stuff."

"Me? I can't carry a tune," said Ingram.

"I'll teach you some farting jokes," said Landa, the sun now cooperating and glinting off his impossibly white teeth.

"And I'll send along some reading material," added Toliver.

DeWitt and handed over a manila packet. "Orders. We had them cut during the ceremony. Signed by Boom Boom here and endorsed by Admiral Halsey."

"It's official," said Landa. "How can you lose?"

"I . . . I have stuff to pack, the ship to think of, my crew."

Landa said, "Your gear is being sent over from the *Maxwell*. You're headed to the *South Dakota* to join up with Admiral McCain, and then you're off. From there, you hop on the plane and," he pointed east, "course zero-nine-zero."

DeWitt pulled out his cigarette holder, plugged in a Chesterfield, and lit up. "I think that's Navy talk for home, Todd."

Landa said, "And don't worry about the Mighty Max. Tubby and I will take good care of her."

Ingram sniffed. "That's what I'm afraid of."

"I appreciate your confidence," said Landa.

Ingram blinked. It was all happening too fast. Then he remembered Landa speaking with DeWitt, Toliver, Sutherland, and Halsey. "You mean you worked this out all the way to the top."

"Even Halsey has heard of you, "said DeWitt. "He was happy to do it. He thinks McCain will enjoy the company."

Ingram gulped. "At least let me say goodbye to my guests."

DeWitt pointed, "Go. Be back here in five minutes. Can't keep Admiral McCain waiting."

30

5 September 1945
North Pacific Ocean
en route to North Island Naval Air Station, Coronado, California

The ride in Admiral Nimitz' four-engine PB2Y Coronado was comfortable but long . . . and boring. Hour after hour of droning interspersed with bouncing and bucking and strapping in and hanging on while trying to smile and look nonchalant.

Vice Adm. John McCain had been in a special bunk and was attended by a doctor, a corpsman, and two lieutenant staffers. The doctor kept an IV drip nearby, and once, three hours outside Wake Island, they actually hooked him up for a while. By the next morning, after their takeoff from Pearl Harbor, the admiral seemed much better, his eyes twinkling.

The weather had calmed, and Ingram walked forward to chat with the cockpit crew. Afterward, as he sauntered aft past McCain's bunk, the admiral spoke. "How's it going, son?"

Ingram smiled. "Fine, Admiral."

"Have a seat."

Ingram was surprised. The admiral had slept well after the doc had given him some knockout drops. He looked to the on-duty corpsman, who gave a quick nod.

Ingram sat in a comfortable chair facing McCain. The admiral had a great deal more color in his cheeks now than he'd had when two sailors carried him through the hatch yesterday. Skinny and short of stature to begin with, his weight had dropped to near one hundred pounds. The rumor was true. *John McCain has given his all.*

McCain asked, "You play cribbage?"

"Yes, sir. A lousy game."

"Well, that makes two of us. Maybe later today."

"I'd like that, Admiral. By the way, I'm Todd Ingram."

"Shit, if I didn't know who you are you wouldn't be on this airplane."

Ingram straightened a bit.

"Ray Spruance speaks highly of you."

"He has been very kind to me." Spruance hadn't been kind at all. Exhausted and debilitated after his escape from the Philippines, Ingram had been posted to a cushy job in San Francisco. Soon afterward, Admiral Spruance presented him with his first Navy Cross in the Pope Suite of the St. Francis Hotel, then turned him around and sent him out to the Solomon Islands as executive officer of the USS *Howell* (DD 482).

McCain nodded toward Ingram's Naval Academy ring. "What class?"

"Nineteen thirty-seven."

"Class standing?"

Ingram pulled a face.

"Come on, I ain't gonna kick you off the plane."

"Forty-eight in a class of 214."

McCain lay back and laced his fingers behind his head. "Well, then, you don't have a thing to worry about, son. Care to guess my class standing?"

"Number one."

McCain laughed. "You are a great bullshitter. You'll go a long way in this man's Navy. You going to stay in?"

"I made it this far, so yes, sir."

"And Jerry Landa's your boss?"

Again, Ingram was surprised. "Yes, sir. CO of DESRON 77."

McCain muttered, "Black-shoe bullshit."

Ingram knew what he meant. They were jousting. Aviator lingo versus surface officer lingo. Aviators wore brown shoes; surface officers wore black. "Sir?"

"I seen you a few times alongside guzzling my fuel oil."

"I saw you up there, Admiral. Thanks for the drink."

McCain's eyes glittered again. "Jerry Landa," he snorted. "Tells great farting jokes. I never laughed so hard."

Ingram grinned.

"Okay, here it is. I graduated 79 out of a class of 116. About as low as whale shit."

"Amazing."

"Yeah, from number seventy-nine to commander, Task Force 38. Can you believe it?" McCain was being modest. He had entered flight school at the age of fifty-two and won his wings. He rose through the ranks of naval aviators to command of all air forces in the dark days of 1942 on Guadalcanal. And he'd won. He'd beaten Yamamoto.

"I can believe it, sir. You did a great job."

"And now you're pumping out more bullshit. You'll definitely make admiral. Maybe even CNO. When you do, I hope you throw crap on all those pinkos on Capitol Hill. Believe me, I saw plenty of 'em when I was running the Bureau of Aeronautics. They can't find their asses with both hands."

Ingram wouldn't back down. "You made a great name for yourself, Admiral."

"Names. You wanna know my real name?"

"I'll bite."

McCain's eyes glittered again. "It's Casper Clubfoot."

"Who?"

"I write adventure stories under a plume de nom."

"Casper Clubfoot," Ingram chuckled. "Nom de plume."

"Whatever."

"With a name like that, your books will sell like hotcakes."

McCain settled back. His eyes seemed to flutter.

Time to go. Ingram rose. "Cribbage later, Admiral?"

"You bet." McCain focused on him. "What's with your wife?"

"That's what I'm going to find out, Admiral."

"From what I hear, she should have a Navy Cross, like you." He gave a phlegmy cough.

"Coming from me personally, Admiral, I'd say that's an understatement."

"It is. Some of her torpedo discoveries hit BuOrd and set them back on their asses. Really brilliant."

"Yes, sir."

"She's still working, right?"

McCain was up on things. "Yes, sir. She's an Army nurse in the psychiatric ward in Fort MacArthur, San Pedro."

"Get her out of the wacko ward. That's probably what's pulling her into it."

"I had the same idea myself, Admiral." Ingram offered his hand. "Thank you, sir, and thank you for letting me tag along."

McCain took it. "You're most welcome. What's her name?"

"Helen."

"Helen. Beautiful name. You give her our love. And come and see us in a couple of weeks. I live on Coronado. Make sure you bring her. On second thought, just send her and you stay home and play pool or something."

"I wouldn't leave her alone with a brown shoe, Admiral."

McCain tried to laugh, but it came out as a deep rattling cough.

"We'd love to come see you. Thank you." He made to move off. "You're going to be just fine, Admiral."

"Don't worry, son. There are worse things than death for some people--take life, for instance." He turned on his side and drew up the blanket.

She picked up on the second ring. "Hello?"

"It's Todd."

"Thank God. You're here."

"Almost."

"Where?"

"North Island, waiting for a ride." Briefly, he explained about his ride with Vice Admiral McCain.

She gave a long exhale. "Your 'aloha oe' made me so happy. When will you get here?"

"Aloha oe." He'd sent a telegram when they stopped for fuel at Pearl Harbor. "Depends on where the ride comes from. I'm logged in for space available here, but this place is like the last night on earth. Guys are pouring in from overseas, and they all want to go someplace." Ingram had never seen so many people in one spot. Hundreds spilling out of the waiting room and into the parking lot, sitting on their duffle bags, waiting for rides to homes all over the nation. He continued, "Outside of that, I wait for the next train, which leaves in," he checked his watch: 5:15 p.m., "a little over two hours."

"Can't wait."

"Me neither." A long pause; static crackled on the line. He asked, "You okay?"

"I have so much to tell you."

"Me too. How's Jerry?"

"Well, I . . . ah . . ."

Her voice. He knew that tone. She was being coy. He imagined her head on the pillow and felt a surge of desire for her. "Spit it out," he chuckled.

"Jeremiah and Mrs. Peabody are reading a book this evening. I believe he prefers to stay there and enhance his reading skills."

"Ah." Ingram yearned to see his son, but for tonight that would be just fine. "Well, I hope she endeavors to challenge and enlarge his intellectual horizons."

"Yes, I'm sure that's what is going on. I believe the subject of their study this evening is Donald Duck."

Again, that tone of voice. Deep, husky. He felt like bursting from the damned phone booth and running all the way up to San Pedro, 120 miles distant. "I--" Someone tapped on the phone booth window. It was a Marine light colonel with lots of salad on his tunic; five battle stars glittered. His face was deeply pockmarked, and his eyes were slits, as if he were sitting behind a water-cooled .30-caliber machine gun hosing down the jungle.

"Gotta go, hon. Here's a lovesick guy wants the phone."

"The hell with him."

"Baby, there's ten guys in line. Six of them are Marines, and they all want to kill me."

"I love you."

"I love you too. Home soon."

"Home soon."

He hated it, but he hung up. Her last words sounded so desperate. He opened the accordion door. The Marine stood there, blocking his way. "Hi," said Ingram.

"Yeah." Grudgingly, the machine gunner stepped aside letting Ingram escape into the smoke-filled lobby. He headed toward his B-4 bag resting against the opposite wall near the "space available" desk.

Someone touched his elbow. "You Ingram?"

He turned. "That's right."

It was a lieutenant (jg) in greens with aviator's wings. "Name's Leonard Hitchcock, sir. You the one headed to Allen Field?"

Ingram's heart soared. "You bet."

"Looks like we're in luck, Commander. They tell me this field is so loaded with aircraft that they're flying out the excess just to make space. So, they detailed me to fly a TBF up to Allen Field, which is home for me and maybe home for you too?" His eyebrows went up.

"That's right."

"Well then, not bad duty for either of us. So, if you don't mind rattling and shaking in the backseat, I think I can promise you Allen Field in a couple of hours."

"When do we leave?"

"Now. There's six of us going out. Just like a Tokyo raid or something."

A quick glance at Hitchcock's blouse showed no campaign ribbons. But that meant nothing. Many veterans preferred not to wear their ribbons. Ingram wore his two Navy Crosses because he'd been ordered to do so by senior officers from Capt. Jerry Landa to Adm. Raymond Spruance.

Hitchcock turned and headed for a door marked Operations. Ingram followed. The young man had a swagger. And his overseas cap was punched down in front and tilted to the left, the eagle and anchor a bit green. Yes, Hitchcock had been "out there."

Hitchcock breezed through the check-in process, looked at the weather, and signed for his airplane in ten quick minutes. No time to call Helen. Then they walked through a door and onto the field to a waiting stake truck. Five other pilots, all in flying jumpsuits, were already on board along with their passengers: a rear admiral, three captains, and a Marine bird colonel. Ingram, a mere commander, felt their cold stares. He turned to Hitchcock and muttered, "What the hell did *I* do?"

The truck started up and bounced out toward the airfield, passing row upon row of parked aircraft. Hitchcock muttered back. "They're pissed, Commander."

"What for?"

"I guess one of their buddies got bumped."

"What?"

"You must have some pull Commander. And I'm not touching that. You seem like a regular guy. But I'm enrolled in Boldt Hall Law School starting next month, so I'm just leaving all this alone and concentrating on flying. Between you and me this is my last flight. They have me tucked into position six, which is okay with me. Hell, life could be worse. One of these ghouls could be ordering me to make a run on a Jap battleship, and I've had enough of that." He gestured to Ingram's medals. "You too, Commander?"

Ingram sighed. "You're right. This is just fine."

Takeoff was delayed for an hour while they waited for mechanics to install a new generator in one of the TBFs. Finally, at 7:45, they took off into a blazing red sunset over Point Loma. Hitchcock's TBF was the last to roll, and it took five minutes to join up. Hitchcock tucked smartly into the number six position of the right echelon.

Quiet. The TBF's R-2600 engine vibration began lulling Ingram to sleep. But then Hitchcock's words came back to Ingram as they droned northwest into the crimson sky: *You must have some pull.*

31

5 September 1945
En route to Allen Field, Terminal Island, California

The formation droned northwest at five thousand feet through a clear and moonless sky, the air soft and smooth as velvet. The interval between the six Avengers was loose, about one hundred feet, and they flew with their running lights on, something forbidden in the war zone. Off to his left Ingram counted the running lights of five ships at sea, also forbidden until a few weeks ago. *Looks like Christmas time.*

Ingram and Hitchcock were quiet for most of the trip, each lost in their thoughts. But their attention was soon drawn by pools of light that grew larger and larger as they flew up the coast. Laguna Beach, Newport Beach, and Huntington Beach slid beneath the Avengers' wings like scattered diamonds. By 9:30 the ground was ablaze with a solid carpet of lights as Seal Beach became Long Beach and Terminal Island, and San Pedro beyond. To the northeast, the dazzling lights of Los Angeles beckoned.

Ingram marveled that there were still places in the world not wrecked and darkened by day and completely lifeless at nightfall.

"What do you think, Commander?" asked Hitchcock.

"Todd."

"Well, what do you think, Todd?"

"Where's the flak?"

Hitchcock laughed. "None tonight. No blackouts. No Japs. No Nazis. Nobody punching twenty-millimeter holes in your airplane. It's hard to get used to."

"You married, Leonard?"

"Leo. No, sir."

"I'm sure you'll do just fine acclimating yourself to this strange land."

Hitchcock laughed. He cut back the TBF's power as the formation slid into a shallow dive to the left. "About five minutes, Todd."

"Boldt Hall, that's pretty good."

"Yes, sir."

"What kind of law, Leo?"

"Me? Well, I'll tell you," Hitchcock leaned forward and flipped levers. Ingram heard a whirr and the landing gear started down. "I had sailors in my squadron getting screwed by these 4-Fs and their finance companies. They repossess cars and foreclose on houses while our guys are out there getting their asses shot off. One of my radiomen had his house taken away with his ninety-year-old mother living there. No mercy. They wouldn't answer any letters, even one signed by the captain. These people are snakes, and I'm going after them. So, I like public service to start. Maybe later, sit on the bench."

"Wow. I'm sure you'll do very well, Leo."

"I hope so."

Gradually, they dropped to two thousand feet until they reached Allen Field, its runway outlined in white lights. Just over the middle, the TBFs did what carrier pilots do; they peeled off every five seconds, each doing a 180-degree turn to line up for their downwind leg, engines at low rpm. The lights of Terminal Island below looked like jewels mounted in ebony.

Ingram thought he should ask. "It's late, Leo. You have a place to stay tonight?"

"I share . . ." another pause and whirring noise as the flaps came down.

"... a pad with a buddy in Belmont Shore, another zoomie. Trouble is, it's kind of crowded."

"Oh?"

"Three WAVES from the Long Beach Naval Shipyard live there too, so space is tight."

"I'm so sorry. Life is hard."

"Yes, sir, it is, but we all have to sacrifice. You know, the war effort."

"Ah, yes, the war effort. I hadn't thought of that."

Hitchcock asked, "How 'bout you Todd, you okay for tonight?" He eased the TBF into a gentle left turn and onto their final approach. Tower and terminal were off to the left, a green "permission granted to land" light flashing from the tower.

Welcome home, sailor.

"Todd?"

"Pardon?" Suddenly, Ingram felt very tired. He hadn't slept well on the PB2Y even though they let him stretch across two seats. The occasional bouncing and anticipation of home had kept him awake. Now, a sudden urge to sleep overwhelmed him as if he were enclosed in a warm blanket. "Say again?"

"You good for tonight, or would you like to bunk with us at the snake pit?" The runway threshold flashed beneath. Hitchcock chopped the power.

"I'm okay, Leo, thanks."

"You sure?"

"Leo, I believe my wife is getting pregnant tonight, and I'd like to be there."

"Ahhhh. Sure thing." Tires squeaked as Leo painted the TBF on the runway.

She wore white, she was warm, she was lovely, she was smooth, she was coy, she was provocative and yet very, very tender. To this she added a touch of Chanel No. 5. He took everything she had, and still she gave more with a laugh and sometimes just a wink. And always, they gave each other a closeness and singularity one could never put into words. It was just there, for them alone, as if it had always existed.

Exhausted from their lovemaking, Ingram rolled over and reached for the alarm clock. His hand brushed against it and it fell to the floor with a crash. "Damn!" He fumbled for his watch and read the radium dial: 2:08.

She ran a hand over his face. "Happens all the time."

"Think it'll still work?"

"It's bulletproof. Like you."

He pulled her close.

Her arm was still around him when he awoke at 4:25. The night was dark and still and moonless. Fred must have figured things had quieted down, because he slept at the foot of the bed.

He turned toward Helen and found her watching him.

She said, "Good morning. You ready for breakfast?"

"It's already right here with me."

She smiled. "So, what do you think?"

"I don't know how to do that."

This time she laughed. "You must have noticed."

He had noticed, but he wasn't ready to get into it yet. "Noticed what?"

"Come on, hon, it's what people don't say that worries me."

Yes, he had noticed almost instantly, the first time he kissed her: cigarettes. But rationality had gone out the window when he burst through the front door. Only the bedroom light was on, and it drew them like moths to a flame. The light went off almost immediately as passion consumed them.

"Lucky Strikes?"

"How did you guess? All your girls must be smoking Luckies."

Now he realized why the clock went on the floor. His hand had hit an ashtray, something that hadn't been there before. That plowed into the alarm clock, and everything went crash.

He sighed. "I hate to think what your mom will say."

"She already knows. She was here last weekend. Dad too. I was scared at first. But they were pretty level about it. Mom knows how I tick, and so does Dad. By the way, Dad wants to know when you're getting out. He needs help at the ranch. I didn't tell him that you're in for life." Her voice held the slightest question.

"Going for thirty if they'll have me."

"Well, I hope the next twenty-two years are easier than the first eight."

"Sorry. Is it okay with you? I'll probably end up with a desk job in East Overshoe, Nebraska."

"I'm not surprised. Sort of expected it. Yes, it's okay with me. But rest assured, I'm getting out of the Army. I have kids to take a care of."

"Kids?"

"We weren't too careful last night, were we?"

Ingram grinned. Then he tried, "What got you going?"

"Smoking?"

"Ummmm."

"I saw an Ingrid Bergman movie."

Ingram nudged her. "You can do better than that."

'Scuse me." She reached over, her arm gliding across his chest like an electric current as she fumbled with cigarette package and lighter. The cigarette lit, she lay back and blew smoke in the air. The effect, he admitted, was soothing.

But his chest still tingled where her arm had touched it. After two puffs, Ingram couldn't stand it. He grabbed the cigarette, stubbed it out, and took her in his arms.

A truck rumbled by at--he checked the clock--6:25 a.m. Outside, a few birds sang in spite of the overcast. He reached for Helen, but she was gone. Where was she? Like him, she should be dead tired. "Helen?"

Something stirred. It was a strange noise. Almost a rattle. It was--directly beneath him! "Jesus!" He sat straight up.

Another rattle and he jumped out of bed and looked underneath.

"My God."

Helen stared back at him, all curled up.

"Honey, what's wrong?"

"I'm cold."

"Come on, baby." He reached. "Let's get you warm."

"Okay."

He slept until 9:45 this time, waking refreshed, sunlight streaming in the window. Helen handed him a cup and saucer. The coffee aroma wrapped around Ingram well before he raised the cup. "Ahhh, wonderful," he sighed, then took a luxurious sip.

"I didn't answer your question."

"Sorry?" His mind swam. *She was under the bed!*

"About smoking."

"Oh."

He sipped while she lit a cigarette and told him about Eddie Bergen. Five minutes later she was crying in his arms. *What do you do with someone crawling under the bed? Oh, God.*

She calmed after ten minutes or so, and he left her resting as he rose, pulled on a T-shirt and a tattered pair of gym shorts, and padded to the kitchen to renew their coffees.

A knock at the back door. A face at the window. Mrs. Peabody. He stepped over to yank open the door. She held his one-year-old son. "Welcome back, Commander."

"Emma! Jerry!" He opened his arms and took the boy in. The child was in his bathrobe and he burbled, his fists thrust straight out. "God he's grown."

The boy looked up at Ingram, his gray eyes wide.

Ingram smiled. "I'll be damned. Kid's a tank."

"No Navy talk in front of that child, if you please."

"He's really big."

"Twenty-four pounds."

Ingram held the boy close. To his surprise, Jerry relaxed his arms and settled his head on Ingram's chest, smacking his lips.

"He likes his daddy."

"Ummm. Hey, come on in, Emma. I'm making more coffee. Then breakfast."

Emma Peabody took a step back. "Maybe later." Pointedly, she looked over his shoulder. "Everything all right?" she asked softly.

No doubt she knows about all this. He rolled his eyes and said, "I'm getting my arms around it."

She exhaled loudly. "Very good. It's really wonderful that you could get here so soon. With you here and Helen on furlough, maybe we can make some progress."

"Furlough?" He darted a glance over his shoulder.

"Oh, well, sounds like you two haven't talked much. In any case, welcome back, Todd." She stepped up and kissed him on the cheek. "Let me know when I can help." With a nod to Jerry she said, "Unlike you, he has had breakfast."

"Now, wait a minute. I just--"

"And he's in clean diapers. So, you should be good for a while." She handed over a paper bag of baby clothes. "And these are washed."

"You're the best, Emma. Thanks for everything."

"Toodle-loo." Emma Peabody walked off.

32

Homecomings are never easy, especially after long absences. Like many newly reunited families the Ingrams discovered that reacclimating to a loved one occurs in at least three phases. Phase one is physical and wonderful, but of course short-lived. The second phase is that uncertain period when lovers examine each other's psyche to see how much or how little they have changed, and if so, what has changed. In phase three they learn how to adjust to the changes. More often than not, things work out, but sometimes disaster follows.

More practical matters accumulate after long absences: dirty windows, overgrown yards, cars in need of repair; in the Ingrams' case the car was a faded blue 1939 Plymouth that needed an oil change and had a leaky radiator. But for Ingram this was all good, something he could throw himself into and see immediate results.

The day dawned clear and blue, and after a big breakfast Ingram turned to. He happily sweated and grunted, mowing and trimming the lawn with a diapered Jerry crawling behind, sun glinting off his little body. Later, Ingram attacked the windows while Helen put Jerry down for a nap. After that, Ingram took the luxury of a nap, then dove into a huge stack of bills.

By six that evening the place fairly sparkled, but they were exhausted. Ingram swilled a beer, took a shower, and walked into the kitchen where Helen laid on a savory pork chop dinner. It seemed strange, almost too peaceful, as they sat at dinner with Jerry pulled up in his high chair, stuffing Rice Krispies in his mouth with both hands. No emergency calls from the bridge, no noon reports, no equipment failures between the salad and main course. No small talk among twelve officers at a green baize–covered table. Just pork chops and applesauce and Helen with Jerry happily spilling milk and banging his cup. At 7:30 they settled back and listened to the *Lone Ranger* with Jerry asleep between them. By 8:30 p.m. they had tumbled into bed and were sleeping like zombies.

The next morning, he was up at 6:45 making coffee and breakfast while Helen changed Jerry's diaper and heated his bottle. "Night feedings," he said, heading for the front door. "Glad that's over. Drove me nuts."

He went out, picked up the paper, and walked back inside looking at the headlines.

Inside, Helen prattled on. "We were lucky. Some babies can't digest milk. It takes a year, maybe two, to grow out of it, and even--what's wrong?"

Ingram sat heavily in the kitchen chair and laid the newspaper before her. He pointed to an article on the front page: "Vice Admiral John S. 'Slew' McCain Dies at Home."

Helen sighed and skimmed the article summarizing McCain's life, from his boyhood on a Mississippi plantation to his attendance at the surrender ceremony on 2 September. "Heart attack. Sad. How did he seem to you?"

Ingram nodded. "He must have known the end was near. You can see it in a man. He wanted to go home the moment the cease-fire was declared on the fifteenth of August. But Admiral Halsey ordered him to stay, insisted that he needed to see the surrender ceremony, the fruit of his labor."

"Stupid."

"Maybe. I don't think Halsey or anyone else other than his doctor realized the severity of his condition. He looked pretty good aboard the

Missouri. He lined up with everyone else at stiff attention. But then afterward, coming back on the plane, he didn't look good. I think he'd had a couple of heart attacks beforehand but just didn't tell anyone." He nodded to Helen's pack of Lucky Strikes lying nearby. "And he was a heavy smoker. That's probably what tipped him over."

She finished her scrambled eggs, letting the remark pass. "We'd better hurry. We're seeing Dr. Raduga at nine o'clock sharp."

"Funny thing. He knew all about you."

She rose. "Who?"

"The admiral. He knew all about your adventures on the Jap barge and your love affair with Lieutenant Commander Katsumi Fujimoto."

"Todd, I didn't--"

He raised a hand. "Sorry. Bad joke. What he knew about was all the torpedo stuff you turned over to BuOrd. He said it knocked them on their butts." He patted her arm. "Congratulations. Seriously. Maybe it's time to take off the wraps. You really should have a medal."

She growled, "How about you? Isn't there talk about a third Navy Cross?"

"I need that like a hole in the head."

"You owe it to them," she said. "All those people who supported you."

"Nonsense."

"Look, Todd. You've been skating on the edge of valor for so long. It's time you stepped up and let people be proud."

"I still think *you* should have the medal."

She checked her watch. "One of these days I may get through to you. But now it's time to hip-hop."

"You think we have time for a quickie before we go?"

"Whaaat?" She jumped up.

"Well, can't blame me for asking."

"Mrs. Peabody is due here any minute, and we have to be dressed."

"Just five minutes?" he grinned.

"Is that all you think about?"

"Frankly, yes."

She threw a slab of toast at him and walked out.

They sipped coffee in a booth at Pete's Drive-in on Gaffey Street, Ingram and Helen on one side and Dr. Raduga sitting opposite. The Friday morning traffic had unsnarled, and the place was quiet. The welders, riggers, machinists, pipefitters, and white-collar workers from Todd Shipyard were over there completing two destroyers, the last of their war production order.

Raduga wore a leather jacket over tan slacks, a white shirt with a bowtie, and shoes that needed a shine. His goatee was neatly trimmed, and his slicked-back hair was pomaded. He reminded Ingram of a Hollywood matinee star.

Helen clanked her spoon on her coffee cup, stirring constantly. Finally, she pulled a Lucky from its pack, lit it, and inhaled.

Ingram and Raduga traded glances. *She's nervous, and she knows we know.* Ingram reached under the table for her hand. She grabbed it and held on. Raduga and Helen had already met twice for psychotherapy after hours at the infirmary before Ingram returned home. She had expected immediate results, but so far, she couldn't see any progress.

Ingram drummed his fingers. *I'm nervous too. Why in the hell is that?*

Dr. Raduga said, "Helen, you can relax. I'm not going to bite you. The whole idea is to help you get rid of these nightmares and the depression, remember?"

She countered, "Depression? I'm not depressed anymore. Todd's home. Everything's fine."

Raduga nodded. "Oh? If that's the case, then maybe I should leave."

"No, no, that's not what I meant," she said quickly. "I . . . I still dream."

"Ummm."

"And . . . under the bed."

"Okay." Raduga looked at a shrugging Ingram. He said, "This isn't going to happen overnight."

She turned on him, her eyes flashing, "It has to. I have a husband and a son to take care of."

Raduga asked, "Have you started your medication yet?"

"The phenobarbital?"

"I believe that's what I prescribed, yes."

"Well, it's the dosage."

"What about it? It's a light dosage."

"Only at night, it says."

"That's so you can be active during the day."

She looked aside, "Well, that's just the thing. I need to be . . . active at night too." Her face flashed with a bit of pink.

There was a prolonged silence. Raduga blinked twice and then he got it. "Delay it for a week and then resume it. Is that all right?" He pointedly looked at both. "Believe me; this will help you a lot. You'll sleep like a log."

"That's what I'm afraid of," grinned Ingram.

She threw an elbow in his ribs.

"Is twice a week, Tuesday and Thursday, still all right with you? Say, six o'clock?" He dropped some change on the table and started to get up.

"Yes."

"Good. Just for an hour. And I've cleared you to come back to work anytime you wish. Not in the psychiatric ward though. You'll be working in surgery."

"Sounds good. I've had some experience there."

Raduga thrust a hand across the table. "I've enjoyed meeting you, Commander. Welcome back. Or maybe I should ask how long are you back?"

They shook hands. Ingram said, "Last I heard, my ship is heading back soon to Hawaii, convoying a slow train of troop ships. I'll meet her there for the rest of the trip." He looked at Helen. "I have another week or so here."

"Okay." She put her hand on top of his.

"Well, then . . ." Raduga started to slide out. "If that's all, I'll . . ."

Ingram said, "Dr. Raduga. I may need your services too."

He stopped. "Oh?"

"Todd?" Helen asked.

Ingram said, "You see, I used to have these nightmares too. I was on Corregidor with Helen. That's where we met. And I saw those poor chopped-up people, some bound to their stretchers in the main tunnel when artillery shells blasted at the entrance, sending dust and smoke all the way through. Some of those guys were so covered with dirt you couldn't tell if they were alive. And they . . ."

"Shhh, baby," said Helen.

He turned to her, "Why am I saying all this?"

Raduga said, "I'm not surprised. So many are in the same situation. And neither of you is a coward. It's just that humans can only take so much."

Ingram tried to stop himself but couldn't. "And then Guadalcanal. We stood toe-to-toe with the Japs. We tangled with a Jap battleship. You know what the inside of a 5-inch mount looks like after a 14-inch round goes through it? You're lucky if you find a jawbone or a bent belt buckle. The rest of the mount looks like hamburger all stuck to machinery. Twelve guys snuffed out," he snapped his fingers, "just like that, to say nothing of the ship on fire and the upper decks littered with dead and dying. Broken men with scalded faces crying for their mothers . . ."

Helen leaned into him. "Todd, honey."

He turned to her. "Did you know Ollie saved my life more than once?"

"You sort of implied it."

"We hated him on Corregidor. He got scared during a Jap air attack and froze up when his shipmates were in trouble. Two of my men died. Not really his fault, but it looked like it. Maybe he could have done something, maybe not. But everybody wanted to kill him, and he let them feel that way. They literally threw him off the dock and into the 51 Boat when we shoved off from Caballo. Everybody ignored him, even me.

"But then I got chickenitis too. There were a couple of times when I froze on the trigger. Once on Marinduque and once when we rescued you. I froze at the trigger. But Ollie was right there backing me up, killing people who were trying to kill me. He saved my life more than once because I became a coward. I really shouldn't be here."

"I . . . didn't know that."

He took a deep breath and looked squarely at Raduga. "This is the first time I've talked about this. And I really didn't mean to. It just came out."

"It's okay, Todd. That's why we're here," said Raduga.

Helen ran a hand through his hair. "You should have said something, Todd. I've been making this all about me."

"Couldn't. Big . . . tough . . . guy."

"Todd."

"I'm yellow." He clinched his fists. "Yellow with two Navy Crosses I don't deserve."

"Todd, come on."

He took a deep breath. "Weeeow. Can you believe this? Shooting off my mouth. I'm sorry." He looked up. "But I think I've beaten it. The belladonna and a caring wife got me through this."

Raduga said, "So, you're okay for now?"

"I'll tell you. Coming home to Helen and not getting shot at helps a lot."

"Oftentimes that's all it takes. But if the nightmares continue, why don't you go to the Terminal Island Naval Hospital. I'm Army, remember?"

"That's a career killer. Someone finds out I'm seeing a shrink and they close the record. Period. I'll get drummed out. This has to be off the record."

"Tell you what, Todd. Let's have coffee again next Friday and we'll talk some more. See how you're doing. But I can't make any promises, especially with the off-the-record stuff. That wouldn't be ethical."

"Pardon?"

"You're Navy, I'm Army, and that's okay. But still, I'm trained and certified to comment and make recommendations on your fitness for duty. I'd be derelict if I found you unfit and didn't do something about it."

"Oh."

"What I can say is that I can keep this off the record unless something is seriously wrong, which in my humble opinion is not the case."

Now it was Ingram's turn to stir coffee. "Fair enough."

33

10 September 1945
Pacific Fleet Headquarters, Voyenno Morskoy Flot
Vladivostok, USSR

Many visitors to Vladivostok, a city of high, rolling hills and sweeping vistas, have compared it to San Francisco. The summer fog that obscured Captain Third Rank Eduard Dezhnev's vision made the comparison even more apt. He couldn't see ten feet ahead as he stepped from the Jeep and hobbled up the steps of the faux-colonial building overlooking Vladivostok harbor. He found it even more difficult to open the front door.

Dezhnev dreaded this meeting with Captain First Rank Gennady Kulibin, commanding officer of the NKVD's special naval forces for the Pacific region, and his CO. Although Kulibin was the son of a Politburo member, he was more of a soldier than a politician, and that gave Dezhnev cause for concern. Kulibin had always been fair, but Dezhnev had no idea what to expect from the sudden summons. This was their first meeting since his disastrous visit to the USS *Missouri* a week ago. For all Dezhnev knew, his body could soon be sailing into a mass grave to join the corpses of the thousands of Japanese and pro–Chiang Kai-shek supporters the Soviets had captured in the last few weeks.

A barrel-chested leading seaman with close-cropped hair sat at a desk in the lobby. Dezhnev expected the man to be half asleep. With the war over, a relaxed atmosphere had fallen over Vladivostok--as it had all over Russia. But not here. This man was on his toes. A thick scar running from his right ear to the top of his eyebrow told the story. *Combat proven. No one to trifle with.*

Dezhnev handed over his ID. The man examined it, checked the photograph, looked Dezhnev up and down, and then handed it back. He picked up a journal and checked a date, saying, "Captain Kulibin is expecting you. Top floor, room 402." He nodded to a flight of stairs.

Dezhnev groaned. It would take forever to negotiate all those steps. "Very well." He pocketed his ID and limped toward the stairs.

"Sir!" The man stood and walked over. "Perhaps you could follow me?"

"What for?"

"There is a VIP elevator." He whistled for an aide to take over, then led Dezhnev down the hall. Taking a key from his pocket he opened a door, revealing an ornate elevator cage large enough for two people. "Perhaps this will be better?" he said studying Dezhnev's campaign ribbons.

"Much better."

The elevator ground and clanked its way to the fourth floor. The leading seaman opened the cage with a nod. "Just push the buzzer on the call panel when you're ready, sir, and I'll come and get you."

"I can make it down all right. Thanks." Dezhnev stepped out and made his way to room 402. He knocked.

"Enter," a voice rumbled.

Dezhnev walked in. "Captain Third Rank Eduard Dezhnev reporting, sir."

The office was small, with a couch on one wall, a bookcase on the other, and books and papers stacked on every horizontal surface. Dirty windows and the fog blocked what would otherwise have been a glorious view of Vladivostok. Captain First Rank Gennady Kulibin sat precariously in a tilted-back chair, his feet propped on a heavily chipped ornate wooden desk that looked as if it might once have belonged to Czar Nicholas II. His tunic hung on a coat rack, and his sleeves were rolled up. "Ahhh, Dezhnev. Come in, come in." He beckoned and lay down a sheaf of papers.

Dezhnev walked in and stood at parade rest.

"Comrade, you are not here to be pilloried, I assure you. Please sit."

Dezhnev sat stiffly.

"Relax, damn it." Kulibin's feet were still up, leaning him back at an impossible angle; his hands were laced behind his bald head. He didn't weigh a lot, no more than 175 pounds on a 5-foot 10-inch frame; otherwise, Dezhnev was sure, the chair would have given way beneath him. A neatly trimmed full beard offset Kulibin's baldness and emphasized his bushy black eyebrows and impenetrable dark eyes. A large black mole protruding from his left cheek made Dezhnev wonder if he picked at it.

Kulibin waved to the fog outside the window. "This weather is for the shits. Can't see a thing. Was it like this in San Francisco?"

"Worse." Dezhnev did his best to look at ease while certain that an operative stood behind him ready to shove a pistol behind his ear and pull the trigger. With great difficulty he suppressed an impulse to turn around and look.

Kulibin repeated himself. "It's all right, comrade. Please." He waved a hand toward an electric coffee pot.

Dezhnev sniffed. The coffee smelled wonderful. "No thank you, Captain. I just had breakfast."

Kulibin dropped his feet to the floor, hitting it with a great thump. His chair rotated forward. "Well, I need a refill, damn it." He rose and walked over to the coffee service and poured a cup. He looked over his shoulder, waving the carafe in the air. "You sure?"

"No thank you, Captain. It keys me up."

Kulibin shrugged, finished pouring, and returned to his desk, again propping up his feet. "Say, you want two tickets to the opera tonight?"

"What's playing?"

"American stuff. *Showboat.*"

Dezhnev knew every song, every line, in *Showboat* by heart. His trainers at Bykovo had shown the film time and time again, immersing their students in American music and films. "Better not. I have an early morning tomorrow."

"Front-row seats. Not a box, but front row."

"I'd really like to but . . ."

"If it's a matter of a date, I could fix you up with Lyudmila, one of our radio girls on the second floor. She's really a hot one and she knows music. Her . . . rhythm is exceptional, if you know what I mean." He winked.

"No, sir. I really appreciate it, but I'd better not."

"Suit yourself." Kulibin raised his mug and sipped, looking over the brim at Dezhnev. "How did your photos turn out?"

"Some didn't."

"Oh?"

Dezhnev knew he was on safe ground at this point. Kulibin would have known about the photographic blunder because Dezhnev had already sent the other roll ahead in the diplomatic pouch along with an explanation of the incident.

He's pulling me through a knothole and wants to see me wiggle. Nevertheless, Dezhnev explained everything in detail, including how Ingram's friends exposed one of his best rolls of film.

Kulibin waved a hand. "We have other photos and intelligence. Don't worry about that."

Dezhnev sat back, an alarm going off in his head. There was something in Kulibin's tone. What else was there to worry about? Sakhalin? As instructed, Dezhnev had allowed the Americans to escape. He could have easily shot them down. So, it can't be about that. *Then why the hell am I here?*

Kulibin sipped his coffee and looked around his cluttered office. Then he said quietly, "This is, ahhh, very sensitive. I had the room swept just this morning."

Swept? What the hell is going on? Again, Dezhnev was bolt upright.

"Yes, look, it's about--all right. I was in Moscow two months ago."

"I recall."

Kulibin was fidgeting. "I didn't tell you this. Your mother was there. It was an opening night."

"What?" His mother had written recently that with victory in the Great Patriotic War, there was a stampede to make movies about beating the Nazis. Although not a young woman by any stretch of the imagination, Anoushka Dezhnev at forty-nine was still beautiful and in demand for mature roles. She had just finished eight weeks of shooting for *Challenge of Darkness*, about the siege of Stalingrad. She'd played the tragic Nikka, wife of a Soviet artillery colonel killed in the final days of the siege.

"Eduard, please. Sit."

Dezhnev didn't realize that he had jumped to his feet. He sat.

"Anyway. There was a party later, and we met and we . . ."

"I see." He knew Anoushka had occasionally seen other men since the death of his father, Vadim Dezhnev, four years ago. But as far as Dezhnev knew she hadn't really been interested in any of them.

"Well, as I said, we met at the party and . . . well . . ."

"I get it."

"Nothing serious, you know."

"Nothing serious."

"Well . . ."

The silence shouted at them. The obviously embarrassed Kulibin was having difficulty. But Dezhnev figured his superior officer didn't need his permission to date Anoushka. His mother was an unmarried woman, a widow among many thousands, and there was a war on. Until now.

Dezhnev kept quiet.

At length Kulibin said, "Something has come up."

"Sir?"

"Beria was at the same party."

"Shit!" said Dezhnev. His heart froze in his chest and the blood drained from his head. Lavrenti Beria was commissar of state security under Generalissimo Josef Stalin and the head of Nardonyi Kommissariat Vnutrennikh del--the NKVD. Beria was the second most powerful man in the Soviet Union. Over the past two decades he had ordered the deaths of millions, including many military officers.

"Take it easy," Kulibin said. "He tried to take her home after the movie ended, but she put him off. Later, at the stage door, he had a couple of goons try to pull her into his car. The word is that she fought them off, screaming, and then escaped when a crowd gathered. Beria was embarrassed and furious and tried to cancel subsequent showings of *Challenge of*

Darkness. But it was such a great success that night that he couldn't bring it off."

Dezhnev ran a hand over his face. Beria's image had appeared less frequently in official photos recently. Especially after word leaked that he often plied the streets of Moscow at night, driving his big armored Packard and pointing out young women he wanted his thugs to abduct. And the goons did it, bringing the helpless women to Beria's soundproof office in Dzerzhinsky Square, where he raped them. Most of the time, the women were turned back to the goons to be released into the streets under the threat of death if anything was reported.

Dezhnev looked up. "Recriminations?"

"As far as I can tell, none. But as extra insurance I had her flown back to Sochi the next day. She is at home now with guards posted."

Sochi was his hometown on the Black Sea. He grew up there. The Dezhnevs had many friends in Sochi. "Guards? Our people?"

"Yes. Don't worry. Nothing obvious. Beria's idiots won't get past if they try."

"That's very kind of you." Dezhnev meant it. "Is there anything I can do?"

"No, not really. I thought you should know about this in light of what I'm about to say to you. The reason for this meeting."

"Sir?"

"Are you sure you don't want coffee?"

"I think I will have some after all, thank you."

Kulibin again thumped his chair down, rose, and walked to the coffee pot. "Strange that we inherited the coffee habit from the Americans. I wonder what else will change."

Wouldn't Lavrenti Beria love to hear Comrade Kulibin say that?

Kulibin handed Dezhnev a mug, then sat and reassumed his tilted-back position. "Big changes are afoot, Dezhnev. Sometime soon, all the commissariats are going to be renamed ministries. The NKVD will become the Ministry of Internal Affairs, or MVD."

"Amazing."

"And they're calling the Ministry of State Security the MGB."

Dezhnev nodded.

"Our friend Lavrenti Beria will be in charge of both."

"Comrade, I--"

"Don't worry, Dezhnev. I'm not interested in politics or coups or breaches of security. I've had enough of wars and fighting and killing. I just want to live a simple life. And I think I know where and how." He looked up.

Dezhnev didn't know what to do. He couldn't help it if Kulibin had fallen for his mother. He shrugged. "That sounds fine with me."

"Yes. I learned yesterday that I am going to be promoted to rear admiral."

"Congratulations, sir."

"But there is an interim assignment." Kulibin steepled his fingers.

Dezhnev waited for a moment, then asked, "What is that, sir?"

"They're giving me a cruiser--the *Admiral Volshkov*, a war prize from the Germans. Previously she was the *Würtzburg*, 5,400 tons. She just arrived, but her skipper took sick. So, I'm on top of the heap now." He laughed, then took a bottle of vodka from a drawer and poured a dollop into his coffee. He waved the bottle.

"No thank you, sir."

"But as I say, it's only interim. When the new replacement skipper arrives, I will be posted to the Black Sea Fleet."

"I see." Black Sea. Sochi. Anoushka. It was all falling into place for Kulibin.

"You, on the other hand, have a career to pursue."

"I'm not so sure now."

"You distinguished yourself with the e-boats. You are Bykovo trained. You did well on Sakhalin."

"But San Francisco . . ."

"Idiots sent you there. Your handler, Zenit, was a dolt. All political training and no military sense at all. No, your record in San Francisco is clear. You did what you were told to do."

That was true. But he hadn't liked betraying his friend Ingram.

"Drink your coffee."

"Yes, sir." Dezhnev sipped. There was a familiar zip to it.

"Yes?"

"It's very good, sir. Thank you."

"It's American: Folgers."

"I thought so. A company based in San Francisco."

"I didn't know that."

"When I was there, Folgers was all we drank. Founded in 1850, I believe."

"Your Bykovo training shines through." Kulibin leveled a gaze. "We need to put you on another path. One that utilizes all your skills and one you will enjoy." He paused. "We are sending you to specialized training. Submarines."

"Sir, as much as I'd like to do that, my foot won't support the physical requirements."

"We're going to change that."

"Pardon me?"

"If Sergei Zenit was a dolt, the doctors who fitted your prosthesis were worse, far worse."

"I couldn't agree with you more."

"We're sending you to America. Under cover, of course. We have a specialist there who can give you a prosthesis that will make your leg like new. Then you can go on to submarine school."

"Where in America?"

"Los Angeles. Your old friend Colin Blinde will be your contact."

"Blinde. Is he in the game for real?"

Kulibin laced his hands over his belly. "As of two months ago. He has given us enough material now that he's in too deep. And he knows it."

"But why? An American rich kid."

"Not so rich. His family owned copper and tungsten mines in Mongolia, of all places--in Dornogovi Province."

Dezhnev gave Kulibin a blank look.

"Right. Dornogovi Province abuts the Chinese border in the south. Communist forces under Mao Tse-tung took some of the land in a border skirmish back in the 1930s; they scooped up the Blinde mines along with a number of other American- and British-owned mining operations. The Blindes' income was cut off. Colin's father is basically penniless. He inherited a fortune from *his* father and did nothing except take profits, build a house on Long Island in a rich place called the Hamptons, and get fat. But the mines are gone, the Hamptons house is gone, and the Blindes live in New York City off a small estate inherited by Colin's mother. It took everything they had to send young Colin to Yale. But he graduated a fiery thinker, and we found him before the OSS did. So far, he has been doing a pretty good job.

"Okay, so I'll be working with Colin Blinde."

"Yes, and we have another task for him as well."

"Yes?"

"Kill Todd Ingram."

34

17 September 1945
Union Station, Los Angeles, California

Roiling clouds hung low over Union Station. The thermometer had hit 101 in the early afternoon, and although it had dropped to 97 by 4:55 p.m., the temperature seemed no cooler to Colin Blinde. An oppressive humidity strangled the mission-style building, and an eerie electricity in the air was unsettling to Blinde as he awaited his contact. *This must be what they call earthquake weather.*

Completed in 1939, Union Station was one of the most modern on the nationwide passenger rail system. Outside were courtyards with lush tropical plants and trees. Broad green lawns surrounded tiled fountains accented by flowerbeds. The grand waiting room inside had Spanish tile floors and a beamed ceiling invited the senses of old California and mission life. Plush back-to-back seats and benches were comfortably arranged throughout.

Blinde scanned left and right, but his man was nowhere in sight. *The damned fool is ten minutes late.*

Blinde had begun to rise when a voice jabbed at him from the bench directly behind. "No need to get up, Comrade. I'm here."

"Wha-what?" Blinde stammered, "How the hell--"

"It's my trade. I've been watching you for ten minutes. You are as you should be: alone. Nobody watching. Now, please sit."

Blinde resumed his seat, his back once again inches from that of the man behind him.

"Where are we, Mr. Blinde?"

Blinde shot back, "Union Station, Los Angeles, California."

"Very funny. Where is the doctor, and what are the arrangements?"

"You are booked into the Los Angeles Orthopedic Hospital under the name Brent Wilson. Your doctor is Walter Sorella, an orthopedic surgeon who is highly acclaimed by the AMA."

"AMA?"

"American Medical Association. Among other things, they validate doctors, clinics, hospitals, and medical procedures." Blinde couldn't resist a dig. "Didn't they tell you about the AMA at Bykovo?"

There was a long silence. "From popcorn to apple pie, I learned a lot at Bykovo. But then we had this little skirmish with the Germans that had to be settled first. So, they cut my studies short, leaving out tidbits about the AMA. What else?"

"Your preparation is scheduled to begin tomorrow. Fittings begin day after tomorrow, Wednesday."

"Very good. And my clothes?"

"In the suitcase next to you."

The locks snapped open and Dezhnev rummaged through the suitcase. "All right. That should do. But where is the money?"

"Sewn into the liner in the top."

"Very good. Now, about this Doctor . . . Doctor . . ."

"Sorella. He helps us from time to time. He examined your x-rays and tells us he can fix things with a new prosthetic that will give you almost normal mobility. You'll be able to walk at a very fast pace, even run, after you strengthen your leg muscles."

Dezhnev exhaled. "Yes, I do believe there is some atrophy there. I expect he can recommend a regimen."

"He will, if you cooperate."

"Yes. I . . . I need this badly."

"Don't worry. Dr. Sorella is one of the best in the nation. He'll have you walking like an Olympian. In ten days you'll be on your way back to Vancouver and Mother Russia.

"The *Rodina*."

"Whatever."

"Don't trifle with me, Mr. Blinde."

"Sorry. Look . . . there's an envelope in the suitcase with directions to Los Angeles Orthopedic Hospital and some expense money. You can best reach the hospital by walking out that entrance and hailing a cab."

"How far is it?"

"About five miles directly south. You can't miss it, just east of Figueroa Street on Flower."

"Pardon?"

"Just tell the cab driver. He'll understand."

"All right. A thorough job. Thank you. Tell me. Todd Ingram lives around here, doesn't he?"

"Well, in San Pedro actually. In Los Angeles Harbor, about thirty miles south of here."

"I see."

Five soldiers walked by singing, duffels slung over their shoulders. One sounded drunk.

Blinde said, "You're not thinking of going down there?"

Dezhnev cracked his knuckles. "I would love to see him again."

"Because if you do and get caught, it would look bad for us all, especially for me and my department. Besides that . . ."

"Yes?"

"I have orders to kill him."

"You do?" Dezhnev was surprised. He hadn't passed on Kulibin's order. And now, someone had gone around him. "How did--?"

"They came to me separately. They're afraid Boring talked to him, which he did."

"But you have the pictures and the diaries?"

Blinde sighed. "Yes. It's not that. If someone intractable like Ingram lets on about the decision to hide the discovery, it would be a great embarrass-ment to the United States and the Soviet Union if it gets out that you are trying to steal it or may already have it."

"Let me see if I have this right," said Dezhnev. "You say Ingram knows everything?"

"Yes, it's like I said. Boring spilled the beans to Ingram. Everything."

Dezhnev changed the tack with, "B-E-A-N-S; that's straight from Bykovo. How do I sound?"

"Like Leo Gorcey."

"Who?"

"A movie star who plays dead-end thugs."

"Gangsters?"

"You should have learned about him at Bykovo. Everybody knows about Leo Gorcey and the Bowery Boys."

"So, a gangster."

"Sort of a good-guy gangster. But yes. It would be embarrassing if Ingram spilled the beans. Embarrassing to both of us."

"What if he doesn't know?"

Blinde said, "He does. After leaving Sakhalin, we had an inquiry at Okinawa. He told us he knew. He even signed a statement."

"Well, if he knows, then everybody else does."

"Only at the highest levels. And they're shutting up. Why didn't you kill him at Toro? You had the chance."

"You would have died in the crash as well."

"I would have expected to have been taken off the plane if you were going to do it."

"Easier said than done. So, I had them shoot wide. I honestly thought the damned plane was going to crash into those half-tracks."

"We were lucky." Blinde ran a finger around his collar as he recalled Radcliff and his hotshot takeoff.

"Plus, we needed instructions from Dzerzhinsky Square."

That meant Beria, their ultimate boss. In spite of the heat and humidity Blinde felt a cold draft. "Well, we now have instructions."

"Indeed." Dezhnev said, "But don't forget that Ingram is almost a national hero. He has two Navy Crosses along with many other decorations. We're taking a big chance. How do you plan to do it?"

"They're sending an asset."

"Who?"

"I don't know yet."

"You'll let me know?"

No answer.

"Mr. Blinde?"

"Yes, all right. I'll let you know."

"Don't be too long." Dezhnev paused. "Rain is coming? A thunderstorm?"

"This is Southern California."

"Meaning?"

"Unlike San Francisco, it's not cold and you don't need an umbrella. Just a roof to duck under for a few minutes until the rain stops."

Dezhnev sighed. "I think I see. Now, speaking of Leo Gorcey, do any movie stars live near the Orthopedic Hospital?"

35

17 September 1945
1627 South Alma Street
San Pedro, California

For days it had been getting hotter and hotter. The air was still and moist, the temperature and humidity tied in a dead heat, with hardly any of the breeze that usually characterized San Pedro's "Hurricane Gulch." The inversion layer rose to 5,000 feet and contained the heat over Southern California like a cap on a giant bottle. Finally, late in the afternoon, a cold front sneaked in from the Gulf of Alaska, defying the predictions of local weather forecasters for a balmy evening perfect for outdoor barbeques. By early evening the cold front had cascaded over the warm air below, causing the unstable warm air mass to rise rapidly, topping out at 31,000 feet in the shape of an enormous anvil cloud nearly 22 miles in diameter and centered roughly over the western end of Santa Catalina Island. Traveling east at a lateral rate of 27 knots, the anvil cloud made landfall at about 8:30 p.m. over San Pedro and marched inland, uncharacteristically building speed as it went. By that time the warm air had reached its dew point and began to freeze into ice particles. The particles fell and eventually melted into rain, generating a large electrically charged downdraft that spilled onto the earth below, yielding lightning and thunder. With the downdraft came first hail and then large droplets of rain.

They ate in the backyard with thunder rumbling in the distance. Ingram had barbecued burgers, and Mrs. Peabody contributed cold bottles of her dark, rich, foamy beer. Helen drank only half of hers, but Ingram and Mrs. Peabody quaffed every drop of theirs, Ingram smacking his lips and saying, "Wow, this stuff has a kick to it, Emma. How do you do it?"

Mrs. Peabody cooed evasively as they ate the last of their burgers. Ingram had just finished his last bite when wind rustled the leaves.

Helen said, "Wind's up. What do you think, Emma?"

"Weatherman said nice evening for a walk. You up for it, Todd?"

Ingram looked up, seeing blacks and grays roiling above. "Normally I'd say yes, but this time it looks like the weatherman is off his rocker. I think we should go inside."

"I think you're right." Helen stood and lifted Jerry from his high chair. "Besides, he needs changing." She nodded at the table. "Do you mind clearing?"

"I'll get it. Don't worry," said Ingram. The low rumbling over the Santa Catalina Channel brought dark memories of the Japanese shellfire he had endured on Corregidor, and later from the Imperial Japanese Navy in the Solomons.

Helen looked at him.

She feels it, too. She got it far worse on Corregidor. "It's okay," said Ingram. "Go on in." He prodded her in the back.

Thunder rumbled again. This time the sky flashed at the horizon. Leaves fluttered past as the wind grew stronger.

Mrs. Peabody said, "Brrrr. What a chill! I think you're right, sweetheart. Time for me to head for my basement and tend to my stock of . . . vitamins." She gathered up her beer bottles, mayonnaise, and half a head of lettuce in a large paper sack and turned to leave. "See you later, kids. Thanks for everything."

"Welcome," Helen called after her. She looked at her husband. "Shake a leg." Her ponytail bounced as she walked into the house, the baby cradled in her arms.

The wind freshened. Ingram packed condiments and silverware into a paper bag as a lightning bolt sizzled on the horizon. He checked to make sure Helen and Jerry were safe inside and then bent to finish up.

As he stooped to gather the checkered tablecloth the wind surged against him, tearing at his clothes and hair. Grabbing the tablecloth and bag, he raced toward the house, reaching it just as the rain hit--first in little drops and then, by the time he swung open the door, in large globs that felt like gelatin. He had barely put the bag and cloth on the kitchen counter when a bolt of lightning lit up the house; it was followed instantly by a loud clap of thunder. With it came a distinctive odor. *Ozone.*

Rain hammered on the roof, the noise almost deafening. Water dripped over the stove, the same place it always dripped. He mentally kicked himself for not fixing it.

Flash--boom! The house shook. Dishes rattled, and a cabinet door over the stove slowly swung open as if pushed by an unseen ghoul.

"You okay?" he called out.

Lightning struck again, the thunder almost simultaneous. The lights went out. He looked out the window and saw only blackness. The whole neighborhood was without lights. *Transformer. At least a couple hours to fix.*

With the next thunderclap the house shook harder. Helen screamed.

Ingram dashed through the house. "Helen? Helen!"

By the light of another lightning bolt he saw her clutching Jerry in the middle of the bedroom. Then she fell to her knees and began crawling for the bed, bending low to duck under it, Jerry still in her arms.

"It's okay," he yelled over the pounding rain.

Another bolt of lightning brought another scream from Helen. He had never heard anything like that sound. Even in combat nobody had yelled like that.

The storm raged overhead as he sat on the floor and leaned against the bed, pulling Helen and Jerry to him. Helen was shaking and crying, and he hugged them close, remembering how cool 1st Lt. Helen Duran had been during those final days on Corregidor in April 1942. Three miles to the north, the Japanese on Bataan were pounding the island with artillery, softening it up for the amphibious attack that came in early May. Every minute, day and night, they fired on Corregidor. Shells shook the Rock steadily, often blowing dust and debris through the Malinta Tunnel and its laterals. Light fixtures swayed, but Helen was always composed, compassionate, and professional, doing her job amid the groans and crying of the wounded and dying. Much of the time they were without anesthesia, and Helen had to comfort her patients, Filipino and American alike, as doctors sawed away at gangrenous limbs.

But now, Helen--cool, competent Helen--was terrified. The baby was crying too, but he didn't seem as scared as Helen. Just crying. Ingram wrapped his arms around them as another bolt danced outside, hitting an oak tree. He thought he heard it split as thunder cracked overhead.

Helen clutched him desperately as the next bolt struck. He wished he hadn't seen her face: a mask of torture, and of fright and anguish. Her breathing was rapid, and her heartbeat was quick. Worst of all, the intense flash made her hair look as if it had turned entirely white. He kissed her hair. "It's okay, I'm here. I love you. I'll keep you safe."

"Wha . . . wha?"

"I'm, here, honey. I love you."

"Uhhh." She tightened her grip. Another bolt brought another scream, and she buried her face in his neck. Between them was Jerry, his arms around his father's neck.

Carefully, Ingram reached up and dragged a blanket down from the bed. With gentle maneuvering he managed to get it around all three of them as the storm cracked and shredded the skies.

Finally, the storm became less and less intense. Lightning still ripped and roared above, but gradually it faded to the southeast as the storm headed for the San Bernardino Mountains. Helen fell into an uneasy slumber. Jerry slept peacefully. Ingram breathed easier as they relaxed while the storm pounded in the distance. He kicked off his shoes and braced himself to his feet, lifting them into the bed with him. He found Helen's cigarette lighter and flicked it on. Jerry was tucked under his left arm and slept the quiet and dearly innocent slumber of the child, his little chest barely moving. Helen was gathered in his right arm, her face now glowing like alabaster, her features gloriously crafted, her magnificent hair again ebony. Her mouth was slightly open. She was entirely at peace. She looked ten years younger than she had half an hour ago, almost as if she'd just stepped out of her high school yearbook.

Ingram watched her for a long time, a smile on his face. Then he gave thanks. Half an hour more of soft rain put them all solidly asleep.

At 4:30 the next morning the power came back on and lights flicked on in the living room and the kitchen. But the bedroom remained dark. They didn't awaken until 7:25, a bright sun announcing a new day with crisp blue skies.

36

Six crossed swords formed an archway outside the Church of the Good Shepherd. At the head of the detail was Jerry Landa's best man, Cdr. Todd Ingram. Across from Ingram was Rear Adm. Theodore R. "Rocko" Myszynski, commander, Destroyer Forces, Pacific Area. Standing beside Ingram was Cdr. Oliver P. Toliver III, an old friend stemming back to their Corregidor days, now with the Office of Naval Intelligence. Flashing his sword across from Toliver was Cdr. Howard Endicott, commodore of Destroyer Division 77.2. Beside Endicott was Lt. Cdr. Eldon P. White, recently appointed permanent commanding officer of the USS *Maxwell*, to Landa's apparent chagrin.

Across from White was Lt. Walter M. Tothe, the bug-eyed operations officer of DESRON 77 and Landa's personal punching bag. Tothe, a ninety-day wonder, had made the mistake of saying he knew the drill for crossed swords. Their practice in the parking lot, however, looked more like a Keystone Cops short than a proper crossed-swords ceremony.

At that point GySgt. Ulysses Gaylord Harper, resplendent in his Marine Corps dress blues, stepped up and bellowed, "Gentlemen! If you'll allow me?" In less than five minutes Harper had the bemedaled sextet drawing their swords smartly and crossing them with precision at a 45-degree angle. When Harper was satisfied, Myszynski exhaled loudly and said, "Looks like we'll be okay as long as we don't stab each other."

The sword detail, beautifully turned out in dress whites, slipped out of the wedding mass five minutes early to be ready when the newly joined Captain and Mrs. Jerome Landa burst through the Church of the Good Shepherd's double doors. The crowd poured out behind and cheered as the Landas passed through the glittering ceremonial arch on their way to a midnight blue 1939 Brunn body Packard cabriolet parked on Santa Monica Boulevard. Their job complete, the detail returned their swords to their scabbards with precision and remained at attention.

Radioman First Class Leo Pirelli stood at attention at the Packard's rear door. The cheering crowd pressed in, showering the bride and groom with rice as they eased through the throng.

"Hut," snapped Harper.

Pirelli yanked open the Packard's door and, with the panache of a vaudeville actor, bowed, whipped off his white hat, and waved them inside. Dark looks caromed amongst the sword detail. Ingram and Harper slapped hands over their eyes.

Tubby White said conversationally, "Last one in's a rotten egg."

Pirelli slammed the door closed and snapped to attention. The car started and the crowd roared as the Packard pulled away, with Landa clearly visible in the rear window kissing his wife.

At the behest of Maestro Arturo Toscanini, Roberta Thatcher, the business manager of the NBC Symphony Orchestra, had been placed in charge of the Landa-West wedding arrangements. Among other things she had arranged for the rental of the Packard, along with the driver, five-foot two-inch Augusto de la Torre, scion of an Argentine road-racing family and now a leading stunt man at Twentieth Century–Fox.

De la Torre pulled the Packard smartly away from the curb as the bride and groom were locked in an embrace in the backseat. The diminutive driver was barely visible above the windscreen of the enormous car, even though he was perched on a thick Los Angeles white pages phone directory. Hunched behind wheel of the enormous Packard, Augusto was supposed to tell his passengers about the champagne in a bucket on the floor, but the two ignored him as they embraced, the only sound the rustling of her off-white satin gown.

"Hell with it," muttered Augusto. He punched the button and raised the privacy window between the driver and the main compartment. Then he goosed the Packard's throttle, tooted his horn, and waved. Immediately, four Beverly Hills Police motorcycle officers roared into place before the Packard with wailing sirens and flashing red lights. Augusto hit the accelerator and popped the clutch, unleashing all 175 horses of the Packard's mighty V-12 engine. He roared up right behind the police, leaving behind a heavy cloud of blue smoke that drifted over the crowd and pitching Captain and Mrs. Landa against the backseat. The screeching sirens and red lights parted a path through the traffic on Santa Monica Boulevard for the Packard. A ragged wedding entourage followed, honking their horns and ignoring other cars and angry drivers shaking their fists.

Following the police, the cabriolet swooped right on North Roxbury Drive, its gears whining as Augusto stomped it, heading toward Carmelita Avenue. At forty miles an hour, Augusto downshifted and turned right on Carmelita, throwing his passengers across the seat against the left panel.

Landa yelled, "Hey!" But the window was up. Landa could barely see Augusto's head.

"It's all right, Jerry," Laura laughed. "Oh, look," she squealed, trying to distract him, "look at that house, just what we wanted."

Ignoring the two-story Mediterranean-style villa, Landa fumed, "I survived a war for this? Where's the damned . . ." he fumbled for the microphone. The Packard flew along Carmelita, madly downshifting for stop signs. De la Torre and his escort "rolled" each of the intersections, bottomed through dips, and jerked into second gear before slowing again. Suddenly Augusto shoved in the clutch and jazzed the throttle, the top of his head tilting toward the left.

"Shiiiiit. Hold on, honey." Landa grabbed Laura just as Augusto downshifted, braked, and cut left onto North Crescent Drive. Bride and groom ended up in a heap against the right side of the compartment as the cabriolet followed the motorcycles up magnolia-lined North Crescent, their sirens ripping at the sun-drenched Southern California afternoon.

At Sunset Boulevard the entourage jumped the red traffic signal and zipped over the equestrian path, ignoring riders who had been stopped by police five minutes earlier. With great panache, Augusto again downshifted to second gear and ascended the sweeping driveway of the Beverly Hills Hotel. With the skill of a jeweler cutting a twenty-carat diamond, Augusto de la Torre eased the Packard to a graceful halt at the hotel's entrance.

Landa tapped on the window.

It eased down.

Landa snarled, "Hey, pal."

Augusto turned with a bright smile. "Welcome to the Beverly Hills Hotel, Admiral. And congratulations to you both."

Landa said, "You ever decide to join the Navy I'll have you cleaning latrines and bilges."

"Oh, no, no, no, Admiral. I will drive your speedboats," he said, white teeth flashing in a smile to rival Landa's.

"PT boats," corrected Landa.

"Sí. PT boats. They are the same."

A uniformed doorman opened the car door and took Laura's hand. "Captain and Mrs. Landa, welcome to the Beverly Hills Hotel." She stepped out into an explosion of reporters and popping flashbulbs.

Landa drummed his fingers for a moment, then caught Augusto's eye. "I'll keep it in mind. From time to time, we do need good PT boat drivers."

"You make me U.S. citizen?"

"We can do that too." Landa got out.

Captain and Mrs. Landa stood at the head of a reception line before the double-door entrance to the Grand Ballroom. Laura looked beautiful in her off-white wedding dress; Landa countered with his glittering Pepsodent smile.

Invitations had gone out to four hundred people, and it seemed to Landa that all and perhaps more had shown up, including more than one hundred officers and men from the ships of DESRON 77, now moored in Long Beach. Both sets of parents were dead, so Maestro Toscanini had given away the bride at the wedding. Now, Toscanini had stationed himself beside Laura in the receiving line, introducing guests to her. Landa retaliated by posting Rocko Myszynski on Toscanini's left to introduce the U.S. Navy guests to him. The line began with Todd and Helen on Myszynski's left. Waiters carrying silver platters flitted along the reception line offering champagne and light hors d'oeuvres. Roberta Thatcher paced behind, checking her watch and keeping things moving with military precision.

Most of the guests had gone through the line when Helen turned to her husband and asked, "Can you believe all this schmaltz?"

"It's not over yet." Ingram nodded to a tall, distinguished-looking man with a mustache, waiting to take her hand.

"Hello." Helen gave a broad smile as the man took her hand and kissed it in grand European fashion. "Good afternoon, Mrs. Ingram. And welcome to my hotel."

Helen laughed. "Your hotel?" Her tone was "Ah, come on."

He clicked his heels and said, "Hernando Courtright at your service, madam." Again, he kissed her hand and looked deep into her eyes. "Please let me know if there is anything I can do to make this special event better for you." Then Courtright shook Ingram's hand. "You are most fortunate, Captain, to have such a beautiful wife."

"And you have a beautiful hotel, Mr. Courtright. Thanks for letting us be here."

Courtright bowed again. "It's the least I can do for our victorious sailors of the Pacific war. Thank you for all that you have done." Courtright moved on to shake Myszynski's hand.

Helen turned pale and mouthed, "I'm sorry."

Landa grinned.

The next three guests were friends of Toscanini's, their gathering a rarity. First was Dimitri Tiomkin and his wife, Rose. Tiomkin was a Ukrainian who had found his way to Hollywood in the 1920s. Laura whispered to Helen Ingram that Tiomkin was an up-and-coming musician who had written the scores for *Lost Horizon* and *The Bridge of San Louis Rey*.

After the Tiomkins came thirty-eight-year-old Miklós Rózsa, a Hungarian who had moved to the United States in the 1930s. Laura whispered behind the admiral's back to Helen that Rózsa had just scored the movies *Double Indemnity* and *Spellbound* using on the latter a revolutionary instrument called a theremin.

"A what?" whispered Helen.

"A theremin. You know, spooky music that makes your hair stand on end."

"Spooky?"

"Scares the daylights out of you."

"Oh." Helen wasn't sure she wanted to be scared that badly. But when she glanced again at Rózsa she saw embers in his dark eyes.

Ferde Grofé and his wife, Ruth, were next. Toscanini and the NBC Symphony Orchestra had just performed Grofé's *Grand Canyon Suite* in Carnegie Hall with Grofé in attendance. "I think MGM flew him out here to score a movie," Laura said to Helen, adding, "You know, the maestro, Tiomkins, and Rózsa are all refugees from Communist or Nazi countries."

To the other guests the three musicians were formal and congenial if rather stiff. But with Toscanini they were jocular and loud with a lot of handshaking and backslapping.

When everyone had been properly greeted, the reception line moved into the crowded ballroom to join the guests enjoying drinks and light music. The Landas were chatting with Todd and Helen Ingram and Rocko Myszynski and his wife when Roberta Thatcher walked up and took Laura's elbow. Roberta was a slender woman more than six-feet tall with blue-gray eyes and silver-blonde hair pulled back severely into a bun. Her tortoise-shell glasses muted the fact that she had been a knockout in her younger years.

"What?" demanded Laura.

"Honey, your face is falling."

"That bad?"

"Just a quick re-do before you go on."

"Okay." Laura smiled at the Myszynskis and followed Roberta to the ladies' room. Helen trailed behind. At Toscanini's behest, Roberta had arranged for a makeup professional to attend the bride. Lorraine Simonds of Twentieth Century–Fox waited for them in the ladies' room. Laura sat before a large mirror while Lorraine fussed and spritzed, a long Pall Mall dangling from her lips.

Roberta paced back and forth. "We're ten minutes behind schedule."

Laura stood and held up a hand mirror. "Who cares?"

"I do," replied Roberta. She stooped before Laura and smoothed her wedding dress. "I must say you look wonderful."

"I feel wonderful."

"I'm very proud of you."

Laura took Roberta by both shoulders and kissed her on the cheek. "Thanks, Bertie."

Roberta straightened to her full seventy-three inches. "Nobody calls me that."

"Oops, sorry. Do I still have a job?"

"As long as you don't mess up your program."

"What's going on?"

"Maestro called this morning to say he has two more volunteers. So, we now have twenty-five of his best."

"Wonderful," Laura said. "Luckily it's a simple program. I do 'Embraceable You.' Then we do 'The Meditation.' After that we do 'Temptation.'"

Roberta interrupted. "Then the maestro does 'The Blue Danube' and everybody dances."

Helen sighed. "Does it have to be a waltz?"

Laura laughed. "Toots, the boogie-woogie comes later when everybody's had too much to drink."

Helen protested, "That's not what I meant. I only--"

Laura smiled, "We're following protocol. Since the maestro is the one paying--"

", NBC is paying," interrupted Roberta.

"We follow their standards," Laura finished.

"Okay. Makes sense to me," said Helen.

Roberta asked, "By the way, who is Eldon White?"

"What?" Laura and Helen said in unison.

Roberta said, "You know, that cute naval officer. The chubby one with short blond hair."

"That's Tubby White, who just took over command of Todd's ship," said Helen.

Roberta said, "Well, he and Jack Carson have found each other. Jack is going to put him on stage as a straight man."

"Oh, God," said Laura. "Jerry will kill him."

Helen laughed, "Let it go, Laura. They'll do just fine."

"They hate each other," said Laura.

"What? I'd better put a stop to this," Roberta said, heading for the door.

"No, no," said Helen. "It's all an act. Do you think Tubby would have ever made skipper if Jerry objected? It's an act, believe me."

Laura drummed her fingers. "Jack Carson and Tubby White. This ought to be good. Okay."

Helen said, "Add Arturo Toscanini, water, and stir, and you have one great party."

"You sure about this?" asked Roberta, her hand on the doorknob.

"It'll be just fine," Laura assured her. "Now, where was I? Oh yeah, is Telfe here?"

"About ten minutes ago," said Roberta.

Helen's eyebrows went up.

Laura explained, "Telfe Rabinowitz, first violin. She'll back me up with 'The Meditation.' And it's a good thing. Otherwise it would fall flat."

Helen said, "Sounds beautiful."

"And that's it," said Roberta.

"No," said Laura. "I'd like to finish with 'Smoke Gets in Your Eyes.'"

"That should work all right," said Roberta.

Laura took her hand. "Corny, but it will be perfect. Then Jack Carson takes over again and closes out with a toast to the bride and groom."

Helen said, "And then we get to do the boogie-woogie?"

"Sorry, sweetheart. The conga line is next. *Then* the boogie-woogie."

Roberta rolled her eyes. "Decorum, Laura. Decorum."

Laura gave a mock curtsy. "Yes, ma'am. Decorum is my middle name."

"Very well. I'll leave you with Lorraine. I need to check on the food."

"We haven't talked for a while," Laura said to Helen after the door closed. You doing okay, hon?" She glanced at Lorraine.

Lorraine Simonds whisked a powder puff over Laura's forehead and said, "Almost done, toots. Go ahead and blab. I can work."

Helen said, "I'm doing pretty well, Laura."

"How well? You still seeing that shrink?" Laura reached under her dress, produced a flask, filled the cap, and knocked it back. "Ahhhh."

"Laura, you're pregnant!"

"Can you tell?"

"You hardly show."

"We don't want people talking." She looked up. "Right, Lorraine?"

Lorraine winked, "No speaka da English."

Laura said softly, "How about the shrink?"

Helen replied, "I think there's light at the end of the tunnel. Remember that horrible thunderstorm a couple of months ago?"

"Oh, sure."

"Well, I stopped dreaming after that. Dr. Raduga called it a catharsis."

"A what?"

"Catharsis. An emotional cleansing. It's caused by a sudden, often frightening event--like that thunderstorm. It scared the daylights out of me and I felt rocky for the next couple of days. But guess what? No more going fetal under the bed. I think it's all behind me. At least I hope so."

"Honey, that's wonderful."

"I do feel better and--"

Landa burst in and interrupted. "Baby, there's a crowd out there that only you can satisfy. Jack Carson is on stage now taking care of things. But I think you really need to get out there."

"Why?"

"Well, somehow Tubby White elbowed his way onto the stage with Carson. He's gonna make a damn fool of himself."

Laura winked at Helen. "Anything else?"

"Yeah, you should see Sergeant Harper."

Laura's eyes narrowed. She didn't trust Marines. "What's he done?"

Landa chuckled, "He signed up that crazy limo driver for the U.S. Marine Corps. Got his signature on the dotted line."

"Well, at least that will get him off the streets."

"Yeah. Safer around here."

"Is that all?"

"My sailors are getting drunk."

"Ouch. That does it." Laura stood. "Sorry, Lorraine, duty calls."

Lorraine squinted, "One moment, toots." She worked a little with Laura's lipstick and then said. "You're a knockout."

"Thanks, Lorraine." Laura stood and smoothed her dress. Helen asked, "Jerry, what if they get out of hand?"

Landa said, "Not to worry, babe. I have shore patrolmen in there ready to whack anyone over the head who gets out of line." He turned to Laura, "Shall we?"

"I'm all yours." Arm in arm, she walked out with her husband.

37

Grand Ballroom, Beverly Hills Hotel
Beverly Hills, California

The enormous crystal chandelier cast a soft glow over the Grand Ballroom. A pastel floral mural with matching drapes complemented the lush greenery visible through the large windows. Tables surrounded a dance floor complete with a lighted stage. The house lights were down, and a single spot captured Jack Carson on stage. He wasn't hard to find. The 6-foot 2-inch comedian weighed 220 pounds and could have done well playing fullback for the Chicago Bears. Behind him was a twenty-piece orchestra assembled by Arturo Toscanini, who stood mutely in the darkness, his baton at his side.

Carson spotted Landa and Laura coming in through the ballroom's massive wooden double doors. He waved a finger in the air and called out, "There they are now, ladies and gentlemen. Our bride and groom--Captain and Mrs. Jerry Landa!"

Applause broke out as the spotlight swung over to highlight the waving couple. Landa widened his smile and the applause grew, his sailors catcalling and whistling from the darkness.

Carson said, "Sage advice for the new groom, Captain Landa. Many a husband has learned an ironclad alibi isn't as effective as a diamond-studded one." The crowd laughed, sailors again whistled, and Carson waved to a set of stairs at stage left. "Right now, I'd like you to meet the commanding officer of the USS *Maxwell*, Lieutenant Commander Eldon P. White."

Again, the crowd applauded, the sailors whistling and stamping their feet as White mounted the steps.

Ingram groaned, "This is going to be a train wreck."

Helen took his hand. "Easy, darling."

Dimitri Tiomkin, who stood next to Ingram, leaned over and asked, "Train wreck?"

Ingram explained, "Jerry Landa is Tubby's boss. They put on a big show of hating each other. They lay off when things get serious. But things haven't been this serious before."

Tiomkin smiled. "Train wreck. I like that."

Ingram muttered, "I hope not."

Tubby's medals and gold braid glittered in the spotlight as he walked up to the microphone.

Carson said, "What do you think, Tubby? Er, I mean Mr. White . . . er, Commander. Oh, hell. Can I just call you Tubby?"

White deadpanned, "Of course, Mr. Carson."

"I don't want to disrupt naval protocol," Carson said.

White looked up to him. "You've got about five inches and twenty-five pounds on me, so you can call me anything you want."

Carson grinned. "You don't look so shabby yourself, sailor. Now tell me, any advice for Captain Landa?"

"Well, I'd say humility is the word of the day for a new groom."

"Humility?"

"Yes, I'd say to the commodore, no matter how well she treats you, always try to be humble."

A few chuckles rattled around the room. Carson asked, "Is he capable of that?"

"Absolutely not." The crowd laughed. The spotlight swung to Landa, who gave a pasty smile, then back to Carson.

"Indeed, humility *should* be the order of the day, Tubby. Commodore Landa has married a very talented lady. You all know that she plays concert piano for Maestro Arturo Toscanini and the NBC Symphony Orchestra." He waved to his left and the spotlight caught Toscanini to loud applause. When that abated, Carson went on, "But many of you may not know that Laura dabbles in popular music and is making a name for herself there as well. She would like to do a couple of numbers for you now. Ladies and gentlemen, I give you Laura West Landa."

The stage lights went down as a single spotlight caught Laura mounting the stage. The crowd pressed in, applauding and whistling. Sailors weaved among them, their shore patrol chaperones carefully watching every move.

She kissed Tubby on the cheek as he walked offstage, then kissed Jack Carson, who made a big show of wiping his cheek. She bowed at the audience and sat at the piano, the spotlight focusing tightly on her.

Ingram felt a draft on the back of his neck and sensed the double doors opening behind him. With a few others he turned to see two people silhouetted in the dim foyer light. One was tall and slender--a woman in an elegant black lace floor-length dress. She was accompanied by a man in uniform.

". . . very happy," Laura was saying. "Jerry and I will honeymoon in Yosemite for a couple of weeks, then he goes back to work for Uncle Sam and I go back to NBC. Lucky for me, Jerry's next duty station is right here in Long Beach on the cruiser-destroyer staff. Did I say that right, dear?" she called.

Landa shouted from darkness. "Good enough for government work, honey."

"Well, I'm glad that it's good enough for you and all of your boys here with us today. Welcome back, sailors, and well done. How fitting for this Thanksgiving weekend. We're honored by your presence here today." She applauded, and the crowd joined her generously.

She pulled the mike a little closer, adjusted herself on the bench, and began playing soft background music. "Jerry and I want to thank Hernando

Courtright and his marvelous staff here at the Beverly Hills Hotel. We couldn't have been more grandly treated."

From the darkness a voice shouted, "Hot springs tonight!"

With an up-tempo, Laura ignored it as two SPs quietly surrounded a freckled-faced sailor. The kid looked barely seventeen years old. Silently they palmed his elbows and escorted him out the double doors.

"And to the maestro, to Roberta Thatcher, and to the entire NBC organization, my undying love. Thank you very much." She held out her arms. Toscanini walked over, wrapped his arms around her, and kissed her.

"Easy, easy; the boss is watching." That one came from Tubby White as the crowd laughed.

Laura continued her soft background music, "And now . . ." She launched into "Embraceable You."

A delicate floral scent enveloped him. Ingram turned and looked into the eyes of a dark-haired beauty. Her hair was done in a French twist, her eyes heavily made up. Her exquisite diamond necklace gleamed and caught the light. Up close she had small creases of wisdom and courage and stamina around her eyes and mouth: late forties, maybe even into her fifties, he guessed. She smiled as if she knew him. Ingram smiled back, perplexed.

Helen dug her fingernails into his palm.

Laura played and sang as Toscanini moved off the stage. In a moment he was beside the woman, kissing her. He said softly, "Anoushka. I'm so happy you could come. Welcome to California."

Her accent was heavy--Russian, Ingram thought. "I'm so sorry we're late, Maestro. This city is so spread out. Our cab got lost."

"Dear, dear Anoushka. Los Angeles is a hard town to understand, especially on a first visit. But you're still scheduled at Warner Brothers tomorrow morning?"

"Ummmm--audition starts at eight tomorrow morning. But where is this Burbank?"

"Warner Brothers' Studio is in the San Fernando Valley."

"Oh, I think I may be there already. We are staying at the Sportsman's Lodge in Studio City." She laughed. "The restaurant is delightful. You catch your own fish and they cook it for dinner. Can you believe that? A car picks me up at seven."

"Excellent, just excellent." Toscanini held her hands to his chest. "Anoushka, darling. All these years. You look as beautiful as ever. I'm so glad you got through it all."

She exhaled. "It wasn't easy."

"I saw *Challenge of Darkness*--a wonderful movie. You're as beautiful in it as you are now."

"Maestro. Thank you. I didn't realize it was playing here."

"The studio found a copy for me. They hope to do an English subtitled version and release it here."

"I wish they would hurry up."

He pulled her close and kissed her forehead. "I want you to meet some good friends of mine, Dimitri and Rose Tiomkin. Dimitri, may I present Anoushka Dezhnev, just in from the Soviet Union."

Dezhnev? Ingram felt as if he had been electrocuted. He spun around and found himself looking into the eyes of Captain Third Rank Eduard Dezhnev.

"You!"

"Good to see you, Todd," said Dezhnev with a thin smile.

While Anoushka Dezhnev, Toscanini, and the Tiomkins babbled on about Soviet Russia and her upcoming auditions, Ingram hissed, "What the hell are you doing here?"

The program had gone smoothly, with Laura now winding up with "Smoke Gets in Your Eyes." Toscanini looked at the stage. "I'm on now. You must have dinner with me, Anoushka."

"I'm not sure if that is possible," she replied.

"Of course it is. I'll be right back. Then we can talk. Now, please excuse me."

"But you haven't met my son," she said.

"I'll be right back." Toscanini wound through the crowd, making it up to the stage just as Laura finished her song.

The stage lights came up and Laura said, "We'll pick it up a bit with a continental favorite: 'The Blue Danube' by Johann Strauss with Maestro Arturo Toscanini conducting."

The crowd clapped and roared as Toscanini beautifully launched his orchestra. The house lights came up a little more as the spotlight swung over to the bride and groom waltzing in the middle of the dance floor. Anyone looking closely could tell that Laura was leading her husband, but Landa did a credible job of faking his part. The guests joined in and began waltzing along with them.

Ingram turned around, half-wishing that Dezhnev would not be there. He was.

"Aren't you going to introduce me to your wife, Todd? She's gorgeous."

Helen registered confusion at the Russian officer who looked dashing in his dress uniform with clanking medals and glittering brass. And he still wore the Alcatraz belt buckle. Ingram made stilted introductions. Dezhnev, the perfect gentleman, raised and kissed Helen's hand.

Helen smiled broadly.

Holding his temper, Ingram said, "Excuse us, Helen." He took Dezhnev's elbow and steered him to the edge of the dance floor. "What's going on?" he demanded.

Dezhnev shook himself loose. "Todd, don't think I don't know how to take care of myself."

"Well, before we figure all that out, tell me what the hell you're doing here."

"Escorting my mother."

"Bullshit. What the hell are you doing here?" Ingram stood close, his chest almost touching Dezhnev's. "You better come up with something, Ivan, or I'm going to have those SPs throw your ass in a paddy wagon."

Dezhnev plopped his hands on Ingram's shoulders and said, "Take it easy. I'm here to save your life."

"What are you talking about?"

"They're trying to kill you."

"What the hell are you talking about?"

"I heard about it just before I left Vladivostok. But it's out of my hands. I can't stop it."

"This is bullshit. Why?"

"I cannot say more except be careful."

"What nonsense."

Helen walked up wearing a puzzled smile.

Dezhnev turned to her and gave an elaborate bow. "May I have this dance?"

Helen batted her eyelashes. "I'd be honored."

38

26 November 1945
San Pedro, California

The Plymouth wouldn't start. The carburetor was flooded, and it was Ingram's turn to drive. He propped up the hood and puttered with the engine. He was sharing a ride today with Cdr. Walt Hodges, the supply officer on the USS *Piedmont* (AD 17), a destroyer tender moored at the Long Beach Naval Station. Ingram's ship, the USS *Wallace* (DD 549), was tied up in a nest beside her going through a long-awaited tender availability. Today and tomorrow were big days: they were re-gunning the ship with five new 5-inch gun barrels, the old ones having been worn out in heavy fighting over the past eight months. Thus, Hodges was not only a good friend; he also held all the cards as far as parts and services from the *Piedmont*.

Sally Hodges drove up in the Hodges' Mercury and let Walt out. With a grin and a wave, she drove away. Shaking his head at Ingram, Hodges said, "So you've been buying that cheap gas on Ninth Street again?"

Ingram muttered, "I wish it were that simple. This damned carburetor needs an overhaul, and the last time I checked there's no good mechanic within miles."

"Hi, Walt," said Helen, walking out with a thermos of coffee.

"Hi ya, sweetheart." Hodges stepped around the car, pecked her on the cheek, and accepted the thermos. "Thanks."

"My pleasure." The Eleventh Naval District had ordered a change from summer khakis to standard blue uniforms last week, and Helen enjoyed the sight of her "two boys" together; they looked so good in blues. "How's Sally doing?"

Hodges rocked a hand from side to side. "Mmm, what can I say? Nine months and no action. The doc may induce labor. She's got an appointment today."

"Gee, and I have all that to look forward to again." Helen patted her belly.

Ingram barked to Hodges, "You ready?"

"Fire away." Hodges got in behind the wheel. "Say when."

"Wait one," muttered Ingram.

Helen poked her head through the passenger window. "Whew! It's hot in here already."

"Blues make me sweat."

"You and Sally should come for dinner Friday night," said Helen, "if you're not occupied with a new baby, of course."

Ingram snapped, "I heard that. You can come only if you get the car started, Walt."

"Oh, yeah?" Hodges jammed down the starter pedal. The engine rolled and rolled before finally sputtering into life. It backfired twice and settled into a smooth idle. "Sounds like Hirohito's revenge."

"Looks like we're having guests for dinner." Ingram plopped down the hood and walked around to Helen. Kissing her on the cheek he said, "Don't work too hard."

"I won't, but guess what?"

"What?"

"Apple pie in the commissary today."

"Oh, man. Bring home a slice?"

"I'll think about it."

Ingram jumped in the passenger seat. "You drive, Walt."

Hodges leaned over. "A slice for me too, Helen?" He jammed the car in gear.

"Sorry, Walt. You're too fat. Maybe one for Sally, though."

"Arrrgh!" Hodges eased the clutch and drove away.

With no wind the air was stale, and it grew hotter inside the Plymouth as they drove onto the *Islander*, the auto ferry connecting San Pedro to Terminal Island. With a blast of its whistle, the ferry got under way for the five-minute trip. Ingram opened the door, "Think I'm going to wash up."

"Mind if I sell it while you're gone?"

"Either that or push it over the side and charge admission." Ingram slammed the door and walked off.

Hodges poured coffee and rested his elbow on the window opening. Outside of the wind made by their trip across the channel there was no hint of cooling. He sipped, sat back, and took a deep breath, cocking his hat over his nose. With a twinge of envy, he thought about Todd Ingram and the other "tin can sailors" on the front line with the real Navy, the destroyer Navy. He knew what they called supply officers like him: pork chops. On the other hand, the tin can sailors romped with the-- "Ouch, damn it," he yelled as a passenger walking between the rows of cars jostled his arm.

"Sorry." The man didn't turn but kept on walking.

Hodges rubbed his arm for a minute, then sipped more coffee.

"Slide over. I'll take it from here." Ingram, smelling of Life Buoy soap, got behind the wheel.

"That stuff will take your skin off."

"Better that than piss off the admiral. I can't shake his hand with grease all over mine."

The *Islander* ducked behind a passing C-1 cargo ship and then made a textbook approach to the Terminal Island landing.

Ingram said a quick prayer and kicked the starter. The engine roared into life and settled down to a smooth idle.

"How's Commodore Landa doing? He still married?" The wedding had taken place two three days ago.

"Last time I checked," Ingram said. "But with Boom Boom, you never know."

39

27 November 1945
USS *Wallace* (DD 549)
Long Beach Naval Station, Long Beach, California

The four *Fletcher*-class destroyers were moored in a nest alongside the destroyer tender *Piedmont* (AD 17), which in turn was moored starboard side to Pier 32 at the Long Beach Naval Station. The *Wallace* (DD 549), flagship for Destroyer Division 77.2, was inside the nest. Outboard of her were the destroyers *Beaulieu, Cheffer,* and *Truax,* all on cold iron, using shoreside services for power. The tired veterans of the Pacific war were finally home for well-deserved maintenance and upkeep. However, DESDIV 77.1, including the *Maxwell,* was still in Yokosuka, waiting to embark GIs for home.

Ingram had relieved Howard Endicott as commodore of DESDIV 77.2 during a half-hour ceremony. Immediately afterward the squadron commodore and his wife, Captain and Mrs. Jeremiah Landa, were piped over the side to the *Piedmont.* They quickly stepped across to the *Piedmont's* starboard side and down the gangway to the pier. Laura's pale green

Cadillac convertible waited at the foot of the gangway. The top was down and luggage filled the backseat. Amid shouts and grins, Landa started the Caddie's big V-8 and eased out the clutch. He was also easing himself into a new life with sophisticated people and sophisticated music--something for which he knew he was completely unprepared.

The *Piedmont* blasted her whistle and whooped her siren while beer cans tied to the Caddie's rear bumper announced the Landas' departure, next stop the Ahwahnee Hotel in Yosemite National Park.

A freckle-faced young sailor had the last laugh as the car pulled away. A garish sign on the trunk boldly stated: "Hot Springs Tonight."

Two days later the *Wallace* and her sisters presented a different sight. Workboats swarmed around the four nested destroyers, delivering supplies, pumping fuel oil, and pumping out waste. Chipping crews turned to with hammers and chisels on the hulls and the upperworks, making a terrible cacophony; they scraped off old paint and brushed on red lead. When they were finished the ships would be painted in the peacetime pattern of haze-gray hull and superstructure with dark gray horizontal surfaces. Sailors carrying spare parts and assemblies from the tender stepped around the scrapers, chippers, and painters. New personnel stepped on board to present their orders to the quarterdeck. All the ships but the *Cheffer* were rebricking their boilers. The workers had finished refurbishing her number four boiler and were now setting safeties, the roar of six-hundred-pound steam ripping at the blue cloudless day.

Ingram and Toliver had a good view of the work from the *Wallace's* bridge, where they leaned on the bulwark and drank coffee. Electronics technicians and radarmen working in the pilothouse were installing two new radar repeaters. But a better show was taking place over the length of the ship as gunner's mates were removing all five of the *Wallace's* 5-inch 38 main-battery gun barrels; intense action, especially off Okinawa, had worn out the liners. The black canvas bloomers had been taken off. Then the guns were elevated straight up. After this, the gunner's mates rotated the barrels a half turn, disconnecting them. Everything was ready to go.

Toliver looked up as the wire cable on one of the *Piedmont*'s cranes dangled over mount 52 on the 01 level. "You did what?" asked he with mock incredulity.

"I said, we bought a house."

"You're still full of Thanksgiving turkey."

"No, I'm not. We bought a house."

"How did you find one?" With millions of servicemen and -women coming home, the housing shortage had become acute. Every one of them seemed to be starting a family and clamoring for a house.

"We were lucky. We're buying the Alma Street house in San Pedro that we've been renting since 1943," said Ingram.

"A house. What the hell for? Your career is just getting started, Commodore. Your next posting will probably be in D.C."

"We need the room."

"Huh?"

"Helen's pregnant. We're going to have another baby."

"Hey, number two. Congratulations, Dad. Do you know when?"

"Doc says next May."

"Amazing. I owe you a cigar."

The two fell silent amid the cacophony. At length Toliver said, "I miss this."

"Say again?" said Ingram.

"Shipboard life. It's simple."

Ingram said, "Most of the time. But remember, there are occasions when you do get shot at."

"Don't I know it? I don't miss the combat at all. I don't know how you stuck it out, Todd. I had to get a medical."

"Oh, horse feathers."

"Sometimes I think I'm yellow. I really don't--"

"Ollie," Ingram interrupted, "you gave it your all. You don't have to worry about being yellow. I nearly cracked out there too. And you saved my butt. I'm sure you'd do just as well, probably better, if you were challenged again."

Toliver rolled his eyes. "Wait a minute. You saved me."

Ingram shrugged. "None of it matters now. It's over. Ships are going into mothballs. People are getting out and going into civilian life. Gun bosses and ship captains are a dime a dozen and the Navy is kicking them out. But you're in a very important billet. And I think we're all a lot safer because of it." Ingram sipped coffee. "Your dad still angry?"

"Never writes. Hardly speaks to me." Toliver looked up and smiled.

"A shame he doesn't realize what a great job his son is doing."

"Sometimes I wonder about that."

"Ollie, damn it."

"Okay, okay, false modesty. Actually, I like ONI." He tried to stretch. "Except the hip is getting stiff. Could be the weather. Arthritis maybe. They may have to operate again. I'm seeing a specialist at the Orthopedic Hospital in downtown L.A."

"Hey! Is it close to Wong Lee's?"

Toliver flushed.

Ingram grinned. "Ollie?"

"Yes, it's close."

"Come on, Ollie."

"Okay, okay. After Jerry's wedding I popped the question. And she said yes."

"You're engaged?"

"That's what I just told you, knucklehead."

"Hey. Congratulations." After a hearty handshake Ingram asked, "Have you told your folks?"

"Can't do that. Dad is mad enough at me. And when they find out I've married a Chinese woman, Dad is going to go through the roof."

"I'm sorry."

"Well, the restaurant's doing fine, and I have a good career ahead. So, we'll be okay financially when he cuts me off."

"You think he'd do that?"

"His lawyers have called me about the first phase--cutting off my allowance."

Ingram felt a twinge of regret. Toliver's allowance had come in handy many times. While on liberty in San Francisco they had partied and acted like fools. And Toliver had bought the Packard that Ingram drove to Ramona to meet Helen's parents. *The end of an era.*

Their eyes locked for a moment, then Toliver looked away. *Subject closed.* Toliver had taken himself out of inheriting his family's millions. Ingram decided not to pursue it. He couldn't. It wasn't his business.

A gunner's mate in dungarees shouted from the top of mount 52 that the crane's wire cable had been attached to its gun barrel. The gunner's mate held up a fist to signal the crane operator high above on the *Piedmont.* Then the gunner's mate slowly twirled his index finger. Slack came out of the cable. It drew taut. Suddenly, the barrel seemed to jump a couple of inches. It was free. The gunner's mate twirled faster and the 16-foot-long barrel rose in the air like a long, gray toothpick.

"There are some things we should talk about," said Toliver.

"I figured. You've had that obsessed look on your face all morning. What's up?"

Toliver let it go. He was serious. "I saw our old friend Eduard Dezhnev at the Orthopedic Hospital."

"What's he doing there?"

"Same thing as me. Getting patched up by orthopedic experts. Seems we have better doctors here than in Russia, especially when it comes to prosthetics. Remember how he used to limp?"

"He was limping on Karafuto, all right."

"Sakhalin," Toliver corrected.

Ingram pressed a fist to his forehead. "Excuse me. Rank reduction to ensign for pissing off the Communists."

"Except Joe Stalin, not Uncle Sam, footed the bill. And they did a pretty good job. Did you see him dancing with his mother?"

"Yeah, between Ed and Toscanini, she had quite a workout. The son of a bitch even had the temerity to dance with Helen."

"How'd it go?"

"We don't talk about it."

They laughed.

Toliver's voice dropped a notch. "I saw you speaking with him. What was it about?"

Ingram watched the gunners for a moment. They had moved down to the main deck and were getting ready to pull the barrel from gun mount 51.

Ingram knew Toliver. There was something in his tone. "You sound more than just a little interested."

"Okay, here it is. First you should know that I'm posted out here, Eleventh Naval District, but I'm working for ONI."

"Terrific."

"Next, there's a great deal of interest in what the Russians are doing."

"I hope so."

"Seems they don't want to stop with the territory they've already gained. Their troops are still mobilized, and the world is their oyster. They want to keep going." When Ingram didn't speak, Toliver continued. "Ugly things are going to happen in Europe with this East Germany, West Germany business. That's just for beginners. We've heard Stalin still wants Hokkaido and is looking for an excuse to get in. He wants to communize Japan and all of Asia. And it looks like he's moving ahead in China now with Mao Tse-Tung."

"That's assuming his army can beat Chiang Kai-chek's."

"Mao has the northern provinces whipped up. His forces were fighting Chiang's before they were fighting Japs. We armed both of them, and the fuse is burning."

"I'm getting tired of all this."

"That's what the Communists are betting on. That Americans will all go home, decommission their ships and planes and tanks, and get fat and complacent while Communists take over the world. And as I said, they're not standing down."

Ingram finished the thought with, "Otherwise they get fat and complacent like us. And Stalin and Mao don't want that."

"Something like that." Toliver rubbed his chin. "Look, Todd, did Ed say anything about what happened on Sakhalin?"

"You sound like this is official; not a casual question."

Toliver exhaled. "Yes, it is an official question. We're very interested in what this guy is doing."

Ingram grinned. "You mean this is a real inquiry with a long case number stamped Top Secret? Guys in topcoats peeking between venetian blinds, wearing dark glasses, writing with disappearing ink and--"

"Todd!"

Ingram shrugged. "Okay, okay. We talked a little bit. He said that he directed the fire away from us when we took off. That's why we didn't get hit. It wasn't luck, according to him."

"Interesting."

"Our landing was a different story. They fired for effect. Said he had orders to do so but that he didn't know I was aboard."

"Nice people, those Soviets.

"Well, by that time I was ready to kill him, wedding party or not."

"But you didn't."

"No, I listened to what he had to say."

"Smart decision. He has diplomatic immunity."

"Right. Just like the good old days."

Toliver nodded.

"He did say something interesting: they're putting him in submarines. I'm guessing that's the reason for the new prosthetic leg. So, he can get around in cramped spaces."

"Submarines? That doesn't make sense."

"It didn't seem to make sense to him either. But that's what they want, so that's what he'll be doing. He starts submarine school soon."

"What else?"

"Well, he's still wearing that damned belt buckle you gave him. Thinks he looks like a movie star."

"We were drunk that night. I'm surprised he hasn't thrown it away."

"He loves it." Ingram lowered his voice. "There is something else."

"Shoot."

"He told me they're trying to kill me."

"What? Who?"

"His people. The NKVD. You know, the Russians' Gestapo."

"Jesus. Are you taking this seriously?"

"Hell, I don't know. It all sounds so stupid. People have been shooting at me since 1941. By more than a few small miracles I, no--you and I--survived all that. And now it's supposed to be over, except now I hear the damned Communists are after me."

"What the hell for?"

"They think I know too much. That I spent time with Walter Boring and learned all his secrets in sixty-five seconds. They don't want me around to talk about it."

Toliver looked away. "I wonder what got them so pumped up?"

"Me too. I can't figure it out. But the little I did see will last me a lifetime. Sometimes I dream about it. I mean guys with their heads cut off, or just heads, or open chest cavities with nothing in them. Our guys. Healthy guys. Looked like they walked in yesterday. Others too. Chinese, Brits, Aussies.

"What did Ed say about killing you?"

"He said he was just passing it on. That he didn't know anything else."

"Is that it?"

He thinks he's doing me a favor. He said that he was supposed to bring the order to the United States for 'others' to carry out. But someone else is involved."

"Who?"

"I don't know. He didn't seem to, either."

"You should have told somebody right away."

"Who?"

"Start with your boss."

"Jerry? He would have mobilized the squadron and sent us to sea. No, I have been thinking about it. But there was so much going on with the wedding and change of command that I haven't had time to do anything."

"Well, I have news for you, Commodore. You don't screw with these people. If they want you dead, they can make it happen."

"Oh, bullshit."

"I'm serious. They've been infiltrating operatives into this country for years, just like good old Ed in 1942 up in 'Frisco."

Ingram fixed Toliver with a stare.

Toliver said, "Really. They can do it."

"Helen? Jerry?"

"I don't know, but I'm going to put a tail on you."

"Shit! You'll do no such thing."

Toliver waved him down. "Sixty days. That's all. You won't even see him, or her. They'll be part of the landscape. They're really good."

"Not you?"

"Not me."

"No peering through my blinds?"

"No. I promise."

"I don't believe you."

Toliver tossed a thin smile.

"What?"

"There's something else. It may be connected."

Ingram sighed. "Here it comes."

"No listen up. It's serious. The State Department is involved."

40

27 November 1945
USS *Wallace*, (DD 549)
Long Beach Naval Station, California

Ingram and Toliver descended the two ladders to Ingram's cabin on the main deck in silence. Ingram gestured to a chair, sat at his desk, and leaned back. "What are you selling, Ollie?"

"How about an all-expense-paid trip to the Orient?"

"Last guy to try to sell me that was Ray Spruance."

"Who won?"

"He did, but he's an admiral. Last time I checked you were . . ."

"Yes, I know, a lowly commander."

"So, tell me about the State Department."

Toliver straightened. "Okay, here's the deal. The Red Cross contacted us about Walter Boring's personal effects. Something is missing."

Ingram had a sinking feeling. "What?"

"A crate."

"A crate of what?"

"Photos. Turns out there were supposed to be two crates, not just one.

"I don't like this."

"Hear me out. This may work to your advantage. The Red Cross contacted the State Department. They tried the OSS, but those guys won't even admit that it exists, so the State Department kicked it over to ONI. From there, it landed on my desk."

"What am I supposed to do?"

Toliver evaded the question. "When does DESDIV 77.2 get under way?"

Ingram rubbed his chin. "We finish our tender availability in the next two weeks, give or take a few days. Then Christmas, then some training, and then on 1 February 1946 we leave for Operation Magic Carpet."

"Where are you going?"

"Yokosuka, to replace DESDIV 77.1. Like them, embark as many GIs as we can, steam in formation with eight GI-filled attack transports, and bring them home. Then DESDIV 77.1 remains here for tender availability.

"Is that it?"

"Well, yeah, then--" There was a knock at the door.

Ingram said, "Come."

A dark-complected Navy commander in working khakis open the door and walked in. He leaned over and made a show of plopping a stack of papers on Ingram's desk. "Here you go."

"How you feeling, Walt?"

"Ugly. I came in today to make sure the paperwork was done on your gun barrels. So, read 'em and don't weep."

"Sorry, Walt. Ollie, say hello to Walt Hodges. He's the pork chop over on the *Piedmont*.

Toliver stood for a handshake, then Hodges waved him back into his chair and turned to Ingram. "That stack, my friend, is for the receipt and installation of five 5-inch 38 Mark 2 mod. 1-gun barrels. I need your signature there, there, and there."

"We can't accept delivery unless you have the bullets to go with them."

"Sorry. That wasn't in the work order. I hear you can find 5-inch ammo on discount at Louie's gun shop on Gaffey Street. Better hurry, though; sale only lasts 'til Saturday."

"All right, all right." Ingram signed and handed the papers back to Hodges.

"Thanks," Hodges said. "Now if you'll excuse me, I'm headed for the barn." He held out a hand. "Don't worry. Sally's picking me up."

"That doesn't sound good."

"So damned tired."

"Still have the runs?"

"Like a fire hose. And I'm getting this cough."

"You better see the doc."

"First thing tomorrow morning."

Ingram gave Hodges a closer look. Dark bags hung beneath his eyes, and he seemed to have lost weight. "Okay. See you tomorrow. Thanks for expediting the paperwork. We'd still be shooting with old barrels."

"You're most welcome." Hodges shuffled out.

Ingram said, "He lives a couple of blocks from me. We take turns driving." Then Ingram sat forward. "Come on, Ollie. Spit it out. What's on your mind?"

Toliver didn't beat around the bush. "We'd like to send you back to Sakhalin for a couple of days."

Ingram felt as if he'd been kicked in the stomach. "Karafuto."

"Not any more. Sakhalin."

"Just a couple of days?"

"Well, maybe three or four."

"And the orders come from?"

"CNO."

"You're kidding."

"I suspect that the State Department is pulling his chain. Somehow, somewhere, you're famous, and they want you back in."

"And you got stuck with telling me."

"I'm sorry, Todd."

"Right. What else?"

Helen was still in uniform as she whipped up dinner. Ingram was seated at their small kitchen table playing quietly with Jerry, who was strapped into his high chair. The more Helen rattled dishes, the more guilty he felt. Her belly was getting larger by the day and he hadn't done much to make things easier.

"Cat got your tongue?" she chirped.

"Ummm."

"I see. Time to feed the beast. I'll have it up in a moment."

"Thanks."

Landa's absence and his new job made Ingram's workdays even longer. He just couldn't manage to get home in time to help Helen. And Toliver's bombshells today had stopped him cold: spies, death threats, orders for Japan. He didn't know what to say.

Turkey soup and turkey sandwiches again. Thanksgiving leftovers. He picked at his sandwich. But Helen had managed to grab a head of iceberg lettuce at Gino's Market, a rarity. The salad made up for what was lacking in the main course.

Then she plunked down two ice-cold bottles of Schlitz.

"Huh? How'd you do this?" he asked, flipping off the caps.

"Gino says hello. He saves these for his favorite customers."

Ingram took a swig. "Ahhhh." *Things are looking up.*

"Kitchen needs painting," said Helen, passing a plate of sliced carrots. She dashed a small smile. "You know. Homeownership and all that. Maybe this Saturday? What do you think, Pop? Pale green? Or maybe bright yellow?"

I have a funny feeling about this.

"Hello? Commander Ingram?"

He looked up. "Oh, sorry. Yeah, pale blue sounds good."

"I said pale green or bright yellow."

"I don't know."

"What is it, hon?" She reached and took his hand.

"Nothing."

"I know. Let's have some coffee and go listen to *Red Ryder*, OK?"

"Sure."

Either the turkey didn't agree with Helen or it was morning sickness at midnight. Maybe it was a little of both. She stumbled into the bathroom and upchucked. But Ingram felt queasy too, and he damn well didn't have morning sickness.

Water ran. She crawled back into bed and snuggled, wrapping her arms around him.

Suddenly he no longer felt sick. He began to relax.

"When do you go?" she asked softly.

"Huh?"

"When do you ship out?"

"Well, I don't ship out. They're going to--say, how do you know?"

"It's me, Helen, remember? I know my family. And when my husband drags around with his nose on the floor and that 'I'm screwed' expression on his face, then I draw conclusions. Okay?"

"Yes, okay."

"So, spit it out."

"I can't talk about it."

"Oh, pretty please, Todd. Pretty please. I won't tell anybody. Well, maybe I can share a little with Mrs. Peabody. And Dr. Raduga. And then there's Sergeant Letenske, the base gossip, to say nothing of Martha Brubaker." She dug at his ribs with long fingers.

"Owww. Cut it out!" He rolled toward her. "Come here."

"None of that."

"I love your mouthwash." He rolled all the way over, held her tight, and kissed her. "What's wrong?" he asked.

"Accelerated respiration rate," she gasped.

"You mean breathing hard?"

"Very good, Todd. You take good notes."

"I remember now. That's what happens when two people--"

"Sorry. None of that until I get over this."

"Says who?"

"The doctor?"

"Come on."

"Old wives' tale?"

"You mean you're planning to vomit while we're in the middle of it?"

"Todd!"

He lay back and nuzzled the nape of her neck. She smelled wonderful. Moments passed. A gust of wind rustled leaves outside the window.

"When are you going?" she asked.

"Sunday."

"How long?"

"Mmmm, a week . . . ten days."

"That's not bad. But it's just temporary, right?"

"Definitely TAD."

"And where is it?"

"Rather not say."

"Japan?"

"Sort of."

"Who's going to mind the store here?"

"Howard Endicott, TAD."

"They've thought of everything."

"Seems like it." He held her close. Next thing he knew he was shaking. "God."

She caressed his head, "What is it? You don't want to go?"

"I don't want to leave you and Jerry."

"Is it dangerous?"

"Could be."

"Then don't."

He really didn't want to go. He held her tenderly and kissed her again and again. Four years of people murdering people was enough. The stench would last a lifetime. And yet . . . "I think this is important."

"Do you have a choice?"

He did, but he didn't want to say.

She rolled her back into him and they settled on their sides.

"What," she asked.

"Pale yellow. That's best. Pale yellow. No, hold on. Make it canary yellow for the morning sun. It'll be bright, just like you."

"I love you."

41

Toliver was quick. By day's end on 28 November he had temporary additional duty (TAD) orders cut for Ingram to report to COMFIFTHFLT on the brand-new USS *Oregon City* (CA 122), now moored at the Yokosuka Naval Base, Japan. Departure was scheduled for the thirtieth: Ingram was to grab a puddle-jumper at Allen Field at 9:30 a.m. for a sixty-minute flight to NAS North Island. From North Island he would fly to Pearl Harbor, Wake Island, and then on to Tachikawa Army Air Force Base in Tokyo to await further orders.

Helen fixed spaghetti that evening, one of his favorite dinners. Helen's secret, passed down from her mother, Kate, was a sauce heavily laced with ground round, garlic, and tomato paste. Whimsically added pinches of seasonings catapulted it into something exotic. She made garlic toast on the side and found a head of romaine at Gino's Market for caesar salad. It was all generously complemented by San Pedro's wine of preference: dago red. After unscrewing the top, Ingram always made a show of holding his nose while quaffing the first glass. After a great expulsion of breath, he would wheeze, "Not bad stuff once you get used to it."

For once, dinner was quiet. They had put Jerry to bed early, and he played quietly in his crib as he drifted off to sleep.

Ingram grabbed a towel to help with the dishes.

"Go on," said Helen. "Time to get moving."

Silently, he plopped the towel on the counter, kissed her on the neck, and shuffled into their bedroom.

Damn it. He reached under their bed, pulled out his B-4 bag, and zipped it open. He was reaching for starched shirts when the phone rang. Helen picked it up in the kitchen. Her tone was steady, noncommittal, all business. Curious, he walked into the kitchen and found Helen bent over a notepad. "It's okay, Sally. I'll set it up. But let me call back to confirm. Right, just hang on. Bye." She hung up.

Ingram said, "Sally going into labor?"

Helen made a couple of notes. "I wish it were that easy."

"What?"

"It's Walt. Doesn't sound good. What was he like today?"

"Absent."

"Yesterday?"

"Looked and sounded like hell. Bad chest cough and still had the runs."

Helen shook her head and started dialing.

"What is it?"

Helen said, "Hello, Sergeant Varela? It's Major Ingram. Who's the doctor on duty right now?" She waited and fiddled with her pen. "Dr. Chandler. Good. Is he there? Surgery? Okay, listen. I'm sending over a close family friend, Commander Walter Hodges, who needs admitting . . . Yes, I know he's Navy. Sergeant . . ."

The man's voice echoed in the earpiece.

"That's what I'm trying to tell you. Yes, it's serious. Bad diarrhea, respiratory problems, and a temperature of 102 . . . No, they tried Harbor General, but they say they're full. Plus, it's too far away. And if my guess is right, Commander Hodges needs immediate attention . . . You can? That's wonderful. I'll send them right over. It's Commander Walter Hodges. He and his wife, Sally, live two blocks away from us and he works at TI with my husband. By the way, she's nine months' pregnant . . . Yeah, have fun. Thank you, Sergeant." Helen hung up.

She muttered to Ingram as she dialed. "Walt has taken a bad turn. Somebody has to see him right away. Sally! It's Helen. Okay, they'll take you. Go directly to the emergency entrance. Sargent Varela will check you in. And you're in luck. Dr. Chandler is on duty tonight. He's one of our best. He'll take good care of you. Grab Walt's teddy bear and get going . . . That's right ... You're welcome. I'll check in on you tomorrow morning. Bye."

"So, tell me," demanded Ingram.

"I think it's bad."

"So, I gathered."

Helen looked up. "Sally's really worried. Walt passed out on the way to the bathroom. Took her some time to bring him around. So now they should be on their way to the hospital."

"Damn. Maybe I should--"

"Maybe you should continue packing, sailor." She grabbed his arm and steered him to the bedroom and his gaping B-4 bag. "You have a job to do. Let us do ours. Walt's in good hands. Dr. Chandler really is one of the best in the business."

Ingram couldn't sleep. It always happened the night before shipping out, whether he was going for one week or one year. He couldn't get used to it. Helen couldn't sleep either, and they lay wrapped in each other's arms until Ingram finally drifted off at four o'clock. The alarm jolted them both awake at 6:30. They stumbled through the motions of the morning's ablutions like robots, washing up, shaving, and dressing, then heaved an overweight B-4 bag into the Plymouth. Mrs. Peabody came over early to help with Jerry. She whipped up omelets and called them to breakfast.

Ingram sat and was soon finished. He stood and pecked Mrs. Peabody on the cheek. "Thanks, Emma."

"Did you get enough?" she asked. Emma's omelets were always good, but today it had tasted like cardboard. "That was really great."

"You okay?" she asked, palming his cheek.

Ingram nodded.

She turned to Helen. "I'm not used to goodbyes anymore."

Helen looked out the window and swiped at her cheek. "Foggy this morning."

Ingram took both of Mrs. Peabody's hands. "Emma, I'm only going for two weeks, three weeks tops."

"Just make sure." She hugged him.

"Do my best. Save me some of your beer. And don't drink too much."

She laughed and said, "Time to check on the little one."

Ingram went to make sure the Plymouth started while Helen phoned the hospital and tried to get through to the emergency room. Finally, she reached someone she knew. After a two-minute conversation Helen slowly hung up.

"What?" asked Ingram.

"No change. He's in a private room with nurses assigned round the clock. Sally's asleep in an alcove down the hall. I'll check on them when I get over there."

He patted her belly and kissed her. "I'm going to put you in an alcove if you're not careful. Promise?"

"Promise." She kissed him back.

Talk was sparse as they headed for the ferry. There were none of the usual derisive epithets as they drove past the ramshackle wooden holding cells on Terminal Island. Six months ago, they had been full of Japanese POWs in transit. Now the place looked abandoned.

When they reached Allen Field's main hanger, Ingram discovered that his ride was a twin-engine Beech JRB-4 "bug-smasher" training plane. The pilot was a Navy captain in a well-worn flight suit with "Pierson" embossed on the right leather patch and gold wings on the left. He stomped up and down and chewed a cigar. "You Ingram?" he demanded.

"Yes, sir."

"You're fifteen minutes late, Commander, and I have a heavy schedule."

"Sorry, Captain."

Pierson jabbed a thumb over his shoulder. "So, I would appreciate it if you would board the aircraft. Now, if you don't mind."

"Yes, sir." Ingram yanked his B-4 bag from the Plymouth and began walking. Helen got out and followed.

"Where you headed?" demanded Captain Pierson.

"San Diego," replied Ingram. "I thought you knew that."

"No, I mean after."

Helen jammed her hands on her hips. "And then Yokosuka."

Captain Pierson seemed to notice her for the first time. "This your wife?"

Ingram turned. "Yes, sir."

"A major?"

"Yes, sir."

"Jeez, she's a knockout."

"Thank you, sir."

"Too bad she's not a WAVE. Where'd you find her?"

"Corregidor, sir."

Three full seconds passed as Pierson stepped up and examined Helen's ribbons. Then he held out his hand. "An honor to meet you, Major."

Helen smiled as they shook. "Thank you, Captain. Likewise."

Pierson turned to Ingram and said, "You're a lucky man."

"Thank you, sir."

"Just remember one thing."

"What's that, Captain?"

He said clearly, "Love isn't love until you give it to someone."

"Makes sense to me, Captain."

Pierson rolled the cigar in his mouth and blurted, "Well then, do it, Commander. Take all the time you want, except hurry up. And don't forget to kiss her." He turned and climbed through the Beech's aft hatch.

Ingram was the only passenger, so Pierson invited him to take the right seat. They flew at ten thousand feet on a clear but bumpy morning as the plane headed for San Diego and NAS North Island. Pierson was hilariously profane, acting more like Jerry Landa than Jerry Landa. In fact, it turned out they knew one another, both having been kicked out of the Mare Island Officers' Club in 1940 when they were junior-grade lieutenants. Pierson turned the controls over to Ingram, so he could use his hands and arms to punctuate his raunchy stories. He had been a dive-bomber pilot in the *Yorktown* (CV 5) at the Battle of Midway. He worked his way up to commander of the carrier air group in the USS *Saratoga* (CV 3). Now, carrier pilots were being retired as ships were put into mothballs. Pierson was looking at either getting out or reverting to the permanent rank of commander if he stayed in.

"What about you, black shoe? What's going to happen to you?" Pierson sat back and lit another cigar as the bug-smasher hurtled through headwinds.

Ingram struggled with the yoke, overcorrecting as the plane jiggled around, its altitude wandering up and down by two or three hundred feet. "Staying in, Captain."

"Why?"

"What else do *you* know how to do?"

"You don't think I'd be good at selling insurance?"

Ingram laughed, and Pierson nodded. "You too?"

"That's it. That's why I'm staying in. I'd be a lousy insurance salesman."

"Here." Pierson flipped switches on the autopilot. "You're headed for Yuma instead of North Island."

"Sorry, Captain." Ingram let go as the autopilot took over and corrected the plane's altitude and course. The ride became much smoother. "Amazing," he said.

"Make a man out of you yet."

Ingram shrugged. "Too much water under my keel to become a zoomie now, Captain."

"Halsey did it; McCain did it. And they were in their fifties."

"That was peacetime."

Pierson's eyes flashed over Ingram's ribbons and his two Navy Crosses. "Yeah, we've all done some of that."

They landed half an hour late. A driver with a Jeep waited to take Ingram to the departure area for the overseas flights. He checked in with the airman there, a redheaded third-class gum chewer who told him boarding was immediate. "I would advise you to step on it, sir." He nodded outside to an R5D with its port inboard propeller turning over.

"Thanks." Ingram grabbed his bag and turned to rush out.

"Oh, sir, this is for you," the airman handed over an envelope with Ingram's name scrawled on the outside.

Ingram grabbed it and quickly walked out the door. Men were gathered about the plane, a Navy version of the C-54, pulling chocks, handing up landing gear safety pins, and making ready to pull away the stairway. Ingram was barely inside when a beefy chief petty officer closed the hatch. After securing the hatch the CPO locked it and then squeezed past Ingram heading for the cockpit. "Welcome aboard, sir. You Commander Ingram?"

"That's right."

"Make yourself at home, Commander." He waved at an empty cabin. "Take any seat; make sure you buckle up, sir. Coffee's up as soon as we take off." He disappeared into the cockpit and closed the door behind him.

The R5D thumped and thudded toward the runway. After stopping and locking the brakes, they ran the plane's engines and then waddled onto the active runway for takeoff. The pilot firewalled the throttles and lifted off with barely half the runway gone.

Point Loma flashed beneath, and the R5D eased into a southwesterly course and climbed. Ingram took off his jacket, loosened his tie, and settled back. As he folded the jacket something rustled in the pocket. The envelope. It was a telegram from Helen. He opened it and read:

WALT HODGES DIED AT 9:02 THIS AM STOP NOBODY KNOWS WHY STOP HIS BODY KEPT FOR AUTOPSY STOP SALLY HOLDING UP WELL BUT NEEDS LOVE AND ATTENTION STOP ALL MY LOVE AND ATTENTION TO YOU FOR A GOOD TRIP AND SAFE RETURN STOP XOXOXO HELEN

PART III

In the dark, men break into houses,
but by day they shut themselves in;
they want nothing to do with the light.
For all of them, deep darkness is their morning;
they make friends with the terrors of darkness.

—Job 24:16–17

42

---

29 November 1945
SS *Marshal K. V. Polochev*
Berth 48, Port of Los Angeles, California

It was nearly one in the morning and activity on the *Marshal K. V. Polochev* was frantic. She was under orders to clear Berth 48 by 5 a.m. to make way for a Matson Lines cargo ship due from Maui at 6 a.m. Although she was only three years old, the *Polochev* looked much older. She was rust streaked, and the low overcast and mist made it look worse as dew dripped from every line, bulkhead, and overhead. Everything on her rust-caked deck was slippery and dangerous. Already, two forklifts had skidded and tipped over, spilling their loads; one of the drivers was seriously injured.

The *Polochev* was a liberty ship manned and operated by the Soviet Union on lend-lease, one of 2,170 mass-produced at 18 shipyards in the United States. At 441 feet overall, she carried 14,474 tons fully loaded and was fitted with 2 boilers and a steam turbine that drove her at 11.5 knots maximum speed. A glance at her hull plating confirmed the *Polochev*'s hard driving over her short lifetime. The hull plates were dished in from countless storms in the unpredictable North Atlantic on the Murmansk run. Her engine, boilers, and evaporators all needed overhauling. But with all this she was still alive--and lucky alive, as her crew liked to say. Once, in a tight convoy, she had combed the wakes of two German torpedoes, one port, one starboard, both of which went on to rip into two other liberty ships.

Forklifts darted from the warehouse to the dock as if possessed, dropping their pallet loads beneath the *Polochev*'s booms. Conflicting shouts in English and Russian tore the air as wharfingers and Soviet sailors wrestled with the pallets, hooking them up to thick lines dangling from the booms. Once connected, the loads were hoisted into the air, swung onboard, and eased into one of the *Polochev*'s five yawning holds.

Karol Dudek waited in shadows of Berth 48's warehouse where he could both keep an eye on the ramshackle coffee shop across the street and monitor loading activities on the *Polochev*. Karol's smooth face and fine, straw-colored hair gave him the appearance of a mousy shopkeeper or clerk. He was dressed like a sailor, though, in peacoat, dungarees, and black watch cap. A sea bag was slung over his shoulder, and in his pocket was his constant companion of three years: a six-inch American switchblade surrendered to him by a Romanian sailor in an alley behind a bar in Piraeus, Greece. Luckily the man was drunk, and he stumbled and dropped the knife. Karol picked it up and went for him. The wide-eyed Romanian became sober quickly and ran screaming into the streets. Since then Karol had used the knife twice: once to kill a Russian tanker and the second time to stab a Warsaw bully who tried to take the switchblade away from him.

An orphan, he had grown up near the Warsaw ghettos, where he made money snitching to the police. After the Germans invaded, he made his money from the Gestapo by reporting people hiding Jews. At age 16 he was drafted into the Wehrmacht, and his 5-foot 7-inch, 140-pound frame made him a perfect fit for rear gunner in an Me 110 twin-engine fighter-bomber. Once he discovered that life expectancy in Me 110s was three months, and less over Britain, he wiggled his way into the Luftwaffe medical corps. He became adept as a physician's assistant treating shot-up flyers, many of whom were unlucky enough to survive crashes with horrible burns and crushed bodies. Morphine and painkillers became his specialty.

In January 1945 the Soviets captured him near Grossenhain Air Base

and threw him into a concentration camp. From Grossenhain they mani-
fested him on a train for Soviet Siberia and the gulags above the Arctic
Circle. But the NKVD discovered his talents just before the train pulled out.
He was medically trained, and in addition to his native Polish Karol spoke
fluent German and Russian and passable English. Instead of Siberia, the
NKVD sent a grateful Karol Dudek to the training camp for spies in
Bykovo, Russia. They decided to try him out at "wet jobs" and sent him into
Berlin's Western Sector on a mission. He performed well, poisoning his
victim with cyanide in a hospital.

The job in America had been his second. He had performed as ordered
and was due to ship out for home on the *Polochev*. But first, his contact.

Dudek's contact was already in the coffee shop, looking around and
checking his watch every minute or so. Karol took a last sweep of the area.
All looked well in the warehouse and in what he could see of the ship.
Except for a bus pulling away, the street seemed clear. So did the coffee
shop. *Time to get going.* He walked quickly across the street and into the
coffee shop. A skinny clerk wiped the counter with a dirty wet towel.
"What'll it be, mac?"

"Coffee, please, two cups," said a voice at the counter. Karol's man. The
two had not met--they had always communicated by telegram--but eye
contact was all they needed. Each nodded in recognition.

Dudek took the stool beside the man, who plinked down a half dollar
as the counter clerk poured coffee. "Thanks, mac." The clerk moved off.

The man wore a roadster cap and a topcoat buttoned up to his chin. He
spoke in terse sentences, half of which Dudek couldn't understand. A scent
wafted around him. Dudek couldn't identify it, but it clearly wasn't a
woman's perfume. Maybe expensive soap. He decided he liked it.

"Are you sure it was him?" asked the man.

Dudek welcomed the opportunity to practice his English. "Who was
him?"

"Your target. Your assignment." He spoke slowly. "Are . . . you . . . sure . . .
it . . . was . . . him?"

"*Da, da.*"

The man exhaled. "English, please, if you don't mind."

"I am sorry. Yes. He was in Navy uniform and drive car you describe."

"And what did you do?"

"I walk from behind and shoot this man here," he pointed to a spot on his upper left arm, "like they tell you."

"Did he see you?"

"No, I just keep walking."

"Did he feel any pain?"

"What? Do what?"

"Did . . . he . . . feel . . . any . . . pain?"

"Oh, no. I think no."

"Very well." Dudek's control reached inside his coat pocket and pulled out a small brown envelope. "As agreed."

Dudek had no difficulty following that. He snatched the envelope and stuffed it into his coat pocket. The envelope carried the man's scent. He did like it, and he wondered how he could find some for himself. "And . . .?" Dudek raised his eyebrows.

"Yes, yes." The man pulled a watch from his coat pocket and dropped it into Dudek's hand. Dudek bent to examine the face.

"Take it easy," the man hissed.

Dudek looked around. Only two other men were in the coffee shop, and both were bent over steaming cups of coffee. Dudek turned his back to them and peered down at the name on the watch's shiny face. Whittaker. *Yes.* He smiled. It was a twenty-one-jewel-movement Whittnauer. All silver with a matching expansion band. The bezel was festooned with timing graduations. Two buttons on the side were for stopwatch functions. He had wanted a Whittnauer ever since he saw one on the wrist of an American pilot who had been unlucky enough to bail out into a group of enraged farmers. But Karol didn't get the watch. Instead, it went to a Wehrmacht sergeant.

"Is this what you wanted?"

"*Da*, thank you." He meant it.

"What of the apparatus?"

"*Was?*"

"English, you stupid . . ." Annoyed, the contact formed a pistol shape with his hand and squeezed the trigger.

"*Da, da.* I throw it over bridge into water. Both of them." That was a lie.

The second ejector was nestled in his pocket beside the six-inch knife. One never knew when such a device would come in handy.

"Good." The man seemed relieved. "Send word when you reach Vladivostok." He eased off the stool and stood. "Have a pleasant trip." He walked out the door.

Dudek slipped the watch on his wrist. With the expansion band, it fit perfectly. His heart soared. He checked the fly-spotted electric clock on the wall then took the Whittnauer back off, wound it, and set it. *Beautiful.* He slipped it back on his wrist, gulped down his coffee, twirled off his stool, and headed out the door. Once outside in the night, he patted his coat pocket, feeling the comforting presence of five thousand American dollars.

A group of Russian sailors jumped off a bus and headed for the *Polochev.* They were loud and drunk. One stopped to pee in the gutter. One look at them told Dudek that neither his money nor his watch would be safe on the *Polochev.* For sure they would bunk him with the riffraff in the forepeak berthing compartment. Both watch and money would disappear. Maybe his life, too. Nor could he trust the captain or the purser. Russians were all corrupt. They would steal him blind and then throw him over the side.

Dudek rubbed his chin. *This does not look good.* And then it hit him. *The hell with that rust-bucket. And the hell with Vladivostok and those stupid Russians; and the hell with selfish and condescending Americans.*

He would exit America the same way he entered: via Tijuana, Mexico, and then go back to Berlin, or maybe even Warsaw, to pick up pieces. Five thousand dollars would go a long way in either city. He could make a fortune smuggling cigarettes, liquor, penicillin, and maybe even women's nylon stockings. With so many shortages he was certain to get rich.

43

2 December 1945
Conference Room B, Headquarters Building
U.S. Army Air Base, Atsugi, Japan

It was cold outside; snow blew in patches, dusting the runways with a brilliant white softness that melted almost immediately and ran into benjo ditches. Ingram stood at the window, drawing his parka around his neck and wondering why the Army engineers hadn't yet figured out how to heat the building. They'd have it fixed by tomorrow, no doubt; meanwhile people were freezing all over the building. He yearned for the warm comforts of Southern California and hoped this would be over quickly. He'd landed yesterday and with eight hours of sleep and breakfast, he felt rested and ready to go.

Instead of reporting to the *Oregon City*, he had been ordered to attend a meeting in Atsugi. *Quiet here.* He was the first one here. He zipped his parka tighter and examined Conference Room B's ornate table. The muted black satin finish on the top and delicate gold trim and scrollwork on the sides shouted power and wealth. A large bonsai commanded the table's middle. Seven elegantly understated chairs finished in matching dark wood with gold trim at the edges lined the sides. The eighth chair, which stood at one end, was not so understated. It had a beautifully carved back with intricate scrollwork. And it was strategically placed so that light coming through the window silhouetted the chair's occupant, making the person's expression inscrutable to others in the room. Whoever sat there had been Atsugi's top Japanese dog, Ingram figured. Pictures in groups of four had once graced the cream-colored woven wallpaper. Only blank spaces remained, the peripheries smudged with yellowish-orange tobacco smoke. Oddly, three bullet holes stitched the wall opposite the table's head.

Ingram was musing on that when the door creaked and Major Neidemeier walked in carrying a well-stuffed briefcase. He looked much more the Army major in his dress uniform than he had in sweaty khakis on Okinawa. He walked directly to the chair at the table's end and set down his briefcase. A tall civilian wearing coat and tie entered next brushing snowflakes off his camelhair overcoat. He had dark, slicked-back hair and a pockmarked face. Somewhere along the way he had broken his nose, which tilted a bit to the right, the tip swollen.

Neidemeier pulled out the ornate chair and sat. Ingram decided not to pull rank and stifled a grin as Neidemeier disgorged papers from his briefcase. He looked up. "Oh, Commander Ingram, good to see you again."

Ingram nodded.

"And this is Harlan Ferguson from the State Department."

Ingram reached across, and they shook hands. Ferguson said, "A pleasure to meet you, Commander. I've heard a great deal about you."

"Thank you, I--"

Two more men walked in the door. The first was a stranger, an Air Corps second lieutenant. Behind him was . . . "Leroy! Good to see you." Ingram jumped up and pumped Leroy Peoples' hand.

"You too, Commander."

"Ahem," grunted Neidemeier.

In his thick Arkansas accent Peoples said, "I ain't too good at this, but please say hello to Lieutenant Richard Lassiter, my new copilot."

Ingram stuck out his hand, "Welcome, Lieutenant."

"Yes, sir, thank you sir. A pleasure." Lassiter was short and stocky with broad shoulders and a freckled red face.

Peoples asked, "Where would y'all like us to sit?"

Ingram waved at the table. "Grab a seat anywhere."

"Okay." Peoples took the chair opposite Ingram.

Ingram said, "Glad to see you have your own airplane, Leroy. And a copilot. What will they think of next?"

Peoples grinned. "Yep. Hauling guys home for Magic Carpet. Nine trips so far--two trips with wounded. But I had a week's layover and Bucky asked me if I wanted in on this."

"You fool."

"Well. This counts toward my rotation. This and two more trips and I get to go home and fly from the other end."

"Leroy, you're working the system."

"Bucky's showin' me the ropes."

"So, how is Bucky?"

"Funny thing. He was detailed for this trip and signed me on along with Berne and Hammer. But then--"

Neidemeier interrupted, "Welcome, Mr. Peoples."

"Good morning, Major," said Peoples. "Isn't Major Radcliff supposed to be on this trip?"

"Something came up. General Sutherland needed a pilot to fly some congressmen up from Manila and I reassigned him."

Peoples slowly nodded. "I see, sir. Well, I reckon we can get along okay without him."

Neidemeier said, "You sound unconvinced, Lieutenant. Don't you feel comfortable with this assignment?"

"Oh, I'm very comfortable, Major."

Neidemeier said, "Because if you're not, you can walk out right now. No hard feelings."

Peoples' jaw sagged.

Ingram interrupted, "From personal observation, I'm sure Lieutenant Peoples can carry out his duties."

"I'm not sure if he's cleared," muttered Neidemeier, rummaging around in his briefcase.

Peoples said, "Hell, I was on the plane that flew Japs to Manila and Todd here to Karafuto--"

Neidemeier held up a hand, "Sakhalin. Our Russian friends call it Sakhalin. You would do well to keep that in mind since you'll be seeing them once more."

"That's interesting," said Peoples. "The last time we saw them they was shooting at us. All in a friendly way, of course."

"Of course. Nevertheless, please keep it in mind," said Neidemeier.

"Yes, sir, I will," said Peoples.

"Good." Neidemeier checked his watch, "Very well, gentlemen. Let's get started. We have only an hour before takeoff." He nodded to Ingram, "Your gear is being packed on Mr. Peoples' plane, Commander."

Ingram nodded. "Thank you."

Neidemeier said, "I would like to introduce Harlan Ferguson, who is posted to the special projects section of the State Department, reporting directly to Secretary of State Byrnes. You should know that Mr. Ferguson used to be Captain Ferguson of the 101st Airborne. He parachuted into the Netherlands with Operation Market Garden a year ago last September and was seriously wounded. He was awarded a Silver Star and two Purple Hearts. After recovery, he was honorably discharged and joined the State Department. We're privileged to have him with us. That said, I'll turn it over to Captain Ferguson."

Ferguson stood. Ingram noticed that his left arm dangled at his side and there was a black glove on the hand. "I have to say that my hat's off to you guys. You've all seen combat and know what it's like. Congratulations to you for surviving the war, and congratulations on your fine service to your country. I'm not going to dilly-dally here. This is a tense situation, and you fellows have done this before and know what could be a simple mission can turn out to be very dicey."

Ferguson held up his forefinger. "First, we need diplomacy. That's why we're sending Mr. Blinde. He's got that in spades. And he speaks Russian and some Chinese, I'm told."

"Blinde is going? Where is he?" asked Ingram.

Ferguson said, "Plane's delayed, Commander. Engine trouble. Should land any minute. But we told the ramp people to direct him directly to

Lieutenant Peoples' plane. He knows the brief and he'll be the on-scene commander."

Ingram said, "I have a hard time taking orders from a civilian when people are shooting at me."

Ferguson nodded. "Absolutely right. If that happens, you take over. And we're sending a squad of Marines again with plenty of weapons, including a bazooka."

Ingram said, "Thank you. That increases our survival time from fifteen seconds to thirty-seven seconds."

Peoples grinned. Lassiter sat poker-faced.

Neidemeier said, "Commander Ingram. Every possibility has bee--"

"Has been evaluated," interrupted Ferguson. "We think we have it all covered. Please let me explain. This mission has been approved at the highest levels of our two governments."

"Really?" asked Peoples.

Ferguson smiled. "None other than my boss, Secretary of State James Byrnes, and Foreign Minister Vyachslav Molotov of the Soviet Union."

"Okay. So, what is it you want?" asked Ingram.

"I thought you knew."

"Something about an extra crate. I was hustled out of town rather quickly."

Ferguson gave a smile. "Well, the Navy can do that to you. Yes, there was a second crate left behind on Sakhalin."

Ingram decided to play dumb. "What's in those crates that's so important, Captain?"

"Harlan, please. I'm a civilian, now."

Ingram said, "As long as you're giving orders, you're still Captain Ferguson to me."

Ferguson smiled. "As you wish." He cleared his throat. "All I can say is that there is information in those crates that is prejudicial to the security of the United States."

Amazing, Ingram thought. Yes, those photos and the cover-up could ruin a few reputations and treaties at home and abroad. World opinion would be scathing. "I see."

Ferguson continued, "Blinde was aware of it, but he didn't have time to let you know because the Russians had, unfortunately, gone over to the offensive."

"I'll say they did," said Peoples. "Made us run like a pack of hounds."

"Well, Secretary of State Byrnes has taken care of that. No rough stuff this time. The Russians are not aware of the missing crate. They think you are coming to pick up Major Fujimoto and his staff. The rest of the Japanese garrison, about two hundred of them, will return on a destroyer, the USS *Maxwell*."

"That's all that's left?" Ingram straightened a bit. "Two hundred out of a thousand?"

Ferguson said, "I'm given to understand there was some bitter fighting."

"Sounds like it."

"I also understand that the *Maxwell* is your former command."

"That's true."

"Good. As we speak she's under way for Toro. She should arrive there late tomorrow afternoon. You will embark the balance of the Japanese garrison aboard the *Maxwell*, which will then set sail for Yokosuka. In the meantime, you will locate and load the second crate on the C-54 and send it back. Also, you should know the tactical situation."

"Has it changed?" asked Ingram.

"Yes and no," said Ferguson. Captain Dezhnev is now in charge of the garrison. He--"

"Dezhnev's back in Toro?"

"Well, yes."

Ingram muttered, "Damn, he works fast."

Neidemeier held up a hand. "I hate to keep jumping on this, but Toro is no longer Toro."

"The Russians are calling it something else?" asked Ingram.

"Yes."

"How 'bout Commietown," said Peoples.

"Lieutenant," said Neidemeier.

"Sorry, sir."

Neidemeier continued, "They've renamed it," he checked a page and then pursed his lips, "Shakhtyorsk, part of the Sakhalin Oblast. Apparently, that's what they called it before the Japs took over in 1904."

Lassiter wrote furiously. Peoples rolled his eyes at Ingram. Ferguson's attention was drawn to a speck of dust on his coat as Neidemeier said, "I'm sorry, but that's how we must refer to it henceforth."

"Yes, I have it," said Lassiter.

Peoples raised a hand.

"Yes, Lieutenant," said Neidemeier.

"May I ask if this here Shakhtyorsk has a beacon?"

"We have diplomatic channels," said Ferguson. "So, I can ask. I'll get right on it as soon as we finish. In the meantime, you should know that the Soviet invasion force is gone, retired back to Port Arthur or Vladivostok. The remaining garrison numbers about five hundred NKVD naval infantry. There is also a station ship: The *Admiral Volshkov*, a cruiser, a war prize from the Germans. She recently arrived as an adjunct to their Pacific Fleet.

Ingram was curious. "Do you have anything on her?"

Ferguson opened a folder and flipped pages. "Hmm . . . she was the *Würtzburg*, captured nearly intact at Kiel; 5,400 tons, 508 feet overall, complement of 534. She carries eight 5.9-inch guns in single mounts. And . . ." he flipped a page, "four torpedo tubes--a twin mount to starboard and another to port, each shooting a 19.7-inch torpedo." He looked up. "Is that enough?"

"How old is she?"

"Ummm . . . built Wilhelmshaven in 1927."

Peoples said, "Nuthin' we cain't handle, right Todd?"

Ingram ignored Peoples and asked, "How about her engineering plant?"

Ferguson said, "Ten Schulz-Thorneycroft boilers, two geared turbines rated at twenty-nine knots. Uh . . . you wanna know about armor plate?"

"Might as well."

"Three to four inches on the sides; two inches on the gun houses; three inches on the conning tower. Tell you what. I'll send this along with the rest of your packet."

"Thank you. Except there's still one problem."

"What's that?" asked Ferguson.

"I have no idea where that crate is. Walter Boring was close to death's door when we pulled him out of there. There was only one crate in the room with him. He didn't mention a second one."

Ferguson asked, "You're not aware of what Walter Boring told Colin Blinde?"

"The only thing I know is that Colin Blinde said he killed Boring," said Ingram.

Ferguson gave a start.

Neidemeier nodded. "He told us Boring was nearly comatose and could hardly breathe. That he gave Boring cyanide to put him out of his misery."

Ferguson said, "Well, it's obvious there's a mix-up here. You two should work it out on the plane, because I'm given to understand that Blinde knows where it is."

Ingram tossed his hands in the air. "Okay. Anything else?"

"Radio procedures," said Ferguson. "We'll have four channels open to you. We want an hourly sitrep in the air or on the ground. And we want a sitrep on landing and on contact with the Russians. Your radio operator has the frequency data."

"Okay," said Ingram. He looked over to Peoples.

Peoples said, "Sounds good to me. We have a full load of fuel; should be plenty to get us there and back."

"Amen," said Ferguson.

There was an uneasy silence. Neidemeier said, "Operations has your weather."

Peoples said, "Already have it, Major. Might be a little bumpy going up." He checked his watch. "I'd like to land before sunset and I'm not sure about the visibility at Toro, er, Shakhtyorsk. If we don't get going now, we're going to need that beacon for sure. So, can we light the fuse now, please, gentlemen?"

Neidemeier said, "Right. You all go board your plane. I'll call operations and ask them to call Mr. Blinde's plane and have the pilot taxi right up to yours."

"Sounds good to me, Major. The sooner the better." They shook hands with Ferguson and walked out.

A Marine gunnery sergeant and his thirteen-man squad were gathered under the C-54's wing chatting with the Air Corps people as the Jeep drove up. Ingram jumped down and walked up to introduce himself. Unlike the refrigerator-shaped Harper, this man was tall and had a large Adam's apple. His deep voice was the clincher for Ingram. The man exuded confidence. He stuck out his hand and introduced himself. "Gunnery Sergeant Horace T. Boland, sir. I've heard a lot about you, Commander."

"None of it good, I expect."

"Better than good. Ugly tells me you're top drawer, and that's good enough for me."

"How is Ugly?"

"Rotated stateside. Camp Pendleton. He's probably swilling beer in Oceanside as we speak."

"Life is hard."

Boland grinned. "That it is, Commander."

Ingram said, "I'm told you have a bazooka."

"Yes, sir. That and some other surprises."

"Such as?"

"Well, I stocked a .30-caliber machine gun, fifty pounds of C-4, twenty claymore mines, and extra rounds for my boys." He winked. "We'll be going out heavy."

"Sounds good, Sergeant. Let's hope we come back heavy."

"That goes for me, too, Commander. Nothing like soft duty."

Boland didn't look to Ingram like a man to run from a fight. "Yeah, I think we should--"

Peoples walked up, checking his watch. "We gotta skedaddle."

Ingram said, "I agree; let's go."

Peoples cupped his hands to his mouth. "Everybody aboard!"

"I can take a hint," said Boland. He turned and howled something to his men. They must have understood because they all gathered their packs and equipment and began boarding.

Ingram was halfway up the ladder when another C-54 whipped over the threshold and flared for a landing. "That's them," shouted Peoples. "Mr. Lassiter, wind 'em up, if you please." He twirled a finger over his head.

Lassiter poked his head out the cockpit window. "Yes, sir." He shouted,

"Clear four!" The outboard starboard propeller began turning and caught, the engine belching blue smoke. Soon the other three were going as well.

Ingram stepped into the cockpit and found Hammer and Berne at their usual stations. "Well, hello. You guys don't give up, do you?"

Berne snorted. "Flight pay is flight pay."

Hammer said, "Good to see you, Commander." He waved a hand. "Here's your hot seat. We wired it this time in case you give us trouble."

Ingram said, "Think I'll sit back aft. There's more room this time."

"Don't tell me we scared you," said Berne.

They all laughed.

Peoples climbed into the left seat and strapped in. "Cain't believe it. We're all buttoned up. Mr. Blinde is aboard and out of breath. Hey, you not stayin' up here?"

"Going aft to spread out."

Peoples drawled, "Peace and quiet for a change."

Ingram smiled. "See you later." He walked out.

Peoples popped the brakes, and the C-54 worked its way down the taxi strip. Then they stopped to test magnetos.

Ingram walked into the main cabin. Blinde was two rows back, stretched across two seats. The Marines and their gear were scattered throughout the rest of the cabin.

Blinde's eyes were closed, and his mouth drooped open.

Ingram walked up. "Hello, Colin. Glad you could make it."

Blinde's eyes snapped open. He blinked for a moment then focused on Ingram. "You!"

"Hell yes, it's me." Ingram held out a hand. Blinde's hand felt like a damp sponge.

"You okay, Colin?" Ingram asked. "How was your flight?"

Blinde turned a shade between pale white and green. An odor of sweat and exhaustion, and even fear mixed with his Aqua Velva. He turned away and looked out the window as the cockpit crew ran up the engines, making conversation difficult. As the plane taxied onto the active runway Blinde said, "The flight was awful. We lost an engine an hour out. The pilots were worried about fuel. It wasn't fun."

What the hell is going on? Ingram sat opposite and strapped in.

Peoples didn't lose time. Engines roaring, the C-54 lunged into its takeoff run. Heavy with fuel and people and equipment, it took a while for the plane to build up speed.

Blinde's mouth moved.

"What?" yelled Ingram over the bellowing engines.

Blinde shouted, "You ... feel ... all right?

44

2 December 1945
ONI Headquarters, Long Beach Naval Station
Long Beach, California

Commander Oliver Toliver III rubbed his eyes and looked out the window. Darkness had fallen long ago, and he no longer heard the frantic rush of workers on the street below and out in the shipyard. They'd already knocked off the graveyard shift. Things were slowing down on the home front. This was the first peacetime Christmas since 1940, and people naturally wanted to enjoy it to the hilt with bright lights and everything lit up and good cheer freely flowing.

But he wasn't in the mood for it. The report in his hand was vague and filled with pathological gobbledygook. He'd spent much of the evening looking up multisyllable medical terms. He sighed and laid down the post-mortem on Walt Hodges. Toliver was as confused now as four days ago when Commander Hodges died. The Fort MacArthur coroner's report was late. And it was inconclusive. He stood, yawned, and stretched. A glance at the Chelsea clock told him it was 6:42 p.m. He clicked off his desk lamp and reached for his coat and hat. The phone rang. He picked it up. "Toliver."

"Commander Toliver. It's Doctor Chandler at Fort MacArthur."

Toliver sat back down and leaned back, his chair squeaking as he put his feet up. "You're working late, Doctor."

"As are you. Glad I caught you."

"I was on my way out. Just finished reading your postmortem on Walt Hodges. I have to tell you that was a real test of my college degree. I could only understand every fifth word."

Chandler laughed. "Well, that report was purposely ambiguous because we really didn't have anything to say."

"Okay. I feel better."

"Now we do have something to say."

Toliver sat up. His feet thumped the floor.

"We're lucky one of our doctors worked at Camp Dietrich--the base in Maryland where they study biological warfare. He experimented with some really strange stuff there. They sent him out here because we were so understaffed with all the wounded coming back. Anyway, he got curious when he heard about the Hodges case and ordered special tests."

"Okay."

"We examined the body further and found something very interesting."

"What, Doctor?"

"A tiny iridium-platinum pellet about the size of the head of a pin. It had been injected into Commander Hodges' upper left arm."

"What did the pellet do?"

"Essentially nothing. It's what was inside that did the trick."

Toliver drew out a pad and began scribbling. "Go on."

"It's ricin. A deadly poison made out of castor beans.

"Ricin?"

That's right. Ricin." He spelled it. "There was a wax plug in the pellet. The wax dissolved when it rose to body temperature, then the ricin flowed out and entered Commander Hodges' body. It doesn't take much of it."

"Poison. Son of a bitch."

"Exactly. Somebody injected the pellet into Commander Hodges' left arm seventy-two to ninety-six hours before he died. Essentially, it made his body shut down. There's no real antidote once the poison gets into the system. We're just learning about it, so once again, I'm afraid I must be vague."

"Ricin." Toliver spelled it out.

"That's right. Commander Hodges was cruelly murdered. It's not a pleasant way to go."

Alarm bells went off in Toliver's head and he shot back to his feet. "How was it injected?"

"Something fairly powerful, spring loaded or air pistol possibly; probably through his clothes unless someone caught him without a shirt. We don't know. Camp Dietrich has no real delivery system for it. Other countries do, however."

"Which ones? Do you know?"

Chandler stammered. "Well . . .

"Doctor, please."

The Nazis for sure. Maybe the Japs, but we're not certain. And--" he paused,

"Come on."

"The Soviet Union has been doing a lot of biomedical research with anthrax and ricin. Soviet scientists have published several papers on it."

"Okay, Doc, anything else?"

"That's it for now. I'll write it up and send it over."

"Thanks, Doc." Toliver hung up and dashed across the room to a clipboard he had scanned that morning--the daily summary of men held in the brig and the charges against them. He ran his finger down a column. Yes, there it was: Karol Dudek, a Polish sailor, had been apprehended by the shore patrol three days ago. They'd come across him as they did their rounds in the Greyhound bus terminal in downtown Long Beach. He looked out of place, and the two SPs became suspicious. They asked for his papers. All he had was a City of Long Beach library card and a USO canteen card. The man didn't speak good English, and they became more suspicious and ordered him to stand for a body search. Dudek pulled a knife and came after them. The man fought hard and almost got away, but a billy club decided the issue and the SPs brought him in.

On his person was the knife, a Whittnauer watch, $5,000 in cash, a life raft inflator, and a seabag with the usual clothing and toiletry items. He carried an out-of-date Polish passport, but the Polish consulate in Washington, D.C., had vouched for him and had turned the matter over to the Soviet embassy in Washington.

ONI had a suite of offices on the second floor. In the basement was one of the two Navy brigs on the Long Beach Naval Station. Toliver phoned the brig downstairs.

"Detention Facility Baker, Chief Derickson, sir."

"Chief, this is Commander Toliver upstairs in ONI."

"Oh, yeah, how are you Commander?" They'd met a few times in staff meetings.

"Good. Say, do you still have a prisoner by the name of Dudek?"

"Wait one, sir." Papers rustled. Then, "Yes, sir, we do. Right now, they're suiting him up for transit to the Soviet embassy in D.C. Flight leaves in two hours out of Long Beach."

"Belay that transfer, Chief. Under no circumstances let him out of your sight."

"I . . . uh, . . ."

"What?"

"We have an order from the State Department. There's a Marine captain and sergeant waiting to take custody."

"Belay the transfer. That's an order. I'll be right down."

"Yes, sir."

Toliver slammed down the phone. He grabbed his hat and coat and hobbled down the back stairs to the basement. The Marine captain and sergeant were seated in the anteroom. Both were in greens and wore web belts with .45 pistols in holsters. Both had two rows of campaign ribbons and looked very capable. With a polite nod, Toliver walked past them and into the station office.

Chief Derickson, a barrel-chested man with silver hair, shot to his feet when Toliver walked in. "Evening, Commander. Do you want to see the prisoner?"

"Yes. Now, please."

"Very good, Commander." Chief Derickson picked up the phone and made the call. He ended with, "And make sure you have two guys on him, big guys . . . Torres and Vestal? They're good. Send 'em up." He hung up and turned to Toliver. "All set, Commander."

"Okay, In the meantime I want to see his belongings."

"Yes, sir." Derickson opened a drawer in his desk, pulled out a paper bag, and emptied it. "Can you imagine, a guy sitting in the Greyhound bus terminal with five grand? And look at this. A Whittnauer watch." He held it up. "I wonder who he rolled." The chief separated the rest of the sack's contents. "Here's his knife, a beauty." He picked it up and pushed the action. The blade jumped out with a resounding click.

Toliver pointed. "That. Is that the life raft inflator?"

"Yes, sir." Derickson pushed it over. The inflator had a black barrel that was about six inches long and an inch and a half in diameter. "That's what he tells me it is, anyway. Have to admit I've never seen one like it."

Toliver picked it up and unscrewed the main section. A carbon dioxide cartridge was secured against the inside wall. He turned it around but found no nozzle. "How does this inflate a life raft?"

"Damned if I know."

Toliver screwed the barrel back in place. He heard a click. "What's this?"

"Sir?"

"There's a ridge at the other end--"

"Chief? Here he is." Two shore patrolmen dressed in blues with web belts and .45s led in a small man in handcuffs. He wore dungarees and a blue chambray shirt, and a peacoat was jammed under his arm. His straw-colored hair was mussed. A fresh bandage was taped over his right forehead.

The man stumbled into the room, his eyes darting about.

"You bet, Chief," One of the SPs rumbled, "He eats like there's no tomorrow."

Toliver walked up to him. "What is your name?"

The man's eyes narrowed and settled on Toliver. "Dudek," he said. "Karol Dudek." Then his eyes continued searching around the room. He stiffened slightly when he saw the table nearby with his money, life raft inflator, switchblade, and seabag.

"Thank you. Where are you from, Mr. Dudek?" asked Toliver.

"*Yeaaaagh!*" the man screeched and shoved Toliver aside. Before anyone could react he was at the table and had his knife in hand.

The room was small, and only one SP could get at him. He charged, billy club raised.

Dudek quick-jabbed the man in the belly. The SP screamed and fell to the floor, moaning and clutching his stomach. Dudek reached down and yanked the wounded SP's .45 from his holster. "Hah!" With a victorious grin he waved the pistol back and forth between the other SP, Toliver, and Chief Derickson. "Back!" he yelled. "Hands up. Now!"

Toliver and the others backed up.

The SP on the floor rose and reached for the pistol.

Dudek slapped away his hand, cocked the pistol, and shot him in the chest. The blast in the small room was deafening, making Toliver's ears ring.

The SP fell to his back, arms splayed and eyes wide open.

Dudek waved the pistol back and forth and then seemed to make a decision. "You next, big officer." He leveled the .45 at Toliver.

Four blasts in quick succession roared from the doorway. Karol Dudek's chest blossomed with large red splotches. The force of the shots slammed him against the opposite wall. With a groan, he tumbled to the floor and was still.

The room was smoky with cordite. Standing at the doorway were the two Marines, their pistols leveled at Karol Dudek. Chief Derickson walked over and kicked the pistol away from Dudek. He felt Dudek's wrist, then his neck. "Done for."

Toliver's head was still filled with noise and cordite. "What's that?"

The chief yelled, "I said, it's curtains, nine innings, lights out. The son of a bitch is dead."

"Got it, Chief."

The SP reached down and checked his buddy. "So is Torres." He nodded toward Dudek. "That dirty bastard got what he deserved." Then he hauled Torres' body to the other side of the room and carefully arranged the dead man's arms and legs. "I'm sorry, Pancho. You was a good partner."

Toliver looked at the Marines. "Thank you, fellas. That was close."

The captain holstered his .45. "Timing is everything."

Others rushed in the room. People crowded in the hallway trying to peek over each other's shoulders.

Toliver said, "Chief, call the coroner and keep everybody out except for our witnesses." He walked over to the Marines and held out his hand. "Toliver, ONI."

The captain said, "Bergstrom, brig commander, and this here is Sergeant Hallen, my top kick." They shook hands. "We heard the scuffle. Sorry we didn't get here in time to save your SP."

Toliver looked over at Dudek's inert form. "He was quick; handcuffs and all, he surprised us."

"For sure," said Captain Bergstrom. "Something weird here. So the Russian embassy in D.C. wanted him? Got an idea." He walked to Dudek's body, dropped to one knee, and forced open Dudek's mouth. After a moment he pulled out a brownish tooth.

"Rotten?" asked Toliver.

"No, sir. This is a cyanide capsule. Meant to be bitten on when captured. Death is almost instantaneous. Did you see his jaw working just before we opened up?"

"To tell you the truth I was scared out of my pants." Toliver was surprised he hadn't wet his britches. He hadn't thought of it at the time, but he sure did now. "But no, I didn't." He nodded to the tooth, "Never seen one of those before. But I've heard of them."

Captain Bergstrom palmed the false tooth. "This is sophisticated stuff. Like he was supposed to kill himself if he was caught."

Telephones were jangling and Chief Derickson was trying to answer them. Two lieutenants barged in, then a four-striper, all demanding answers from Derickson.

"What else did he have?" Toliver wondered aloud. With Bergstrom and Hallen he walked over to the table to examine Dudek's belongings again. He picked up the black barrel, screwed it tight, and looked again at the ridge.

"Just for kicks." Toliver aimed it across the room and thumbed the little ridge. "*Phhhfft!*" The barrel jumped in his hand. Something plinked against a glass-framed photo of the battleship *Maryland* across the room and then rattled on the desk beneath.

"What the hell?" said Bergstrom.

"I'll be a . . ." The three walked across the room. The other officers and Chief Derickson joined them. The photo's glass cover was cracked. "This thing has a kick to it." Toliver bent down to find a gleaming little pellet on the desk just below the picture. "Chief, you have an envelope?" He held out a hand.

"Yes, sir." Derickson yanked open a drawer and handed one over.

Using a paperclip, Toliver poked the pellet into the envelope, then sealed it.

"What do you think, Commander?" asked Captain Bergstom.

"I don't like what I think. Chief, did you count the money?"

Derickson said, "Yes, sir. Five grand. Couldn't you do a number at the track with all that? Think of it. Del Mar in the summertime. Horses prancing in the surf. And the dollies. Lotsa dollies. Hubba, hubba." He picked up the money and waved it.

Toliver said, "Yeah, Hubba, hub--" He sniffed. That odor. Only a faint tinge, but it was there: Aqua Velva. On both the money and the envelope. "Son of a bitch!"

"You okay, Commander?" asked Captain Bergstrom.

Toliver barked, "Chief, get the Fort MacArthur Infirmary on the line. Doctor Chandler. Hurry!"

Derickson stepped to his desk and picked up the phone.

Toliver sniffed again at the money. "I'll be a son of a bitch."

45

3 December 1945
En route to Shakhtyorsk, Sakhalin Oblast, USSR

As Peoples had predicted, the weather was bumpy. They flew under a high overcast at ten thousand feet only to look down on a hoary mist obscuring the seascape. It got worse as they approached Sakhalin, with the overcast blotting out the sun and darkening their surroundings.

Small talk had long been exhausted. The Marines kept busy, and Ingram envied that they had something to do. Rifles and pistols clacked as they were fieldstripped, the Marines running the actions. Ammo boxes and field packs were examined and reexamined as they closed Sakhalin. Time and time again, Sergeant Boland polished his binocular lenses while his radioman fiddled with his equipment, checking frequencies and poring over codebooks.

With darkness falling, Ingram walked to the flight deck. Right now, Berne, the navigator and radioman, was the most important man on the plane. Every hour or so he checked in with Atsugi while updating his navigational plot.

Peoples turned in his seat, "How ya doin', Todd?"

Ingram said, "Middling to unfair."

"That means you're anxious. We're doin' just fine, so you don't have to worry." Peoples winked and returned to his controls.

"I'll try." Ingram leaned over Berne's shoulder, "How's it look, Jon?"

Berne fiddled with radio dials. "Eh, win a few, lose a few. Atsugi rogered our sitrep, so we're okay in that department. But the navigation is for the birds. I haven't had a fix for the past four hours, and we should be making landfall pretty soon."

Berne raised his voice, "You get that, Leroy? All dead reckoning. No guarantees."

Peoples turned slowly in his seat. "DR roger, Jon. So, tell me somethin'. We're still on autopilot. Do you think we should take it off?"

"No, I--"

"Then we'll go with what you got, Jon."

Peoples was dead serious. Ingram had to hand it to him. The man was putting his trust in Berne and letting him know it--a real confidence booster. Peoples wasn't a Bucky Radcliff, but in his own way he had become a good leader.

Berne gave a broad smile. "I appreciate your vote, Leroy. Still, no guarantees."

Peoples said, "Your recommendation is guarantee enough. Now, get busy and give me a time, course, and speed to let down in this muck. Any luck with their tower yet?"

"Nothing yet. I've been trying every five minutes. They just don't answer."

"Are we transmitting properly?"

"Checking it five ways from Sunday, Leroy. Radios are working all right."

"What does Atsugi advise?"

"Same as last time," said Berne. "They say 'use your own judgment.' The bad news is that we're almost out of voice range. When we start down we'll be on CW for sure."

"Okey, dokey," said Peoples.

A moment later Berne said, "In 4 minutes, at 1517, descend to 1,500 feet and maintain present course, speed 135. There should be no obstructions around the field for at least 20 miles."

"Very good. Mr. Lassiter, if you please?"

"Yes, sir." Lassiter began calling out the landing checklist.

Hammer rose. "Might as well tell 'em now." He went to the door and called for everyone to buckle up and prepare for landing. Then he returned and sat. He leaned over and said, "That goes for you, too, Commander." He nodded to the jump seat.

"Thank you." Ingram sat and buckled up.

Peoples asked, "Is 1517 still good, Jon?"

"Sure is."

Peoples counted off on his fingers and then chopped the power. Moments later he eased the yoke forward and said, "Flaps fifteen when I give the word, Mr. Lassiter."

"Flaps fifteen on your word, sir," said Lassiter. Soon he reported, "Passing through 5,000 . . . 4,500."

"Flaps fifteen."

"Flaps fifteen," replied Lassiter. He reached down and tweaked the lever. The plane bucked with the lift as the flaps lowered.

"Jon, give Atsugi a sitrep, please," said Peoples.

"Roger." Berne twirled dials on his radio equipment. "Lost them on voice. Going to CW."

"Right," said Peoples. When the altimeter read 1,500 feet Peoples called, "Okay, speed 135. Gear down."

"On its way," said Lassiter, throwing the lever.

"Flaps twenty."

"Twenty," said Lassiter.

With the others, Ingram looked out the window. It was nearly pitch black; he couldn't see a thing.

Peoples said, "Try Shakhtyorsk again and keep working it."

Berne gave an eye-roll. "Yes, sir."

"We've been here before, Commander," said Peoples. "You cain't trust these bastards, remember?"

"How can I forget," said Ingram.

"What do you recommend, Mr. Berne?" asked Peoples.

"Pucker up and be ready for anything," said Berne.

"Descending to five hundred feet," said Peoples calmly, again pulling back the power.

The cockpit became quiet with the engines at idle. Ingram and Hammer traded glances as they realized Peoples was acting as if he were riding a bicycle down Main Street.

Hammer mopped his forehead with a handkerchief, "Shit, we don't have an altimeter setting."

Ingram pulled his strap tighter. He knew that the C-54, in poor visibility, could fly into the ground without the proper altimeter information provided by the tower.

Lassiter said, "I wonder if--"

"Mr. Lassiter, please!"

"Yes, sir. Sorry, sir."

Ingram knew how they felt, and he envied them as he did the Marines; they all had something to do. All he could do was hang on and pray and think of Helen.

"Five hundred feet," called Lassiter.

Peoples pulled back on the yoke and eased in some throttle. "Runway three-four?" he asked.

Berne said, "Affirmative, three-four. And according to this we should be on top right now."

"Going to 250 feet," said Peoples, leaning forward, peering at black cotton.

Suddenly, wisps of gray shot past and they saw the ground. "Hey!" said Lassiter. "There. Ten o'clock."

Indeed, Berne had planted them on their downwind approach to the airport. Over their left shoulders they spotted runway. Slick with moisture, it glistened in the dimming light.

Peoples called over his shoulder, "Son of a gun, Jon. Fine job. Damned fine job."

Berne fairly beamed. "All part of the service, Leroy. You'll get my bill."

"Except, where the hell's the lights? There's no lights at all," said Hammer.

"Yeah, no beacon," said Lassiter. "How's that for diplomacy?"

Ingram caught something at the edge of his vision. He looked aft and spotted a long, narrow shape off the coast. The Soviet cruiser. The *Admiral Volshkov*. Barely visible, she was anchored about a thousand yards offshore.

Peoples saw it, too. "There's your German cruiser."

"Strange," said Ingram.

"What?" asked Peoples.

"She's not showing lights either. Anchor lights are required. Especially in peacetime. Even our ships in Japan show lights now. What the hell's going on? No beacon, no lights. Nothing." He swept a hand toward the horizon. And I don't see the *Maxwell*."

"Would she have her lights on?"

"Don't see any reason why she wouldn't. Tubby White knows the drill."

"You still want to go in?" asked Peoples.

Ingram thought it over. "We've come this far. Might as well."

"I smell a skunk." Peoples turned the C-54 onto the base leg.

"Do we have a choice?"

"Don't think so. But I'm glad we have them jarheads," said Peoples. He eased yoke and rudder and put the C-54 on final approach.

"I'll say. They'll be the first ones out," said Ingram.

"Okay, final checks, if you please, Mr. Lassiter."

"Jon, what about the Commies?" asked Lassiter. "Anything yet?"

"Nothing," said Berne. "Hold on. Sending a sitrep. Whoops! Now what? A long one coming in. Whoa. Priority. For Mr. Ingram's eyes only. Amazing." Berne bent over his code key and tapped with his left hand while writing the message on a blank pad with his right.

"What's amazing, Jon," demanded Peoples.

"It's . . . top priority . . . top secret, and . . ." Berne twirled his pencil trying to keep up. ". . . Never seen anything like it. Damn thing's in plain English."

"Get it down, Jon," said Peoples.

"Doin' my best."

Peoples eased off some power and called, "Full flaps."

"Coming down," said Lassiter.

Peoples barked, "Landing lights. You got landing lights?"

"Sorry." Lassiter threw a switch and the haze before them became opaque. But now they could make out the numerals 34 painted at the runway's threshold.

They were five hundred feet from the runway when Berne said, "Got it." Then, "Jeez." He keyed his acknowledgment as the plane flashed over the threshold.

Peoples chopped throttles and the C-54 began to flare.

Berne reached over and handed the message to Ingram. "Best you look at it now, Commander."

"In a minute." Ingram snatched it away and jammed it in his pocket just as the C-54 touched.

"Holy shit! Damned thing is still there," said Peoples.

A glance toward the runway's end told the story. The wrecked M-16 half-track was still in the middle of the runway, about three quarters of the way down.

The C-54 bounced and then held. "Flaps up *now*, Mr. Lassiter."

"Got it," said Lassiter, yanking the lever up.

With some lift gone, the plane settled on its mains; then the nose came down. Peoples began a delicate dance on the brake pedals, knowing the C-54 could easily go into a skid on the slick surface; maybe even a ground loop.

"Come on," he urged. The dark gray hulk of the M-16 grew larger in the windshield. "Git your butt down."

One hundred yards to go: the C-54 was still moving, its nose dipping as Peoples stood on the brakes.

"*Yeaggh!*" Peoples yelled. "Cut the damned power. Everything off. All master switches!" He yanked back the mixture and throttles.

Lassiter flipped off magnetos. Hammer frantically flipped off fuel switches and everything else he could find.

"Brace yourselves!" yelled Peoples.

The C-54 drew to a halt ten feet from the half-track--so close they couldn't see it below the nose.

"Shit!" said Hammer.

Lassiter whacked Peoples on the back. "Great job, Skipper."

Peoples said, "Aw right, aw right. We need power. Hammer, reengage master switches and start number two immediately."

"Yes, sir." Hammer flipped switches. Soon he and Lassiter were spinning the port inboard engine. Immediately, it burst back into life. The cabin lights and instrument panel blossomed as the generator came back online.

"Welcome to Karafuto, lads," said Hammer.

"Sakhalin, you jerk," said Berne. "We mustn't insult our comrades."

Peoples opened the cockpit window and stuck his head out. "Brrrr. It's cold out there."

"See anybody?" asked Ingram.

"No, sir." He slid the window shut.

Ingram's left hand was shaking. So was his right. He flexed his fingers, making them work. Then he unbuckled, leaned forward, and said, "Good landing, Leroy."

"Almost crapped my pants," Peoples said. His left hand was shaking, too. He saw Ingram flexing his fingers and grinned. "They say any landing you walk away from is a good landing," he said. "Trouble is, we haven't walked away yet."

"I'll go with that," said Ingram. "Time to get going. I want to get the Marines on the ground ASAP."

"Makes sense to me," said Peoples.

Ingram walked aft and found the Marines on their feet, checking their gear, ready to disembark. He looked about the cabin but couldn't find Colin Blinde.

Squeezing past two Marines, Boland said, "If you're looking for that civilian, he's already gone. Pulled a ladder and scrambled out the hatch the minute we stopped."

Indeed, the hatch was open. Cold wind ripped at them from the near-darkness.

"He say anything?"

"No, just skedaddled."

"Okay." Ingram said, "Get your men on the ground, Gunny. They have parkas?"

"Yes, sir."

"Good. Tell them this was not a nice welcome and to be ready for anything. Set up a perimeter around us. And that means live ammo."

Boland stared at Ingram for two seconds. "Who are the bad guys?"

Good question. "Anyone who threatens us. Outside, right under the nose, you'll find a burned-out M-16 half-track that we took out on our last visit here. The Russians promised peaceful terms this time, but they haven't moved the half-track. No lights, no welcome, no nothing. It's a boondoggle. So, don't trust anyone right now. Check passwords carefully."

"Will do, Commander."

Ingram spun, looking forward. Berne and Peoples were right there. "We need to turn this airplane around and get ready for an immediate departure. How do we--"

Berne grabbed him and hissed, "First, you have to read the damned message, Commander."

46

---

3 December 1945
Shakhtyorsk Air Base
Sakhalin Oblast, USSR

Berne stepped close. "Now, Todd. It's really important."

Boland tugged at Ingram's elbow. "We're going out now, Commander." He passed over a walkie-talkie. "Find me with this."

"Thanks, Gunny. On your way." Ingram turned to Berne. "Think you can raise the *Maxwell*?"

"If you don't read the damned message, I'm gonna raise the dead."

Ingram flushed. "Forgot all about it." He dug the flimsy from his pocket. Berne had written the message in pencil on a blank pad as the C-54 bucked and bounced its way on the downwind and final legs. Some of the words were smudged, but all in all Berne had done a creditable job.

INGRAM--EYES ONLY--INGRAM--EYES ONLY
TOP SECRET
FM: ONI-11NAVDIST

TO: INGRAM, ALTON C, CDR, USN
DTG: 03111746Z NOV 45
CC: SECSTATE
COMONI
COMFIVEFLT
COMII
COMDESRON 77
COM DD525
SUBJ: BLINDE, COLIN

1. HODGES, WALTER, CDR, USN, MURDERED.
2. BELIEVE HODGES MISTAKEN FOR YOU AND ASSASSINATED VIA
RICIN INJECTION: EXOTIC POISON.
3. ASSASSIN WAS FOREIGN NATIONAL, CAUGHT AND KILLED, LBSY.
4. COLIN BLINDE WAS HIS CONTROL. RPT: COLIN BLINDE WAS
THE ASSASSIN'S CONTROL.
5. APPREHEND BLINDE. RETURN HIM CONUS ASAP WITH
PHOTOS.
6. IF (5) NOT PRACTICAL, YOU ARE AUTHORIZED TO TERMINATE.
TOLIVER
BT
INGRAM--EYES ONLY--INGRAM--EYES ONLY

"Holy smoke." Ingram caught Berne's eye. "Can you authenticate this?"
Berne grabbed the message. "Do my best, Commander."
Ingram called after him, "And see if you can raise the *Maxwell*."
"Will do, Commander."
Ingram turned and shouted out the hatch, "Sergeant Boland."
Boland's voice echoed up, "Sir?"
"I'm coming down." Ingram started down the ladder. Bitter cold ripped into him, and he realized he didn't have a jacket as he reached the ground. *Stupid*. Boland must have thought so too because he said, "Freeze your ass off, Commander."
"Look, that civilian who jumped. His name is Colin Blinde."
"Sir."

"I just got a message from ONI. This bastard is a spy, a traitor, and a turncoat. He is to be apprehended. Put the word out to your men. If they see him, grab the son of a bitch. Don't worry about being polite."

Boland's face darkened. "Got it. Do you want to send out a search party?"

"My guess is that he's gone over to the Russians, so I don't think we have a chance of nabbing him right now. Plus, I think we're going to need everybody here, Gunny. At least for the rest of the night. Agree?"

"I do, Commander."

"Okay, set the perimeter. I'm going back inside to find a jacket and send a couple of messages. Also, we have a ship coming in."

"What ship is that, sir?"

"Tin can. The *Maxwell*."

"The *Maxwell*, huh? Destroyer? Tubby White?"

Ingram stopped two rungs up the ladder. "You know Tubby White?"

Boland gave a shallow grin. "Tubby White the PT-boater? Right?"

"That's him."

Just then, two Marines wearing winter whites merged from opposite directions and spoke with Boland in low tones. Boland muttered, ". . . passenger . . . Colin Blinde," along with other instructions. They nodded and disappeared back into the darkness. Boland said, "Perimeter's secure, Commander. Hundred yards each direction. As far as we can tell, nobody's out there. No sign of Colin Blinde."

"Very well."

Boland continued, "Lieutenant White saved my ass down on Bougainville. Came inshore and picked me and six grunts up right off the beach while the Japs threw everything they had at us. Two of my men was wounded, and he got them out too. He's got real guts."

Ingram nodded. "Yep, that's Tubby." He climbed up halfway. "Oh, and Gunny, can you send out some recon to see what we're up against?"

"Consider it done, Commander."

The thick overcast hid the moon and stars, and there was no wind to stir the bushes around the marooned C-54. The cockpit was nearly as cold as the outside with the engines shut down. They all wore mittens and heavy parkas, and vapor shot out when they spoke. From the cockpit they could see over the low berms lining the airstrip and out into the blackness of the Sea of Japan. They saw nothing where they knew the *Admiral Volshkov* was anchored. Peoples instructed a couple of Marines to pull the plane's props through every hour lest oil freeze in the crankcases.

After two hours a tiny glow popped up on the horizon to the southeast. The glow grew brighter and larger and eventually separated into a ship's red and green sidelights and white masthead lights: the *Maxwell*. The men waiting in the cockpit found it comforting that an American ship was nearby, especially because it was the only light in the otherwise complete darkness.

Then Ingram heard a welcome sound: an anchor chain rattling through a hawse pipe, which meant the anchor was plunging through the icy depths and digging its flukes into a soft muddy bottom. The *Maxwell*'s running lights flipped off, and seconds later her anchor lights went on, bathing the forward section of the ship in a soft radiance.

Berne tapped his CW key as they watched. Finally, he stopped and said, "Atsugi authenticated the message about Mr. Blinde, Commander."

"Okay, thanks, Jon," said Ingram.

The other three looked at him, their faces saying, "What the hell is going on?"

Okay. Ingram held up the message and read it to them. "You all know him. Can you believe it?"

"Never did trust the man," Peoples said. "Damned Yankee prances around like a French poodle. And smells like one too."

"Let's hope we catch the son of a bitch," said Lassiter. "An American! With people like that, no wonder the Commies are giving us fits."

Berne grabbed his earphones. "I have the *Maxwell* on voice, Commander. Here." He passed over the headphones and a microphone. "I know he's only about a mile away, but our Army-Navy liaison ain't too hot at this angle. The connection is intermittent, but it's the best I can do. Use this squelch knob if it gives you trouble."

"Thanks, what's our call sign?" asked Ingram.

"Apprentice two-six," said Berne.

Ingram gave a thumbs-up and then said into the mike, "Crackerjack, this is Apprentice two-six, over."

"Crackerjack, over." It was Tubby White's voice.

Ingram said, "Crackerjack, be advised reception for Apprentice two-six very unfriendly. No lights, no reception committee. Also, one of our passengers is a Benedict Arnold and has jumped ship, over."

"Apprentice two-six. Understand your last. Have much ONI traffic for you regarding Benedict. In particular, you should be aware--"

A loud buzzing in Ingram's earphones blotted out White's voice. He gave them back to Berne, who flipped switches and turned knobs. Finally, he said, "Looks like we're being jammed."

"What?" demanded Ingram.

Berne pointed in the direction of the cruiser. "That bastard is jamming us. All frequencies. We can't get out. Nor can we receive."

Peoples opened his window and shined a flashlight at the ground. "Well, if it's any consolation to you, I believe we can turn the airplane around if we don't run number two engine. Looks to me like we can barely clear the half-track. So, we can get out of here any time we like."

Ingram rubbed his chin. "Yeah, I would agree with that. We should think about the safety of your airplane and crew. With the *Maxwell* here, no sense risking you guys. You want to go?"

Peoples eyed his three men, then said, "Shucks, if it's okay with you, Commander, we'll stick here a bit longer, especially since Ivan is jamming the radio. You may still need the Confederate Air Corps for a thing or two."

"Thanks," said Ingram. Then he asked, "Say, do you have a signal light?"

Hammer opened a small cabinet and fished around. "This do the trick?" He held up a hand lantern.

Ingram said, "Right, let's rig it up. Is that a hatch up there?"

"Yes, sir. We can open it up and--"

"Sheeyat! Look at that," shouted Peoples pointing out the window.

The cockpit glowed as a searchlight's pencil beam shot from the Soviet cruiser and bathed the *Maxwell*'s forward deckhouse in a hoary brightness. A second searchlight flicked on, playing over the *Maxwell*'s after deckhouse.

Lassiter said, "What the hell do they expect to accomplish by that?"

"Just being assholes," said Hammer.

"What do you think, Commander?" asked Lassiter. "Does the *Maxwell* have a chance against her if it comes to a fight?"

"You mean as in a street fight?"

"Well, yes."

Ingram said, "The *Volshkov* is three times the *Maxwell*'s size and has nearly twice the armament."

"What can she do, then?" asked Berne.

As if in answer, the *Maxwell*'s stack-mounted searchlights flicked on, illuminating the Russian cruiser.

"All right!" said Peoples.

They gasped as the searchlights probed and dueled into the night, each playing over the other's ship as a policeman would play his flashlight over a gang of criminals.

The plane jiggled, and Sergeant Boland appeared in the cockpit doorway looking like Nanook of the North in his white snow parka and trousers. The hood was up, vapor erupted from his mouth, and frost coated his eyebrows and nostrils. "Gentlemen."

"Gunny, how is it out there?" asked Ingram.

"Patrol returned, safe and sound," Boland said.

"Good."

"Surprise. This place is damned near empty. No more than fifty to seventy-five men ashore. And they're just guarding Jap prisoners bivouacked in a camp about five hundred yards due north, right near the pier. It looks like they're getting ready to load out because there's three fifty-foot personnel boats tied to the pier along with a barge. But get this. Everything is gone except for about twenty trucks and some mechanized, including a half dozen T-34s and as many M-16s. But there are two 105-mm fieldpieces at the end of the runway, fully manned and with plenty of ammo."

The searchlights continued their intricate dance as Boland went on, "The headquarters is empty."

Ingram looked up. "That is a surprise."

"And no sign of Benedict Arnold."

"That's not a surprise."

"Hey!" Lassiter pointed at the *Maxwell*. In the frosty light they saw a living room–sized American flag unfurled, run up, and two-blocked on her starboard halyard.

"I'll be gaw-damned," said Peoples.

Ingram felt a surge of pride. "Her battle flag."

"That Tubby White?" asked Boland.

"That's him."

"He don't screw around," said Boland.

"That the fat little guy with us on the *Missouri*?" asked Peoples.

"Yes. He was your host for the day aboard the *Maxwell*."

"Guy has guts," said Berne.

Ingram smiled to himself, wishing Landa could see this. "Indeed, he does." *I'm going to put the little son of a bitch in for a medal.*

"That's it for now, Commander," said Boland.

"Thanks, Gunny. Return to your men. I still want to hold tight on the perimeter until morning."

"Yes, sir." Boland walked out.

Ingram muttered, "The rules are changing." To Hammer, "Okay, that light ready to go?"

"Yes, sir."

"Know how to use it?"

"I can, sir, but I feel certain, Marco Polo here can do a better job."

Of course. "Jon, can you send a flashing-light message to the *Maxwell*?"

"You mean out the hatch?"

"That's the idea." With Hammer's help he reached up to unclip the escape hatch.

Hammer plugged in the light and handed it to Berne, who asked. "What do I do?"

"Smile for the Commies," said Peoples.

"Up yours, hillbilly," said Berne.

Ingram said, "Flash 'dog five.'"

"That's letter dee and then a numeral five?"

"Right. They should respond with the same thing. And keep trying. They're busy out there with all that damned search lighting."

"Okay." Berne stepped on a foot brace and raised himself halfway through the hatch.

"How's the weather out there, big Jon?" asked Peoples.

"Screw you."

They laughed. Peoples cupped his hands to shout--

"Hey! Here we go. They roger dog five followed by able two-six. That's us. What now?"

"Okay. Send 'Tubby, MT 5 shoot one star.' Got that?"

"Tubby, MT 5 shoot one star."

"Right. And then wait for a roger."

"Freezing my ass off." Berne began clicking his signal lantern.

"Don't worry. I'm sure Mr. Peoples will put you in for a Silver Star," called Hammer.

"Over my dead body," said Peoples loudly.

"That's the spirit," said Hammer.

Berne yelled down, "Leroy, when I get out of this, I'm going to beat the crap--ho, wait a minute. I have a roger from the *Maxwell*."

"Good. Now, sign off and come on down, Jon." Ingram and Hammer grabbed Berne's elbows and lowered him to the flight deck. Quickly they secured the hatch.

Berne's eyebrows and hair were frosted. His teeth chattered as he said, "B-b-blanket."

Hammer stepped aft to a locker, drew out a blanket, and wrapped it around Berne's shoulders. "Sorry no booze, Jon."

Berne shivered. "I'm sure you have some stashed somewhere, you stingy bastard."

Blam! A gun fired from the *Maxwell*.

Seconds later a star shell puffed gently into the night well beyond the Russian cruiser. Swinging on its little parachute, the flare eased down, fully illuminating the cruiser for the *Maxwell*'s gunners.

"What's to keep them from shooting back?" asked Peoples.

"I don't think so," said Ingram. It was a gutsy move, Ingram knew. But the *Maxwell* had the drop on the Russian cruiser at the moment. She would be mortally wounded if gunfire broke out now. He repeated, "I don't think so."

The cruiser's searchlights flicked off.

A half minute later the *Maxwell* turned off her searchlights. Then her anchor lights flicked off. With all the lights out, Shakhtyorsk was once again plunged into darkness.

Good. Ingram turned to Hammer. "Got another blanket?"

Hammer opened a locker. "All you need, Commander." Then, "Oh my, oh my, what is this?"

"What?" they demanded.

Hammer reached in and carefully lifted out a bottle of brandy. "Who would ever do such a thing?"

47

4 December 1945
Shakhtyorsk Air Base
Sakhalin Oblast, USSR

"Commander, we got trouble." It was Boland whispering in Ingram's ear.

"Huh?" Ingram tried to straighten up, but he was cold and stiff from being wedged in between two passenger seats.

"Commies. Outside, sir, when you can." Boland disappeared.

Ingram checked his watch: 7:42. Nearly sunrise. Gray light was already filtering through the C-54's windows. *Damn!* He had overslept. He'd wanted to be up before dawn and outside with the Marines. They must be half frozen by now.

He reached over and shook Peoples. "Leroy. Off and on."

"Huh?"

"No time for talk. Time's a wasting." Ingram shook off the blanket, rose, and jammed his feet into his boots. Grabbing his hat, he headed for the ladder.

He scrambled down, finding Boland waiting for him. Silently, the sergeant pointed past the M-16 and down the runway, toward the coast. In the distance a ragged line of soldiers walked toward them on the runway. More were bunched at the edges. It reminded Ingram of a suicide charge; they could have easily been mowed down. Except among the men were two M-16 half-tracks with quad .50-caliber machine guns. And behind them was a staff car.

The ladder jiggled as the cockpit crew scrambled down. Vapor escaped their mouths as they gaped down the runway. "Commies playin' chicken," said Hammer. They looked at Ingram.

Five minutes, no more.

"What are your orders, Commander?" Boland asked.

The realization that it was up to him hit Ingram like a bucket of ice water. He'd been faced with decisions in the heat of battle many times. But on those occasions his training and experience had taken over, telling him what to do. And if not that, then instinct. His escape from Corregidor and travel through 1,900 miles of enemy-held territory had been mostly on instinct.

But this was a new situation. What was supposed to be diplomacy could be escalating into a deadly conflict. Two sovereigns who were supposed to be at peace with one another, who were supposed to be friendly nations, were suddenly shaking their fists. And Ingram was in the middle. Friends or not, He realized that they were now standing on the soil of the Union of Soviet Socialist Republics, and the Russians could do any damned thing with him they wanted. It made him feel naked and defenseless. And Boland was asking for instructions.

American naval officers from John Paul Jones to James Lawrence to Oliver Hazard Perry to George Dewey had made decisions under similar circumstances. Like them, he was the on-scene commander. There was no one else to turn to. He, Cdr. Alton C. Ingram, USN, had to decide. Worst of all, he might have to order one or more of these brave men to their death. How ironic. After a bitter four-year war, it was peacetime. Yet here he was with a gun to his head.

His first priority: their safety. Second priority: the mission, which didn't look too promising right now, especially since the Russians had two 105-mm cannons dug in at the far end of the runway plus a seemingly inexhaustible supply of those damned M-16 half-tracks. And that was to say nothing of the Russian cruiser anchored offshore.

Back to priority one. Ingram asked, "Still have that bazooka?"

"Yes, sir."

"Line up on the M-16 on the right and take it out when I give the word."

"Yes, sir." Boland raised his walkie-talkie and gave instructions.

The Russians kept advancing.

"How are your men, Sergeant?"

"Freezing their asses off. But they're okay. They have proper gear for a change; good Alpine winter stuff."

Closer. He could hear the rumble of the half-track's engine.

"Good. After we're done with this set up a plan to rotate them, so they can have chow and rest up."

"Sounds good to me, sir."

Just then, the half-track on the right fired a burst from the quad .50 machine gun over their heads.

"What the hell do those bastards think they're doing?" said Peoples. He, Lassiter, Hammer, and Berne took cover behind the burned-out M-16.

Ingram said, "Sergeant Boland. Commence fire; bazooka only. Take out the left half-track. But don't reveal your other positions."

"Got it." Boland yelled into his walkie-talkie, "Able six, *faaahrrrrr.*"

The bazooka round whooshed downfield, went straight through the half-track's windshield. It exploded with an enormous blast. A great plume of dust, dirt, M-16 parts, and bodies twirled through the air. Some of the Soviets soldiers nearby were knocked down and lay where they fell. Others crawled slowly away, some being helped by comrades.

Ingram barked, "Line up on the second M-16 and get ready."

Boland howled into his walkie-talkie.

The second M-16 began a turn, apparently to escape, but someone ran from the command car and blocked its path. Then he ran up to the driver's side and shouted at them, his hands on his hips.

Boland said dryly, "Now's a good time, sir, with that stupid officer standin' there in plain sight."

"Not yet." The quad .50s were more or less straight up in the air. "If he levels that thing at us, then I'm going to--" A familiar sound cut him off:

aircraft engines. He looked behind him and saw three four-engine aircraft approaching, flying no more than thirty feet above the runway nearly wingtip to wingtip, pulling large trails of dust. They flashed overhead, making their world one of thunder and vibration. The aircraft in the center was a C-54. On either side were B-24J Liberator bombers. They blasted over the Russians and were gone.

The cockpit crew cheered and waved their arms.

"Looks like we have an air force," muttered Boland."

"Damn! It's Bucky!" Peoples waved.

"How can you tell?" demanded Ingram.

"The sumbitch is sideslippin'."

"Not only that." Boland stepped out into the middle of the runway and pointed.

Ingram followed his gaze. The Soviets were in full retreat. The command car was gone, and the remaining M-16 bounced into a clump of bushes and disappeared.

In the distance, the B-24s begin to orbit the *Admiral Volshkov* at about two thousand feet while Bucky Radcliff lined up for another run down the field.

The next decision was easy. Ingram yelled. "Leroy! You and your men get on that aircraft and get out of here."

Peoples trotted up. "Hold on. What about you and your Marines?"

"We have the Navy and those B-24s to take care of us. Now, get going while the getting is good. Start that damned airplane and," he nodded in the opposite direction, "I suggest you point it that way."

Peoples said, "You sound like a damned pilot. Okay, Todd. Thanks." He pumped a fist. "Let's go, boys." While the others scrambled, he held out a hand. "Godspeed."

Ingram said, "You too, Leroy. Now, get the hell out of here." He slapped Peoples on the butt. The Marines pulled the props through a few strokes while Peoples and his crew scrambled up. Hammer stayed behind and dashed among the landing gear, pulling safety pins and chocks. He tossed them through the hatch and followed them in. Peoples slid open his cockpit window and called, "Stand clear. We're going to kick up a hell of a lot of dust."

Boland walked up as Ingram yelled back, "Good luck, Leroy. And thanks again."

Peoples pulled a face. "I pale in the presence of two naval heroes."

"Correction, sir," growled Boland, "I'm a Marine."

Peoples grinned, shook his head, and called back, "Whatever. Thanks for everything, Gunny. What do you think the Commies will do when we start cranking engines?"

Ingram said, "We'll check with the outposts and let you know. Safe trip home."

"That's the easy part."

Engines droned in the distance, and the men on the ground turned to see Radcliff's C-54 heading down the runway, much slower this time. The gear was down, and the flaps were lowered, as if coming in to land. Just before the C-54 got to them, a weighted bag fell out the rear cargo hatch, thumped down on the runway, and skidded to a halt seventy-five yards away. Then the C-54 flashed overhead and was once again gone, its landing gear and flaps retracting.

Boland raised his walkie-talkie. "Able three, can you recover? . . . Roger."

A marine in a white camouflage suit ran out of the bushes, snatched up the bag, and jogged toward them.

Boland said, "Pony Express, sir."

The Marine handed it over.

"How you feeling, son?" asked Ingram.

"Not bad, Commander. Err . . . are those Commies coming after us?"

"Not if I can help it. Actually, you guys just fired the shot heard round the world."

"Are we in trouble, sir?"

"Not at all, son. Thanks for taking care of us."

"You're welcome, sir."

Boland nodded, and the Marine jogged back to his post.

Ingram said, "Your men are going to have a story to tell, Gunny."

Boland chuckled, "I can see it now. Amaya telling his grandkids, 'Hey, I fired the shot that started World War III.'"

"Good aim."

Hammer hollered down from the open hatch, "Watch out. Fire in the hole and clear one!" Then he hoisted up the aluminum ladder as the propeller for number one engine began to turn.

Boland led Ingram over to the runway's edge as the engine caught, backfired, erupted great quantities of blue smoke, and then finally evened out. Engines 3 and 4 started in short order, coughing and snorting.

Boland jammed the walkie-talkie to his ear as the engines rumbled. "What?" he yelled. Then, "Hold your position . . . that's affirmative . . . roger."

Boland turned to Ingram and hollered in his ear. "That was able one." He pointed toward the coast. "They caught a two-man team crawling up with an RPG. They had two rounds."

Ingram yelled back. "What'd they do with them?"

"Tied 'em up. Do you want to shoot them?"

"Leave 'em there. We don't have time for prisoners. Let Ivan find 'em."

Even with the engine noise, Boland's tone was the equivalent of an eye-roll. "Yes, sir." He lifted his walkie-talkie and gave instructions.

Radcliff made another pass. Someone waved from the aft cargo hatch.

Ingram and Boland watched closely as Peoples gunned number one engine to pull it over the burned-out M-16.

Suddenly, Boland crossed his fists. Peoples throttled back and hit the brakes.

Boland scrambled onto the wreck and turned a hand wheel. The quad .50s, which had been pointing upward, slowly lowered to zero elevation. Boland hopped out of the wreck. He and Ingram eyed number two engine and its still propeller. They looked at one another and nodded. Then they looked up to Peoples and gave a thumbs-up.

Peoples nodded and punched some power into number one engine. The C-54 rolled and began a 180-degree turn, the left wing clearing the wreck by no more than nine inches.

Halfway through the turn, Peoples started number two engine. The plane finally finished rotating and lined up on the runway, its nose dipping as Peoples braked to a stop. Methodically, the cockpit crew did magneto checks, running systematically through each engine.

Ingram yelled over the noise, "Okay, Gunny. Any more bandits out there?"

Boland did a comm check and nodded. "Looks okay, Commander," he yelled.

"Good." Ingram and Boland walked around opposite the pilot. Peoples slid his window back and waved. Ingram clasped two hands over his head and shook them.

In rapid succession, Peoples lowered the flaps and ran up all four engines while standing on the brakes. The air was filled with thunder as the four R-2000 engines delivered full power. Dust twirled down the runway toward the beach and the Soviet line.

Meanwhile, Bucky Radcliff lined up for another run down the airstrip.

Peoples glanced at Ingram and with two fingers to his forehead tipped a salute. He popped the C-54's brakes just as Radcliff roared over the threshold. With Peoples fairly rolling, the two planes zipped past one another in opposite directions like lumbering barnstormers at a county fair. Ingram and Boland waved as Radcliff blasted over. Fifteen seconds later, Peoples wobbled into the air, having taken up the entire runway. Ingram strained to see if Peoples had used Bucky Radcliff's flap trick to bounce into the air, but he couldn't tell.

The C-54 rose and gained speed; the wheels started retracting.

"Will you look at that," said Ingram.

"Sir?" asked Bolan.

"Typical Leroy."

"What's typical?"

Ingram pointed. "He's side slipping."

48

4 December 1945
Shakhtyorsk Air Base
Sakhalin Oblast, USSR

Ingram reached inside the bag Bucky had dropped and pulled out the message. It was scrawled on the back of an engine maintenance list:

Todd,

State Dept. worried with the Soviet radio jamming and no sitreps from you. In light of this, Atsugi relays from State to scrub mission and come home. Get Leroy in the air ASAP. Four destroyers en route to help. ETA tomorrow 0600.

We're in contact with Tubby, who stands ready to pick you up. Just wave or flash a light from the beach and he'll send in his putt-putt. Avoid the pier to the north. Lots of activity there. Troops milling around, many being loaded on a barge.

Better yet, try your walkie-talkie with Tubby. You might raise him if you climb to a high place--maybe the control tower.

Getting low on gas and have to scram. B-24s too. Good luck.
Bucky

As if on cue, the two C-54s blasted down the runway, wagging their wingtips. Radcliff's plane was the closest, and he slid open his cockpit window and waved. Ingram waved back. The two B-24s circled lazily at the other end of the runway. Soon they all formed up, climbed, and turned to the south, the drone of their engines fading into the distance.

Ingram jerked his attention back. He should have thought of it sooner. "Gunny!"

"Sir!"

"Major Radcliff thinks we can raise the *Maxwell* on the walkie-talkie."

"We've tried."

"He says go to the top of the control tower."

"Ummm. Might work. Still a little beyond our range, though."

"What do we have to lose?"

"I'm with you, Commander."

"Okay. Let's pull back and stake our perimeter around the control tower. Then send someone up and give it a shot."

"Yes, sir." Boland picked up his walkie-talkie and started bawling instructions. The Marines emerged from the bushes in twos, formed up, and crept along the edge of the runway toward the base headquarters buildings. Soon they were below the wrecked control tower.

To Ingram, it seemed too quiet. No birds, nothing. Just the Marines gathered about, gray skies, low mountains in the distance, and the burned-out hulk of the M-16 near the far end of the runway. He caught Boland's eye.

The sergeant shrugged then called softly, "Villari, you and Amaya go topside and try to raise the *Maxwell* . . . er, what's her call-sign, sir?"

"Crackerjack," said Ingram.

"Got it, Villari?"

"Crackerjack. Got it, Gunny." With his M-1 in one hand and the five-and-a-half-pound walkie-talkie in the other, Villari made a careful ascent up creaky steps with Amaya close behind. Seconds after they disappeared inside, the bushes rustled across the field as if whisked by a strong wind and NKVD soldiers poured onto the runway. In a matter of seconds there were twenty, thirty, then a hundred, at least. They wore long overcoats and fur caps, and most were armed with PPSh submachine guns.

Quickly the Marines ran their bolts to chamber rounds in their rifles.

Ingram called, "Sergeant, have them stand down."

"Sheeyat," muttered Boland. His .45 was out, and he'd likewise run the action with a loud clack.

"Sergeant Boland. There are well over a hundred Russians around us. No use all of us getting killed. Our time will come. Have your men stand down. Now."

"Bastards," muttered Boland. He slowly holstered his .45 and then said, "All right, ladies. Form up. Two ranks. Dress right. Now!"

They looked at him in disbelief.

"I said now, damn it!"

The Marines formed two ranks as ordered. Boland called them to attention and right shoulder arms. Standing before his squad, he did an about face, saluted Ingram, and barked, "All present and accounted for, sir." He winked, both knowing two were still up in the control tower.

A group of Soviet soldiers gathered beneath the tower and yelled up. Villari didn't respond. One of the soldiers fired a burst into the tower's floorboards. Still no response.

Ingram said bitterly, "Get him down, Gunny. If he's still alive."

"Let's hope so." Boland cupped his hands and yelled up, "Game's up, Villari. Get on down here."

Nothing. The soldier aimed his weapon again.

"Villari, damn it," yelled Boland.

"All right, all right, Gunny." A shadow flicked across the gaping floorboards, and Villari clumped down the stairs. As soon as he gained the ground, three Soviet soldiers grabbed his rifle and walkie-talkie and shoved him roughly toward the command bunker. Villari winked and gave a barely visible thumbs-up as he passed.

Amaya is still up there. And maybe still alive. And Villari had just indicated that he'd made contact with the *Maxwell*. *Brave men. The Russians were going to chop them to pieces. And maybe that burst got Amaya.* He just didn't know. Villari hadn't let on.

"Knock it off." Villari must not have liked the way he was being pushed. He turned and shoved the Russian behind him.

The soldier backhanded Villari, who drove a fist into the soldier's face. Blood spurted from the Russian's nose and he fell to his knees howling in pain. The other Russians fell upon Villari and began beating and kicking him. Soon the Marine was doubled up. But they kept kicking. The other Marines broke ranks and charged into the Soviets. With a heathen growl, Boland charged into the mess.

Ingram ran after Boland and jumped on the back of an enormous Russian who was about to whack Boland on the head with the stock of his PPSh. The man growled and tried to peel Ingram off with the swipe of a powerful arm. But Ingram wasn't finished. He hung on and bit down hard on the man's ear. The Russian screamed. He pulled out a pistol, a 7.62-mm Nagant, and began blindly firing over his shoulder. Ingram ducked, pushing the pistol away each time it blasted, bullets screaming past his nose and ear. He knew he couldn't hang on much longer. Someone else wrapped his arms around Ingram's waist and tugged mightily. Another pounded his back and kidneys. Ingram kicked backward at him.

A command car roared up and ground to a stop. Someone fired a submachine-gun burst in the air. The fighting subsided. One by one the Marines were hauled to their feet and pushed into a group. Ingram let go of the monster's ear and fell to the ground. Teeth bared, the man turned and raised an enormous boot to stomp him. But he stopped at a shout from the command car.

"*Prekratite seychazhe!*" Stop this at once!

Ingram was roughly hauled up and shoved beside Sergeant Boland, both men wheezing and out of breath. Boland had the beginnings of a magnificent black eye.

Two men stepped from the command car. First out was Captain Third Rank Eduard Dezhnev. He was followed by a thin, balding man wearing a dark gray overcoat and garrison cap. He had close-set eyes, a full beard, and a big black mole on his left cheek. His shoulder boards were gold with three stars: a captain first rank.

Six Soviet soldiers walked up and began throwing the Marines' weapons onto a pile. One soldier held up a hand and stopped another from throwing the bazooka on the stack. With a broad smile, he ran his hand over the bazooka's barrel and then hoisted it on his shoulder and walked away.

"Lend-lease!" shouted one of the Marines.

"*Da. Spasibo*" Yes, thank you, the man shouted back

Dezhnev walked over to Ingram, "What the hell, Todd. Can't you take no for an answer?"

Ingram's lower jaw throbbed, and his swollen lips made it hard to speak. He wiped blood from his mouth. "We had a deal, remember? Your Foreign Office approved this trip."

Dezhnev offered a handkerchief. "The terms were changed, and we never received an answer from your State Department."

Hands braced on his knees, Ingram was still panting. "That's bullshit! And where are the Japanese POWs? We are supposed to take them home."

"Ahhhh, that's one of the problems. Our Foreign Office has decided to keep those men. They are aggressors and have illegally occupied Soviet territory. We cannot release them until penalties are assessed and reparations made."

"What? Reparations? What sort of malarkey is that?"

The other officer stepped up. Dezhnev said, "May I introduce Captain First Rank Gennady Kulibin, overall commander of this operation and commanding officer of the *Admiral Volshkov*.

The man saluted stiffly and said, "*Kak vy poshevayete?*" How do you do?

Ingram stood to attention.

Dezhnev hissed under his breath, "It's customary for officers of peaceful nations to exchange courtesies, such as saluting."

Ingram said, "Please tell this man, Ed, that U.S. naval personnel don't salute unless they are covered. And if I'm not mistaken, that's my garrison cap on the ground over there that your animals are walking on."

Dezhnev shouted at one of his men. A Russian soldier stooped, picked up Ingram's garrison cap, brushed it off, and walked over and handed it to Dezhnev. It was passed to Ingram. "Okay?"

Ingram put on his cap and adjusted it. "Next, I don't show courtesy to people who break promises. And you've done that in a most unfriendly fashion. You didn't show a beacon as you promised, making our landing difficult and dangerous. And now you tell us you're not releasing the prisoners to us as originally agreed."

"But I just told you--"

"I demand to see Major Fujimoto."

Dezhnev looked down. "I'm sorry, he's dead. Shot while trying to escape."

"Bullshit! When did that happen?"

"While we were all in Beverly Hills enjoying champagne at Captain Landa's wedding."

Ingram felt his blood run cold. "Shot while trying to escape?" He waved his arms. "Escape to where in this godforsaken country?"

"Yes."

"Yes, what?"

"Don't push it, Todd."

Ingram's fists doubled and he threw a glance at Boland. Then he nodded toward Kulibin and said, "Tell this son of a bitch that excuse doesn't work with us. Tell him to keep his animals away from my men or there *will* be reparations. And not the ones you're thinking of."

Kulibin's eyes narrowed.

"He speaks English, I see," said Ingram. "I'm glad he understands me." He stepped up to Kulibin. "Captain, I'm telling you to return our equipment, including our arms, now."

"*Nyet,*" said Kulibin, stepping closer until they were almost nose-to-nose.

Ingram said, "Captain Kulibin, our governments had an agreement for me to come here in peace and return with the Japanese garrison. You've reneged on that promise and--"

Dezhnev shouted, "Todd, stop. You don't know what you're doing."

"And if you don't return me and my men, with our equipment, to my ship, then this becomes a major international incident. You saw just two B-24s." He pointed up to the tower. "My lookout was able to contact the *Maxwell* and tell them what was going on. Four American destroyers are on their way: ETA oh six hundred tomorrow morning. So, make sure you have an early breakfast because it'll be your last. They're going to obliterate you and your damned Nazi ship out there. And if that's not enough, Commander White will have called in B-24s, B-17s, and B-29s to make sure nothing is left." He looked at Kulibin. "Your days of kissing commissars' asses are over unless you do what I say."

Kulibin rocked back and forth and hooked his thumbs in his belt.

Dezhnev said, "He's really pissed off, Todd. You went too far."

Inwardly, Ingram felt he had too. He'd been taking too many Jerry Landa lessons and it had gone to his head.

He was ready to apologize when Kulibin stepped back. "*Da, da.*" He shrugged and turned to walk away. "*Do svedaniia*" Goodbye. He waved his hands in the air and said something to Dezhnev. Then he walked to his command car and leaned against the fender. He pulled out a pack of cigarettes and laid one on his lower lip. An officer stepped over and lit it for him.

Dezhnev said, "I don't believe this."

"Believe what?"

"He just gave in. Tell your men they can have their arms and their equipment back."

Ingram yelled over, "And turn off the damned radio jamming too."

Dezhnev hissed, "Todd, damn it. Quit while you're ahead."

Kulibin called over, "*Da, da.* Hokay."

"And the bazooka. Right now."

"*Da, da.*"

This has been too easy. "All right." Ingram yelled to Boland, "Gunny!"

"Sir!" snapped Boland.

"They're returning our weapons and gear. Have your men grab their stuff and fall in across the runway right there."

"Yes, sir." Boland turned and bawled at his men. In a flurry they attacked the pile of weapons and equipment and pried the bazooka from the hands of a reluctant Soviet soldier. In two minutes the pile was reduced to nothing. They fell into a single rank, one or two Marines still dabbing at blood running from cuts and bruises on their faces.

Ingram said, "By the way, where's Mr. Blinde?"

"In the command bunker, waiting for you," said Dezhnev.

"Just like that? No excuses?"

"You scared the hell out of him. He thought you were dead. He decided to get out while the going was good."

"You're talking in riddles," said Ingram. Images of Walt Hodges and then Sally flashed through his mind; they had barbecued hamburgers with the Ingrams in Mrs. Peabody's backyard. They drank Mrs. Peabody's beer and got silly. And again Sally, soon to be mother of a fatherless baby. *You're getting hot.* He controlled his breathing and jammed his fists in his pockets.

Dezhnev stepped close, so he couldn't be overheard. "Remember when I said at Landa's wedding that they're trying to kill you?"

"Yes."

"You didn't take me seriously, did you?"

Ingram knew what he meant. Unfortunately, he had read Toliver's message too late--after Blinde had left the plane. "No, I guess I didn't."

"Well, I'll let him explain it to you. Then you must leave."

Ingram said, "This I gotta see."

49

4 December 1945
Shakhtyorsk Air Base
Sakhalin Oblast, USSR

Dezhnev and six Russian soldiers escorted Ingram to the camouflaged entrance of the Japanese command bunker. Dezhnev stopped. "He's inside."

"You're not coming in?"

"No. I'm to wait out here." Dezhnev lit a cigarette, something he did when he was nervous.

"What's going on, Ed?"

"Todd, just go in there. Be nice and keep your mouth shut."

"My orders are to return him to the United States."

"That won't happen."

Ingram's eyes swept over Dezhnev and his NKVD soldiers. They were tall and intelligent looking, and one or two looked as if they understood English. He was outnumbered in more ways than one. "All right." He turned and went inside.

Three portable lanterns provided the only light in the room. It was barely recognizable from the last time he had been there. Furniture was tipped over, cabinet drawers left open, papers strewn about. The large map table was tipped on end and lay against the far wall.

A figure was bent over a desk examining something. Ingram couldn't see who it was in the dim light. The man raised his head as Ingram started across the room. He turned. It was Colin Blinde.

"Come on in, Todd."

Ingram sniffed and said, "Your Aqua Velva and the rest of your gear went out on the C-54."

"I'll get by."

Something rustled behind Ingram. He looked behind him to see two Russians in leather jackets. One wore a slouch hat. The other had a blond crewcut. Both men were large, but the blond was enormous--at least 6 feet 5 inches and 250 pounds.

"Your friends?"

"In case you develop a bad temper."

"That could happen. You might say treason aggravates it."

"Todd, look. I'm leaving now. You're staying here. I wanted to tell you what this is all about."

"Finally, someone is giving me the dope."

"It's simple. I'm claiming what was mine in the first place."

"You have a funny way of claiming things. Walt Hodges was about to become a father."

"Who is Walt Hodges?"

"The man you killed--excuse me, the man you had killed."

Blinde stood straight and rubbed his chin. "What do you mean 'had killed'?"

Ingram said, "The torpedo you had do the job for you with that poison. Ricin. Is that what you call it? It seems your boy was a foreign national who got caught. And now he's dead, by the way."

Blinde sat heavily. "I . . . I can't go back."

"What made you think you could?"

"I didn't know until you just told me."

It hit Ingram that Blinde had been planning to return to OSS after this and pick up right where he left off. But Ingram had just told Blinde the essence of Toliver's message that he'd received on landing here. Blinde realized the game was completely up. He could not return. Then came the horrible realization that Ingram had overplayed his hand. He'd popped off like loud-mouthed Jerry Landa. Instead, he should have acted stupid, like Dezhnev said. *I just signed my own death warrant.*

A chair squeaked in a far corner. Someone was over there in the shadows sitting on a crate. Seeing Ingram's stare, he stood and approached, pulling on gray gloves. He walked a complete circle around Ingram, trailing a faint odor of garlic. It was Kulibin, the captain who had agreed to release the Marines. He barked several Russian phrases at Blinde.

Blinde said, "He's impressed with you and compliments you for your tenacity, Todd."

Ingram demanded, "Just tell him to let us go."

"May I introduce Captain First Rank Gennady Kulibin, commanding officer of the *Admiral Volshkov*?"

Ingram stood still. "We've already met."

"Oh, I see. Well, isn't it military courtesy to acknowledge his presence? After all, he outranks you."

Ingram looked over to the two goons in leather. The shorter man covered him with a pistol. "Tell him, Mr. Blinde, that military courtesy went out the window when he refused to honor an agreement between our two governments. And courtesy is certainly not called for when one of your thugs is pointing a pistol at me."

Kulibin's eyes narrowed.

"Easy, Todd," said Blinde.

Ingram was worked up. "And what would you know about military courtesy, Mr. Blinde? How much military service did you give to your country? What uniform did you wear?"

"I had a deferment."

"Well, why doesn't that surprise me? What kind of deferment, Mr. Blinde?"

"Flat feet."

Ingram slapped his knee. "My, oh, my! Flat feet. I'm so sorry. But you ran pretty fast right after the plane landed yesterday--flat feet and all. Out the door and down the runway like an Olympic sprinter. I was really amazed when--oof!"

A lightning bolt of pain raced up Ingram's back. Someone had hit him in the left kidney. He half-turned and saw the larger of the goons behind him with a doubled fist. He sank to his knees before the man could deliver another blow. He squeezed his eyes closed and braced himself from falling all the way. But then a boot was planted in his back. It pushed, and he was flat on his belly. He whiffed garlic and looked around to see Kulibin, a corner of his mouth rising, shoving him down with his boot. Quietly, he asked Blinde a question.

Blinde replied in Russian. To Ingram he hissed, "Todd, you must answer if you know what's good for you."

"Well, what the hell does he want to know?"

"He wants to know about Karol Dudek and the life raft inflator."

"Who? Life raft what? What in the hell is he--*eyaaaaagh!*" He screamed as another boot stomped his left kidney. Everything went dark.

Ingram awoke lying on his back. Water was pouring over his face. He looked up into four shadowy outlines. Blinde leaned in close. "You claim you don't know who Karol Dudek is?"

Ingram smacked his lips. "You can kick all you want, but I have no idea who that is."

Blinde spoke to Kulibin in Russian. Then he leaned back and stood. The two goons bent over and hoisted Ingram into a chair. He gritted his teeth as they jounced him down.

"Relax, Todd," said Blinde.

"Relax? You and your thugs are beating me up. I'm going to be pissing blood for weeks."

Blinde nodded to the big goon. The man lifted Ingram's chin and poured water in his mouth. It tasted wonderful. "Why are we here?"

Blinde asked, "You're sure you don't know who Dudek is?"

"I've been sitting in damned airplanes for nearly four days. Who the hell is Dudek?"

"How did you learn about ricin?"

"It was in a message I got just before we landed. By the way, you're under arrest and are ordered to return with me on charges of treason."

Blinde paid no attention to Ingram's gallows humor. He stared at the wall, his eyes unfocused. "They know. Now what can I do?"

"Who knows what, Colin?"

"You don't understand."

"Try me."

"My dad was a Texas wildcatter. He did all right, but then came the depression. We lost everything. Everything except six copper mines in Mongolia that came down to us through my grandfather. Then the Japs seized the mines and we were left with nothing. Now Dad sponges off my mother's small inheritance, living in a two-story walkup in Brooklyn. They do nothing but argue all day. Dad drinks a lot. Mom sits in a corner and looks out a window." Blinde looked into the distance.

"After Pearl Harbor we were in the thick of it. Like Dad, I had thought everything was lost until I met Walter Boring. Boring was shrewd. He knew Mao Tse-tung; he knew Chiang Kai-shek; and he was on close personal terms with Hideki Tojo. How could we lose?"

Ingram was beginning to see. "He got them together."

"Well, no. He simply brokered a deal."

"With whom?"

"Tojo, basically. Boring was playing Mao against Chiang Kai-shek. So Boring got Prime Minister Tojo to turn the mines over to Mao after watching the two drive up the price. Our cut was paltry. Five million in rough diamonds. And Walter's share was half."

"And the diamonds are . . ."

Blinde pointed. "There. That's the second crate we came to retrieve in the name of an outraged free world. The Japanese unwittingly used it as one of the four legs to support that map table. Walter didn't realize it until he saw the crate as he was being carried out by your men." He pointed to the upended table against the wall. "Five bags in the bottom."

Ingram felt sick standing near this man. Blinde had killed Walt Hodges and who knows how many others. And all this ghoul could think about was his diamonds lying beneath a stack of grisly photographs. "So you tortured it out of him."

Blinde stared into the distance.

"It wasn't a mercy killing. You killed Walter Boring to find out where the crate was and steal his share."

"Um."

"Except now, of course, you're going to split it with your captain there and those two goons. Who else?"

"Nobody else. And those two are very capable NKVD agents. Please say hello to Oleg Lepechn," he gestured toward the blond giant, "and Matvie Borzakov." Lepechn glanced at Ingram and brushed dust off his leather coat; Borzakov stepped under a naked lightbulb, revealing a thin, pock-marked face.

Ingram waved, "So pleased to meet you all."

Kulibin went back to the crate and sat.

Ingram asked, "Please tell me one thing?"

Blinde checked his watch. "Time to go."

"Where does Eduard Dezhnev fit in all this?"

Kulibin chuckled from the corner.

Blinde said something to him in Russian.

Kulibin laughed again.

"What?" asked Ingram.

Blinde said, "Oh, it's a little joke."

"Okay. You want to tell me?" asked Ingram.

"It depends on what his mother does."

"Whose mother?"

"Dezhnev's mother, of course. Anoushka. Comrade Kulibin has been trying to get her into bed for months."

It hit Ingram. "Anoushka. Anoushka Dezhnev. The actress?"

"That's her," said Blinde. "Very sexy. She's in Hollywood right now making movies. Do you know her?"

"I met her at Jerry Landa's wedding. But if . . ."

"If she doesn't come around, then her little boy goes to Lubyanka sooner rather than later."

"Where's Lubyanka?"

Blinde said, "Political prison in Moscow run by the NKVD. Prisoners rarely come out alive." He said it with a finality that seemed to make the whole room black. Even Kulibin across the room faded from view.

"I don't understand. Dezhnev is a highly regarded officer, is he not?"

Blinde said, "Not anymore. He's working for you, the Office of Naval Intelligence."

"What?"

"You didn't know?"

"Know what, damn it?"

"You should ask your buddy Toliver."

"Speak English."

"Except I don't think that will be possible now."

"Why not?"

Kulibin sauntered over and tapped Blinde on the shoulder.

Blinde said, "We must leave, Commander. I wish we had met under different circumstances."

"Not me."

Kulibin clapped his hands and called, "Oleg."

"*Da.*" The big blond thug walked up and slapped Ingram hard. His leather jacket squeaked while he tied Ingram's hands with telephone cord. Then he pulled a pistol from the small of his back, a German Walther 7.65-mm PPK. Oleg's enormous hand made the pistol look like a toy. He ran his hand over the action and cocked it.

"*Nyet,*" Blinde shouted. "*Podozhdi poka my uidyom.*" Wait until we leave.

"Hokay." Oleg lowered the pistol, set the safety, and stuffed it back in his waistband. Then he wrapped tape around Ingram's mouth.

Ingram's nose was swollen from the fighting, and it was already hard to breath. He squirmed and kicked his feet and growled.

Again, the Russian backhanded him.

It was all Ingram could do to will himself to be quiet, to stop breathing hard, to quell the panic rising in his throat.

Blinde and Borzakov each took an end of the crate and picked it up. Kulibin stood by passively, his hands behind his back, watching Ingram as if he were a bug on a microscope slide.

Blinde said, "I'm sorry, truly I am." He nodded to Borzakov and the two men carried the crate out the door. Kulibin lingered for a moment, then tipped two fingers to his forehead and followed.

Is this it? Ingram's heart must have been pumping at 220 beats a minute.

His head throbbed, and he sensed Oleg moving around like a caged animal. What the hell was he doing? Cigarette butts! The idiot was picking up Japanese cigarette butts and stuffing them in his pocket. Then he opened desk drawers, peering at documents. Some drawers he dumped on the hard-packed clay; a few papers he stuffed into a leather briefcase. Seconds turned into minutes as the man quietly canvassed the room, then the bunkrooms off to the side, one of which was where Ingram had originally met Walter Boring.

Oleg emerged from the bunkroom, walked over, and patted Ingram down, removing everything from his pockets. Nothing seemed to interest him, and he pitched it all on the ground: he didn't take Ingram's watch or his Naval Academy ring.

The Russian swept the room for a long moment with steel-gray eyes. Finally, he looked down at Ingram and smiled. He reached back and pulled the Walther PPK from the small of his back as if he were tugging out a handkerchief.

Lightning bolts danced in Ingram's head. He felt cold and hot at the same time and jerked against his bindings. Like a wild-eyed cow in a slaughterhouse, he knew his time had come. His breath came in short gasps. He couldn't sweat enough; he couldn't cry out. The realization hit that he had just seconds to live. All he could think of was how cruel life had been to him and how short it was. Helen swirled in his mind, and he thanked God for her. She was the best thing that ever--

"Goodbye, Yank." The Russian raised his pistol and pointed it right between Ingram's eyes. His thumb traveled to the safety.

There was a blast. Ingram, waiting for death, wondered, *Shouldn't I be dead?* But it was Oleg Lepechn's forehead with a neat hole in it, not his. Blood and gray matter spewed out the back of his skull. With his eyes wide open and knees locked, the giant fell straight back to crash among rolled-up charts and a pair of overturned chairs.

A man stepped through the entrance. Ingram's heart jumped. It was a Russian dressed in a fur cap and heavy overcoat; a PPSh submachine gun was slung over one shoulder, an M-1 carbine hung over the other. He was crouched in a two-handed stance, and a wisp of smoke rose from the muzzle of his .45. He quickly swept the pistol over the rest of the room.

Vapor puffed from his mouth as he walked into the bunkrooms and checked them carefully. Looking from side to side, the man walked up to Oleg, stooped, and put two fingers on the corpse's carotid artery, making sure Oleg really was a corpse.

Satisfied, he looked up at Ingram, stood, and walked over.

Ingram squeezed his eyes shut.

50

4 December 1945
Shakhtyorsk Air Base
Sakhalin Oblast, USSR

Instead of a cold gun barrel against his neck Ingram felt the tape being carefully peeled from his mouth. His eyes snapped open. It was a U.S. Marine. It was . . . "Ah-Amaya," Ingram stammered. He gasped and sucked in large breaths of cool, wonderful air.

"You okay, Commander?" Amaya asked, shedding his Russian overcoat. He threw off the fur cap and plopped on the helmet that had been hanging from his web belt, his eyes all the while sweeping the room.

"Get me out of this Amaya."

"Yes, sir." Amaya whipped out his bayonet and easily cut through the telephone cord.

Ingram rubbed his wrists. "How did you manage this?" He stood, feeling wobbly.

Amaya grabbed Ingram's elbow to steady him. "They're gone. They loaded our gear in the command car and had the gunny march the boys down the runway. They turned right and headed for the Rooskie pier."

Circulation returned. Ingram's wrists and ankles glowed and itched with new life. "Thanks Amaya," he pushed away and stood on his own.

"That's not all."

"What?"

"I heard the Russian officer tell the gunny that they'll give us a ride back to the *Maxwell* and 'poof,' we'll be gone."

"That sounds encouraging. But tell me what made you decide to come after me?"

"After they marched off the squad, the remaining Rooskies fell in and headed back."

"How many?"

"Umm, twenty, maybe thirty guys. But the command car didn't leave right away. It just sat there with the engine idling."

"I wonder why?"

"I'm not sure. But up in the tower, I got worried. I saw those Rooskies take you to the bunker. You walked in, but you didn't come out."

"Can you see the bunker from up there?"

"Yes, sir. Not the entrance, but the top of the bunker and some trenches around it. So, I'm thinking about all this when their top kick decides to send someone back to check the tower. They were marching away when this guy climbs up the ladder right to the top. You should have seen his eyes when he saw me. Big as saucers. So, I bopped him on the head. Not a sound. Then I put on his stuff and climbed on down. I just marched past the two guys in the command car and into the brush."

"What made you come here?"

"Me? Like I said, you weren't with those Russians when they came back. And later, that civilian, Mr. Blinde--he's workin' for the Commies, right?"

"That's right."

"So, Mr. Blinde and this other civilian came back carrying a crate. And right behind them is a Russian officer. He looked important."

"Skipper of that Russian cruiser."

"So that's it. This other guy with Mr. Blinde was dopey looking. He was wearing a black leather jacket and some sort of mobster hat; kind of like Al

Capone. So, they loaded the crate on the command car and took off. Hell, I didn't know what to do. But I kept thinking about you and decided to come here and . . ." he waved at the corpse.

On the trip up from Atsugi, Ingram had watched Private Amaya laughing and cutting up with the others. He was an eighteen-year-old from New York with sandy hair who spoke with a Brooklyn accent and had a lopsided grin. He looked as if he had just started shaving. And now, in an instant, Amaya had become a man, looking every inch a Marine. His face was at once very serious and yet relaxed, confident but vigilant. His eyes darted everywhere, the pistol still poised.

"I owe you my life, Amaya. Thank you," said Ingram.

"Well, I suppose it's my job, sir."

Ingram's knees still felt shaky, and he knew it wasn't from being tied up. *Time to put on a good face.* "And well done too. Here, give me a moment." Ingram stooped, picked up the PPK, and stuffed it into his belt at the small of his back, Oleg style. Then he checked Oleg's pockets, finding an extra clip for the pistol. There was an ID kit inside Oleg's jacket. A strange-looking metal badge and a wallet--very thin, no rubles, just a crinkled photo of an elderly couple. Then he picked up his own belongings that Oleg had cast aside. Standing, he said, "Okay."

"How are we going to do this, Commander?"

"I'm working on it." Ingram hadn't the foggiest idea.

⸻

It was late afternoon by the time they finished creeping the length of the runway. They turned north for the pier and . . . Amaya raised a finger to his lips. "Shhh."

They stopped. It was one of the 105-mm gun emplacements. Two of the crew sat around a small bonfire warming their hands. Another was drawing a canvas cover over the barrel. Three more were loading gear on a truck while a lone soldier walked the perimeter with a rifle over his shoulder, occasionally stamping his feet.

Ingram whispered. "Packing up?"

"Looks like it."

Silently, they eased around the gun emplacement, giving it a wide berth.

Someone shouted. An engine started nearby. Then another. Then many. The ground shook with vehicles on the move. Ingram muttered, "What are these guys doing?"

More vehicles rumbled nearby. They came to a break in the brush and saw a muddy road. As they crouched in the underbrush two T-34 tanks, four M-16s, and four trucks swept by, their gears clanking as wheels and treads churned through the mud. Ingram looked at Amaya, who shrugged. The convoy petered out, and they waited for a moment making sure the road was clear.

"Now." Ingram said. They dashed across just as another tank clanked around a bend and snarled past. He looked back. The tank hadn't stopped. Nor did any of the ten trucks that sloshed by afterward.

With stealth no longer necessary, Ingram and Amaya made their way through tall grass and up to the top of a berm. Below them lay the pier. It extended about three hundred feet into the Sea of Japan, where twelve knots of wind whipped up waves, a few topped with whitecaps. To their right, the *Admiral Volshkov* lay a thousand yards off the beach. To their left, the *Maxwell's* graceful lines stood out as she swung at anchor, her battle ensign now stowed and her flag flying at the fantail. A low gray shape bobbed around her bow and swept down her starboard side--the *Maxwell's* motor whaleboat patrolling around the destroyer in slow, lazy circles. Ingram muttered, "What I wouldn't give for Boland's walkie-talkie."

Amaya glanced at Ingram as if to say, "Wishful thinking."

A large, slab-sided logging barge was moored near the far end of the pier. Groups of ragged soldiers stood or sat on the barge. Ingram soon realized they were Japanese soldiers, the remainder of the garrison originally promised to the Americans. But the Japanese were heavily guarded by Soviet troops on the pier who stood fast and kept them covered with their PPSh submachine guns.

Closer in, two dark gray 36-foot personnel boats bobbed alongside the pier. Red flags emblazoned in gold with the Soviet star, hammer, and sickle drooped from tall staffs mounted on their transoms. Soldiers moved about on the pier, loading boxes and gear on the boats.

Ingram nudged Amaya.

"Sir?"

"Our ticket home." He nodded toward the squad of Marines standing on the opposite side of the pier, their rifles and equipment stacked before them. They were surrounded by twenty or so Russian guards poised with submachine guns. Sergeant Boland walked inside the perimeter, looking his tormentors up and down as if he were reviewing them at the Marine barrack at Eighth and I Streets in Washington, D.C.

"Gunny," rasped Amaya.

"Yep."

Ingram started to rise when something caught his eye. Colin Blinde and Gennady Kulibin were settling onto white cushions in the stern of the nearest boat. Borzakov stood amidships watching two sailors lash the crate atop the engine cover. Satisfied, Borzakov waved to Blinde and Kulibin, braced a foot on a gunwale, and deftly stepped back onto the pier. He stood stiffly as sailors cast off the boat's lines. Kulibin and Blinde were deep in conversation and barely noticed Borzakov as the boat backed away from the pier and then lunged forward, leaving a cloud of greasy blue diesel smoke. The NKVD man paced up and down on the pier, head hidden under his slouch hat, hands jammed in his jacket pockets.

Ingram watched the boat head out into the chop. One of the finest and most promising young minds in the United States was on board that craft. Colin Blinde had been given the advantages of a respected family, a superior education, and entrée into society at the highest levels. Indeed, he had the confidence of his government. Squandered Blinde family riches of the past had reached forward and twisted this young man and shrouded from him the ability to distinguish between right and wrong. He was incapable of caring or understanding the epic proportions of what he had done: he had betrayed his country. It was abject greed in the name of resuming his family's fortune and restoring the Blinde name to whatever former glory it had enjoyed . . . and buying another house in the Hamptons.

Ingram thought of simple, likable Walter Hodges and what Colin Blinde had done to him; and to Sally and their child. And others as well-- Boring for certain, and he didn't know how many others. The blond young man bobbing up and down in those waves, heading toward the *Admiral*

Volshkov, exemplified what can go wrong in a civilization at its apex, even the United States, a proud nation at the top of its game.

The din of truck and tank engines grew. The air was filled with diesel smoke and occasional shouts. "These guys are on the move," said Amaya.

"Looks like it. You ready?"

"I'm with you, sir."

They stood. "Okay. Just remember to stay behind cover as long as possible. We don't want to give these people too much time to think."

"Got it."

They found a path and walked down the hill into what looked like a vehicle park. The group appeared to be breaking up as a command car peeled away leading six trucks, two M-16s, and three tanks onto the road toward the mountains.

They came upon a lone tank, a T-34, its unmuffled engine rumbling loudly. Ingram nearly stumbled into a man in dark, grease-stained overalls and leather helmet. The tanker wiped his hands with an oil-stained rag. "Oops," Ingram sputtered.

"*Da?*" The man asked. "*Otkuda ty prishyol?*" Where did you come from?

"*Spasibo,*" Ingram tried.

The man shouted. "*Stoi tam!*" Wait right there!

Ingram turned, smiled, spread his hands, and said, "Sorry, we're in a hurry." To Amaya, "Come on."

They dashed into the park, racing between trucks and an occasional Jeep. Ducking around a command car, they walked onto the pier toward Boland and his squad. Ingram heard angry shouts behind him.

Russians walked past. One or two stopped, astonished that two Americans strolled nonchalantly among them. The shouting from behind grew closer.

The tanker.

"Keep walking," said Ingram, bumping into a Russian rating.

"Bet on that, sir."

Twenty yards.

Boland's ears picked up the commotion. Quickly, he took it all in as soldiers descended on Ingram and Amaya from three different directions. He roared at his squad, "All right, you sissies, fall in."

They looked at him, bewildered.

"*Fall in!*"

A corporal still stood motionless, his hands on his hips.

Boland growled, "That means now, pissant, on the double. Two ranks, *dress-rihyet--hess.*" Then, "*Dee-tail, ten-hut!*"

The Marines snapped to attention.

"*For-arrrrd--mark time--harch!*"

Boland screeched out the cadence, completely smashing his words, "*Lehp...lehp...lehpha-right, lehp.*"

Getting the idea, the Marines marched in place, stomping their feet loudly, kicking up dust.

The Russians looked from the squad to the commotion around the two Americans and back to the squad. It was enough. Ten seconds later Ingram and Amaya popped through the crowd. Amaya took a position in the second rank, Ingram before the squad.

Boland growled, "*Houn-off!*"

In unison, the Marines shouted, "*One! Two! Three! Four! One! Two! Three! Four!*"

Russians pressed in on all sides watching Boland's parade. The tanker burst through the crowd and reached for Ingram.

"*Nyet, nazad!*" No, stand back!

At once, the tanker stopped and took a pace back.

Captain Third Rank Eduard Dezhnev walked through the gathered Russians and stood before Ingram. Quietly, he said, "That's enough, Todd."

Ingram caught Boland's eye and drew a finger across his throat.

Boland growled, "*Deeee-tail, halt!*" Then, "*Par-haaaaade-hest!*"

Ingram said to Dezhnev, "Do you wish to inspect my men?"

Dezhnev moved close and said quietly, "Very funny. You have one chance here."

"What's that?"

"Just load your gear and get on board that boat as fast as you can. Shove off as soon as you're ready."

Ingram turned and called the order to Boland.

Boland dismissed the men and they turned to, loading their gear.

As they watched, Dezhnev asked, "What happened back there? Why didn't you come out with Colin? And where's Lepechn? Borsakov is going crazy looking for him."

Ingram looked out into the crowd. Borzakov was speaking with a young naval officer, waving his arms.

"Oleg won't be coming back."

"What the hell do you mean?"

"Oleg is dead. We killed him. He was going to kill me."

"This is nonsense."

"Face the facts. And I hate to tell you this, but your cover is blown."

Dezhnev turned to him. "What are you talking about?"

"Blinde and Kulibin know about you and that Toliver is your control." Ingram was guessing at this point, but the look on Dezhnev's face told him he had hit home.

Ingram continued, "And your boy Gennady." He pointed to the *Admiral Volshkov*. "You should see what he has in mind for you."

"Go on."

"I can't put this to you very delicately, but he wants to send you to this nice little resort in Moscow called, Lub . . . Lube . . ."

"Lubyanka?"

"Lubyanka. Yes, that's it . . . if your mother doesn't go along with what he has in mind. I'm guessing they'll do it anyway because of your relationship with Ollie."

Dezhnev looked down. "He has been after Anoushka for months."

"Well, apparently he's tired of waiting."

"Shit."

"Yes. Deep shit."

Dezhnev's shoulders sagged. "It's . . . like . . . I've been trying to tell you, those are sick people out there." He pointed to the cruiser. "I'm trying to do the right thing."

"Well, I'm sorry to say we have someone just as sick out there with him. His name is Colin Blinde."

Dezhnev straightened. "You too, Todd. They intend to kill you. They're going to sink the *Maxwell*."

"What the hell? How?"

"Tonight. After sunset." Dezhnev checked his watch. "In about an hour and a half when it's dark and there are no witnesses. Kulibin intends to fire a full spread of torpedoes at the *Maxwell*. That's why they want you out there. Everything gone in one big explosion. Poof."

"He can't do that."

"Oh, yes, he can. These are Soviet waters. He'll claim it was aggravated. With all this cargo plane nonsense he can make a case. We were harassed. They fired on us last night--"

"That was an illumination round."

Dezhnev raised a hand. "Nevertheless, they fired a shot at us. It'll be tied up in international tribunals for years. Kulibin's family has strong contacts at the most senior levels. He'll get away with it."

The audacity. Ingram refused to believe it. "This is crazy. Are you sure?"

"That flag business last night embarrassed him and made him really angry. They were abandoning this base anyway and will now finish the job by sunset." He swept his arm at trucks grinding over a hill. "That's about the last of them. We'll be completely gone. Tonight is reserved for the big show with the *Maxwell*."

"That truck convoy. Where are they going?"

He pointed east. "We're sending everything over to Leonidovo on the east coast. A much better airfield with direct access to the Pacific."

"You're saying he really intends to do this?"

"Nobody around to testify. Nothing here by morning except empty vodka bottles."

"Son of a bitch."

"There's more."

"What could be worse?"

Dezhnev pointed to the barge. "See that?"

"Yes."

"No, I mean look closely."

A group of heavily armed Russians moved among the Japanese prisoners, pushing them onto the barge's deck and fussing around their feet.

"What are they doing?" asked Ingram.

"That, my friend, is a fine example of one of the highest achievements of the Soviet Union. They are tying each prisoner to a six-hundred-foot length of anchor chain flaked on the barge. After sinking the *Maxwell*, they intend to connect that anchor chain to the *Admiral Volshkov* and pull it off the barge."

"Drag them off the barge? Drown them?"

"Shhhhh. Keep your voice down. Yes. Isn't that brilliant? Captain First Rank Gennady Kulibin has discovered a way to solve a troublesome logistics problem involving the difficult task of the care and feeding of Japanese prisoners of war. Now he gets rid of it in one fell swoop. He thought of it last night and received Beria's permission this morning."

"Who is Beria?"

"Lavrenti Beria: commissar of the NKVD. Second only to Josef Stalin."

"These really are a bunch of sick bastards."

"I agree. So, the question remains, what can we do?"

"We?"

"I serve my country, Todd, as you have seen in the past. But I don't serve these animals."

"We're in this together?"

Dezhnev lifted a corner of his mouth. "You should have believed me to begin with." He took a step back and jammed his hands on his hips. "Any ideas?"

"Ever since you said torpedoes I've been thinking of something. It may work."

"*May* work?"

"If it doesn't, we're screwed."

51

4 December 1945
Shakhtyorsk Air Base
Sakhalin Oblast, USSR

In spite of the deep overcast Dezhnev knew the sun was close to setting. There were no shadows and it was getting dark. Time to get moving. He yelled to Borzakov, "I said I am taking these men back to the tower to recover some of their radio equipment. There are codebooks there and I want to confiscate them."

"How are you going to do this?"

"We march out there, pick up the radio equipment, and march back here." Dezhnev lowered his voice. "That's where you come in, my friend."

"What do you mean?"

"When we return, I will be 'examining' their radio with you next to me. That's when I will pass the codebooks to you."

Borzakov rubbed his chin. "It could work." Then he asked, "How did you learn of all this?"

"I overheard them talking and convinced them we could go back to recover the codebooks. We will return in twenty minutes. In the meantime, make sure the rest of them get aboard the boat and out to the destroyer so they can offload their gear. Believe me, we'll save time."

"What about these men here?" protested Borzakov.

"Our coxswain will tell the Americans to send their motor whaleboat back and pick them up.

"But--"

Dezhnev stood close, their noses almost touching. "This could be an intelligence coup, for you, comrade. People in Dzerzhinsky Square will be very pleased."

"But these men have their rifles. Who authorized that? And what if . . ."

"What if a handful of Americans go up against us? What then?"

"I . . ."

"We'll squash them like bugs." Dezhnev waved his PPSh.

"I don't know . . ."

"Comrade, we're out of time."

Borzakov sighed. "All right. Go ahead." He stepped aside.

Dezhnev turned to Boland. "You may proceed, Sergeant."

Boland puffed out his chest. "Aye, aye, sir. *Deeeee-tail. Ten-hut!*"

The men snapped to attention.

"*Hight--shoulder--harms.*"

Six M-1 Garand rifles were yanked from the ground and plopped on the Marines' right shoulders.

"*For-aaaaarrrrd . . . harch! Leph . . . Lehp . . . Lehp ha-rih lehp.*" The remaining Russians cleared a path as Boland marched his men past the 36-foot shore boat. Ingram and the other Marines were already on board, their gear stacked high. The mooring lines were taken in; the engine roared, and the coxswain twisted the boat from the pier and then backed away. For an instant, Ingram and Dezhnev locked eyes, Ingram with crossed fingers jammed to his chest, Dezhnev with the slightest of nods. Another member of Dezhnev's detail was Pfc. Edwin Amaya, who winked at Ingram as he marched past.

The Russian sailors watched Boland, his six Marines, and Dezhnev march down the pier and onto the coast road.

The whaleboat growled through the waves on the way out to the *Maxwell*. The Marines' gear had made the boat a bit top heavy, and it rocked drunkenly from side to side.

The closer they came to the destroyer, the better the view of the *Admiral Volshkov*. From the pier they had seen only a stern aspect as she swung at anchor. As they approached the *Maxwell*, the single-stacked cruiser was unveiled in a broadside view, her sleek German lines graceful, functional, and deadly. A cold wave of apprehension swept over Ingram as he realized Dezhnev was right. The cruiser's two portside torpedo tubes were trained out and aimed at the *Maxwell*. Each mount carried three torpedo tubes, making a total of six torpedoes aimed at the *Maxwell*. Each torpedo was most likely a German-design G7a, 21-inch, 44-knot torpedo with a warhead packing 617 pounds of hexanite high explosive. The little 2,100-ton destroyer would be vaporized in one salvo. Also, it hit Ingram that if the *Maxwell* tried to weigh anchor or train out her own guns or take any other defensive action, Kulibin would fire early to remove the threat.

He looked to the rapidly darkening sky. *Hurry*.

The Russian coxswain backed the boat's engine as it slid next to the accommodation ladder dangling over the *Maxwell*'s port side. Tubby White stood above on the main deck, hands on his hips. Beside him was Andy Markham, the executive officer, and Julian Falco, the gunnery officer. Several sailors crowded behind them.

Ingram turned to a short, bull-chested lance corporal and said, "Karzarian, we have exactly ninety seconds to get our men and gear off this boat. After that, I'm shoving them off."

"Aye, aye, Commander." Karzarian called to his men and they began tossing their gear up to the waiting sailors.

Ingram scrambled up the ladder, throwing a salute first at the flag and then at Tubby White. Not standing on formality, White demanded, "What the hell do those Commies want?"

Waving Markham and Falco over, Ingram said, "There's not much time."

"I gathered that," said White.

Ingram said, "Get your men to GQ, but don't sound the alarm. I don't want them to notice anything out of the ordinary."

"I've already done that."

"You have?"

"Todd, what would you do if you had six Commie torpedoes pointed right at you?"

"Good, except don't exercise the gun mounts. Just keep them at ready air. And nobody visible in the topside 40- or 20-millimeter mounts. I don't want the Russians to figure out what we're trying to do. And get a couple of boatswain's mates ready to slip the anchor."

"What the hell? Cut my anchor?"

"That's the idea. And have main control ready to answer all bells. And Tubby, very important..."

"Shoot."

"Make sure no one on the weather decks is visible to the *Admiral Volshkov*, especially the guys on the foredeck."

"Yes, sir." White turned to a talker and relayed the orders to the bridge.

Ingram turned to Falco, "Can you have all mounts load a round of AP and stand by for salvo fire?"

Falco asked, "You mean ram them too, sir?"

"Absolutely."

Falco and White locked eyes.

"Do it, Julian," said White.

"Aye, aye, gentlemen." Falco took off at a dead run for director 51.

White said, "Todd, except for the 20-millimeters, all the topside 40-millimeter mounts are manned and ready. But they're to be stooped down behind the gun tubs, not visible to the cruiser."

With a roar of its diesel, the Russian shore boat backed clear, spun, and steadied on a course for the *Admiral Volshkov*. In a glance, Ingram saw that his six Marines were on board the *Maxwell*, their gear piled against a bulkhead.

Ingram caught Karzarian's eye. The lance corporal reached in a pack, pulled out a walkie-talkie, and walked over. "Will this do, Commander?"

"Thanks, I hope so. Is the battery okay?"

Karzarian checked a tiny dial. "Says it's up to full charge, sir."

"Okay." Ingram held up the walkie-talkie and keyed the mike. "John Wayne, this is Roy Rogers, over."

He switched to receive. Nothing. Ingram listened again.

"... Roy ..." Static.

"John Wayne, your signal weak, over." He looked at Karzarian.

The corporal shook his head.

Suddenly Boland's voice boomed, "Wagons are circled. We're ready."

Ingram yelled, "Hear you five by five. Commence fire!" To White, he nodded toward the bridge, waving Karzarian to follow. They had just stepped on the open bridge when they heard a report from the beach.

Ingram peeked over the bulwark in time to see the 105-mm shot land well over the *Admiral Volshkov*. Grabbing a set of binoculars, he rose up and looked again. The men surrounding the *Admiral Volshkov*'s torpedo mounts were looking forward, not bent over their sighting mechanisms.

Ingram keyed the walkie-talkie mike. "This is John Wayne. Down two hundred, right one-fifty--over."

"*Zzzzzhhhhr!* ... one-fifty! Out."

Again, the 105-mm boomed from shore. The round splashed alongside the cruiser's bridge, raising a tall column of brownish-gray water.

"Not bad for a bunch of jarheads," said White.

Ingram glanced at Karzarian.

Karzarian's eyes twinkled. "Boland's done some can-cocking in his time."

"Well, it shows." Ingram bellowed into the walkie-talkie, "Right fifty. Fire for effect!"

"*Zzzgggh!!*" The 105 boomed.

Almost simultaneously, the aft turret of the *Admiral Volshkov* belched out a salvo toward the beach.

Falco shouted from the director. "Torpedoes in the water."

A 105-mm round landed on the *Admiral Volshkov*'s 01 deck, blowing away her single stack.

The aft mount barked back.

White jumped to the pilothouse and shouted, "Foredeck, slip the anchor. Main control, all ahead full." He looked at Ingram, "You ready to shoot at a bunch of Commies?"

"They fired at us first," said Ingram.

White bunched a fist and yelled up to director 51, "Mr. Falco!"

Falco's head popped from the hatch. "Sir?"

Pointing at the *Admiral Volshkov*, White barked, "Guns free. There's your target."

On the bow, one of the two boatswain's mates swung a sledgehammer and smacked the pelican hook releasing the anchor chain. Then he ran aft for the protection of the deck house as the anchor chain raced like a writhing black snake from the chain locker with a resounding clatter; its bitter end capable of killing anyone in its path.

At the same time, Tubby's full-ahead bell was transmitted from the bridge to main control in the forward engine room. The enginemen were ready and instantly spun their wheels, cracking the throttles. The *Maxwell's* screws dug in and she surged forward.

Boland's next round landed near the *Admiral Volshkov's* bridge, flinging wreckage and bodies high in the air.

Ingram couldn't dwell on that now. The sobering reality was that torpedo wakes were racing toward the *Maxwell*. Except there were only four torpedoes. Where were the other two?

One passed ahead, missing by no more than twenty yards.

Another raced by well astern, its white-streaked wake trailing bubbles.

The next passed just twenty yards aft of the *Maxwell*, still building speed. Ingram's heart sank. The next torpedo headed right for the forward fire room. There was no dodging that one. He gripped the bulwark tightly. *Dear God.*

The torpedo hit with a loud clank.

Karzarian recovered first. "No shit! A dud."

Ingram crossed himself. Others on the bridge did the same.

Falco had shifted all five of the 5-inch gun mounts to automatic control, linking them to the main battery director in deadly synchronization. He swung them to port, and now the 16-foot-long barrels were laid directly onto the *Admiral Volshkov*. He yelled down from the director. "On target. We have a solution."

White called back, "Where are you aimed, Mr. Falco?"

"At a spot right under the number 1 turret." For show, he held up a portable brass gun trigger connected by a thick rubber cord to the inside. "Why?"

Normally, that would be an impertinent question, but these two had worked together for a long time and were complete professionals. "Just curious," said White.

Ingram, urged, "Tubby they still have two more torpedoes to fire."

White yelled, "Commence fire!"

Falco squeezed.

The ship recoiled as all five of the 5-inch guns belched a 54-pound armor-piercing projectile equipped with a base-detonating fuse at a muzzle velocity of 2,600 feet per second. The projectiles reached the *Admiral Volshkov* in 1.1 seconds, all impacting within a 20-foot diameter of where Falco's giant optical sights were aimed. The *Volkov*'s foredeck blazed with light. Then her bridge. A gigantic plume of black smoke gushed from where her funnel had been. With an enormous *crack* the ship rose ten feet, spewing wreckage and streaming columns of smoke and bodies, the light shimmering and suddenly glowing with the intensity of a hundred suns.

With the others, Ingram ducked behind the bridge bulwark as the shock wave slammed over them, pummeling their ears, their bodies, their clothes with a blast of hot air. Red-hot chunks of shrapnel clanked and fell among them, one piece glancing off Ingram's shoe and sizzling to a stop just three feet away, burning into the painted deck. *Amazing.* Ingram stood and looked at the *Admiral Volshkov.* Except she wasn't there. Only a heavy cloud of thick white smoke and churning whitecaps remained. *I'll be damned.* To his left, Ingram saw the Russian 36-foot shore boat running in circles. Nobody was at the controls. It was like a child's forgotten toy. Finally, a lone Russian sailor struggled to his feet, his silhouette barely distinguishable in the fading light.

White rose beside him. "Would you ever believe?"

"I'm as astounded as you are," said Ingram.

"How are we going to explain this?"

"I don't know, but for now let's get to the pier, pick up our Marines and the Japanese POWs, and head out to rendezvous with those four cans. I have a feeling Ivan won't want to tangle with a group that size. One maybe, but not all five of us.

White barked, "Boatswain's mate of the watch, turn on the running lights. And set the special sea and anchor detail." He pointed. "We're mooring to that pier, port side to, so break out some dock lines and fenders."

The boatswain growled, "Yessir," and got on the PA while flipping on the running lights.

White called, "Mr. Woodruff, take the conn and make that pier over there, port side to." He turned to his talker, "Tell Mr. Markham to pass the word for the crew to prepare to receive prisoners."

Ingram said, "You sound like a hard-ass skipper."

"Learned from the best." White stood close. "You know, you look like shit."

"I'm okay," said Ingram.

"Yeah, still tough as nails. Come on, lay below to my cabin and hop in the rain locker. You'll still look like shit but at least you'll smell better." He thumbed at a cut over Ingram's eye and called to his OOD, "Mr. Woodruff, have the corpsman lay to the captain's cabin on the double."

"I said, don't bother."

Tubby said gently, "Go on, Todd. We can handle this."

"Okay."

EPILOGUE

Forgive your neighbor's injustice.
Then when you pray,
your own sins will be forgiven.

—Ecclesiasticus 28:2

4 December 1945
USS *Maxwell* (DD 525)
One thousand yards off Shakhtyorsk Air Base
Sakhalin Oblast, USSR

Darkness had fallen as the *Maxwell* approached the pier. With the heavy overcast, there was no moon or stars. The wind had abated and there was no groundswell either. With no pitching or rolling, it seemed as if the ship was imprisoned in a black velvet chamber. Signalmen played the destroyer's powerful searchlights up and down the dock, finding smoking junk and Russian soldiers wandering aimlessly. The wreckage was worse at the pier's end, the end closest to where the *Admiral Volshkov* had lain at anchor.

On the bow, two boatswain's mates swung a lead line as the *Maxwell* eased near. She gently bumped the pier and came to rest with about eight feet of water beneath the bow and ten beneath the fantail. Sailors jumped over to catch mooring lines and make them fast to bollards.

Hurry.

Tubby sent the pharmacist's mates and the Marines over to begin recovery of the Japanese prisoners. Dazed Russians stumbled among them but were easily moved aside by the Marines. Beginning with the worst cases, the Marines first untied the Japanese from the anchor chain and made ready to carry them across. Those who could walk boarded the *Maxwell* on their own. American sailors helped send them to the warmth and safety of the mess deck.

Meanwhile, Ingram showered in the captain's main cabin. His clothes were a mess, but he and Andy Markham were about the same size and a clean khaki shirt and trousers awaited him when he stepped out. Also waiting was Eddie Geer, a second-class hospital corpsman, who dressed Ingram's cuts and bruises. Ingram hustled Geer out, knowing the Japanese would need his services more.

Keeping in mind that the few Russians left on the pier might still have some fight in them, Ingram stuffed Oleg's PPK into a fresh duffel coat and walked on deck. Japanese soldiers were everywhere; some talking quietly in groups, some moaning, and some lying silently on stretchers. Canvas tarps covered a few from head to toe. He walked over a makeshift gangway and across to the barge and found Boland talking to Amaya.

Ingram said, "Well done, Gunny."

Boland said matter-of-factly, "We were lucky." He nodded out to where the cruiser had been anchored. "Those Commies couldn't hit the broad side of a benjo ditch."

"Apparently not. And apparently we could."

"Never seen anything like it. That ship went up worse than anything I saw at Guadalcanal. And man, it was rainin' shrapnel."

"Same with us. We got a lot of hot metal. Did you know they shot torpedoes at us?"

"You're kiddin'."

"Three missed and one hit at the forward fire room. It was a dud. Otherwise it would have been curtains."

Boland shook his head. "Life does things like that to you."

"That it does." Ingram waved to the barge. "How much longer?"

Boland said, "Actually, we have them all untied, and the ambulatory ones are across. It's moving the wounded that's taking the time."

"Better make it quick. We have to get out of here."

"What's the hurry?"

"Aside from the fact that the Russians are most likely on their way back, the tide's going out and we'll be sitting on the bottom soon. The captain tells me we have about twenty more minutes, then we have to scram."

"We can wrap it up chop, chop, Commander. Don't worry."

"Okay."

"By the way, see those two guys over there?" Boland pointed to two people standing next to the ship. One rested his foot on a bollard.

Ingram barely made them out in the gloom. "Yes."

"One is Mr. Dezhnev, and if you don't mind my saying, I'm glad he's on our side. He's one hell of a shot with a 105. And he played that artillery gun crew to where they were putty in our hands."

"That's good to hear."

"The other guy is a Japanese major; I think he was the garrison commander here. He was one of the first we untied."

"I'll be damned. Thanks, Gunny." Ingram walked over to the two men. A Navy blanket was draped around Fujimoto's shoulders and his hands were wrapped around a steaming coffee mug.

Dezhnev recognized him first. "Welcome to the first annual Tri-Parte Conference."

"Ed, good to see you." He shook hands with Dezhnev. "That was a nice job back there."

"Well . . ."

"My gunnery sergeant says you're pretty good with a 105. And coming from a Marine, that's high praise."

Dezhnev gave a slight bow. "Glad to be of service."

Ingram reached for Fujimoto's hand. "And Major, what a wonderful surprise. They told us you were dead."

Fujimoto still wore the eye patch, but the Fu Manchu mustache was gone. He nodded toward the barge. "I thought I was about to be, with all that metal and junk falling on us."

"Anybody hurt?"

"I don't think so. But big pieces splashed all around us." He stamped his feet and worked his arms, muttering, "Circulation. Everything feels like cotton."

"How long have you been tied up?"

"At least twelve hours." He added, "My garrison here originally consisted of one thousand men. But there were hard battles over the past weeks. Then the Russians started toying with us, knowing that we were out of food and water. Now we are barely two hundred."

Dezhnev looked away.

"I hope we can save those who are left," said Fujimoto.

"We're trying our best," said Ingram. Then he changed the subject. "Your brother will be very pleased."

"How is he?"

"Much better."

"Strange," Fujimoto said. "We were never close. Father wouldn't permit it. Now, I think we will have to be."

Dezhnev said wistfully, "Take it from me: love your brother. I never had one and I wish I did."

Fujimoto sighed, "I was taught to have a warrior's spirit. Everything so . . . stoic . . . so much self-sacrifice . . . so much dedication to the emperor. And those things are not so bad. But now . . ."

"Now?" Ingram urged.

Fujimoto took a deep breath. "After tonight, I don't know."

"I don't either," said Dezhnev.

Fujimoto's eyes glistened. "Then we are two." He lifted his cup in a silent toast and drank.

Dezhnev looked ashore. "Hear that?"

"What?"

"T-34s. You have less than ten minutes."

Ingram listened and heard the ominous rumble of diesel engines and the squeak of treads. "You're right. Let's go." He turned to leave.

Dezhnev stood where he was.

Ingram said, "Come on."

"I'm sorry."

"What the hell? What are you doing?"

Dezhnev spread his hands. "I serve my country."

Fujimoto said, "Come on, you damned fool. They will tie you to a stake and fill you full of holes before the night is out."

"Come on, Ed," said Ingram.

Dezhnev shook his head. "I said I serve my country."

"Nonsense," shouted Ingram.

They started at a six-second blast from the *Maxwell*'s foghorn. The echoes had barely stopped when sailors ran down the gangway and headed for the bollards, slipping off dock lines.

The tanks rumbled closer, sounding as if they were just around the corner.

Ingram yelled. "We can't wait."

"Go!" shouted Dezhnev.

"You're not coming with us?" Ingram was incredulous. "They *will* shoot you."

"I'm not coming. Go, you damned fool."

"But--"

Dezhnev yelled, "Don't worry, I'll take my chances."

"He needs something more than that. Give me a pistol," said Fujimoto.

"What?" shouted Ingram.

"A pistol. Do you have a pistol?"

"No . . . yes." Ingram reached in the small of his back and produced Oleg's PPK.

"Fine." Fujimoto grabbed the Walther, cocked it, and shot Dezhnev in the left arm.

"*Owwww!*" Dezhnev tumbled to the dock, grabbing his arm. Blood oozed between his fingers. "*Chort voz'mi, eto bylo bol'no!*" Damn you, that really hurt!

Fujimoto said, "Sorry, but you now look like an authentic casualty."

The foghorn sounded again. Then a shout from the bridge, "Todd, damn it! I'm backing down in the next ten seconds."

Ingram shouted back. "On our way and kill the running lights!" He reached down to Dezhnev and took his hand. "Adios, amigo." Taking the PPK from Fujimoto, he passed it over. "You may need this."

Dezhnev gasped between gritted teeth, "Thanks, killjoy. Goodbye. We'll meet again."

"Hope so." Ingram touched Dezhnev on the shoulder then stood and ran, Fujimoto close behind.

The sailors finished lifting the dock lines off the bollards and cast them back on board the *Maxwell*, then ran for the safety of the gangway. Two more people followed. The first was Major Kotoku Fujimoto of the Imperial Japanese Marines. The last was Cdr. Alton C. Ingram, U.S. Navy.

Tubby White wasted no time. He ordered all the *Maxwell's* topside lights doused and backed the destroyer away with a two-thirds bell. Once clear of the dock, he changed to a full bell. The ship gained sternway into darkness and the protection of the night.

Ingram walked onto the bridge, finding Tubby bent over a radar repeater. It rendered a beautiful picture of a ship safely away from shore and out to sea. Tubby ordered left full rudder and a two-thirds counter-clockwise twist. Once the ship lost sternway, he shifted the rudder until they were headed fair into the Sea of Japan. With that, he rang up turns for seventeen knots on a standard bell and steadied on course two-five-five.

Russians raced onto the pier and began shooting at where the destroyer had disappeared. Captain Third Rank Eduard Dezhnev stood among them, firing bursts of his PPSh submachine gun into the air.

An out-of-breath Matvie Borzakov rushed up to him. "You damned fool. Look what you've done."

"I? What have I done?"

Borzakov waved toward where the *Admiral Volshkov* had been. "Our ship is gone, along with her captain and crew and a valuable asset. One would think you were working for the Americans." He peered at Dezhnev. "What happened to your arm?"

Rifle shots burst all around as men fired sporadically after the ship. It was difficult to hear. "What?"

"Your arm," Borzakov screeched. "What happened?"

"I have news for you, Matvie."

Someone found a machine gun and began spraying bullets into the night.

"What?"

"You are right. I am working for them."

Borzakov said, "Is this a stupid joke?"

Dezhnev added, "No joke. As for what happened to me, I found Oleg's pistol."

"What are you saying?"

"Here it is." Dezhnev pulled out the PPK and shot Borzakov in the chest. Twice. The man fell to the ground, reached toward him, and then was still.

A minute later, three T-34s rumbled up to the pier. The tanks fired wildly into the night at the invisible destroyer. Although the gunners couldn't see, one round zipped between the *Maxwell*'s stacks and hit the ocean beyond, raising a tall water column and dousing the quarterdeck. The other thirty-five or so rounds the three tanks fired missed by at least five hundred yards.

The shooting petered out, and soldiers aimlessly wandered up and down the pier; who or how many, Dezhnev didn't know. It was too dark to make a count. Dezhnev stumbled against some oil drums and peered into the blackness. He could barely see his hand before his face. For certain, nobody would be able to describe his role here tonight. But just to be sure, he moved farther from Borzakov's body, then threw the PPK into the water.

He looked out to sea, realizing the utter foolishness of his actions. *America. Freedom.* An independent, creative, and robust way of life sailed away with that ship. All he ever wanted--all any decent man ever wanted. He could have gone with them. The door was wide open. And yet, he had turned aside. A short time ago he would have jumped at the chance. But for some reason he didn't understand he had remained behind in this hell.

Sergeant Boland had easily captured the 105's gun crew and had left them bound and blindfolded. None of them knew of Dezhnev's role tonight. He might just get away with it. That thought was of some comfort as the tanks secured their engines. Trucks rattled up, troops disembarked, men shouted. More tanks rumbled up. Getting organized. Soon, flashlights popped up on the beach, their beams waving in the air and on the ground, picking out a path. Cautiously, men began walking out on the pier.

They'll be here, soon. Better to be found on the ground than on my feet.

He let himself fall against a stack of crates. As he lay there waiting to be discovered, he thought about Fujimoto. They really were two of a kind, he realized, just as Fujimoto had said. Fujimoto was as passionate about Japan, as flawed as it was with its bushido code, as Dezhnev was about Russia, the *Rodina.* Yet, the major had instinctively grasped what was needed in this situation. A stupid gunshot wound to carry Dezhnev through all this.

The *Maxwell's* foghorn ripped at the night in a long, mournful blast; its echo rolled over what had been the coastal plain of Karafuto and was now Sakhalin.

Ingram. Dezhnev grinned. Either Ingram was giving him a Bronx cheer, or he was saying goodbye. Deep down, he knew it was the latter.

Do svedaniia. Goodbye for now, old friend.

ACKNOWLEDGMENTS

There's no doubt that people are the essence of it all. Our friends, our relatives, our spouses and children, our bosses, teachers, coworkers, healthcare providers, casual acquaintances, even those we don't count among our friends. They drive the engine that allow us to exercise our talents and eventually, accomplish a goal or two – maybe even more if the good Lord is with us.

I am no exception and boldly admit that I constantly turn to these people whether or not I'm in trouble. Their comfort and talents overwhelm me. Over the years, they have contributed to my works in more ways than they will ever know. Among them, in no significant order are:

The flying scenes were greatly enhanced by Daniel Truax, Captain, USN (retired) and my old friend and corsair jockey Dick Bertea formerly a pilot of the United States Marine Corps. Commentary about U.S. Navy organization, tactics, and equipment, came from "Tin Can Sailor," David Ramsey, Rear Admiral, USN (retired) along with kind advice from another old friend, submariner, and fellow author, George A. Wallace, Commander, USN (retired). Yet another friend and contributor is fellow "Tin Can Sailor," Terry Miller, Executive Director and Editor of the National Association of Destroyer Veterans. I would be remiss if I didn't mention a wonderful friend, yachtsman, naval aviator, and patriot, Captain Randall J Lynch, Commanding Officer, Naval Station, Great Lakes, who helped with naval customs and usage.

When medical problems came up, I once more turned to Dr. Russell Striff and Fred Meister, Ph.D. Elsewhere, I received fine counsel from Bob Bailey, Robert G. Mahan, and Beverly Hills Police Chief David L. Snowden. Also, my hat is off once again to Susan Kechekian of USC's Department of

Slavic Studies, for her help in Russian translations not only here, but for her fantastic help with the second novel in the Todd Ingram series, *A Code For Tomorrow*.

As always, my wife, Janine, is not only a great editor (something I re-learn every time I go through this) but also a marvelous and loving partner for which none of this would have occurred, to say nothing for all of the wonderful events in my life.

Also, to you, my readers thank you, and thank you, and thank you, for your support, encouragement, critique, and e-mails over the years. Truly, it is you, my friends, who keep me going. And if you're interested, please see the other Todd Ingram novels on Kindle or Amazon.

Please don't hesitate to visit my website at www.JohnJGobbell.com for commentary on my novels, including photos of actual people places and military equipment portrayed herein. As always, mistakes herein are mine alone, many times called to my attention by your kind e-mails. Please keep it up.

JJG
John@JohnJGobbell.com

ABOUT THE AUTHOR

JOHN J. GOBBELL is a former Navy Lieutenant who saw duty as a destroyer weapons officer. His ship served in the South China Sea, granting him membership in the exclusive *Tonkin Gulf Yacht Club*. As an executive recruiter, his clients included military/commercial aerospace companies giving him insight into character development under a historical thriller format. An award-winning author, John has published eight novels. The books in his popular Todd Ingram series are based on the U.S Navy in the Pacific theater of World War II. John and his wife Janine live in Newport Beach, California.

Sign up for John J. Gobbell's newsletter at
severnriverbooks.com
johnjgobbell@severnriverbooks.com

Printed in the United States
by Baker & Taylor Publisher Services